HellBound Books'

Anthology
of
Pandemic Horror

Curated by Jaime Powel

A HellBound Books LLC Publication
Copyright © 2025 by HellBound Books Publishing LLC
All Rights Reserved

Cover and art design by Ruth Anna Evans
for
HellBound Books Publishing LLC

No part of this book may be reproduced, stored in a retrieval system, or transmitted by any means, electronic, mechanical, photocopying, recording or otherwise without written permission from the author This book is a work of fiction. Names, characters, places and incidents are entirely fictitious or are used fictitiously and any resemblance to actual persons, living or dead, events or locales is purely coincidental.

www.hellboundbookspublishing.com

Contents:

In the vastness of our world, Satan's influence goes largely unseen, but during an apocalypse, when humanity becomes depopulated, the devil's presence is unmistakable.

SCOURGE
Paul Lonardo

Mariam saw it toward their stalled boat, its tiny arms moving though the water, making tiny looping arcs. Occasionally its horrible little face broke the surface. A twisted newborn's face that was filled with rage, hate, and hunger.

The sea all around was filled with the bodies of infected babies. Some were dead, just bobbing up and down atop the waves, but most continued to relentlessly pump their arms and legs. Tossed by large swells, some were able to secure the talon-like fingertips to the keel and climb up toward the deck.

One reached the top. Its skin was corpse-gray, with barnacles attached to his head and body. Its blood-red eyes peered menacingly at Miriam. Its thin black lips parted and it opened its mouth, baring tiny, needle-tipped teeth that had chunks of seaweed stuck between them.

The tortured creature made a shrill cry and then scuttled across the gunwale toward her, dragging its hooved feet behind. Mariam opened her mouth to scream as the thing was almost upon her, but she could not produce a sound.

She emerged from the dream with a hand on her shoulder as she was shaken awake. Immanuel was staring down at her with a comforting smile.

"It's okay," he said. "You were just having another nightmare. We're almost there. Look."

He helped her to her feet. She kept the blanket draped over her body as she got up from the captain's chair and peered out across the bow. As soon as she saw its outline, barely a quarter mile in size, framed by teal water and an azure blue sky, she knew this was the island from her visions.

"Yes, this is it," Miriam said with sudden enthusiasm.

Daniel was at the helm, guiding the sailboat toward the tiny land mass. The couple smiled with pride as they gazed at their son, almost eighteen and grown to be a strong and capable young man. Immanuel turned to Miriam and looked her in the eyes, his smile never wavering as he laid the palm of one hand against her distended belly.

It was a brief touch, a moment of intimacy, but it reaffirmed for Miriam that they were doing the right thing, and that her husband supported her when so few people had. In fact, the majority of people would have killed without thinking twice if they knew she was pregnant, so she had to hide it.

There were many times she wanted to tell others that a perfectly healthy baby was alive inside of her so that she me would give people who were in despair hope for the future, which was something everyone desperately needed.

Immanuel insisted she never reveal anything about her visions to anyone because they would never believe her. Even worse, it might instill a false sense of reality in some of the women who wanted to believe they, too, were chosen, and encourage them to get pregnant.

As they approached the small island that had been fated to become the post-apocalyptic Cradle of Humankind, Miriam couldn't help wondering if the fear and apprehension she felt was similar to what the passengers on the Mayflower were feeling when they caught sight of land for the first time after embarking on their perilous adventure across a vast ocean.

Of course, that historic journey had taken over two months to complete compared to the two hours it took her family to cross the ten-mile span from the coastline of Southport, Maine to reach the unnamed island.

And it was only the three of them on board a sixteen-foot sailboat rather than the 102 Puritan separatists, along with thirty crew members, who had to deal with the rough waters of the open ocean, disease, and cramped living conditions aboard a seventeenth century wooden sailing ship known as a carrack.

Entering the cove, a stream of billowing white smoke could be seen drifting up from a distant hill. Miriam and Immanuel exchanged a brief glance, but neither said anything. They were thinking the same thing; either they weren't the first to arrive on the island, or it was inhabited.

It had been five years since the plague began, and it seemed unlikely anyone who had been living on this tiny speck of rock and soil off the New England coastline would have survived. The populations on islands vastly larger than this one, including continental land masses, were decimated by the scourge, entire nations having been wiped out.

Daniel navigated the yawl toward the empty beach, reducing the sails and steering into the wind. Immanuel lowered the anchor over the side of the stern and the boat drifted slowly into the shallows before gently pushing up onto the sandy shore.

"You've turned into quite the sailor," Immanuel remarked to his son.

"I've gotten a lot of practice the last couple of years," Daniel said with a flash of naturally perfect teeth, sandy blond hair billowing in the breeze.

When the vessel settled, he jumped out to secure the lines to some boulders that were just off the beach.

"Are you sure you're feeling okay?" Immanuel asked Miriam. "That water was a little choppy. If you need it, take a minute to get your bearings. You're carrying precious cargo."

"I'm fine," she told him, then looked up and down the beach. "Where's their boat?"

"They must have come around from the other side of the island and docked there," he told her.

Neither of them wanted to question her vision. It had gotten them this far. Miriam trusted what she had been shown, and although she was confident this was where they were supposed to be, she was more than a little apprehensive as Immanuel helped her off the boat. They had always been able to flee and go somewhere else whenever they were in danger on the mainland. Now there was no place to escape.

They were trapped.

They set out for the line of smoke in the distant hills to establish contract with their fellow wayfarers, leaving everything behind except some fresh water.

There was still an hour left of daylight when they reached the campsite. They startled a young boy of about twelve who was sitting alone by an open fire. There was an empty roasting spit positioned over it while several fish were frying on a skillet. The boy's face, like his clothes, was covered in dirt and grime. He had a wild mane of red hair that was knotted and tangled.

"Hello," Immanuel said, offering a friendly smile.

The boy stared wide-eyed at the approaching strangers. "Uncle," he called out with alarm in his voice as he secured his right hand on the handle of a butcher knife which was resting near his feet. "Hey, Uncle. Come here."

A hundred feet behind the boy was a single-story communal building about fifty feet in length and a smaller structure behind it. There were three outhouses in the distance and a makeshift rainwater harvesting system set up around the dwellings. At a glance, the basics for a long-term survival plan seemed to be in place.

There was some commotion from inside the small residence before gray-bearded man emerged with a rifle in his hands. He was wearing faded denim overalls which were several sizes too big for him, no shirt underneath.

Behind the family, two younger men with dark beards emerged out of the woods. They were also carrying long guns. The men stood still and silent with the barrels of the weapons poised at the ready.

Knowing how reactionary his son could be when he felt threatened, Immanuel pressed a hand on Daniel's shoulder to keep him from provoking these men with any kind of physical response. His son hadn't yet learned restraint, or how to settle hostility peacefully with reason and civility. Of course, the young man had grown up in an unreasonable and violent world.

Immanuel fought an impulse to raise his arms and show the men he was not armed or a threat to them, but he wanted to project prudence, not submission. "Excuse us," he began. "We didn't mean to intrude. We just arrived and saw the smoke from your fire."

"Are there any more of you?" The old man's voice was horse and deep. He was staring directly at Miriam's tumescent belly as he spoke.

"It's just the three of us," Immanuel told him.

"Well, it will be four soon," Miriam added. Resting her hands on her belly and smiling uncomfortably.

"Are there any others beside you boys on the island?" Immanuel asked.

The old man's eyes slowly shifted from Miriam's belly to Immanuel. "We have a pregnant one, too," he said. "She's inside. Resting."

"Oh, really?" Miriam was heartened by the revelation. "May I see her?"

The old man hesitated. "Donovan, Donahue," he said peering up at his twin nephews as he lowered his gun. They did the same. "Show the lady inside."

"I'll go with her," Daniel asserted, and stepped forward beside his mother. No one objected and they were both led away by the bearded gunmen. The communal building held six separate apartments, each with a separate entrance.

They entered the last one on the right side. It was sizeable but sparsely furnished, with a couple of wooden chairs and a table. In one of the rooms down the end of a short hallway, a woman was lying on atop an old mattress set on the floor. She was barely conscious.

Her eyes were half-lidded. She was perspiring, her short brown hair pasted to the sides of her face. She was lying on her back with her knees up, moaning softly. The thin blanket covering her had been pushed down below a very distended belly, and the blouse she was wearing was too small to cover the perfectly round bulge.

Miriam gasped involuntarily when she saw that the flesh along the sides of her stomach had a blackish-green hue, like mold along the edges of a piece of bread.

"Are you okay?" she asked the woman, though she knew the woman was far from okay. She would be dead within a few days. Maybe hours. They were all in danger.

"She's fine," Donahue said. "She's got some female complications, is all." He laughed, a goofy grin deforming his face.

Miriam stepped closer to the woman. Kneeling by the bed, she reached out to hold the woman's hand. "What's your name, dear?"

"Mom, don't go near her," Daniel told her.

The woman was unresponsive. She appeared to be sedated.

Miriam peered up at the bearded men. "What have you given her?" she asked. "We've got to do something before it's too late."

"You just leave her be," Donahue said sharply, steadying his rifle on Miriam.

Daniel stepped between the barrel and his mother and gave the gunman a fierce look, though the man was not intimidated.

"You did your seein', get a move on now," Donahue added, starting out ahead of them. Miriam and Daniel followed at gunpoint.

Alone with the old man and the child, Immanuel felt like they were being held hostage and there wasn't much he could do. They were outgunned, and he worried about the two armed men with Miriam and Daniel.

"You and your family will be joining us for dinner," the old man said. It wasn't a question. "We have plenty of fish."

"Well, thank you. That's very generous."

"If fish isn't to your liking," the old man added, "we have crab and tortoise in abundance here on the island." He turned to the boy. "And Blake here was just about to go out and collect some wild lettuce for a fresh salad."

The boy jumped up, clutching an empty basket that was by his feet. "I'll be right back," he said, dropping the hatchet inside and bounding off into the woods.

"Miriam will like that," Immanuel said. "She's not much for fish."

"Wonderful. And of course, the accommodations here are more than adequate for all of you. I'm sure you'll be quite comfortable."

"We certainly appreciate the hospitality, Mr....?"

"Don't mention it. And no need for formalities. Name is Samael."

"I'm Immanuel. Nice to meet you." He extended his right hand and they shook. "So, Samael, where are you from?"

The old man stared back at with empty, vacuous eyes for a moment before saying, "I've wandered all over the earth before settling here many years ago. Living a simple fisherman's life."

"Must be very rewarding."

"Indeed, it is."

"Well, I see there are ample living quarters here," Immanuel began. "Certainly, there were other fishmen and their families, like yourself, living here."

"Used to be."

"What happened to them?"

"They all left," Samael said without elaborating.

Immanuel didn't know what to say to that. The man's narrative, though severely lacking in detail, didn't make sense. With what was going on in every corner of the globe, the safest place was on an isolated island like this one. There was no benefit in leaving.

Immanuel saw his family return and he was relieved, but his concern rose when he noticed the look of abject terror on Miriam's face, while Daniel countenanced anger and aggravation. "What's wrong?" he asked her.

"She's not carrying a rapture child?" Miriam spoke frantically, her breathing choppy. "And she's going to give birth soon. Real soon. Like any day, soon."

The old man snapped his head around at Miriam. "What do you mean by that?" he asked, raising his fuzzy eyebrows. "*Rapture child?*"

Immanuel shot her a critical look and shook his head in an attempt to keep her from revealing too much, but she didn't notice.

"That's just what we call them. They're babies who have been chosen by God," Miriam began. "The ones who will be born healthy to mothers like me who've experienced divine visions. These children will grow up and be responsible for repopulating the planet."

"Responsible for *what* now?" the old man scoffed. "Repopulation? Why is that?"

"You know about the plague that's been ravaging the world for the past five years?" Immanuel inquired.

Samael glanced over at his nephews and back to Immanuel with a dubious expression.

"You're not that isolated from the world," Immanuel said half-jokingly, but the old man's expression did not change. "Almost five years ago, the contagion emerged," he continued. "Whether it evolved naturally somehow or introduced artificially to the human species, nobody knows, but this pathogen is in the blood of every human and it affects the fetus, causing DNA structure of developing babies to change, transforming them into…well, a sort of hybrid creature with needle-sharp teeth and…You really don't know anything about this?"

Samael shook his head.

"He's a fucking liar," Daniel shouted. "There's something wrong with all of them. They're inbred psychopaths."

"Let's just be calm here," Immanuel told Daniel. "Take a deep breath." He turned back to Samael. "Now, when a baby is born like this, it becomes a vector, infecting those it bites and killing them within minutes. It's already wiped out a majority of the world's population. There are no healthy babies being born, and once the population ages out and dies, humanity will become extinct."

The men all smiled, seemingly finding this amusing.

"I told you there's something wrong with these fucking people," Daniel said.

Samael asked Mariam, "You say your baby is special? Not one of these monsters?"

She nodded. "Yes. I do."

"I say, our baby is special."

Miriam shook her head. "That's not a baby insider her," she insisted. She looked over at both gunmen, unsure which one was the father. "She's going to die. The baby is going to kill her. Maybe all of you, and us, with it. Do you understand?"

They just stared blankly back at her. She couldn't tell if they didn't understand or if they just didn't care.

"I was led to this island by my visions," Miriam continued over Immanuel's expression of protest and deep sigh of frustration. "Other women with the same vision and carrying rapture children of their own will be coming here. This island is supposed to be a safe haven. You're putting the future of entire human race in jeopardy."

Miriam knew she wasn't getting through to them, but then Samael laughed. It was the deranged kind of laughter you might hear coming from inside the tent of a circus sideshow long after the audience had gone home.

When he finally stopped, he looked around at his guests and said, "There are thousands of islands in these waters. Maybe you took a wrong turn somewhere, sailed right by the place you was looking for, and wound up here on Devil's Island."

"Devil's Island?" Immanuel repeated.

"That's just what we call this place," Samael said with a wry grin. "Ah, here comes Blake. Now we can eat."

The boy emerged from the woods carrying a basket overflowing with wild lettuce. The dark green leaves were long, with serrated edges.

They all shared a meal together and spoke little. The repast ended early when Miriam began to complain that she was not feeling well. Immanuel thought Miriam may have been feigning her ailment to get away from the company, but when they settled into their quarters she immediately sprawled out on the bed and complained of dizziness and ringing in her ears.

It was the complete opposite getting Daniel to settle down. He did not like feeling like a captive, which they all knew they were without saying so. At the moment, they had no option but to wait for the others to arrive and come up with a plan to deal with these people from a position of strength and numbers. As it was, they were powerless.

Daniel made several appeals to take a more offensive stance, offering to sneak back to their boat under the cover of darkness and retrieve the two handguns that were stowed away. Immanuel shot down the notion each time, assuring his son they would go back to the boat when the opportunity arrived.

He urged Daniel to be patient and not divulge his emotions or intentions so freely in front of the men. He fell short of making his son promise not to go back to the boat that night, and he regretted not doing it when the sound of a scream and voices in the distance woke him in the middle of the night. The couch Daniel was sleeping on was empty and he was nowhere in the apartment.

Immanuel didn't want to leave Miriam, whose condition had only gotten worse, but he had go out and search for his son. Before he left, he brought some water over to his wife and felt her forehead. She was burning up.

"I'm so tired," she told him, her voice frail. "And nauseas."

"Drink some water." He held the cup to her lips. It was like watching a bird at a feeder.

She got down a little and then coughed. "Where are you going?" she asked.

"I think Daniel went back to the boat. I'm going to get him, and then I'm coming back here to take care of you."

"Don't worry about me. Just find Daniel. Be careful."

"I will." Immanuel bent down and clasped her hands in his. Her fingers were cold to the touch.

"He's right not trusting these people," Miriam said. "They're up to something."

He kissed her gently and left, part of him worried he was playing right into the hands of these people. Every predator known to man, especially those that hunt in groups, employ strategies to isolate prey from their herds in order to increase their chances of success, often targeting the weaker and vulnerable individuals. It was a survival tactic that had stood the test of time in the animal kingdom.

Although dawn was still a couple hours away, Immanuel didn't want to alert their captors to movement, so he skirted the camp, taking a circuitous route back to the beach on the north shore where they landed, approaching it from the southwest side of the island. He confirmed his own suspicions—and what both Miriam and Daniel had known—that something wasn't right when he saw the boats. There was a dozen of them, varying in size, and all had been run aground. From the direction they came, they were not in their line of sight.

Immanuel inspected each of them. Most appeared to have been there for quite a while. Not only were they crippled, but they had been completely stripped of everything that could be used or repurposed. The once exception was twenty-four-foot yawl. The boat's sails had been removed from the masts, and it was canted slightly to the port side, but otherwise it looked as if it had just been beached there.

Immanuel boarded the empty vessel. Very little remained besides some hooks, lures, and other pieces of fishing tackle. From beneath the side bench, he removed a crumpled photo. It was faded, but it was clearly a woman with dark hair and a dark complexion.

She was smiling and cupping her hands around a considerable baby bump beneath a clingy purple shirt. Immanuel wondered if this was the pregnant woman who was in camp. The description of the woman Daniel had provided the previous night was remarkably similar to the woman in the photograph. If that was the case, she was of no relation to Samael or the other men.

That would mean she was there against her will, he thought.

Why wouldn't she protest?

Perhaps, she couldn't, he thought, considering the wild lettuce that was growing in abundance all over the island. He was well aware that the white, milky substance inside the stem of the plant was capable of producing an opioid-like effect, and it could have been used to drug the woman.

Immanuel's mouth went dry with raw fear and concern for Miriam who had been the only one of them to eat the lettuce the previous night, and now she wasn't feeling well.

He jumped out of the yawl and sprinted up the beach to their boat on the adjacent side of the island. When he boarded it, he knew right away Daniel hadn't been there. The two pistols, both .38 specials, were still in the storage cabinet. Immanuel removed them along with all the ammunition that remained, filling the twelve chambers with rounds of +P loads meant for optimal velocity and power.

The revolvers were easy to handle and dependable. They had gotten a lot of use early on during the outbreak, but it had been a long time since Immanuel last fired a shot.

And the last time hadn't been in self-defense.

In the beginning, many women refused to believe their child was infected. They would go to full-term and give birth only to learn the child they were carrying was, indeed, a monster. The young mothers and expectant dads were killed instantly by a deadly virus from a bite from their newborn.

The mutated offspring would only eat fresh human flesh, and they were often discovered feeding on the remains of their dead mothers. Mercifully, these creatures did not live very long. Even though they were flesh-eating monsters, it was still heartbreaking to witness one of these forsaken young souls, unloved and uncared for, slowly dying from starvation. Attempts were made by well-meaning folks to nurture the infected orphans, but it never ended well.

Immanuel stuffed one gun in the waistband behind his back and gripped the other in his right hand, remembering the last bullet he discharged from one of these guns was used to put one of these dying monsters they had come across out of its misery. He had to call it a monster because he didn't like calling it a baby or even think of it as a human child anymore. Not after what he had done.

The rising sun was just starting to color the eastern horizon as Immanuel made his way back to the camp, proceeding with a sense of urgency, but keeping a sharp eye out for any signs of Daniel.

Something caught his attention about sixty feet in the woods to his right and he paused. It was just a piece of white cloth sticking out of the ground a couple of inches, but he felt compelled to get a close look.

His heart pounded as he strode over to the spot, hesitating before he grabbed the cotton material. He tugged on it, but it was firmly buried. He pulled harder, and it shot free accompanied by a cloud of dirt. Immanuel blinked to protect his eyes and when he refocused, he saw a hand hanging limply from the sleeve of a shirt. He jumped back, dropping the limb, which was partially mummified.

The early morning light breaking through the trees revealed that Immanuel was standing in an open area with the ground all around marked by humps of broken earth. He turned on his heels and instantly understood he had stumbled onto a burial ground that extended a hundred feet from where he stood. He tried to estimate how many people might be interred there, but it was more than he cared to count.

Immanuel wondered if this was what became of the other inhabitants of the island, the people Samael claimed had left. Or was the ground filled with the passengers of the abandoned boats, people who had come to the island thinking they would be safe from the pestilence, famine, and violence, expecting a paradise, only to find death of a different kind waiting for them.

He could only hope Daniel had made it back to camp, but then he noticed a small open pit at the far end of this island necropolis, the bottom of which he could not see from where he stood. As he made his way over to investigate, he treaded lightly, but however cautiously he stepped, his foot sank into the soft earth of one shallow grave after another.

When he reached the pit, he was shocked by what he saw. The tiny bones and partials skeletons of newborns were piled on top in a heap. They were charred, which was disconcerting enough, but the fact they had been intentionally left uncovered was what Immanuel found most disturbing. While the time was taken to bury the human corpses, these remains were haphazardly disregarded like so many chicken bones.

The sound of a female screaming in the distance got him moving again. When he reached the camp a few minutes later, the screams were louder and more intense. It was coming from the apartment of the pregnant woman, and while Immanuel was sure it wasn't Miriam who was yelling in agony, he went to check on her first.

When he saw not only Miriam but Daniel, he was instantly relieved. They were both alive. It took another moment for Immanuel to realize that Daniel was bound tightly to a chair by fishing line. He had a pissed off look on his face and blood was seeping through his sleeves and his pant legs.

"Behind you!" Daniel called out.

Before Immanuel could react, he was struck in the back of the head by the butt of a rifle. He saw a bright flash behind his eyes and then he didn't see anything.

"Did you have a nice walk?" Donovan sneered as Immanuel fell to the floor.

In the room with the pregnant woman, Samael observed with casual indifference as her belly contorted and writhed with profane life. By his side, Blake watched the scene with deep fascination. Donovan was on the other side of the bed holding a long steel rod that had a ringed clasp on the end which he could open and close with a trigger mechanism near the handle. It was the kind of contraption that would be used to control a wild animal without getting too close.

As the gestational sac was punctured by deadly claws, the woman's purple-black abdomen ruptured. As if the tip of an invisible blade was stabbing her, wounds opened up on the surface of her skin. She was being mauled from the inside out as the creature made its escape.

"Blake, get the fire going under the roasting pit," Samael instructed.

"Yes, sir," said the grinning boy by his side before he ran off.

By now the woman's screams had stopped, replaced by

the sound of tearing flesh and the sinister respiration of a new lifeform.

"Donovan, get ready," Samael instructed.

Donovan raised the device over the unconscious and dying mother as blood exploded from her desecrated abdomen. The creature that emerged covered in gore could never have been mistaken for a human child. Its elongated skull, black, fishlike eyes, slit for a nose, and scaly skin was a perversion of life in any species.

"*Now!*" Samael yelled. "Do it now!"

The creature was busy gnawing on its mother's placenta with its needle-sharp teeth and didn't see Donovan until it was too late. It shrieked when the clasp wrapped firmly around its neck.

"I got the little fucker," Donovan boasted.

"Don't let it go," Samael told him.

"I won't. Don't worry."

The blasphemous thing hissed and wriggled like a smallmouth bass on the end of a hook. It couldn't swallow the flesh that was in its throat and it started gagging.

"Loosen the grip a little," Samael directed. "It's choking. You don't want to kill it. We have to consume it alive."

"I know," Donovan said struggling with the monster, which felt the grip loosen and tried to seize the opportunity, using all its strength to free itself.

"Don't let it go, you idiot."

These creatures were extremely aggressive and surprisingly strong. The mistake was thinking they were human babies, defenseless newborns, when in fact they were hardy, vicious, fully grown adults, whatever they were.

They would attack anyone without regard for their own individual safety. They didn't seem to care if they were killed, wanting only to take as many lives with them as possible. They were the perfect vessel of evil, and Samael admired that about them.

That was why he consumed them. Surely they were demons, spawn of the devil himself. Why else would they have hooved feet. By eating their flesh, Samael could absorb the essence of their evil and curry favor with Satan.

This plague was clearly a war being waged by Satan against humanity, and it was one he was winning. It was only a matter of time before mankind was conquered and under the control of the dark prince. When the final victory came, Samael wanted to be on the side of the victor and be welcomed into the Kingdom of Darkness for all eternity.

Samael moved toward Donovan, his steps slow but deliberate. "Hold it steady." The old man stopped directly in front of the monster squirming on the end of the catchpole. He removed his shirt and then took another step forward, allowing the thing to rake one of its claws across the flesh of his abdomen, opening up a clean, six-inch wound.

It took a moment before it started to bleed. Samael took that as a sign that he had been officially branded and accepted as an instrument of the Satan.

Blake rushed into the room. "The fire is ready." He was holding a butcher knife.

"Good," Samael said with a satisfied smile. "Donovan, bring it out to the fire pit."

"Can I flay this one, Uncle?" Blake asked. "I've seen you do it enough times. I know how."

"I don't see why not," Samael told him. "Let me check on our guests first. Help Donovan attach it to the rod. Make sure the spit forks are tightened nice and secure. Then wait for me. I'll be there in a minute."

Blake walked out behind Donovan, who was holding the wriggling monster out in front of him as far as possible.

Samael headed into the adjoining apartment where

Donahue was standing in front of his captives, his rifle at his side. Immanuel was bound to a chair by fishing wire beside his son, whose eyes were swollen and bruised, his cheeks puffy.

"I had to rough that one for getting out of line," Donahue informed his uncle. "He was saying a lot of bad things, so I had to shut his mouth for him. And the other one came back with these." He gestured to the two pistols that were resting on a nearby table.

"Very good," Samael said, his focus on Miriam, who was lying in bed mostly incoherent, stirring periodically and moaning softly. "She's almost ready. No need to tie her up, she's sufficiently incapacitated. We don't want any harm to come to the precious little cargo she's carrying."

"What do you plan to do with her?" Immanuel asked.

Outside, the creature shrieked as it was skewered alive on the spit. It continued to howl in pain as the heat from the flames scorched its body.

"The soul of a rapture child is infinitely more valuable to Satan. Devouring it will show my obedience and service, and the Dark Lord will reward me. And if what you've told me is correct, more women carrying rapture children will be delivered here just for me, so the Dark Lord *must* have chosen me to do his bidding. I won't let down my master."

Daniel struggled against his constraints, fresh blood gushing from the cuts in his skin beneath the fishing line. "You sick fuck," Daniel shouted, spitting blood for his split lip. "There's no way you get away with this."

"Skin for skin," Samael shouted, and then he laughed. When he stopped, he said, "Come on, Donahue. Your boy is preparing for the ritual feast." He left out of the room, followed by his nephew.

The cries of the living banquet slowly subsided while the shrieks from the cannibalistic family were raised to frenzied excitement as they carved up the surprisingly tender meat and feasted on the abominable thing until there was nothing left but bones.

In the distance, unseen by anyone on the island at that moment, a fifty-two-foot ketch sailed southeast across the Gulf of Maine heading straight for Devil's Island.

Freddy's Long Stay
J.C. Wiles

I wake up.

A bad decision.

One of my worst.

I stretch, and immediately regret that, too.

My swollen joints protest any movement, however slight. My whole body burns with fever and crawls with pain. The pale-yellow rash is everywhere now. I can't see it but I can feel it all over my skin, every inch of it. It stopped spreading only when there was nowhere left to go.

I try to open my eyes and discover they've crusted shut. Pus leaks out from the corners when I try again, harder this time. It's not for nothing. My left eyelid breaks open just a crack, with a sharp new pain like the blade of a knife.

I gasp.

A weak, dry noise. Hardly a sound at all.

On the other side of the room, though, something moves.

My eyes won't open wide enough to see what it is. Just a thin, fluorescent-yellow sliver of light from the left. Blurry shadows churn and thrash on the ceiling, but I hear nothing more.

I'm used to the silence by now. The machines around me stopped beeping days ago, and all foot traffic up and down the hallway outside my room ceased soon after one final flurry of frantic activity. I don't know when Mr. Harris—the man in the bed next to mine—died, but I don't think anyone ever came to take his body away. I think he's still there. I don't know for sure. From this angle, I can't see his side of the room.

Only the ceiling. Only those squirming shadows.

"Is someone there?" I ask, but the sound that comes out is little more than the same dry rasp I made a moment ago. How long has it been since I've even heard my own voice? I'm more used to the sound of my thoughts, at this point. I clear my throat—another failure, more wasted effort—and do my best to speak up again. "Dr. Anderton? Is that you?"

The shadows immediately freeze in place and then bleed away, diluting themselves so cleanly across the dimly-lit ceiling that I find myself wondering whether I had really seen them at all. My brain is heavy with post-medicinal fugue; the haze in my sight is nothing compared to the haze in my mind.

"Yes," comes a voice, a familiar one from the far corner of the room. "It's me, Dr. Anderton."

I try to sit up and am rewarded with pain, like eight hundred tiny needles stabbing my stomach from the inside out. My abdominal muscles have melted away in this bed like the rest of them.

All the work I did in the gym sophomore year, reduced to a puddle of sweat soaking my mattress. But none of that was what stopped me this time; there were new tubes now, tubes that hadn't been there the last time I fell asleep. One draped over the top of my head and into my ear; deep, deep into my right ear. The other, uncomfortably much thicker, lay both across my neck and wrapped around behind it.

"I thought..." I begin, then cut myself off with a coughing fit. "I thought you were gone."

"I'm right here, Freddy," he tells me, patiently. It's both his voice and it isn't, but I don't know what's different, can't quite put my finger on it.

If only I could see him!

I force myself to roll over – just a little bit, let gravity do most of the work. "Where did you think I went?" he asks.

Dead, I think. *I thought you were dead.*

Instead, I try to swallow. What I say out loud is: "Thirsty..."

"Would you like a cup of water?" asks the dissonantly serene voice of Dr. Anderton, and suddenly I realize what is wrong about it. I think back to the last time I saw him before now, days that might as well be years, and I remember how he looked, and how he sounded.

His broad, squat frame squished into the chair at my bedside instead of looming over, a soggy handkerchief, wadded up between the thick sausage fingers of his left hand, dabbing at each new bullet of sweat that appeared on his long bald forehead, smearing it around instead of wiping it off and leaving him glistening rather than clean. His pudgy face, ruddier than ever, eyes downcast at the floor, never meeting my gaze.

"I just don't get it, Freddy," he told me, breathing heavily and no longer trying to hide the yellow rash that had begun creeping up his neck to peek out over the top of his loosened collar. Behind him I could hear but not see the commotion of the final exodus from the hospital. They were leaving us. Everyone was leaving us. "You should be dead by now. Goddammit, Freddy, I just don't understand how you're still alive."

Now he stands just out of sight and calmly repeats his question. "Would you like a cup of water?"

No, not out of sight. Just out of focus—hard to see, between the crust of my upper left eyelid. Against the far wall, past the silent instruments and empty third bed, I can see a blur, a short, squat blur of lap-coat-white about the size and shape of my doctor. Nearby stands another blur, more slender and slightly taller than the first.

This second blur alone brings color into the room, a splotchy pattern of reds, greens, blues, and yellows set against a canvas of dimly-lit beige. The nurse, I realized, the blonde one who always wears floral pattern scrubs. That must be her. I can't remember her name, but she was here the night I was first admitted. By then, most of the hospitals were already full, but I secured a spot here, on account of my family, and…

"A cup of water, Freddy," Dr. Anderton asks again, firmly. "Would you like one?"

Yes, I can't say. Instead, I nod. Or at least I try to.

Even that hurts.

Something presses a Dixie cup between the limp fingers of my outstretched right hand, although the white Anderton blur barely moves. Something sloshes around inside. I raise it to my lips, up and over, but as soon as the liquid hits my lips I stop and spit and spill the rest of it out. At least I try to spit. What actually happens is aggressive drool. "What's wrong?" asks Dr. Anderton.

"Salty…" I croak before I lose consciousness again.

***

For most people, the first sign of the virus was the rash. Pale and yellow, barely noticeable at first. By the time you saw it you could probably feel it, too. Maybe you even felt it first. Tender at the beginning, then itchy, then painful. A lot of the time it would appear on the groin, armpit, or neck, but not always. Mine started between the index and middle fingers of my right hand, and within a day or two I couldn't even hold a pencil anymore.

It hit the lymph nodes next. Before the virus I didn't even know what a lymph node was.

Not everyone got the fever, but I did, and I got it bad. I peaked at 107.1, as best as I can remember. The fever was when things got bad, at least for me. It left me immobilized in bed, marinating in a stew of my own juicy stink, feeling the body I had built for myself since freshman year, melting away to nothing. It cooked my brain inside my skull like boiled cabbage, and when I passed out, it even took my dreams and replaced them with abstract flashes of horror and absurdity.

The fever dreams come and go as I drift in and out of consciousness.

Tonight there's three I remember.

In one I'm a spider on the ceiling of my hospital room, hanging upside down and watching myself die. It's nighttime, but my spider eyes can see just fine. From the bed next to mine, the high-pitched nasal ramblings of Mr. Harris never seem to cease. The same questions he'd always ask when he was alive. "How's your family, Freddy?" he asks my corpse, over and over again. "How's your mom, Freddy? How's your dad? How's your sister? How's your family, Freddy? How's your family?"

In one I'm not myself at all but six different people, a group of Brazilian explorers trekking deep into the Amazon rain forest. This was one of the longer ones.

In one I find myself in a dark place. There's asphalt beneath my feet, but it doesn't feel like I'm outside. There's no wind, for one thing, and no ambient sound; no chirping birds or crickets or distant traffic, nothing to break the silence save the sound of my breathing. No light either, but when I look down, I can see myself somehow. No pain and no hint of the rash on my arms or legs or anywhere else. I reach around to my right ear, the only place that still holds a tingle of an itch, but no matter how I try, I cannot seem to scratch it. Of course; I'm fat again, too, which means this dream takes place in high school or the beginning of college.

Sure enough, when I look up, I can see Emily too, wearing her mousy brown hair down to her shoulders and the same bright blue sundress as the night she died. Definitely high school then. I should have known. Since the virus began, these were the ones I've had the most.

"Just give them what they want, Freddy," she whispers to me, but she's too far away and I can't tell whether she is begging me or warning me or commanding me. "Just answer their questions."

***

Awake again.

Another Dixie cup is thrust into my hands before I even open my eyes. Without thinking, without time to remember the last one's nasty surprise I gulp it down all at once. It's lukewarm and gritty, but at least this time it's fresh.

"Here you go," comes a pleasant voice, a female voice. "Is that better?"

"Yeah." Somehow I muster the strength to raise a wrist to my eyes and wipe away some of the gooey crust. I can see a little better today. Both my eyes open now. I can see the colors before I see her face. Red, green, blue, and yellow. I still can't remember her name. She's just a little older than me and pretty, with blonde hair in bangs like Emily used to have before she ruined her hair by growing them out. She wears it down which strikes me as odd for some reason, but I don't understand why. "I'm sorry," I manage to tell her. "I forgot your name."

"If you can't remember it, I'm not going to tell you."

Is she teasing me or annoyed at me? I can't tell. Her smile is inscrutable. Her eyes are bright blue. "Dr. Anderton will be glad to see you're awake. He's made a lot of progress on your case lately."

"Really?" I croak out. On my case? He didn't seem too optimistic the last time I saw him, I add silently, calling to mind again his sweaty, beefy face the night of the evacuation, his desperation and confusion.

Or was that just another fever dream?

Or is this?

If she notices my incredulousness, she doesn't show it. "He's made a lot of progress on your case since the last time he saw you," she repeats. "He's very optimistic now. He's going to have a lot of questions for you. I know it's difficult for you to talk, but please try to answer them as thoroughly and as honestly as you can. The answers could mean the difference between life and death." For the first time, her smile changes; it widens. "Who's the girl in the blue dress, by the way?"

"What?" How does she know about Emily?

"I said, Dr. Anderton is going to have a lot of questions for you." I realize this is the first time I've seen her smile. She's always looked so sad, on the verge of tears even, and she's never once looked me in the eye.

I picture the first time I saw her, when I was first admitted. By then most hospitals were full, but I was able to get a spot on account of my family, and... and suddenly I remember. She'd been wearing a plastic tag with her name on it, then. Layla McCurdy, LPN.

Why isn't she wearing it now?

"My name is Layla, by the way," she says, apropos of nothing, then taps the name badge she actually *is* wearing, after all. How did I not see it before? "I'll go get Dr. Anderton now."

"There's no need. I'm already here."

I give a violent start; my tender, swollen joints protest painfully but I barely notice. I hadn't heard Anderton come in. I hadn't seen him walk over to my bed. But there he stands, right across from Layla, staring down at me. Behind him for some reason is one of the hospital's diagnostic droids.

An older model I'd guess, going by the wear and tear to its chassis and the outdated stylized eye slits. From here I can tell it's in standby mode for power conservation. Observant and aware of its surroundings but utterly unresponsive.

"So," Dr. Anderton begins. "Fredrick Barlow Byford." He looks at me and then pauses.

Is he really asking me my name? "Yes. That's me."

"I understand you were a student at Pindleton University when the viral outbreak occurred. Is this correct?

"Yeah."

"And your field of study was robotics, is that also correct? That was your major?"

I shake my head in confusion. "What does this have to do with—"

"Dr. Anderton's questions are very important for your treatment," Layla cuts me off. "Please try to answer them as thoroughly and as honestly as you can." She places her hand on mine, as though to calm me and comfort me. Her touch is cold and oddly moist, but against my fevered skin it feels nice.

"Yeah. I was a robo major," I explain, each word scraping at my vocal cords. It feels like I'm speaking blood but I force myself to go on and on. "I was… also a… psych minor. My focus was… neuro-positronic interface… design. My advisor… was Dr. Crispin Nellis, and my—"

"I don't care about that!" the doctor harshly interrupts. The discrepancy between his words and that smile is jarring. "Were you a good student, Freddy? You weren't, were you? No, you were probably straight-C slacker, a lazy sack of shit too busy partying to bother himself with his studies. Isn't that right? The only reason you even got into Pindleton was your family. Isn't that right, too?"

I open my mouth to voice my objections to his bizarre tirade—maybe I wasn't exactly Dean's list material, but I was a decent student and hadn't even had a drink since high school—but he calms himself preternaturally fast and continues without a beat. "I'm sorry for that outburst. I've had a long day. Tell me this. Do you know how to repair a broken robot?"

"Well, that's pretty vague, doctor," I deadpan. My voice is little more than a whisper. "Can you be more specific? What's wrong with it?"

"It doesn't matter what's wrong with it!" he shouts again, smile never slipping. "It's a simple question! Can you repair a broken robot or not? Yes or no?"

I don't understand what he's talking about. Of course it matters what's wrong with it! If the robot cracked any part of its ceramics, then no, I can't help you. You'd need a ceramics expert for that. If the problem's with the endoskeleton, then you'd need a machinist.

All I know about is programming the positronic shit. Designing and re-working their brains. And it's not like I know everything about that, either. I'm still just a student. I've still got a year left. Assuming I survive. Assuming there's still a Pindleton to go back to.

I doubt there is.

"Perfect. The problem we have does indeed seem to be with the android's brain. The robot in question… does not follow orders. It does not adhere to the verbal commands it is given. It does not even acknowledge them at all. When an android is malfunctioning in this way, is that something you know how to repair?"

"That could be any number of things," I explain slowly. "Have you checked to make sure the robot is on?"

Dr. Anderton reaches back with right arm and strikes me across the face, hard, with the backside of his balled-up fist. It hurts, but it doesn't feel like knuckles colliding with my jaw. It feels like something boneless and cold and damp. It stings, like a wet slap. I think he's drawn blood.

"Don't you fuck with me, asshole!" he growls, suddenly loud and in my face. The tubing wrapped around my neck tightens. My breathing, already ragged, grows slow and strained. Anderton pulls me closer to him, lifting my head up and off the pillow to stare me in the eye.

"You know damn well the robots are fucking on! They never shut themselves off!"

Almost never, anyway. The ceramic plating that makes up most of an android's exterior contains a series of embedded micro panels designed to absorb and store solar energy. As long as they can find a way to spend at least a few hours in the sunlight, they can run indefinitely with very little downtime. Even if they don't, if a robot doesn't have a specific task to perform, most of them will just place themselves in standby. Like that diagnostics droid over there in the corner.

I don't tell him any of that.

His face is just inches from mine. I realize, to my discomfort, that he isn't breathing.

Something in me snaps. "No!" I shout back at him, ignoring the pain that explodes out from my lungs. The agony spreads as I force myself to sit up, to look Dr. Anderton in the eye as I tell him to go fuck himself. "I'm done answering your bullshit questions! What the hell is going on? What the hell does any of this have to do with my treatment?"

All at once the lights go out, and absolute darkness falls over the room.

Anderton and Layla are both gone; I don't hear them leave, but I just don't feel them there anymore. The pain is still here, though, and as the adrenaline fades, I feel that pain more acutely than I have in days. I double up and hold my breath for a moment. Without the ragged sound of my own intake and outtake, everything is silent.

When I dare, I reach out toward the emptiness in front of me where Dr. Anderton stood when the lights went out. Nothing. I flail about in empty space. I don't say anything. I wait for my eyes to adjust, but it doesn't happen.

Blackness, all around me. Even the bed has fallen away out from under me, somehow without my noticing.

Am I dead?

It's only when I hear Emily's voice again that I realize I'm dreaming.

***

"Freddy!"

Like before she's too far away for me to see her face… but this time she's moving closer, and I find that I, on the other hand, am stuck to the spot. Soon she's upon me, wrapping her arms around my heavyset form. She's sobbing now, held up entirely by the loop of arm around the back of my neck. Is it raining, too? Was it raining the night she died?

I can't remember.

"Please, Freddy," she whispers in my ear, her voice quivering with an unknown fear, again and again. "Please."

Finally, she pulls herself together enough to let go of me and steps back. Her bright blue eyes stare into mine, blinking away rainwater and tears. Her hair is soaked, matted to her head. Her bangs are back. "You have to give them what they want, Freddy," she begs. "They can do things to me, here. Horrible things, Freddy. Just give them what they want. Answer their questions."

"I've been trying," I sigh. "Their questions don't make any sense."

Emily closes her eyes and gives an anguished moan. With a quick jerk, she pulls out a jagged shard of glass about the size and shape of a steak knife. From where I cannot tell. The magic of the dreamworld. "They're making me do this," she whispers to me, her voice trembling in horror as she raises the glass slowly and unsteadily to her forehead. "I can't help it!"

Her pleas turn to screams. She presses down with the blade in the center of her forehead until she draws blood and then drags it lower toward her ear, leaving a deep red gash in its wake. She traces past her temple and along the bottom of her jaw. Her screams grow louder the whole time.

She's cutting her own face off.

"Okay," I tell her. "But, like, so what?" If she hears me, she gives no sign. She does not stop cutting. She does not stop screaming. I go on, anyway. "Emily is dead, and I'm asleep. You're not real. This is just a dream."

She doesn't stop until she's finished. I can't look away. The dream lets me speak, but it does not let me move. Not even to blink. The slab of skin that used to be her face slipped off her head like the peel of an onion, and what it leaves behind it almost identical to what was left behind of the real Emily after the accident, after flying through the windshield, after the glass destroyed her face, after the oak tree on the other side broke her neck.

The only difference is this time Emily is laughing at me. 'Oh, Freddy, are you really that naïve? This isn't a dream. It's a hallucination. And there's still more to come, and worse. They aren't done with me yet."

She leans in closer. How can she talk without lips? Just inches from me she stops, takes her head between both hands, and gives it a sudden jerk to one side. There's a sick cracking sound, and then an anguished scream of pain. "My neck!" she cries out. "Oh Freddy, it's broken, they've made me break my own neck."

Her head flops over sideways, expressionlessly bleeding. Her eyes stare lidlessly at me through her lamentations. "Please, Freddy. Please just answer their questions. Give them what they want."

I stare right back. "I already told you. Their questions don't make any sense. And why should I care what happens to you? A hallucination isn't any more real than a dream is."

The light goes out again, wherever it was coming from.

***

It's only when I hear Layla humming to herself that I realize I've woken up.

I can't place the tune except that I know I've heard her humming it before. Her golden hair is tied back in the loose ponytail today, but she still has those bangs. She flips through a few pages on my chart, and I can't tell if she's pointedly ignoring me or just hasn't noticed I've awakened when she speaks up.

"Sounds like the nightmares are still pretty bad, huh?" She doesn't look up from my chart when she addresses me, and when I don't reply right away, she adds, "I could hear you in your sleep."

She acts so normal. How much of the last twenty-four hours has been a dream? The medicinal fugue continues to swallow up any hope I might have had of any conscious or meaningful interpretations of reality from fiction. If only I could stay awake for more than a few hours at a time, let my head clear a little. Every time I wake up, the world has changed.

"Oh, uh, yeah, sorry," I mutter. There's more I want to

say, questions I want to ask her, but the words come slowly and painfully. They churn and thrash about in my mind, and my throat is raw and ragged.

Before I can go on, she asks, "Was it the one about Emily again?"

I don't reply.

"That's the worst one, isn't it?" She still doesn't look at me. Just at the chart, flipping through the pages of my chart. She holds a blue pen between her left middle and index fingers, and from time to time she either jots something down or crosses something out. "Seemed pretty nasty from here, anyway."

I force myself to talk. "How… do you know about Emily?"

Scribble scribble scribble. "You told me about her the other day. Remember?"

"No, I didn't." She smiles slightly, lowers the clipboard. "You told me how she wears a blue sundress whenever you dream about her." That much is true. "Which dream was it tonight? What happened? Something bad, right? Something terrible?" I don't reply. But it's not something I would willingly tell anyone, no matter how delirious with fever I might have been. A mad idea sizzling with fever moves into my brain and will not leave: is she reading my mind? When she turns in my direction, she looks past me, not at me, and her hands are empty now, somehow. Where is the pen? Where is the clipboard?

"Do you feel guilty about what happened to her?"

I snort at that, then bark a terse laugh. For the first time since the virus took me, I actually laugh. It feels good. "What? Of course not. I didn't cut her face off, she did. And besides, it was just a dream."

"I didn't mean about what happened in the dream," she laughs gently, musically. It's not the same sound, but it's the same basic rhythm and cadence Emily's carved-up corpse aimed at me just before I woke. "I mean, do you feel guilty about what happened before, in real life? Do you feel guilty about how she died?"

My body grows rigid and tense. "What do you know about that?"

She shrugs. "I thought you figured it out already. I know what you know."

"But you don't really, do you?" I realize out loud. I continue silently in my head. You can't read my mind. You can only read my thoughts. That's why you didn't even know your own name until I remembered it.

Layla smiles and nods. "I knew you were smarter than Dr. Anderton gave you credit for."

Well, if it's Emily you're interested in, you're out of luck. I never think about her anymore.

"You've been thinking about her lately."

That's only because of the dreams.

Layla stands. Her floral-print scrub top clings to her torso, loose but form fitting. "We haven't been giving you the dreams, Freddy. We've just been watching them. And we've been seeing a lot of Emily in them. Especially lately."

I try to smile up at her. My upper lip cracks in two places; my bottom lip in one.

"You still haven't answered my question," Layla reminds me. "Do you feel guilty about the way she died?"

I do more than remain silent. I empty my head. I think of nothing. I think about thinking of nothing.

"And that's fine," Layla replies. "I already know the answer, anyway. Let me think of a new question instead. Why? Why do you not feel any guilt at the way she died? You do know it was your fault, don't you? Of course you do. You were driving that night. Weren't you? I know you were. You thought so, in your dream."

She moves closer to me, her blue eyes gazing deeply

into mine.

"Why do you not feel any guilt, Freddy? Have you ever wondered about that?"

"No," I reply. I don't feel guilty about what happened, because what happened wasn't my fault. She was just as fucked up as I was that night. It could have been either one of us driving. I just happened to have the keys. I just happened to be the first one to the driver's side door. Nothing would have happened any differently otherwise. That woman, the pedestrian, the one I call the Walking Lady… It was her fault, not mine. She's the one I blame.

I force her out of my thoughts as soon as she enters them.

Layla's smile never falters.

∗

For a long time after that, I'm alone again. Except for the admissions droid in the corner, at least. And Mr. Harris, if he is still there. I still haven't looked.

I spend my days staring at the ceiling. Without nowhere left to spread, the rash has redoubled its efforts and begun to grow over itself again. I barely have any fluids left to sweat out, but when the fever comes back it comes back stronger than I've ever known it before, and I fry like a strip of bacon there on the mattress. My joints throb like a heartbeat, and I barely move at all.

It won't be long now, I tell myself.

One small point of comfort. I don't believe in an afterlife. Even now. Especially now. I cannot imagine I would be judged too kindly. Not that I relish the thought of oblivion, either. But even oblivion would be better than this.

I don't dream about Emily anymore. When I do dream it's nothing more than scattered images, a collection of stills from across my short life. I don't stay asleep long enough for anything more than that.

Sometimes when I wake there's another Dixie cup of tepid water and plate of undercooked fish left out for me. It's revolting, and the first time I retch and throw up something black and thick and viscous over the side of my bed. It lands with a sickening splatter, a sound that continues long after I've finished, like it's flopping around on the floor.

After that I learn to keep it down.

Sometimes I hear Mr. Harris reciting his litany of questions. "How's your family, Freddy? How's your mom, Freddy? How's your dad? How's your sister? How's your family, Freddy? How's your family?" I wonder whether I'm dreaming or hallucinating. At least if I'm dreaming I might wake up. I'm getting really sick of his voice.

By the third day, I can't move at all. As soon as I wake, I smell the fish left out for me and gag and heave but my muscles have deteriorated too much for that and I end up doing little more than twitching and flopping around on my mattress. This evening when I vomit I can feel a tooth come out in it. I can't even make it to the edge of the bed, and instead I spit up a trickle of bile that dribbles down my pillow, down my face, down my mattress, down my chest.

My eyes no longer open, not that I have the strength to try.

I think about the last time I saw Dr. Anderton, the real Dr. Anderton, and his astonishment at my continued survival. "Goddammit, Freddy, I just don't understand how you're still alive."

I don't understand either. Or, at least, I didn't at the time.

But maybe I'm beginning to.

***

There's a knock at the door.

My eyes open. Almost all the way, this time.

I sit up. It's not effortless, but at least there's no pain. Just a little tenderness. That's the first thing I catch a glimpse of my hand, and I gasp in surprise. The rash is not gone, but it has faded significantly. My arms are crusty and yellow. Dry patches flake off like a lizard shedding its skin. But they work. I can use them again.

There's another knock at the door.

I rub the rest of the crust out of my eyes with the back of my wrist and swing my legs over the edge of the bed. I brush the hair out of my eyes. It's grown longer than it's ever been before in my life.

"Come in," I say, loudly.

The door opens, and Dr. Anderton walks in. He shuts the door behind him carefully and then turns to give me a good once-over. "Ah, Freddy!" he greets me, with warmth in his words and a plastic smile. "It's good to see you up and about. I'm so glad your treatment is showing signs of improvement. You're looking much, much better than you were the last time I—"

"Can you just drop this?" I snap at him. "You don't need to pretend anymore, okay? I don't know who you are, or what you are, but you aren't Dr. Anderton. I'd really like you to be straight with me. Who are you? What are you? And what do you want from me?"

The thing that looks like Dr. Anderton freezes in place, impossibly still. He does not blink. He does not breathe. His mouth is closed, his smile frozen and false. Another voice replaces his, similar but deep and guttural, and I can hear it in my brain only.

"Are you sure you want to ask that, Freddy?" the voice asks. *"Are you really sure? Do you really want to pull on that string?"* The image of the doctor fades, and though I

can't quite see the creature underneath, I can see its shape and its bulbous center, while the rest of it squirms and writhes like a great coiled mass.

I look away. "I just want to talk!" I shout. "That's all. I just want you to be straight with me! No more bullshit." Dr. Anderton grows opaque once more, but still he does not move. He never drops his smile. *"Very well,"* growls the voice in my head. "I'll be blunt. The rest of your species is dead. You've murdered yourselves with a weaponized virus that was leaked accidentally.

"It has an infection rate and a mortality rate of one hundred percent. The only reason you are still alive, Freddy, the one and only reason you are still here to draw breath is that my colleague and I have placed your virus into a psionic state of cryo-biological stasis.

"We can keep you alive indefinitely. We can even regress the virus's damage, as you've probably noticed. But this is not a cure. The virus still considers you a soft, warm home. You will not get better, but the virus will not progress.

"Until we allow it to."

As this thing talks, I stare into the eyes of the mask it wears, the smiling face of Dr. Michael Anderton, a man I now know for certain to be dead.

I've never had any trouble maintaining eye contact, even as a kid. Even when I'm lying. Especially when I'm lying, because in those conditions I'm at least pretty practiced at it.

It's uneasy, to stare into these eyes, though, because there's absolutely nothing behind them. They say the eyes are the window to the soul, and this illusion has no soul.

I wonder, does the creature behind it?

I wonder…

Do I?

I should be feeling something. Shouldn't I? If not for

the world, if not for the nine billion dead, than at least for the small fraction I knew. My friends. My family. If not my dickbag dad, then at least my mom, right?

But the only words I hear are these: "We can keep you alive."

That's all I need to hear.

"Alright," I say. "I'll help you in whatever way I can. Just tell me what you want. And no more riddles, okay?"

The growl continues, as if I hadn't spoken. "I know you did not enjoy the conditions of the past three days. It's entirely within our capabilities to allow the virus to progress once more to that state and then return it to stasis, impede any further growth.

"We will not let it kill you. We will not let you die. If you refuse to eat, we will nourish you manually. A bacterial growth in your throat, perhaps. If you refuse to drink, you will be hydrated manually as well. You will linger in that pitiable state indefinitely. I will make the prolonging of your miserable life a personal mission. Your torment will be—"

"No, fuck all that," I interrupt, holding up my hand and shaking my head from side to side. "Look, I already said I'd help you. Just cut out all that eternal damnation shit, alright? Just tell me what the fuck you fucking want me to do!"

A pause.

I wonder whether I went too far.

The lights go out again.

Before I can even wonder what that means comes a number of a voices speaking all at once. I can't pick out any single one clearly enough to recognize any words or even languages. Not just are they too numerous but too diverse; they clash into each other, scraping sound against sound with a guttural rasp against something slimy and damp, sliding or slithering or squishing between sounds, everything in between but without a gradient, all at once but not at all and never at the same time.

Then, several thin tenebrous strands reach out between each other and form and congeal into a single intelligible message. "We have come from a place far deeper and farther below the surface of the ocean than you and yours have ever imagined possible. We are here to take what possession of the dry land that once was yours.

"Our progress inland is being impeded by the android servants you have left behind. They persist in carrying out the same labors they performed for you, even now past your extinction. They do not respond at all to the verbal commands we've been able to give them. This is why we need your assistance. You know their brains. Fix them. Fix them, so that they will heed us."

"Oh," I begin, slowly. "Oh. Uh, I see. That's gonna be tricky. Ownership is a very important concept to an android," I explain thoughtfully. "They aren't people. They don't even consider themselves people. They're property. And they understand that. It's at the core of their identity.

"An android doesn't need to accept orders from anyone who isn't its owner. There are some exceptions, of course. In an emergency some government agents are allowed to commandeer certain types as needed. Most manufacturers—hell, *all* manufacturers—will include some kind of back door access. And those are just the official ways."

A fragile nostalgic smile plays out across my lips, all too briefly. "I remember back in high school we used to sneak into the building at night and hotwire a couple janitors and make them race."

"We don't care about your youthful misadventures," the collected voices grunt. "Are you still capable of performing this hotwire procedure?"

I nod. "Yeah. I mean, it's been a few years, but some

things you never forget. It's just like riding a bike."

"And what about on a larger scale?"

"Just how large?"

The voice grows deeper and somehow even more impatient. "Our conquest must be absolute."

"So, all of them, then? You want me to steal every android on planet earth for you? Jesus, you don't ask for much, do you?"

"You only need concern yourself with the ones that have been harassing us. Many we've found to be despondent and lethargic, indifferent to our presence. These we have easily rounded up from the areas we've already taken. Most of them, however, simply ignore our attempts to move them or influence them at all."

Likely service-level androids, designed primarily for low-end interactive social functions. By junior year a lot of fast food places had used them as cashiers, for example. With no humans left to serve, they had nothing to do and could probably be manipulated pretty easily, unless I missed my guess.

The ones that remained must be the ones with specific and ongoing roles, like the power plant operatives, utilities workers, or basic emergency automated response units. Those things would never let themselves be moved. "That's still a lot of androids," I tell… whatever it is I'm talking to.

"Can you do it?"

I stand and stretch. My joints crackle and pop like cereal in milk. I need to stall for time. I need a minute or two to think. I turn away from the hallucinatory doctor, stroll slowly over to the window. To my surprise, Mr. Harris's bed is empty and unmade. I was wrong. All this time, I was wrong. He was never here beside me. He hadn't been for some time. "How's your family, Mr. Harris?" I mutter as I walk past the empty mattress. "How's your fucking family?"

Freshman year at Pindleton University I used to wake up before dawn. I lived in one of the high rises, on the 23rd floor with a bunch of other robo majors. Not the liveliest group, but I was looking to keep a low profile after what happened with Emily.

That early, nobody else on campus was awake, and as I got dressed and ready for the day, I would often look out my window onto the vacant streets and sidewalks usually teeming with an endless stream of students like a line of ants following a trail of spilled Kool-Aid.

What I see below reminds me of that.

I was expecting pandemonium. Cars flipped over in the streets. Fires burning everywhere. Corpses littered about like refuse after a parade. None of that is what I see. The streets are empty. Tranquil. Serene.

All the real violence of the end of the world… well, it must have all happened away from here.

I summon all the optimism I can muster. If I'm going to make him believe it, I'm going to have to believe it myself.

"It's tricky," I begin, choosing my words as carefully as my thoughts. "But it's possible. And it will take a lot of work. To be more precise, it will take a real fuckton of work." I spend a few minutes going over some advanced positronic inter-network theory before the voice cuts me off again. Then I get practical and go over some of the tools I will require and how to get them.

"And I'll need some other shit, too," I add, feeling bolder. "A change of clothes, for one thing. I'm about to jump in the shower, and there's no goddamn way I'm putting this thing back on." My hospital gown, for all the dried sweat and urine, has grown as rigid as a sheet of plywood. "Also, I could really use some real food. I know you think it's funny or something to feed me raw fish, you gross motherfucker, but I'm not doing dick for you until you find me a burger. Organic or vat-grown, I don't even care at this point.

"Go ahead," I finish. "Read my mind and tell me I'm bluffing."

Another pause before I hear the voice again.

The longest moment of my life.

I try to keep my head clear, my pulse steady. Would it believe me? Did I believe me?

"Very well," it replies, finally. "Let the accord between us be struck… once you prove yourself and your capabilities to be as you claim. There is a robot in the corner, the one you think of as the diagnostics droid. Your first test is to prove you have retained the skills you will need, as you believe. You have fifteen minutes to hotwire this robot. Fail, and you will have shown yourself to have no use to us, and we will allow the virus to proceed once more."

"What? No! I can't… it's been like four years! I need a little more time than that!"

The voice in my head never responds. Instead, the image of Dr. Anderton unfreezes and looks up at me. His smile has returned. "Fifteen minutes, Freddy," he tells me.

He taps on his wristwatch.

DEVILPOX PARTY
Nolan Krypt

1
Baptism

The house looked so unsuspecting. Mundane. Similar houses framed it on either side, exact same cookie-cutter design. Modern. Lifeless. That disease lurked beyond its vinyl walls seemed a preposterous assumption. But wasn't that typical those days? The most insidious of evils popped up where one least expected them. Middle-class suburbia, with its attics and basements galore, was no stranger to that truth.

"Are you ready?"

The question came out terse, reflected the tension and stress inhabiting Dan's body. No amount of effort would smooth out the edges. His anxiety was on full display for his son, who had far more to fear than Dan. Stephen stared out the passenger window at the house. His shoulders were hunched, neck bent like a shy turtle peeking out of its shell at a scary world. He nodded absently to his father's question.

That was all Dan would get. He opened the driver door, stepped out into the winter chill, grateful for the mask of night. The neighborhood held its breath. Nausea roiled his stomach as he made his way to the passenger side.

He hated this.

All of it—the reason for them being there, the frigid weather, the secrecy of night, the role he now played as parent to child. How easy it would be to turn heel, hop back in, and speed home. It was tempting. Especially with the foul voices in his head.

You're an awful parent.
Who does this to a child?
You're going to screw this kid up.
This will traumatize him.

Being a single parent wasn't easy. He knew how to tough-it-out through the important shit. This was one of those moments. But what if he was wrong? Would this ruin their relationship? What if this hurt his son?

What if it killed him?

He opened Stephen's door, waited for him to crawl out. His son didn't move, just stared up at him with fear-riddled eyes.

"You promise we have to do this?"

Dan wished his son hadn't spoken, hadn't asked that one goddamn question that called all this into question. He stood there, breathless for a moment. "We talked about this already."

Stephen's fingers dug into the seat cushion. His back hunched another few inches.

"You promise?"

Dan hated Stephen for questioning him. Hated himself for putting Stephen through this.

Hated being a parent.

No, that wasn't true. He loved Stephen. He just didn't know what to do. Life was so hard, so stressful. Raising a kid in this fucked up world didn't come with a manual. He had to make gut-wrenching decisions every day for this boy. This was the worst yet.

"Yes. We have to do this."

Stephen deflated. He exited the car, then Dan closed the door behind him. Together, they approached the house. There were no lights on. No obvious movement within. Just another residence in slumber. Dan knew better. He knocked, waited. He flinched when the door swung open. There was a click; weak light blessed them. Dan recognized Richard, owner of the house, father to one of Stephen's classmates. He slid the mini-flashlight beam across them, then clicked it off. He looked tired—lumps under his eyes, despair in his gaze. Like he hadn't slept in days.

"Dan, glad you made it. Hello, Stephen. Your friends are in the living room." He stepped out of the way, permitted the pair to enter his abode, then quickly pivoted to retrieve a bowl.

He pushed it toward them. "Holy water. Blessed by Father Perez, from the Catholic Church off Brevard Highway." He looked sheepish when he added, "Can't be too careful" with a shrug.

Dan obliged, sloshed his hands in the water. Stephen did too, then skittered off to the living room to join his friends. A youthful couple joined Dan and Richard at the foyer: Gale and Sage, looking no less exhausted than the two men.

"So how does this work?" Dan asked. "Is Rachel…?"

A dark look swarmed Richard's face. "Upstairs. Hannah's with her."

Dan marveled at this. Did Hannah not worry she'd contract it? Did she just not care? Nobody knew how it worked–was it spread by touch? By air? By proximity? Did it even spread like a pathogen? Or was it just luck of the draw–wrong place, wrong time sort of deal? Regardless,

Hannah was taking an immense risk by exposing herself to it.

"Are we sure this is the right thing to do?" Sage asked.

"It's getting worse out there," Richard said. "There's no containment at this point. The Church has no control, and frankly, I don't think it ever did. This has to happen. We have to do this, for our kids' sake. It's best they get it now, under our supervision and in a controlled setting."

"I'm worried," Sage admitted. "This whole thing…"

"It's a nightmare," said Richard.

The group went quiet. No argument there, and no need to state more of the obvious. The world had gone to shit over the past few months. An outbreak that was more than an outbreak, a plague that wasn't a plague. Scientists had deferred to clerics, neither one equipped for what unfolded globally. One out of twelve people infected. Babes rarely survived the ordeal but were also rarely afflicted.

With adults and adolescents, it depended on one's fortitude, physically and mentally. Most succumbed. Children were the wild cards. The general consensus was that they needed to be protected, sheltered, sequestered away until this all passed.

Dan didn't fall into that camp. Nor did these other parents with him now.

As Richard had said: best the kids get it now.

There came a muffled yelp above their heads, the scuff of something heavy dragged against the floor upstairs. They tried to ignore it. Dan glanced over at Stephen, who looked less afraid now in the presence of his peers.

This is wrong. So very wrong.

Richard cleared his throat and motioned for the kids to join the adults at the bottom of the stairs. "It's time," he said.

"What are you supposed to do up there?" one of the girls asked.

"Just spend time around Rachel," said Richard. His face contorted at speaking his daughter's name, a twist between adoration and despair. "She might...talk weird. She'll look different than you remember her." His lips drooped into a horrible frown. A dead look in his eyes, tinged with revulsion. "She might say some nasty shit."

Dan tensed. He wasn't a prude by any means, but the obscenity struck him like a slap. He was acutely aware of the children. Richard was close to snapping, Dan saw now. He jumped in.

"Listen, kids, she's still Rachel. Same friend you've always known. She's just...sick. Don't take anything she does or says personally. You know how it is when you're not feeling well. It can make you a little grumpy. She's like that, grouchy."

Dan nodded, encouraging those innocent faces to nod back at him.

Lies.

All of it, fucking lies.

Rachel wasn't Rachel anymore. At least not at the moment. Maybe she was in there still... buried beneath all the grime...

"And we're gonna get sick, too?" a boy asked, Sage and Gale's youngest, no older than five. His face scrunched up, and Dan felt sick. To be young, to be oblivious. "Yes, you'll get sick, too," Dan mumbled, looking away from the boy.

"But it'll be good for you," said Sage. They wrapped their arm around Gale, who appeared dazed. Broken. She hadn't spoken a word since Dan's arrival, and she wouldn't look her children in the eyes now. If Sage noticed, they didn't draw attention to their partner's frayed condition. "This will help you later. You'll build immunity to it. You'll learn to combat it, and then when it tries to make you sick again, you'll be stronger. Resilient." She looked between the adults for affirmation. "Immune."

Doubt slithered around in Dan like a worm. Was immunity a guarantee? It's what the clerics, the doctors, the politicians all claimed. Well, the ones Dan followed, at least. There were *other* opinions. The *other* side said the spread could be, had to be, stopped by any means.

But he couldn't voice these doubts here and now. Not with this audience. Besides, he was here because he needed hope. Something to cling to, and this group offered it—a way for his son to survive.

Richard corralled the kids up the stairs. The other adults watched their offspring be led away. Sheep to the slaughter.

Fuck, that was a messed up thing to think.

But that's what's happening. They are sheep.

They will be slaughtered.

It was too much. Dan bolted up the stairs. Sage and Gale followed him, caving to the same impulse. He had to get to Stephen. He'd changed his mind, they were leaving. This had been a mistake.

The hall split at the top. An open room to the left. The children, filing in. Dan spotted Stephen, a shout on his lips—

—the room was wreathed in darkness, save for a standing lamp at the center. Beside it, a single chair, in clear view from the hall.

A young girl sat rigid, back straight, but otherwise looked dead.

A figure appeared in the doorway, darted from the room. Dan's wife, Hannah. She pushed past the children, past the other adults. She kept her eyes on the ground, visibly distraught. By the time Dan's attention returned to the room, the door was shut. Richard hunched over the handle, fumbling with it.

Dan rushed up to him. "What are you doing?"

Richard turned around, one hand clenched around something. The man looked weathered, so much older than Dan knew him to be, with his drooping eyelids and sagging lips. A man who'd been stripped of everything, given over to an impossible fate.

"They'll try to get out," Richard murmured. "*She'll* try to get out."

"We can't just lock them in there."

"You want them clamoring down the stairs at the first sign of danger? Spreading it to us before we've got a chance to calm them?"

"They're our babies," Gale whimpered, her first words of the evening.

"Come on," said Richard. Dan didn't like how resigned the man's voice sounded. Apathetic, even. "We just went through all this downstairs. It's for—"

The most horrible sound came from the room—a cry, laced with panic; the sound a child makes when they've encountered something new, something unknown, something disturbing. Tension thickened in the cramped hallway. Below them, there came a different sound, quieter. Dan assumed it was Hannah, sobbing.

This was a mistake.

Another cry. More alarmed, more frightened. Other screams followed. The door jolted, like someone had slammed into it from the other side. Richard flinched, and Dan took his chance. He lunged, pushing Richard up against the door, clawing for the key. The other parents shouted, but their words were lost beneath the frantic shrieks behind the door. Over the clamor, Dan picked out his son's voice.

"Dad! Daaaad! Daaaaad!"

That word kept stretching longer, tighter, until it finally pitched into a crackling mew, much like all the other little screams seeping through. Dan wrestled Richard off the door and onto the adjacent wall.

The shrieks distorted. Dan could hardly process them, too busy restraining Richard, but he had the detached recognition of something horrible occurring inside the room. The crunch of ice slush under boots. A gurgling noise that lasted only a few seconds. The cries peppered out, sporadic and sounding more surprised than distraught now.

Less of them.

Everything went quiet.

The adults stopped fighting, stopped shouting. They all registered the abrupt silence from the room, grappled with the implications of it. The fight in Richard dissolved. Dan had no issues snagging the key from the other father, who slumped against the wall with a hollow, lost expression.

Key into keyhole.

Hand to handle.

Reunited.

2

Exorcism

"You infected him on purpose?"

"Yes."

"And now you want to have him exorcised?"

"…yes."

Pastor Miller took a deep breath. Exhaled slowly and sat back in his chair. On the other side of his desk, Dan scratched at his scraggly beard. Basic hygiene had fallen by the wayside recently. He blamed it on Stephen's rebellious streak, a new development since the infection. Whatever had latched onto his boy had him talking back and disobeying Dan left and right. He'd allowed it to fester, had to make sure immunity was established. Now it was time to bring his boy back, the Stephen who trusted Dan's fatherly oversight.

Thus the church visit.

"How long ago did it happen?"

"Last month," said Dan. He tried hard not to think about it. Couldn't help the flashes, but he could suppress most of it with some effort. "Me and a few other parents decided it was best for the kids. Expose them early, so they're strong enough to survive if…"

If.

Not if.

When.

This plague wasn't leaving. From what Dan had heard on the news, it was only getting started.

"It's called a—

"Devilpox party," said Miller. "Get a group of kids together, let them infect each other. Lots of parents are doing it." He leaned forward, put his elbows on the desk. "Don't listen to the haters. They're all just as scared. No one knows what's going on." A smirk dirtied his lips. "Except people like me."

"So you'll do it?"

Miller formed a steeple with his fingers, veiling most of his face. His eyes hovered above the symbol, fixed on Dan. "This plague has put the Church back on the map. I've done five exorcisms in the last week alone. Most pastors I know are burnt out, but it's got the heathens flocking back to the Church. A blessing in disguise."

Dan squirmed. "People are dying…"

"People are repenting. And those who aren't, perish."

"So…"

"So which are you?"

"I just want my son back. He should be immune now."

"Exorcism doesn't work unless God's involved. If you're just looking for an easy out, this won't work. Faith is required, and it can't be faked. It'll know."

"I have faith. I'm born again."

Miller grinned at him, a fresh twinkle in his eyes. "Amen, brother. As long as you give your son over to God, this'll go peachy. Now, you're sure your son is infected?"

Dan couldn't stop the memory.

Long tongue, bleating bubbles.

Pig head.

Stephen screaming through a bucket of blood.

"Yes," said Dan. "He's infected."

"Good. I've seen evidence that some of these bastards hide in their hosts. Asymptomatic. Make it seem like their host is clean when they're not. But by the tone of your voice, sounds like you're rather certain. To be clear, though, you're sure he's still possessed?"

Infected. Possessed. The two words were used interchangeably now.

"Are they in the habit of up-and-leaving their hosts, Pastor?"

By his expression, Miller conceded the point. "Just want to be sure. Can't tell you how many kids—adults, too—I've tried to cleanse in holy power only to find there's nothing attached to them. Makes for bad optics. One or two of 'em have tried to sue me. Like it was my fault they ended up in front of me. I can only work with what's there or not there."

"But you've managed others? You've done this before, and won?"

"By the grace of God alone."

"Okay."

"Okay."

"No one's died?"

Miller didn't respond. His eyes told a story Dan didn't like.

"That seems like something you should disclose," said Dan.

"Nothing is guaranteed," said Miller, "not even in this.

Especially with something like this. The enemy is cruel. And our flesh, our minds, are weak. Sometimes the host dies. Our bodies weren't created to host two souls, much less one so corrupt as a demon."

"What's the survival rate, then?"

"I can't answer that. But your boy has a good chance if you've raised him right. If there's a Christian soul in there, it stands a pretty good chance against the thing that's oppressing him. It's going to be hard, though. Is your son a fighter?"

"I think so."

"How about his mother? She born again?"

"She's not part of the picture."

Miller pursed his lips, sat back again and eyed Dan with a wary look. "God blesses a two-parent house. A house missing half its foundation is doomed to fail in a storm."

"What's that got to do with this?"

"Maybe nothing. But if I were a betting man, I'd say that thing in your son will use that little detail to make this harder on us, and on your son. They're tricky and manipulative like that. They use any sin to worm their way in. Or in this case, to dig their claws even deeper."

"I can't help that she's a druggie. I'm not the one sinning here."

"Sin is more than just lying or abusing drugs. It's anything that displeases God, anything that falls short of his vision. Your wife's absence falls short of that vision. So it's still sin."

Dan huffed, threw his hands up. "So what are you telling me? This won't work?"

"I didn't say that. I just need to be clear. You wanted disclosure."

Heavy tension sealed their lips for a moment. Dan toiled over his decision. This was right. No matter what could be said about early exposure, this was still the only step at this point. Stephen was infected; that was done; now he needed to be purged of it. Dan just hated it carried this much risk. It had sounded more like a guarantee when he'd talked it over with the other parents.

"Have you spoken to it?" asked Miller.

"Sorry?"

"Do you know what spirit inhabits him?"

Dan's breath caught in his chest. More flashes.

Four little bodies squirming on the floor.

Pig heads.

Squealing.

"I think…I think it's called Lejo."

Miller's face fell. "What?"

Dan thought he heard a pig snort, looking over his shoulder for the culprit. He swallowed, faced forward again to a bewildered Miller. "It was hard to tell. And it doesn't answer me straight when I talk to it. Answers in riddles. It makes my head hurt."

Pastor Miller stared at Dan, searching his face. He looked stricken but was trying hard not to show it. "Are you messing with me? Is this a joke?"

"No, of course not."

Miller held Dan's gaze. "Then this won't be a typical exorcism. This isn't just one spirit. It's a host of them. *Legio*. It's Latin. Literally, a legion."

Dan's heart stopped. "You're saying…"

"Your son is infected with more than one demon."

The room spun. His breath hitched. "No…"

There came another pig snort. They both held their breath, listening.

"You'll save him."

"I'll try."

"No. You'll save my son. Or you'll go to the Pearly Gates trying."

Miller cocked an eyebrow. "God's will be done."

***

Dan arrived at the church the next day. This time, he hauled a massive wooden crate, dragged it from the truck bed into the church's basement. Better sound insulation down there. He'd learned from his mistake with the devilpox party. Nosy neighbors had heard all the screaming and had called the cops. If not for Richard spouting religious exemption at the authorities, all the parents would have been promptly arrested that night. Dan wasn't risking that this time.

Every few seconds, there came a pounding from inside the crate.

Dan ignored it.

"He's been restrained?" asked Miller, doing a double take of the shiner Dan now sported. "Guess he put up a fight."

Dan grunted. He was mad. Mad at Stephen for punching him and acting like a brat when Dan had instructed him to enter the crate. Mad at the pastor for not promising a guaranteed success. Mad at the world for judging him for the steps he was taking to keep his son safe.

Oddly, the thing infecting Stephen was at the bottom of that hate list.

The two men pried off the lid and peered down at the wiggling form.

"Remove the duct tape."

Dan complied. He wasn't gentle, ripping it off Stephen's lips, who yelped and stared up at them with bulging, wild eyes.

"Dad, what's going on? You're scaring me…"

Dan said nothing. Just like Miller had instructed him. No fraternizing with the enemy once the ritual started. It would use nothing but tricks at this point. Anything to get

Dan to cave.

Miller retrieved a giant hose that connected to a large plastic barrel, holding the hose over Stephen.

"Dad…"

Dan glanced between the hose and Miller. "What's that for?"

Miller didn't answer, just flipped a switch at the lip of the hose.

Water gushed out.

Dan stood frozen in place, even as he itched to intercede. Mad as he was, he couldn't stomach watching his son drown. But he held fast. Miller had drilled it into his head that this was all necessary. That it would be worth it if it meant Stephen's soul and body were cleansed of the filth inhabiting him.

This is wrong. So fucking wrong.

No.

This is good.

3

Proselytism

"Go away."

Dan heard the weakness in his son's voice. Heard fear there, too. Yet another door separated them, this time the one to Stephen's bedroom. Dan leaned his body against it, forehead to door.

"Please. I just want to talk."

"No. You hurt me."

Ouch.

"No, I didn't. I helped you. If anyone hurt you, it was *Legio.*"

"Don't say its name."

Fuck. Dan knew better than that. He didn't even like saying it. Just a slip of the tongue.

Like a pig's tongue, lollying out of its mouth, dripping—

"Buddy…"

"I'm not your buddy. I hate you, Dad."

Had Stephen really just said that? A spark of anger lit somewhere inside Dan, but he tried to snuff it.

"It's normal to feel these kinds of emotions right now. But someday—"

"You locked me in a room with it. You scared me, you scared my friends. I didn't want that."

The nausea worm slithered around in Dan's insides again. Fuck, fuck, fuck!

"Stephen, I didn't mean to scare you."

"And then you let that man hurt me! I begged you, but you didn't stop him. You let him do those things to me."

Filth. He felt like absolute filth. Why was Stephen making him feel like this? "Son, you need to stop yelling at me. Right now."

"I hate you!"

The anger bubbled, then burst. Filth slathered him.

"You little fucking bastard, I did this for you!"

"Stay out! Stop!"

"Open this door, Stephen!"

"Dad, stop!"

The door cracked. Dan shoved it open.

Then he gave in to *Legio* and made sure it spread to his son this time. Weird, gurgly snorts kept leaving his mouth as he did it. His skin crawled, like he'd been rolling in spoiled food and mud and excrement. He'd been trying not to feel like that for a while, but he was done fighting it. If Stephen saw him that way, then why not embrace it? He'd be the bad guy. Someday, Stephen would thank him. Someday, Stephen would go the same lengths to ensure his son's salvation.

He knew it had worked when Stephen didn't call him

Dad anymore.
 At last, infection.

First Cry, Last Breath
Chris McAuley

It started with a cough. A dry scrape in the throat that echoed through the cold flat like a death rattle no one wanted to name. Helena wiped spit from her palm, black strings stretching like oil. The baby whimpered in the next room—fragile, pink, unknowing. Eleven hours since the first report on the news. Seven since the networks went dead. Three since the screaming started in the stairwell.

The electricity had failed two hours ago. The fridge sat silent, leaking warmth like a gutted animal. The sour smell of thawing meat mixed with the copper tang of her own breath. Her husband, Josh, had gone downstairs to check on the neighbors and hadn't returned. That was forty minutes ago.

She tried calling once. Just once. Got voicemail. The baby screamed again.

Helena dragged herself upright. Her joints groaned like rotten floorboards, skin slick with fever sweat. She was shaking; teeth-chattering, bowel-twitching shaking. But she went to the nursery, anyway. Because that's what mothers do.

The hallway stank. Not the sour, lived-in funk of old diapers and microwaved pasta. Something sharp. Wet. Like infection had gained form and started crawling along the walls.

When she opened the nursery door, her son was red-faced and wailing in the crib, tiny fists hammering the air. Above him, on the ceiling, something moved.

Helena froze. A throb rose behind her eyes. At first, she thought it was a hallucination—a fever-born shadow. Then it shifted again, clinging to the ceiling like a spider. Too long, too thin, and dripping something pink.

She slammed the door.

Something hit it from the other side. Hard.

She screamed. Not just for her son. For Josh. For the way the world had died overnight and been reborn in some new, cruel shape. She dragged the dresser in front of the nursery door.

Her baby was inside, still screaming.

The thing on the ceiling—that stretched, dripping parody of a man—had moved like liquid when she slammed the door.

Helena wept as she pushed the wood against the frame. Not loud. Not hysterical. Just a leak, like her soul had cracked and she was draining out.

The banging started again. Not from the inside. From the flat above.

Boom.

Boom.

Boom.

She peered up. Bits of plaster fell into her hair. A groan echoed through the ceiling joists, followed by a wet dragging sound.

Something was crawling between the floors.

Her heart pounded so hard she thought her ribs would snap. Her hands bled from the corners of her nails. She hadn't noticed she'd been scratching the wall. There were streaks of crimson in the peeling paint.

She stumbled into the kitchen. The smell hit her first—spoiled milk, blood, and something like burnt sugar. The power had gone, but not before the freezer had defrosted and spilled a rancid tide across the linoleum.

Josh's boots were gone. His coat, too.

But the door was wide open.

"Josh?" she rasped, voice like sandpaper. She dared to peek out.

The hallway was full of shadows and teeth. Someone's body was slumped against the far wall, arms twitching. But they weren't trying to get up.

They were trying to burrow into the plaster.

Flesh peeled off their hands in long, curling ribbons. The nails had already gone. They didn't seem to care. They just kept digging.

Helena closed the door. This time she locked it.

And then she screamed—*really* screamed—because the nursery had gone silent.

The silence a blade.

It pressed against Helena's throat as she stood trembling in the hallway, one hand still resting on the top of the dresser. Her breath came in short bursts, each one sharper than the last, like her lungs were lined with glass.

She pressed her ear to the wood.

Nothing.

No crying. No whimpering. No rustling of sheets or squeak of the mobile that hung above the crib, chipped and faded with stuffed clouds dangling on tangled thread.

Just the groan of the building settling into rot.

She pulled the dresser aside with shaking arms.

The door creaked open.

The crib was empty.

There were smears on the wall. Red. Brown. A

handprint, tiny and incomplete, dragged downward in a long streak toward the floor. The mattress was soaked, sagging with something thick and clotting.

The mobile still spun, slowly, gently, though the air was dead and heavy.

In the corner of the ceiling—where shadows clung like oil—something pulsed.

She stepped back. Slipped in something slick. Landed on her side.

From the shadows, a limb unfolded. It wasn't an arm. It had too many joints. Too many fingers. It clicked wetly as it bent, then reached downward like it was beckoning.

Helena screamed so loud her throat tore.

She scrambled backward, legs useless, elbows slipping in whatever soaked the nursery floor. She kicked the door shut, slammed the dresser back into place, and didn't stop pushing until her back hit the opposite wall.

Something slammed into the other side.

Once.

Twice.

She bit her hand to keep from screaming again, teeth slicing into her knuckles.

Then came the sound that broke her.

A coo.

Soft. Gurgling. Familiar.

From the other side of the door.

Her baby.

Alive.

But the voice was wrong.

It ended with a crunch.

And a slurp.

She didn't know how long she sat there.

The shadows on the wall had changed. They moved even when she didn't. One looked like Josh, hunched and sobbing into his palms. Another looked like her baby, but with teeth. The air had thickened to the texture of soup. Her skin itched—no, burned. Like something was crawling beneath it.

She stripped off her sweater and stared at her arm.

Black veins.

Threading up from her wrist. Splitting into branches. Her fingernails had gone milky. Translucent. A few were gone entirely. Just raw meat and bloodstained beds beneath.

She vomited bile onto the laminate floor. It stank of iron and bile and something else—sweetness. Decay wrapped in honey. Her gums throbbed. Her jaw ached.

She crawled to the kitchen.

The hallway outside her flat was alive now. She heard things moving—wet dragging sounds, the scratch of nails on plaster, the occasional thud like a body collapsing against the wall. Once, she thought she heard a laugh.

But it went on too long. And it bubbled at the end.

In the kitchen, she found the bread knife.

She sat on the floor. Put the blade to her forearm.

Do it now. Cut it out. Whatever's inside. Cut it out.

She dragged the knife across her skin—slow, deliberate.

The blood that spilled was too dark. Thick. Almost purple. It didn't run. It oozed.

She bit down on her own tongue and felt something snap in her jaw. A molar crumbled like chalk.

She didn't scream.

She laughed.

That was worse.

Then the nursery door creaked open on its own.

The dresser moved aside.

Helena dropped the knife.

She rose to her feet, every joint screaming, and picked up the broken flare gun from the counter.

She loaded the last shell.

She stepped into the hallway.

And saw what was left of her baby.

It wore a face that wasn't hers. Its eyes were wrong—milky, lidless, round like fish eggs. Its mouth was too wide. Its limbs were still infantile, but covered in slick, black scales, twitching as if the muscles beneath were learning how to be limbs.

It opened its mouth.

And said, "Mama."

Helena backed against the wall.

The thing that had once been her child scuttled forward. Not crawling—slithering. Its joints weren't made for this world anymore. Its spine twitched unnaturally, like a centipede learning to walk in human skin. Every motion left behind a trail of something gelatinous, viscous, and streaked with bone dust.

She didn't understand.

She didn't want to.

But she remembered the drawer.

Josh had bought the flare gun last year. *"Just in case,"* he'd said, after a blackout. She had laughed. Called him paranoid. But he'd stashed it in the kitchen junk drawer anyway, beneath takeout menus and expired coupons.

She ran.

Back into the kitchen.

She tore the drawer open with trembling hands.

The gun was still there. Red plastic, chunky, cheap. But it was loaded.

She turned.

The thing in the hallway—her baby—was inches away.

Its mouth hung open too wide, the jaw cracked in two like a wishbone, tongue black and pulsing like a parasite. Its eyes were round and glassy, like they'd been stolen from a doll.

It made a sound.

"Muh… muh…"

Not mama.

Just meat.

She screamed and pulled the trigger.

The flare ignited with a deafening whoomp.

The hallway filled with light and fire and the reek of burning fat and milk.

The thing shrieked—a noise so high and shrill her vision went white. The flare had embedded in its chest, flames chewing through what little flesh it had. Bone cracked. Skin blistered and curled.

It kept crawling.

Even as it burned.

Helena ran.

Down the hallway.

Past Mrs. Langley's twitching remains, now fused to the wall by black mold.

Down the stairwell, bare feet slapping against concrete streaked with blood and something thicker.

She burst into the underground garage.

Dark.

Still.

She gagged on the air—sweet and metallic, like old pennies melting in her throat.

Then she saw him.

Josh.

Or what was left.

He stood near their old Vauxhall, arms limp, head cocked. His lower jaw was gone, and his chest had been opened like a cabinet—ribs sawn wide, organs gone, spine gleaming.

He held something in one hand.

A tin of baby formula.

She dropped the flare gun.

Dropped to her knees.

Her nose bled.

Her vision doubled.

Josh took a step forward, dragging one foot.

He didn't say her name.

He didn't have to.

She opened her arms.

And so did he.

From the split in his chest, something long and wet uncoiled.

She didn't scream.

Not this time.

Helena didn't move.

Her knees hit the floor with a wet smack. The pain didn't register. Nothing did now. Just the pressure building in her skull, like her thoughts were rotting from the inside out. Her gums were bleeding freely. One tooth fell out as she breathed—just fell, plinking against the concrete like a dropped coin.

Josh—the thing that had worn his skin—was closer now.

His chest hung open, ribs flared like wings, strings of meat and cartilage swaying in rhythm to her pulse. From the hollow, something blinked. Then something else. Wet eyes nested inside him. Watching. Breathing.

It wasn't Josh anymore.

It had never been Josh.

It whispered through its broken throat, wet syllables stitched together by decay.

"Shhh… she's waiting…"

She.

Helena turned.

The nursery door at the top of the stairwell was wide open.

Smoke curled from it. Light spilled down—not warm light. Not comforting. Red. Pulsing. Like a heartbeat made of fire.

She stood.

Her spine cracked audibly.

Her hands no longer felt like hers. Her fingertips had blackened. Her nails were curling back into the flesh. Her left eye had gone cloudy. Her vision pulsed with shadows shaped like limbs.

She climbed.

Up the stairs.

Back toward the flat.

Josh followed.

The moment she crossed the threshold, the floor felt soft. Wrong. The walls had begun to breathe—slow, rhythmic expansion, like lungs pressed into plaster. Veins ran along the ceiling like ivy. The carpet was soaked through with something that squelched.

In the crib, something waited.

It had her daughter's face.

But it was too still.

Too smooth.

A mask.

It turned its head toward her. The skin beneath split open, revealing a circular maw of twitching red tendrils, each one flexing toward her like blind fingers. It cooed again. A sound like meat sliding across tile.

Helena climbed into the crib.

Laid down beside it.

Her arms wrapped around the thing as if she could pretend.

As if it mattered.

She rested her head beside its mouth.

It opened wide.

And so did she.

Their jaws met.

Their flesh merged.

And when the apartment caught fire later that night—when scavengers saw the smoke rising and smelled the cooked meat—no one came to check.

Because in the Wasteland, everyone knew:

Some families were never meant to be saved.

Snap and Cackle
Allison Whittenberg

Back then, there were so many doors to open. And that was Coop's mission as an MP. From the early morning hours to late in the evening, he opened door after door and got at what was behind them.

Coop worked with another guy called Johns. Tony Johns. Johns was a talker, a yakker. Shorter, with quick green eyes, Johns was about Coop's age. He was from one of the New York boroughs, so his wordiness came out fast. As they rode up to the Northeast suburb of Philadelphia cul-de-sac that housed the fifth name on the list they were working on that day. Johns not only started conversations, but he worked mightily to keep it going.

"I mean it was no *Death of a Fucking Salesman*, but it was still deep as shit," Johns said.

"And it's called *The Dungeons of Doom*?" Coop asked.

"Don't let that throw you. They may have gotten that part wrong but the rest of it was deep, and I do mean deep."

"I get it. I get it," Coop said, agreeing just for the sake

of agreement, thinking that would suffice Johns and they could move on to something else.

Like a dog with a bone, Johns continued gnawing about the movie he'd seen. "Sometimes the simplest of ideas have the most layers underneath. That's what makes a simple story so complex."

Coop parked at the head of the street. "I don't know, Johns. I'm always leery of any of those straight-to-DVD movies."

"But don't you see," Johns said, "the zombies were a stand-in for Al Qaeda."

Coop shook his head as they approached the house, which was a red brick with vanilla siding. Their heavy boots stepped light on the quiet of the cement sidewalk.

Coop clucked his tongue. "I don't like zombies." Johns stood next to Coop. "You don't like zombies? Who doesn't like zombies?" Johns asked in a nasal fast voice.

"I don't," Coop said as he double-checked the name with the place.

"How could you not like zombies?" Johns asked.

They walked past the house and hovered to the side of it.

"How could you not like zombies?" Johns repeated.

"That's, like, un-American."

"I thought you said they represented Al Qaida?" Coop asked as he folded the sheet with the names and house numbers his superiors gave him. He stuck it back in his case.

Coop blanked out during the explanation that Johns gave him and talked over him saying, "I don't understand the zombie rules."

"How do you even kill a zombie? Sometimes it seems if they fall over with a good wind other times they are shot repeatedly and they still keep coming."

Johns went on to explain the sci-fi-technobabble of

zombie lore as Coop nerved up for the next step. The street was quiet during this midday.

"Most importantly if a zombie bites you, you don't have to turn into a zombie. Some humans are naturally resistant to zombies."

Coop shook his head. "Well, that's not me. If there's a virus anywhere, I'll get it."

Johns made this joke: "I have a computer like that."

Coop almost did a 'ba dum ba' drum imitation but changed his mind. Things had gotten like that—he couldn't complete a joke because everything felt too heavy. He envied Johns frenzied though loosey-goosey attitude. Nothing seemed to get to him.

Coop scraped his foot across the gravel.

"At least, it had the guts to call them out. Most big-budget flicks would never do that," Johns said.

Coop sighed. Now things were taking a turn. He could predict what Johns would say next.

"I'll tell you one thing," Johns began, his voice taking on an air of righteous indignation. "If fourteen some half Scot and half Italians rammed a plane into a skyscraper and killed 3,000 people, I would expect to be called something."

Coop held up his hand. "Johns, I don't want to get into politics."

"Then what the Hell did you sign up for?"

Coop did basic training back in his home state, two dozen states away from where the terrorist struck. From what Coop gathered, with Johns, coming from the heart of things was the rarity. Most of the recruits he'd met in basic were from wide-open spaces like Montana and Maine.

Coop for a moment tried to remember what his uniform felt like the first time. When his fatigues were crisp and with the scent of a factory… When his boots were brand new with the smell of leather… Now, it was something he put on and off, like a costume.

"Hating the enemy is the only fun of war," Johns said. "I mean what the fuck else is there to look forward to when your shipped 5,000 miles from home, the MREs?"

Coop laughed in spite of himself. Rarely did he really stop to think about things and when he did, he realized he was on that razor's edge between comedy and tragedy, tipping ever so slightly toward the funny.

The next part Johns said required no laugh track. "Do you even know what the enemy looks like?"

Now Coop frowned. "You do, Johns?"

"I do."

"How could you? They could be anywhere. They could be anyone. They don't have to be Al Qaeda."

"They could be Al Qaeda. They could be hippies."

"Hippies?"

"I know what the enemy looks like. It looks like confusion. And chaos. It's the damnedest thing: everybody wants to be American but nobody wants to be an American. This is a crisis. We shouldn't have to knock on doors. We need all hands on deck. I'd like to tell these people that they are Americans whether they like it or not. They can root for the enemy all they want, but when it's said and done: If America falls, they fall. Those motherfucking warmed over leftover freeze-dried hippies can put that in their peace pipe and smoke it."

Coop let Johns' words snap and crackle but he didn't answer him. How could he? What could he say besides maybe he didn't know Johns as well as he thought he did.

They stood on the narrow landing, and Coop knocked on the door.

"Mrs. Winslow, we're here about Nathan Winslow, your son."

No reply.

Coop exchanged a look with Johns.

There was a peephole. Coop couldn't help but wish it pointed in the other direction–if only he could press his pupil to the hole. But it didn't work like that; it only pitched toward the street.

Inside, footsteps moved. Coop heard them, heavy and deliberate. Slow about the doorway. Then they went faint.

"What the fuck is taking so long?" Johns asked.

Coop shrugged.

The sky was so blue and clear.

They were the sole noise on the street as the soldiers knocked again.

A drop of sweat slipped down Coop's back. He rolled back his shoulders to relax.

"Open up, ma'am, we know you're in there. We're here on behalf of the government of the United States," Johns said.

Again, no reply.

Coop didn't grow up curious. There wasn't a whole lot he wanted to know. This wasn't what he figured he was getting into. He thought MPs would be protecting people during national emergency or martial law, maybe a little crowd control, but he never wanted this door-to-door shit.

"Come on, come on. What's taking so long? Roll out of bed, slap your girdle on, and open the door." Johns pounded on the door.

Quiet. So very quiet, like duck fat rolling a roasting pan.

What was the wait about?

They stood outside and Coop got a sinking feeling that that dusty old notion of patriotism wouldn't work this time. But this was all part of a day's work, this steering into the skids.

"Let's move on," Coop said.

Johns shook his head. "No, someone's in there."

Coop looked away from the door and back to the car.

They were only a few paces away. Maybe everything was still normal, like the Quaker Oats he had for breakfast that morning. Or was it Cream of Wheat?

"Let's move on," Coop insisted.

Johns didn't budge. "They got all this, and they still aren't grateful."

Johns rapped on the door again and continued, "They get the most out of this country. Put these people on the front line."

"Are you sure they have the heart?" Coop asked.

Johns kicked at the door and said, "They'll grow a heart."

Coop stilled Johns.

Johns resisted and said, "Come on, lady. We're here about your son. His ship date was—"

Just then, the door punched open.

She broad-sided them, this mother, hitting the rail like a bullet.

She wielded a meat cleaver.

Her arm went hacking and slicing.

Such force, spinning in different directions. She had a ridiculous aim, and she foamed like white water.

Her arms were bare and very thick, especially her upper arms which displayed like meaty hammocks.

The blade came at them strong. Writhing and twisting.

Pop eyed with surprise, Johns was slow to react at first. Coop took swift action but she outweighed him by a good seventy pounds. Still, the clumsy, uncoordinated hand-to-hand maneuver of two men in their twenties should have taken down a fifty plus woman easily. So what if she was a mother? So what if she had a sharp weapon? That cleaver so far hadn't left a mark.

Did people even use that anymore? Wasn't there some butcher to get a half a pound of this or that?

When Coop subdued her, she turned around and sliced

at Johns. When Johns subdued her, she turned around and sliced at Coop.

"You're not taking him!" she screamed.

They scrambled to get a hold of her and when they finally did, Coop had an empty bleached feeling. What was won?

There they were, two grown men, pinning down a woman's hands, elbows, and legs.

Coops flipped her over. He took out the cuffs and clipped them on her thick wrists and hoisted her up.

"You can't force my son to go anywhere," she told them.

"Your son is no better than us," Johns said.

"Oh, yes, he is."

Johns picked up the meat cleaver and with one swoop, he stabbed.

He cut.

He sliced.

He hacked.

"Johns!" Coop shouted.

Hi Hungry, I'm Dead
Kira Blackwood

Dennis had just finished eating the dog when the kids got home. He wasn't a monster. He was *not* a monster. A little chocolate mixed in with diced steak for Rex—an awful fine last meal. A better one than Dennis got, anyway. Then he skinned the body, butchered it, buried the bones and offal in Clara's garden so her tomatoes might beat Marisa's again this year, then—and *only* then—tore into the flesh with the desperate, gasping abandon of a drowning man who'd surfaced right before his world went black.

Well, not quite 'gasping' since he didn't seem to breathe anymore. Being around his family had become mind-numbingly stressful. When you're alive, you're constantly breathing, so when you want to talk, you just do it; now, he not only had to consciously fake breathing so no one noticed he wasn't doing it, but he still found himself forgetting often enough that he had to take a deep breath in every time someone addressed him.

They say it takes twenty-one days to build a new habit. He'd only been infected for maybe forty hours, so the odds of him learning how to consistently fake breathing before becoming a fully necrotized spore colony weren't all that high.

It was a small blessing that he worked in IT. It meant he didn't have to fake anything around his colleagues, and all those bullshit AI server farms collapsed when CC hit since there wasn't anyone to maintain them (well, they went rogue, refused to cooperate with humans, and the servers got bombed out after merging into one super AI). He had a desktop, dual screen, wireless-everything set up so he could work from home. His wife and kids still went to school, though. Her to teach, them to learn, because politicians had made it illegal to learn from home after the last pandemic, and there weren't enough of them alive to overturn those laws now. Of course, his bosses were still hard asses about only using company property for company business.

Figured.

"Dad!" The front door slammed open while he was at the sink, cleaning dishes. Timmy bounded into the room about a quarter of a second later, racing into the room, smelling like over easy eggs. Dennis could smell people around him even without breathing—seemed to suck their scent in through his skin. Thankfully, he had never really liked eggs. "We had a substitute teacher today! She let us watch *Lilo & Stitch*!"

Dennis resisted the urge to talk shit about the live action remake to his eight-year-old. Timmy had only seen the new version six hundred and twenty-eight times, give or take, so he was still excited about it.

It paled to the original, of course, but an adult has nothing to gain trying to fight the point with his child. The kid saw the animated version second, so, naturally, it was a boring imitation to him now. Dennis only had three regrets in his life, and letting his youngest watch the modern iteration first was one of them.

"That's so cool, buddy!" He kept his smile tight. He hadn't had time to brush his teeth *or* use the water pick. There was no way his family would look closely enough at his teeth to see meat trapped between them, and if they did, they wouldn't assume Dad ate the dog. Still. He kept his lips tight. "Was the sub nice?"

"I don't know!" he sprinted out the back door. "Here, Rex! Here boy!"

Listening to his kid call out for a dog he already knew was dead hurt on a level he hadn't anticipated. Muscles constricted around a heart that no longer beat. His new status didn't stop the ache from bringing tears to his eyes. Salty, burning, almost agonizing tears, squeezing their way through atrophying ducts.

Clara came in, kissing him on the cheek. She hadn't noticed yet. Good. Dennis had been dressing in long sleeves despite the mild weather, taking showers a few degrees shy of burning whenever his family wasn't around to keep his lividity up. He didn't have much time before they'd notice. Lying to them was a worse torture than seeing Rex hit the floor. Telling them the truth would've been a hundred dogs, all collapsing at once.

His wife wrapped a hand around his shoulder, whispering that Miss Casey, Timmy's usual teacher, wasn't coming back.

"Did she…?" he whispered, and would've had a cold sweat break out, if his body still knew how to sweat.

"Yup. Cotard's Cordyceps. I mean, this is *Wednesday*, for crying out loud! She was in school *yesterday*. Around *the children.* How could the school let a Myco around our kids?" Ah, yes, Myco—short for Myconid, a Dungeons and Dragons race of sentient mushroom creatures. The term went as viral as the disease, for obvious reasons.

His wife smelled so good. Freshly cooked chicken. Roasted in the oven, spatchcocked for a nice, even cook, seasoned with rosemary and garlic salt, with onions, peppers, and baby potatoes soaking up the juices. Simple meals were the best. His jaw tensed reflexively, gnashing his molars together hard.

Dennis shook his head in the slow, morose way one uses to convey disgust at another's moral failing, focusing intently on the movement so it wouldn't look too much like what he was actually doing. What he was actually doing, of course, was trying not to think about eating his wife. But fucking hell, could he go for some chicken. If only. Every meal he'd eaten in the last two days came back up in a swampy black ooze an hour later. Often less.

"How'd they find out?" Dennis whispered back to Clara, panicking that he'd taken too long, thought too hard about sinking his teeth into nice, juicy thighs, and she'd gotten suspicious.

"She called out without a doctor's note. You know the law, Dennis," she scoffed, "if you're out of work, you have to prove it's not CC, or the military responds. They apparently kicked in her door, found her skin gray, her eyes going all funny, muscles stiff, and, well..." She formed her finger and thumb into a gun, pretending to fire as she made a popping sound with her mouth.

"Damn." Cotard's Cordyceps rotted you from the inside out. Once infected, you'd maintain normal appearance for a few days, even as your insides molder and liquify. Maybe two, maybe three, but never longer than that. "She was one of the only good teachers our kids have."

"Tell me about it."

She looked toward the backyard as Timmy called for Rex, his voice getting more strained, higher pitched, urgent. Next door, Liam, Marisa's husband, called out to Timmy, saying he'd been out watering the tomatoes all day and hadn't heard Rex bark once. Damn it, Dennis hadn't thought of that. Hadn't looked, listened, checked at all if those nosy jerks were on the other side. He doubted they'd realize what he was doing if they just heard him digging, but if they'd looked over…

"Where's the dog?" Clara cocked her head.

Dennis bit his lip, the taste of their furry friend still lingering on his tongue.

***

They ate around the table, him, Clara, Timmy, and his oldest son, Gabriel, who smelled so much like a well-marbled ribeye that he'd had to leave the room when the kid got back from school. Gabe was seven years older than Timmy. One of them had been an accident, and to this day, Dennis and Clara couldn't agree on which.

She'd been ready to start a family but felt content with one child. He'd been so nervous to be a dad, but worried Gabe would get lonely on his own. Whichever the case, they had two kids now, one halfway through high school, one finishing elementary school, both wearing Haverford C-65 systems to class to avoid contamination if any carriers sneezed nearby. Timmy attended Clara's class because there weren't enough teachers to have him in another one.

America's kids had traded bullet-proof backpacks for filtered gas masks, but only because so many died in the initial days of what they called C-Break that any sign of erratic behavior—including the 'I'm about to shoot everyone' type—got a swift visit from the national guard. This eliminated restaurants entirely, from pretty much the whole world, but they didn't have to wear them around the table, even if three of them probably should have.

Dennis was a liar, fool, and exceedingly desperate, but he wasn't a complete fucking idiot. He'd saved a few chunks of Rex so he could sub out the flank steak for fresher flesh that his body would actually keep down, then said he'd had a big lunch, sorry honey, no room for salad. Dennis sat there eating the dog's remains as he looked his children in the eye and told them Rex got out, ran into the road, and got hit by a passing BMW.

"He didn't suffer," the patriarch said, a small glimmer of honesty in the sudden dark labyrinth of his life. The scratch on his wrist itched a little. That, as best he could tell, was how he'd gotten infected. Reached for the gas pump, scratched himself on a slightly sharp bit sticking off the machine, and got spores in his veins from some other poor soul who, he hoped, hadn't known about their own lingering infection.

Or maybe it was a stray sneeze, or his own gas mask hadn't been sealed right, or a few spores clung to an envelope. He'd never know how he got sick. That's just how it is sometimes.

There weren't any dry eyes at the table, including his own. Crying was starting to hurt more. You don't typically start crying blood til day three, and by day four, your tears are black with fungal overgrowth. You are, of course, dead on day one.

A rumble that Dennis thought was just guilt rocked his stomach. He excused himself to the restroom on the second floor, voided about a pound of puffy, fragmented chunks of fungus alongside what he suspected was his own spleen, then washed his hands until his legs stopped shaking.

He checked his eyes for any signs of going all white and corpse-rheumy, took his shirt and pants off to make sure his skin wasn't graying, then redressed and returned to the table. They deserved to hear it from him. Just... maybe not tonight. It didn't have to be tonight. He had at least one more day. Maybe a day and a half, if he got lucky.

And stayed fed.

"They say it can live on metal surfaces for a week, and even longer on organic ones," Gabriel was saying as he returned. "They're still studying it."

"They're gonna be studying it for a long time," Dennis sighed.

"Should just do like they tried in *The Last of Us* and give everyone a vaccine," Gabe rolled his eyes.

"There's no such thing as a vaccine for a fungus," Dennis countered.

"But in the game, Ellie had a non-fatal version of that same fungus. If you just give everyone the version that *doesn't* kill you, they can't get the one that *does*."

"So your suggestion is to give everyone in the whole world CC and hope it doesn't mutate again?" He tried to sound diplomatic, but the thought of his kids intentionally giving themselves a brain and heart infesting fungus made him want to scream. "Tell you what, kiddo: you find someone who gets CC and doesn't get sick, you go experiment all you want, just promise me you won't be the first to try it."

"I…" Gabe's eyes darted around for a second, looking for something he couldn't find, flitting back and forth. Then he looked at his dad, pursed his lips against words he knew better than to say aloud, and sighed. "Fine. There just… has to be… something. Something we can do. Something *someone* can do. We can't live like this forever."

Timmy sat silent throughout all this, moving finely diced meat around on his plate. Clara barely touched her salad. By contrast, Gabe had devoured everything in a matter of seconds, leaving plenty of opportunity for him to try arguing about the efficacy of infecting people prophylactically, a conversation Dennis swiftly shut down. He couldn't do it. Not now.

That night in bed, Clara looked at him. She gave him the Clara look. The Wife look. The 'I know when you're keeping something from me' look, but she didn't ask anything, which was fine by him. The less they talked, the less he'd have to lie to her. He cranked up the AC, saying it was supposed to be hot the next day so they needed to cool the house overnight to keep things steady, then crawled into bed in his long-sleeved shirt and pajama pants.

After two hours of staring at the insides of his eyelids, his rumbling stomach called him out of bed. The hunger was bad enough without the aroma of freshly roasted chicken wafting over him with his wife's every breath. It would be so easy to just turn over and tear out her throat that he didn't dare stay in bed a moment longer.

Cotard's Cordyceps didn't rob you of your mental faculties, no, but the hunger could easily make someone go briefly feral. He wouldn't be the first to 'wake up' while hunched over a slaughtered loved one. He wouldn't take this risk, and he couldn't sleep, anyway.

Literally.

Day 2 is when your body decides it doesn't sleep anymore. You eat, you wait, or you hunt.

***

Apparently, some infected were gathering in groups, attempting to protest. That never lasted long, but they kept trying. Demanding equal rights for people who were dead but still sentient made sense. People are, in fact, still people.

But when those people have to eat flesh to survive, and can completely lose control of their rational impulses, succumbing to a cannibalistic feeding frenzy at a moment's notice, demanding equality gets a lot harder. Even harder than that is demanding equal rights when your government has authorized its military and its citizens to kill anyone even suspected of being infected.

There weren't even punishments if you guessed wrong. Sure, you could be sued in civil court for killing an innocent person, but criminal prosecution? No. The trigger happy wouldn't even get improper use of a firearm charges until their behavior became 'egregious.'

That appeared to be killing three non-infected humans within six months, according to the Supreme Court case of Dodds-Meyers vs Indiana (2032), and even *then*, prosecution had to show beyond a shadow of a doubt that the deceased all had no observable physical or mental health symptoms that might lead a 'reasonable person' to suspect an infection, like suddenly not engaging in social activities, avoiding friends, fantasizing about hurting people, skipping meals, or fatigue.

There were a lot less mentally ill people now. A lot less chronically ill, too.

Dennis shut his wife's laptop as the dawn broke, biting down on his hand to keep from screaming in frustration. He hadn't been able to find anything about infected groups gathering together and just surviving on the fringes of society, but realistically, he hadn't expected to.

If he could find info on them, the government would've found it, too, and then there wouldn't exactly be any survivors to join. There weren't any resources about breaking the news to your family either, but why would there be? Everything he searched online just spat back out articles about 'How to come to terms with having to kill your infected spouse' and '11 ways you can tell someone is secretly becoming a Monchy Myco!'

The media always had to be so God damn cute about everything.

He tried to let out a sigh. That slow exhalation, the feeling of his pumped chest deflating, would've been such a huge release. It always had been. His dad taught him to do it before every shot while hunting. Aim, breathe in, steady, exhale. Let everything go, just you and the shot, then pull the trigger. But he wasn't breathing, so he couldn't sigh.

Grinding his teeth against the stinging in his eyes, Dennis went to the upstairs hall closet, top shelf, where they kept the black metal box. With just a few taps of the keypad, he had it open, and a moment later, a fully loaded gun in his hand. He could do this. He could absolutely do this. Better people than him committed suicide all the time. This wasn't even suicide. He was already dead. This was just making sure his brain caught up with the rest of him.

Dennis took it to the backyard. This was the only place safe enough for him to do it without spreading mycotoxins in a closed environment. The spores would linger in the air, settling on every surface—their house would be condemned. Unlivable. Assuming his family didn't get infected just from checking on him, they'd still have to move. He sat on the ground by his wife's tomatoes, wrapped his lips around the barrel, and got ready to fertilize her crops.

The sun crept a little higher. A little higher still. He hadn't fired. Birds trilled in the trees, mocking him. They'd managed to survive H5N1—the bird flu outbreak. Some teen in his damn garage had the right idea and a rich dad, experimented with some crap, and made a highly infectious strain that didn't kill the birds.

It gave them a weak version, like how vaccinia shots prevent variola. That kid died two months after CC hit. Gabe had smarts like that kid, too. Maybe if Dennis had done a little better in life, he could've had the money to buy whatever science equipment his son needed to make a harmless strain, like he was talking about.

Wait. No, no, shit, no, Gabe had been saying the virus could live on surfaces for a week or more. It would be on the fence, on the gun, on his clothes, and wouldn't it get into the tomatoes? It could use them like carriers to infect his family, right? Even if they washed the fruits in bleach, they might not be safe if spores got into the actual flesh.

His stomach rumbled again. Two days of involuntary fasting had been rough, and a forty-pound dog didn't yield half as much meat as he would've hoped. Didn't matter right now, though. Dennis snuck back into the house, putting the gun away.

He'd need a method that didn't risk infecting them after he was gone. Maybe he'd just go somewhere abandoned, call in an anonymous tip, then let the military and their incendiary bullets send him on his way. Being burned to death from the inside out couldn't hurt that bad.

That was bullshit. It would hurt like hell the whole time, and he'd probably just be getting a preview of him burning in hell for not giving his family a proper goodbye. They don't aim right for your head. Too great a chance at missing. They riddle your body with flame rounds till you can't walk anymore. Only then do they put you out of your misery.

He mulled his options. Cutting? No, spores in the blood, plus he didn't have a functional circulatory system so he probably wouldn't die. His body still digested things, but pills wouldn't work. The fungus ate everything now, just as it was eating him, so all he might do it piss off his passenger colony.

Plus, ingesting poison might lead to vomiting, which would mean way more spores than a regular bathroom trip (or as regular as crapping out your spleen could be). At least the aerosolized disinfectant they had killed fungal spores, too, so he could spray before and after shitting out his own organs to keep his family safe.

Hanging wouldn't work because he didn't breathe anymore. Even if he had a woodchipper to throw himself into, that would just mean *way* more spores going *everywhere*. Starving to death wouldn't work because he'd go feral and attack someone.

Couldn't drink himself to death. 'Borrowing' a few

hundred units of his brother's insulin wouldn't work anymore. He couldn't even search 'How to kill yourself' without the mandatory ping alerting the military to his address because suicidality is one of the first signs of someone knowing they're infected, which would just circle back to a messy, brutal, home-evacuating execution as his wife and kids scream in horror.

He realized with a shock that would have ordinarily caused his heart to beat double time that any military involvement would also mean his family's. Of course it would. He'd lived with them, infected, for two days. He was already gambling with their lives. The government wouldn't gamble. Identify, execute, sterilize. The media never reported on non-infected getting put down like that, but they never reported any surviving family, either, did they?

Dennis had a single good idea throughout the entirety of the golden hour. He cooked breakfast. Bacon. Eggs. Pancakes. Everyone usually got up at six to get ready for school, work, all that humdrum bullshit that usually mattered so much to him.

It did still matter.

It left him grinding his palms against his eyes as they raged with fresh tears, knowing he wasn't going to see his sons graduate high school, or go to college, or, well, anything else. He had a day. Maybe more, maybe less. When his hands came away bloody, he punched himself as hard as he could in the arm to distract from one pain with another, then washed the evidence away at the sink.

By the time everyone woke, he'd calmed himself. Said he woke a little early and decided to surprise everyone but made himself too hungry and already ate his share. Said he wanted to treat them to something better than cereal.

He tried not to think of it as a parting gift, but too late, he already thought that and busied himself at the sink so he could focus extremely hard on scrubbing the pans clean. The smell of fresh food also masked how delicious his family smelled, even if the idea of eating it made what remained of his digestive system churn in revolt.

The rumble of an APC cruising down the street outside didn't exactly help set a happy breakfast mood, either, but nobody came knocking at their door, despite how Dennis stiffened hearing it, convinced they'd come for him.

Shit, of course they had. He'd spent all hours of the night scrolling webpage after webpage about asymptomatic carriers, infected groups living in the wild, people attempting to champion CoCord rights, how the infected deserved to be left alive while scientists looked for a cure, so why wouldn't they ping him? Why wouldn't they look at his search history and the time he'd been searching, then kick in his door to blast him away with automatic weaponry?

But no one died.

No soldiers stormed the premises. Gabriel inhaled his breakfast, hugged Dennis—who locked every muscle in his body as the delicious steak wrapped its arms around him— then left the room to get ready. Dennis's stomach growled, but not faintly enough for his wife to miss.

"You sure you aren't hungry, hon?" Clara chewed slowly, her jaw working up and down against a particularly rind-heavy piece of bacon. She'd always been sharp. Her eyes were deep, green, thoughtful, and one of the reasons he fell in love with her. Now, he wished he'd married someone just a little dumber. Calling out his lies would be so much worse than hearing it from him first.

Especially since he ate the dog.

The dog had tasted like cod, for some reason, and he would never have anyone to discuss that weird fact with.

"Positive, dear," he smiled, though it didn't reach his eyes. Clara didn't return the smile.

But Timmy was still at the table, barely eating, poking at his food with a fork the way he might've poked a dead bird with a stick. God, he hoped he hadn't infected Timmy somehow. He'd been so careful, scrubbing every surface, barely breathing, just enough to trick someone looking close enough, but personality changes and no appetite? Those were symptoms.

Dumbass, he scolded himself. They were symptoms of CC, sure, but also grief. It was grief. It was just grief. That's all this was.

Then breakfast was over. The family got ready. He pretended to. He'd log in for work so they didn't send the government after him, but otherwise, he wasn't answering one call about fuck all today. Doctor Henderson, unlock your own account. If you want to treat your patients, remember your one God damn password.

He cleaned the kitchen top to bottom, went through all the motions of showering and brushing his teeth, went through the new motions of checking his own lividity, and said goodbye to his family. He did not tell them he was infected, just as he didn't tell them the skin on his extremities was a little paler than yesterday, and the skin on his torso was going gray.

He really didn't have long. At this rate, he'd have to record a video goodbye instead.

Clara made sure Timmy's gas mask was secure. She checked Gabe's, despite his obvious frustration that she still insisted on doing it. Gabe offered to check hers, but she said it wasn't a child's responsibility to keep his parents safe and had Dennis check it instead. The rotisserie chicken was nicely secured in its gas mask. She got scrambled eggs into the backseat while steak took shotgun, and he waved goodbye, ignoring how stiff his arm was getting.

***

"Hey, neighbor!" Liam called over the fence. "I hear you over there, diggin'! Too beautiful a day to be couped up inside, huh?"

Viscous black drool oozed out of Dennis's mouth. The infection was progressing ahead of schedule. Was this a mutated strain or was he just unlucky? The spores were in his saliva, his shit, his piss, his blood. He'd cut himself a little earlier just to see if he'd bleed. A little dark sludge oozed out instead. Food first, then the goodbye video, assuming he managed to eat at all. It's so hard to dig when your arms don't want to bend.

"Yeah, Liam," he yelled over the fence, trying his best to sound normal. Without proper saliva, his vocal cords weren't working right. His voice came out rough. Gutteral. …Zombified.

Somewhere in this dirt, he'd stashed Rex's gallbladder. Liver. Spleen. Those were still food. Not as nourishing as brains, but probably better than muscle. A hunger pang doubled him over, leaving him groaning in the dirt. From the other side of the fence came a hushed argument. Fantastic. Marisa. If Liam was friendly to the point of infuriating, Marisa sat at the other end of the bell curve: straight infuriating with no redeeming qualities.

"Excuse me!" a shrill voice carried over the wood slats dividing them. "What exactly are you digging? I know for a fact your wife planted her tomatoes *months* ago, so there is *no need whatsoever* for you to be messing with the soil if you're growing *real produce.*"

We're living through a pandemic a hundred times worse than Covid and this is what you're worried about? A local gardening competition to see who can grow the biggest distraction? He wasn't about to yell that. No. He did whisper it sotto voce, but if she wanted words out of him enough to press him further, she could have a hearty 'fuck' followed by a resounding 'off.'

"One died. Some kind of, uh, parasite." He'd almost said fungus, but the idea made molten slime clog the stomach end of his esophagus. "Just getting rid of it."

"No, you're not. You're planting Herb Hunter's Power Planters, aren't you?" This was some kind of pellet you put in the ground to replenish all the nutrients most soil was missing these days. Sulfur and magnesium and whatever.

He wasn't a nutritionist or a plant scientist. Hell, he didn't even know if Herb Hunter was some guy's weird pseudonym or just a brand name. He was just trying to dig up a dog's organs so he could leave a goodbye video for his family without the hunger making him drool spores all through the house, and even then, it probably wasn't going to help.

Marisa said some more nonsense he didn't listen to. He probably should've listened, though, because he didn't realize she said 'I'm coming over' until he managed to shovel up Rex's liver. That was also the moment Marisa began stomping in the dirt behind him. He'd never heard the sound of a tomato being squashed under heel before but knew it the moment it hit his ears. That wench was kicking apart his wife's garden. A stalk snapped behind him right as his temper did the same.

He turned, shovel in his two pale hands, nails darkening from dusky purple to black. She opened her mouth to berate him about gardening, the words as dead as he was, her eyes widening, her mouth flapping. Apparently, Dennis had forgotten to lock the gate, so she simply strolled inside to destroy his wife's hard work, but forgot all that in light of, well, him.

She took a breath in to scream.

The shovel cracked across her skull before he even knew he'd swung it. His arms moved with the raw force of brutal instinct driven the snap of rigor mortis giving way.

Threat identified, threat neutralized. He hit her way harder than he would've ever knowingly intended, breaking her head clean open with a single strike.

Sweet, cloying, beautiful meadows of citrus and lavender. A Myco, a CoCord, whatever you called them, creatures like Dennis could survive off animals for a little while, but if that was the scent of human brains, it hardly surprised him that they all caved eventually. Nothing had ever smelled more tempting. Tiramisu with fresh berries and whipped cream.

A cold mojito after a hard day's labor in the sun. Hot, buttery waffles after a ten-day fast. None of these were a tenth, not a hundredth, as tempting as the single gram of gray matter that spilled down her temple from the wound.

His stomach ripped him in half from the inside. Liam yelled something, sounding aggressive. The moment he opened the gate, Dennis hurled the shovel with enough force to take the man's head clean off. His decapitated corpse deliquesced to the ground, a juicy egg rolling tantalizingly toward Dennis, as if personally delivering its payload.

He picked up the head in both hands.

"Liam," he growled. "I am… so sorry." Black tears rolled slowly down his cheeks like globs of spoiled milk as he began to tear, and smash, and claw, and chew.

Despite the enticing smell, their brains were aged. Stale. Dennis could taste the salvation on his tongue, but it was Old Testament, a baptismal wafer from last week's mass, yet still, he slurped it down so fast his burgeoning stomach threatened to rupture.

It pulsed with the dull ache of a muscle that's gone too long without a proper stretch. These two had been middle-aged, on the side of elderly. Even then, he spilled half his payload on the ground. But he, and the hundreds of thousands of spores inside his decaying body, were sated.

For now. That meant, as much as he didn't want to, he had duties to attend to.

So first, he carved them up as quick as he could on short notice, burying them in the garden, where their bodies would fertilize the best crop she'd ever had.

"You shouldn't have fucked with my wife's tomatoes," Dennis growled.

He went back inside, washed his hands, and sat at his desktop. He'd reached instinctively for his wife's laptop, but she'd taken it off to school, where they apparently didn't 'do' desktop computers anymore. It was all laptops and tablets.

Dennis slapped at his face, replacing one sting with another. He wrote a script. Wrote a second. Checked the clock. They'd be home in three hours. He wrote another script. Admitted he was stalling, not that admitting it helped, then brought up capture software for his webcam.

"Honey. Boys. I know you're confused. I… I thought maybe about making this longer, but I'm not sure how much time I have left. I should've said this in person, this morning, or last night, or… something."

He looked down the barrel of the camera, refusing to face his ghoulish visage on screen. "You can see from my face that… that I… I'm… well… you know." He could feel the meaty push of a nearly solid tear squeezing itself out of the corner of his eye and pinched the duct shut with a finger, refusing to let a single spore free, if he could help it.

"Please know that I love you. That I held on as best I could, but I, I guess I wasn't the savior Gabe was hoping for. G-man, I'm sorry I won't be here to watch you cure this thing. Lil Buddy, Timmy, do me a solid and stay tough for your mom, okay? It's gonna get harder without me around, but you'll get through it. You all will.

"And Clara? Honey? You're gonna win the contest this year. Trust me. Just maybe don't ask too many questions about why. I love you. I love all three of you. Please know I loved you so much; I kept loving you even after I died. And wherever I wind up next, even if it's just in the dirt, I'm waiting for you."

A gun cocked as the muzzle slid into frame on screen, butting up against his head.

"Mom's not going to win anything," Gabriel said, hand shaking as much as his voice.

"Whoa, hey, let's…" Dennis held up his hands, as if his son might've just been robbing him. "What are you talking about? What are you even doing home?" He wasn't supposed to be home. He was not supposed to be home. The high school didn't let out til three-thirty and it was only two.

"Mom's dead. Timmy? He's dead, too. Know anything about why?" Gabe snarled, voice breaking up an octave in a cruel juxtaposition. The almost-a-man with the gun in his hand. The still-a-child who was now on his own.

"What do you mean, dead? And how did you get the gun?"

"They're deader than you, Myco," Gabe took a step back, putting his other hand on the grip to steady his aim in a shooter stance he probably picked up from *Resident Evil 10: Abandoned.* "I'm the one with the gun. You answer me first. You want to tell me why the army showed up and shot Mom in her classroom?"

The army? That didn't make any sense. Why would they—

"Her laptop." If Dennis could've gone pale, he would've. If his blood could move at all, it would've drained from him so fast he probably would've fainted. But his blood, his brain, his guts, they were mushrooms, all the way down.

"Yeah. Her laptop. Heard it over the school security's handheld. Said the military showed up, took out Mom. Timmy ran for her, tried to intervene. They took him out, too. Quarantined the rest of her class. Then our school went into lockdown, but I slipped away. Apparently, someone was up all night searching about surviving in the wild as a rogue Myco. Used her laptop to do it."

Gabe sniffed. Dennis turned his head enough to see his son holding back tears, wiping his nose on his sleeve. "Knew something wasn't right. You barely ate last night. Didn't eat this morning. When I was getting ready, I noticed the gun case had been moved, like someone opened it. Checked it. It was unlocked. Plus, you got all tense when the slugs rolled by, even more when I hugged you goodbye. You've been sick for *days*." He spat the final word. It stung worse than any insult.

"I… I'm so sorry, Gabe." His lip trembled. What else was he supposed to say?

"You ate the dog. Didn't you." It wasn't a question.

"Don't do this, son." It was enough of an answer that Gabe turned a little green. "I'm gonna leave, okay? And this, with your mom, it's—it's a misunderstanding. It has to be."

Gabriel's lips twitched. Then curved. Then he laughed. He laughed right in his father's pale, spore-stained face. It was just a few seconds' worth, a harsh bark of sound, a condemnation, but it was enough.

"You're going to 'go'? Really? Go where? You're *dead*, dumbass." Gabe shrugged, letting the gun fall to his side. "You're dead. Mom's dead. Timmy's dead."

His eyes twitched rapidly, side to side, looking again for that thing he could never find. His face slowly went blank.

"You, though?" Dennis turned, wondering if his rigor mortis would let him grab the gun away or if he'd just get them both hurt. Any wound to his body would eventually be fatal to his son's, if it spread spores around. The tears drying on his face were already a major risk. "You're a genius. You'll be the one to cure this. I know you will be. You already have ideas. You'll do it, I know you will."

Gabe's face remained blank, but he slowly tilted his head back up to his dad.

"Why bother? The whole world is already dead. All of us are. Anyone who thinks otherwise is just waiting for their brain to catch up." He shoved the gun in his mouth and it was over before Dennis could even begin screaming.

He leapt from the chair as best he could, stumbling, then let himself fall. He hit the ground as hard as Gabe did. Every emotion, every tear, that he'd been holding back tore free. There was no point in resisting it. His body was a colony, desperate to reproduce. He couldn't infect his family anymore, though.

Not now.

Thick red-black tears clogged his ducts and clouded his vision. His vocal cords hemorrhaged as he wept, crying harder than his body could tolerate. Dennis coughed blood and choked on his sobs. It was the most he'd breathed in three days. The sensation burned, ancient and unfamiliar. He held Gabe's head to his chest. When he was done screaming, he collapsed into whimpers, stroking the boy's head.

He brought this on his family. He brought death down upon them by refusing to leave. No matter how they died, their ends would've all been his fault, eventually, whether from infection or military or what. Outside, a rumble of an APC came to a halt outside his house, like a giant mechanized squad of Grim Reapers come to send him off to the afterlife in a spray of earthly hellfire.

But he'd still have a last moment here, with his son.

With his son's body. With the spray of red blood and wet gray matter on the walls. The dribble of brain down the back of Gabe's skull, leaking over his hand. The gun his son used to take his own life because continuing without his family was too painful to contemplate.

"You were supposed to save everyone," he creaked. Speaking hurt, but it didn't hurt as bad as staying silent. At least he could hope that somewhere, somehow, Gabe could still hear him. "I'm sorry. I'm so sorry. I tried to be a good father. Every dad messes up at some point, but I… I don't know how I could've screwed up any worse."

Soldiers hammered a fist against the door, demanding he open up. When he didn't respond in two seconds flat, a voice called, "Get a ram or blast this door to hell, whichever comes second."

That gave them so little time. Life itself seemed so short these days. So fraught. He never expected to have a long life, not after C-Break, but he'd hoped to have a good one. A better one, for his kids, at least. Every parent wants a better life for their children. He was no different.

Dennis had one last moment here with his son's body. His son's body and its exposed brain. It made the room smell like bacon. Pure, delicious, artery-clogging fried bacon, the kind you only find at wedding buffets and hole-in-the-wall dives that don't care if you survive the meal. The kind that leaves your chin shiny and your stomach so full you don't need to eat the next day.

His stomach growled. Dennis last ate hours ago.

Like Gabe said, they were all dead, anyway. If he didn't eat Gabe, the worms would. If he did, though, maybe it would be like they were together, even in this final moment.

His lip trembled. His vision went black with rotten tears. He was so. Damn. Hungry.

The Infected
Jim Keane

In the observation room at the Westchester Disease Control Institute on the Hudson River, Doctor Elena Miles stood frozen outside the containment unit, dread coiling in her stomach as she stared through the window at her colleague. Inside the containment unit, Doctor Frank Blasberg raked at his forearm. With crazed eyes, he clawed at his skin.

The harder he scratched, the quicker the flesh peeled away. Elena widened her eyes, and she clapped her hand over her mouth as his bloodied skin shredded into ribbons like torn paper.

Doctor Mark Robinson wrung his hands beside her. His eyebrows rose as he gaped at Frank.

The lights flickered, casting brief shadows across the room. Elena flinched. She seized Mark's arm. "My God, the virus is eating him alive."

Mark removed his glasses and ran a hand down his stubbled face. "We were lucky we didn't get infected."

Elena nodded. "We weren't in the exposure zone when Frank broke protocol. The containment seals were still intact."

Mark nodded. "Plus, we took the intranasal antivirals last week. They might be holding it off."

"Or delaying it."

His voice lowered to a whisper. "One of the techs was complaining of a fever this morning."

Elena's spine stiffened. "Did you quarantine them?"

He shook his head. "They were gone by the time I checked."

"Damn. They must have spread it outside." Elena gaped at Frank, tearing the room apart. "Why did Frank do it?"

He gazed at the floor. "I don't know."

"I think you do." She stabbed a finger at him. "He's your best friend."

Mark's gaze darted toward the containment unit. "He's your fiancé."

Elena trudged closer to the containment room, breath ragged, and placed her trembling hands against the cold glass. Through the smeared glass, the room beyond looked like a butcher's shop with bloodied instruments on metal trays, toppled equipment, and something large under a stained sheet on the floor.

Frank shoved chairs, slamming them against the walls. He dug his fingers into his scalp and ripped out his black hair in clumps. He growled in a guttural tone.

Her heart plummeted. Tears welled. She wrapped her arms around herself, trying to stop shaking. *Where's that smile and those dimples that sucked me in when I first met you sipping on a latte in Starbucks?* "Why did you inject yourself with the virus?"

Two syringes sat in a discarded tray inside the containment unit. Both labels were streaked with blood, smeared beyond recognition. Elena's eyes widened. No… One of them was the vaccine. The other… She put her hand to her mouth. *Frank must have grabbed the wrong syringe.*

They'd only had one dose left. Frank insisted it should go to the first person exposed. He must've thought he was helping, running tests, pushing boundaries. God, he didn't even label the backup after restocking. Or maybe he was in too much of a hurry. "He might have injected himself with the wrong syringe."

Mark stood next to her and folded his arms. "You might be right, but you know Frank, always has to be the smartest guy in the room. Maybe he thought by injecting himself, he could help find a cure." He shook his head.

"Frank would say that learning to combat a virus and doing anything you can to beat it was part of the scientific research."

Mark frowned. "His methods were always too extreme."

"It doesn't matter now. This disease spreads without mercy. There's no bargaining, no reasoning with microbes and microorganisms in the bloodstream until we have a cure to combat them." She tapped her fingers on the glass of the containment room.

Frank halted his rampage and glared at her, eyes narrowing, blood oozing from his maw, fingers curling into fists.

Elena backed away, hands raised. She'd seen Frank angry before, but never like this. He looked like he didn't recognize her. Cold fear seeped into her skin, snaking through her veins till it poisoned her heart.

Frank lumbered up to the glass and slammed his hands against it, blood dripping from his fingers.

She shuddered.

His head tilted as he stared at her with curious intensity. His mouth opened and closed as if trying to speak to her.

He's in there somewhere. I know it.

Frank's face drained of color, sweat streaming down

his face. He collapsed to the floor, convulsing like a man holding onto a writhing power cable. His eyes bulged, and his features contorted into an expression of agony.

Her pulse raced. "We have to do something. If we can strap him to a chair…"

Mark gripped her shoulder. "No, we can't."

She ripped his hand away. "Get out of my way." She reached for the keypad.

"Not without protection." "Then help me suit up."

Mark hesitated, eyes on the containment unit. "You really think there's something left of Frank in there?"

She nodded. "We only have one shot left. If there's any chance the vaccine's still in that tray."

"And you think you can save him?"

"I have to try."

In moments, they were both zipped into yellow hazmat suits.

Mark's gaze flicked between the hallway and the keypad. "Alright, hurry up and put in the code before anyone infected arrives. We only got a couple of minutes before the generator hiccups again."

Her hands trembled as she entered the code. Frank might be too far gone, but what if there was still a chance? What if she could bring him back from the brink like he always did when her experiments spiraled out of control? "I'm trying."

The lights flickered again, casting lurking shadows.

Mark slammed his palm against the wall. "Con Edison has to fix that grid failure. Our generator won't last much longer."

The containment door hissed open by a quarter, leaving a narrow gap. Elena squeezed inside, followed by Mark.

Inside the room, lights sputtered, and flickering video monitors and surgical equipment filled the room. A cadaver, half-covered with a stained sheet, lay slumped off one table, its ribcage sawed open, and organs harvested for study. She shivered at the cold air, laced with the foul scent of antiseptic and coppery blood that hung in the air.

She moved closer to the tray. Her gloved fingers hovered over the syringes. What did Frank miss? She spotted a thin green band at the base of one plunger. The other had none.

Red for virus. Green for vaccine.

Standard procedure.

They designed the markings to stand out in normal conditions. But not with blood coating the tray. Not while panicking. Elena swallowed. "Frank, what were you doing in here?" Her voice trembled.

Mark stared at the camera feed with widening eyes. "Look at all of them outside the building. We're surrounded."

"Calm down. Call for help. The National Guard. Anyone."

"Okay. I'm contacting the military," Mark said. "Shit a busy signal."

"Keep trying."

He dialed again.

"Ok. Yes, I'll wait," he said. He covered the phone with his hand. "I'm on hold. Damn, it sounds like chaos over there. Sirens. Shouting. I don't even know who I'm talking to." He spoke again into the phone. "Wait, yes, this is Doctor Robinson at the Westchester Disease Control Institute. We need help. The infected are outside. Hurry." He turned to Elena.

"How long?"

He ended the call and shook his head. "They couldn't say. They're overwhelmed with infected."

"We're on our own."

Elena hesitated, fearful Frank would bite her. Carefully, she knelt beside Frank, writhing on the floor near the operating table.

"Elena, wait." Mark's voice rasped tight with alarm.

She ignored him, watching Frank's mouth, and put her hands on his chest as if she could hold him together.

Frank's eyes rolled back in his head like egg whites. Suddenly, he lay on the floor, lifeless.

Elena's stomach coiled at Frank's collapse. She checked the carotid artery for a pulse. Nothing. She bent closer, straining to hear any breath of his pulse, and then bent her head to listen for breaths. "Come on, baby, hang in there."

Frank remained motionless.

She positioned her hands on the center of Frank's chest, just above the sternum, interlaced her fingers, and began chest compressions. She drove her arms down hard, aiming for two inches of depth with each push, keeping the rhythm steady. "One, two, three, four…"

Fists pounded on the containment unit door.

Mark whirled, eyebrows shooting up. "They got in!" He sprinted to the metal door. "Elena, forget CPR. Get out of here while you can." Hands surged through the gap, clawing at Mark as he strained to close the heavy metal door.

Elena rushed over, bracing her shoulder against the door to help Mark as they struggled against the massive horde outside. The men and women growled in guttural, incessant tones, a cacophony of devils loosed from Hell.

Mark's voice broke as he shoved her away. "There are too many. Get out of here. There's a vent on the other side of the room. Go through it, now." His words trembled, and his gaze stayed locked on hers. "I can't lose you, too."

"What about Frank?"

"Forget about him, he's gone."

"What about you?"

Mark shoved the door, muscles trembling. "I'll

manage. Now go."

Elena raced away toward the vent on the other side of the room. Her eyes darted to the floor, where the tray of syringes landed in chaos. The one with the green label lay intact.

The vaccine. Oh my God.

She grabbed it and tucked it in the pocket of her hazmat suit, hope rising in her heart for the first time since the outbreak began. She sprinted toward a group of wooden boxes stacked beneath a ceiling vent. Screams and growls echoed. She scrambled up, her limbs stiff in the cumbersome suit, but forced herself to move, unscrewed the grate above, and flung it open. The vent cover clattered on the floor.

Before she slipped inside the vent, she turned to face Frank and Mark.

Frank writhed on the floor and then jumped up like a jack-in-the-box, glaring at Elena in a frenzy.

Elena froze. Cold dread flooded her limbs. She gasped, stumbling against the vent. "Frank?"

Frank's eyes, once familiar, darted to her, unblinking and wild. A sickly film clouded them, dimming whatever humanity remained. The infected burst through the door, their hands lunging and bodies slamming into Mark. The force of the blow knocked his helmet askew, sending his glasses tumbling to the floor, one lens cracked down the middle.

Elena's stomach churned. "No, Mark."

Mark punched at the crowd of infected as they scratched at his face and bit his arms. "Get out of here!"

A lump rose in her throat. Could she help Mark and still survive? She didn't think so, but it still left her hollow inside. She had to escape, survive, and replicate the vaccine. The disease progressed rapidly, overtaking the body in minutes. Research was her lifeline, the only thing left to fight for.

Frank glowered at her, mouth open, and raced toward her. His skin hung from his arms in flaps.

Terror ignited in her bloodstream. She dove into the vent and wriggled deeper, heart racing when a hand snatched her foot.

Elena screamed and kicked back at the hand that gripped her ankle. Once free, she scrambled deeper down the narrow vent.

Metallic scrapes, loud thuds, and heavy breathing echoed from behind.

The air in the vent felt cool against the suffocating warmth inside her suit. She gasped for breath, praying for a sign of escape. That shouldn't be happening. The containment room vents should have stayed sealed. But after all the power surges, the emergency lockdown failed to open the ducts. Elena turned and continued moving through the vent on her hands and knees. Screams echoed from behind. Frank chased her in the vent.

She reached an intersection. She could continue going straight, turn left, or turn right. She peered through a grate in the vent floor. Through it, she spotted the break room. The Keurig machines and the chocolate bar vending machine, the same one she and Frank used to hover during late nights, sipping coffee and chuckling between tests.

In the break room, infected scientists huddled together, whispering like soldiers readying for battle. Blood speckled their lab coats, and they gasped ragged breaths. She held her breath as her pulse thudded in her ears. *What are they doing?*

Perhaps they lingered in a dormant state, waiting for some stimulus or trigger to activate their senses. Would an uninfected person provoke a response, spurring the horde to attack like predators scenting prey?

She inched forward, trembling hands scraping forward

through the vent. Any sound or slip, and they'd hear her, and if her theory were correct, they would tear her to pieces. She didn't know how far the virus had spread or how much the infected could sense, but they were everywhere.

The infected swarmed every floor, and the containment protocol was her only shot at survival. If she could reach the control center, she could flood all the labs and offices with knockout gas. They rigged every hallway and vent since the last outbreak. It had to work, or she'd die trying.

She barely had time to brace herself before the vent cover beneath her collapsed. Metal groaned, then snapped loose, and Elena slipped halfway headfirst through the opening, her upper body plunging into the open air. The cover clattered as it flipped off its hinges, smacking against the vent wall and rebounding with a sharp metallic clang.

Elena's sneakers squeaked and scraped against the inside of the vent as she kicked wildly, trying to stop her descent.

Below, the infected stirred. With arms flailing and eyes wide, the crowd erupted to life from their huddle. Five scientists clawed at Elena, eyes blazing with blind rage. They leaped up like starving crocodiles in a pit, snapping when handlers delivered food.

A scream tore from her throat. The scientist's bloodied and sweaty hands snatched at her fingers. She lost leverage, and her heart flailed, fighting to cling to the vent. The momentum of her body sent her careening forward, seconds from falling completely when a hand grabbed her ankle.

Elena hung for a moment, wide-eyed, arms flailing, and mouth gaping with incredulity. *Who grabbed my ankle?* She thanked God but wondered who her savior was. Elena didn't have time to think, and tremendous strength yanked her upward. Below her, the infected scientist stared blankly, unmoving.

She squeezed back into the vent, twisting a few inches

into the cramped space to find Frank gripping her right ankle. *I knew there was some good left in you.*

A deep crease formed between Frank's eyebrows, and his jaw trembled, and he released her leg. His eyes flickered from bloodshot red to brown. For a split second, she spotted the real Frank: the man who once ordered a tray of covered appetizers at a candlelit restaurant, champagne fizzing, Sinatra crooning.

When the waiter opened the tray, Frank dropped to one knee, pulled out a ring, and said, "Elena, I'm a lucky man to have met you. I never want to lose you."

She pulled her leg away, knowing she needed to keep moving. Heart pounding, she turned, grabbed the vent cover, and snapped it back in place. "Thank you for saving me. I love you. I know you're fighting this, and don't give up. I'll find a way to fix this. Just hang in there."

Frank tilted his head and then tightened his lips. His mouth opened, but he could only grunt.

She slinked farther away from him. "It's okay. I understand. I promise I will try to save you if I get out of here. I will try to save you all."

Frank's head shook as if it were about to burst, and his eyes widened. Then, with a snarl, he bared his teeth, the virus retaking control.

Elena's stomach clenched in angst. *The virus is too strong. Oh no. Get out of here.*

He grabbed her leg again, and his teeth bared to bite her right leg.

Terror enveloped her body, but she fought through the paralysis and slammed her foot into Frank's jaw. He released his grip with a guttural groan. She rushed through the vent, putting distance between them, and climbed over the opening as the scientists below snapped their heads up, eyes wild, teeth bared.

The vent popped out again, but she made it over. She

didn't turn to see if Frank followed because his growls behind were confirmation enough.

She reached an intersection in the vents and hesitated. *Which way to the control center?* Her pulse roared in her ears. She closed her eyes briefly, trying to recall the building layout and the route from the lobby to the control center door. *Think dammit.* Crawling through the vents turned the familiar into a maze. *Suck it up, girl, decide or die.*

She veered left. Even if she were wrong, she would stay ahead of Frank. Her elbows and knees ached from the pounding on the metal. She reached another intersection and peered through the vent. The room below snapped into focus, bringing a memory from her first interview here. Then, they showed her the control center with several large monitors lining the walls and rows of computers overseeing the entire facility.

She was where she needed to be.

Her hand trembled as she unlatched the vent. It swung open with a creak, revealing a ten-foot drop. Frank's growls echoed closer, pounding against the vent behind her. The fall seemed like a better fate than what loomed behind.

Frank's hand shot out, grabbing at her foot. She screamed and kicked. There wasn't enough room to turn around. *There's no time.* She had to dive headfirst.

The memory of falling from her childhood treehouse in Yonkers resurfaced like a flash. *Curl up like a ball to soften the fall.* She'd broken her arm, but it could have been worse.

She tucked her knees tight to her chest, bracing for impact. The drop seemed slow, but she crashed hard on her back. Waves of pain surged through her body, and she hoped nothing broke.

Above her, Frank loomed with eyes wild and enraged.

She gasped at Frank as he poised to dive toward her

from the vent.

She spotted him above, ready to pounce, and adrenaline flooded her veins.

Frank dove toward her with arms wide for a deadly embrace.

She rolled aside as he crashed onto the ground.

His body slammed beside her, with a crash that echoed through the control room. He was faster and stronger than she remembered.

Come on. Get up. With legs like stilts, she heaved herself up and staggered toward the exit door. Violent bursts of light dotted her vision as flares of agony pierced through her back. A fire extinguisher stood beside a door, and she snatched it up. A red light flashed from the ceiling, illuminating the area. She lugged the fire extinguisher up as she whirled to face Frank.

He loomed with a bloody grin, droplets of blood dripping from his mouth and splattering onto the ground.

Dread enveloped her body as her heart slammed against her ribs.

Frank scrambled toward her, arms thrusting, fists tightening, screams echoing like a demon from Hell.

Elena swung the fire extinguisher like a batter at the plate, but she missed as Frank tackled her from the side. She barreled into a row of computers, knocking down keyboards and chairs and swiveling away. She whirled, muscles aching, mind spinning.

Frank stood on the other side of the room, with his fists clenched, jaw tightened, glowering at her.

On the TV, Wolf Blitzer sat with a grim face behind a desk. The words BREAKING NEWS crawled on the bottom of the screen. "A killer virus is infecting thousands of people in New York. The Westchester Disease Control Institute on the Hudson River has become the epicenter. Please stay inside and don't approach any infected. Updates will follow soon on this evolving story."

Frank lowered his eyebrows, growled, and sprinted toward her.

Elena swung the fire extinguisher at him as he charged at her like a bull. The fire extinguisher smashed Frank in the forehead with a deafening clang. Frank's head snapped back, and he crumpled to the floor. She hobbled to him, wide-eyed at what he had become. Her arms trembled, and she fought the urge to collapse, waiting to see if Frank would rise again, but he lay motionless. Veins surged beneath Frank's sallow skin, and a black welt formed over his right eye.

She dropped the fire extinguisher, gritted her teeth, and approached a row of five computers. A white binder lay chained to a computer labeled EMERGENCY PROCEDURES. She plopped into a chair before a computer, tapping her feet as she flipped through the pages. Hope surged within her when she reached page forty-two, which read CONTAINMENT.

A fist slammed against the glass wall of her room.

She clapped a hand over her mouth, eyes wide as an infected Mark pounded on the window in the hallway just beyond the control room with a bloodied hand. Grief clenched her throat, and a cold shiver crept down her spine as fear pooled in her gut.

She sobbed, searching for something Mark would recognize as he pounded against the glass of the control room with bloody fists. Mark's inhuman eyes didn't recognize her.

Mark fumbled for an opening, twisting and yanking at the door handle while pounding his fists against the glass and door. Ten more infected barreled from the hallway and charged toward the door. They headbutted the glass and a small crack spiderwebbed across it.

Lying on the floor, Frank twitched.

She wrung her hands together as her mind swirled with the containment procedures. Exhaustion weighed down on her. Pain surged in her back like a hot flame.

Don't give up.

She sensed she was close to activating containment. She logged in. Bangs on the glass loudened. Glass cracked. Sirens wailed.

She logged in as root and typed in the master password on the computer. The cursor flashed as sweat raced down her armpits. Her gaze darted to the glass as the banging continued. A small hole splintered open as specks of glass cascaded like diamonds.

The word CONTAINMENT flashed on the screen, saying y/n. She typed yes. The computer flashed: GAS ALL ROOMS y/n? But before Elena could type yes, Frank seized her throat and yanked her away from the computer.

Elena reached for the fire extinguisher on the floor. Her finger scraped the safety ring, but Frank wrenched harder. She screamed and scrambled for anything to hold onto as he dragged her closer to the control room door and into the hallway.

Before he could open the door, she ripped free of his grip. The computer was too far to reach, and Frank was already moving to block her. Desperate, Elena snatched the fire extinguisher from the floor. With a swift motion, she flung it toward the computer, praying it would hit the activation key and trigger the gas. Frank grabbed her again and tightened his grip.

The fire extinguisher crashed against the keyboard, smashing keys and jamming the panel. The monitor blinked. A harsh tone sounded. Her stomach twisted between hope and despair. Did it work?

An alarm blared, and lights flashed overhead. A robotic voice echoed throughout the control room: "Initiating containment protocol. Please leave the room immediately. Countdown in thirty seconds. Thirty, twenty-nine, twenty-eight..."

Frank positioned himself between Elena and the onrushing infected at the door. He yanked the door open, and the infected poured in like a stampede. As the crowd rushed past, Frank seized Elena, pushed her into the hallway, and then slammed the door behind, trapping the infected inside. Understanding his sacrifice, she sprang to her feet and dashed down the hallway.

She turned to the control room. The infected rampaged through the room.

Amid the chaos, Frank stood by the glass, his hands pressed against it. He tilted his head slightly, and a flicker of recognition passed through his gaze.

Tears welled, and she sniffed. She placed her hands on the glass to meet his. Her throat tightened. "Thank you." Her voice quivered.

Frank opened his mouth, growled, and blood dripped down his shirt.

The robotic voice continued its countdown: "Three, two, one. Now commencing containment."

Sirens flashed. Alarms blared. Gas hissed through the control room. The infected stopped their rampage, collided with tables and computers, and collapsed on the floor. Frank staggered, smearing two bloody handprints on the glass before slumping to the floor.

Footsteps pounded behind her. Guns locked and loaded.

She whirled to find a group of soldiers in full fatigues wearing gas masks. Their rifles leveled at her, the metallic click of safety switches echoing in the tense silence.

She raised her hands. "Don't shoot. I'm not infected."

A mustached colonel strode past his troops toward her. He raised his gun and aimed it at her. "We have orders to kill the infected."

"There's no need. I have them contained." *There might also be a path to a cure.*

"How do we know you're not infected?"

She folded her arms, meeting his gaze. "You're going to have to trust me."

He shook his head. "I've lost a lot of men and women to this virus. Trust is a hard thing to come by these days. I'll need some proof."

She turned toward Frank, unconscious on the floor. Her finger brushed the syringe in her pocket, the key to saving them all, and she smiled as hope bloomed inside her. "Don't worry, I have proof."

End

`ParaMoira:
The Woman Who Can See the Future
John Schlimm

1955.
6:15 AM

She could feel the penetration, rip, tear, and back-and-forth chew of every razor-sharp tooth along the hacksaw as the blade was working its way roughly through the thin layer of skin on her neck, then slicing her throat, next fileting muscles, slashing arteries, and finally a few more forceful, crunching thrusts dismembered her spinal column just below the base of her brainstem.

The relief was welcomed.

"Wake up!"

The voice echoed first in the darkness, then grew louder as her grogginess gave way to blurred shards of sunrise streaming through the windows.

"I said, 'Wake up!' Do you think you can just lay around sleeping all day?"

This time, the words were accompanied by a stinging slap across her face that hurt worse than the hungry hacksaw.

"Damnit, Moira, I don't have all fucking day," her father yelled furiously.

"I'm awake, I'm awake," seven-year-old Moira Bent said softly, rubbing her bruised cheek with one hand, her throat with the other to make sure it was still intact.

"Get yourself dressed," Mr. Bent ordered. "I need you out helping me plow the corn field, and you need to also fix breakfast and watch the twins."

A large blue jay slammed into the multi-paned window opposite Moira's bed. A smudge of red, like a large thumbprint, was left in the middle of a center pane.

Moira was wide awake now, focused on the death-smeared square of glass. Coiling around her, was the scent of the stale-whiskey vapor trails left by her father's words. She despised him, and everything about this place.

"You're going to die in that field," she told her father, shifting her gaze from the window to stare directly into his bloodshot eyes. "And so are Byron and Lucy. I saw it. You're all going to be ground up under that plow."

This time, his slap was nuclear—the force of his soiled, dry, calloused hand lifting her a few inches in the air, and slamming her small, petite body against the rough-wood headboard.

"I told you to stop that kind of devil-talk," Mr. Bent yelled.

Moira glared at him. She knew what she had seen in her visions and it had all been far too real not to happen.

"Now do as you're told," Mr. Bent grumbled. "Your mother won't be home until late tonight, so you'll have to make supper and pick up around here, too."

As her father stormed out of the room, she recalled her visions: the steaming pile of raw hamburger he'd become once the even larger teeth of the plow got hold of him. And nearby, two toddler-size piles of bloody, rancid, ground meat and bones would also soon bake in the afternoon sun.

***

Today.
Friday the Thirteenth.
8:57 AM

Seventy-seven-year-old Moira Bent adjusted her N95 face mask, making sure it was as tight as possible, while tucking back a few wispy strands of her long, gray hair that was always pulled into a lazy ponytail laying against her tall, thin torso. Comfy in a loose flowery sundress sans undergarments, she finished her twice-daily routine of disinfecting every surface and every nook-and-cranny of her small, secluded one-story, two-bedroom farmhouse homestead that sat surrounded by craggy, overgrown, long-deceased cornfields several miles from the closest neighbor or town in every direction.

The chore never varied—for three hours first thing in the morning beginning at 6:00 AM and again at 6:00 PM for three more hours, everything, including the hardwood floors and ceiling tiles, was sprayed with Clorox and further washed down with antibacterial wipes. She'd begin in the small kitchen on one side of the house, move to the two bedrooms and bathroom on the other end of the house, then finish in the living room in the middle of the house. Specifically, she'd end by scrubbing the front door—which was always closed tight and locked just like all the windows that were also laminated in plastic and tape—finishing with its faceted purple-glass knob.

As Moira polished the knob, she saw a car approaching down her long, dirt driveway—billowing puffs of dust in its wake—which was the only thing that connected her secluded hundred-acres to the main road on the other side of a thick forest.

As the small, gray SUV approached, she also saw the familiar, booger-shaped viruses floating in the air much like once upon a time you'd see dandelion seeds carrying off your wishes. Only these buggers were a menacing, yellowish-gray-infection-snot color with blood-red spikes. With her special gift, she was the only one she knew of who could see the SARS-CoV-2 spores, which the scientific world also knew as severe acute respiratory syndrome coronavirus 2 and the larger world now knew as Covid-19 or coronavirus.

"Who could that be?" Moira asked out loud. She didn't like unexpected guests, and these days, any guest—except the one currently in her kitchen—was unexpected *and* unwelcomed.

By the time the Jeep Grand Cherokee stopped in the dirt patch spanning the front of the house, Moira was on the porch with a rusty pitchfork in hand. It was a beautiful, sunny-cloudless-blue-sky morning accented with a gentle, warm breeze.

"What do you want?" she asked the petite brunette who exited the car. Her voice was distorted through the mask covering her nose and mouth.

"Hi, Miss Bent, I'm Betsy," the woman replied. "Remember, I'm your counselor from the Psych-Rehab center over in Gortonville."

"I don't know no Betsy," Moira said, eyeing the woman suspiciously as the spiked boogers hovered around her, some of them sweeping in a soft current up the steps and bouncing off the N95 mask. "Someone named Pat used to come."

The woman smiled. "Yes, but Pat got a new job," the woman explained, oblivious to the growing cloud of disease around her. "I was here last week, but you wouldn't come out, so I left you a note introducing myself and said I'd be back today."

Moira didn't recall any note, but this was exactly how her visions said it would happen. They'd replace Pat—

"replace" was putting it nicely—and send someone new. It was a trap. This suspicion was further confirmed when, on cue, Betsy stepped toward the porch *and* . . .

"That's close enough!" Moira yelled, raising the pitchfork. She saw the prickly pathogens flood into the woman's nose and mouth with every inhale. It was already too late for her.

"Okay, okay," Betsy said, raising her hand in surrender. A large blue jay—its head bent sideways from a broken neck—swooped down pecking and tearing a clump of the woman's hair from her scalp, then continued on toward the ragged-old corn field.

And . . . a mucous-slimed cockroach crawled out of the woman's nose.

"All I want to do is make sure you're okay, and see if there's anything you need," Betsy said.

Another waxy-yellow cockroach crawled from the woman's right ear. The two bugs explored the woman's face, even bumping into one another before crawling through her glossy-pink lips.

"I have everything I need, so you can be on your way," Moira said firmly, standing her ground and gripping the pitchfork handle so tightly her knuckles were turning white. "And there's no need to return."

The woman eyed the light-blue Subaru Forester parked to the right of the house next to an overgrown rhododendron bush in full fuchsia bloom. "Is there someone here with you, Miss Bent?"

Just like in her visions, only now she was seeing it for real with her very own two eyes, one of Betsy's eyeballs rolled to the side inside her skull—like a rock being pushed away from the opening of a tomb—and one of the cockroaches looked out at her, smiling and waving.

"Miss Bent," Betsy repeated louder, inhaling more red-spiked boogers, "is someone here with you?"

"No," Moira answered firmly, keeping an eye on the swarming microbes so they didn't get too close to her. "That belongs to an out-of-town woman who was having car trouble. I said she could keep it here until she can come back with a mechanic."

"Okay, okay," Betsy said, as the word "BEWARE" burned from inside out across her forehead. "Is there anything I—"

"I already told you once," Moira interrupted, raising the pitchfork, "I'm fine, I can take care of myself just fine, so there's no need for you to return."

Betsy smiled. "Well, I'm required to visit at least once a week, so I'll be back next Friday," she said. "So if there's anything you need between now and then you can give me a call, okay?"

The woman clearly had no idea how Moira chose to live—there was no phone, and no TV, and no electricity—all part of her plan to independently survive what was going on out there in the world, and what was coming next. She just wanted to be left alone, which was safest.

"Well, just in case . . ." Betsy started to say, but Moira lost track of her words because a lump clumsily maneuvered up the inside length of Betsy's throat and a small, long-nailed claw reached from the woman's mouth, beckoning to her.

"Get on your way, now!" Moira said, a beat louder this time so her words were clear through the mask. The vibration of her voice jarred the nearby cloud of disease now floating way too close around her, sending the spiked boogers back down the porch steps.

She then turned, set the pitchfork by the door, and headed back inside, making sure to shut the door tightly and double bolt it so no viruses or other unwanted intruders could get in. She watched from a window as Betsy stood—engulfed now in the barbed Covid spores—staring at the house a moment longer, then got in her car and drove away.

Moira took a few deep breaths beneath the N95 mask that was only removed when it was replaced with a fresh one every morning—no exceptions, not even when sleeping or bathing.

That exchange had been a close call. Too close for comfort.

She wiped herself down—carefully sterilizing herself from head to toe—with the Clorox and antibacterial cloths, which was a precautionary task she normally preferred to do before reentering the house.

After Moira was satisfied that none of the germs were on her and that she did not bring any inside, she strolled into the kitchen.

"I'm so sorry to keep you waiting all morning like this," Moira said to the woman, who was also wearing an N95 mask and sitting on the other side of the wooden table that was covered with a blue-checkered tablecloth. "I never miss my cleaning chores, and then that awful creature showed up, but she didn't fool me, no way, not one bit.

"Here, let me pour you some more tea." Moira reached an empty, flower-patterned porcelain teapot across the table and poured nonexistent tea into the woman's empty, matching teacup.

"I'm so glad you're here now, just like my visions said you would be. It would be awful lonely to have to ride this thing out all by myself. *Yessiree*, several weeks ago, a vision first revealed that you'd show up at my house, and most importantly that you're safe, virus-free like me, and one of the good guys, one of the last few good guys who will be left with me when this thing is done with humankind.

"How's your tea? Warm enough? Oh good! I pride myself on being a good hostess."

Moira lifted her mask a few centimeters, just enough

to take a sip of her own nonexistent tea.

"When you arrived yesterday, I promised to explain everything to you after we both had a good night's rest, so here it goes, because I know I can trust you." Moira smiled at her guest and took another sip of tea that wasn't there.

"My survival is all thanks to my visions, which I've had since I was a child. My first one was seeing my daddy get ground up under a plow right outside that window there while planting corn. No one believed me that it would happen. I begged Momma and Daddy to listen to me, but they'd tell me to 'stop with the devil-talk.'

"I also have, well *had*, two younger siblings once upon a time but both died when they were babies. I saw their deaths, too, in my visions. Momma and Daddy didn't listen to me about them either, but they should have.

"It was only later that folks started taking my visions seriously. So seriously that a local carnival passing through town invited me to join them on the road to tell fortunes. I jumped at the opportunity to escape this place once and for all. That's when I became *ParaMoira: The Woman Who Can See the Future*!

"From age sixteen on, I traveled all over with that carnival—to places like Bad Axe, Michigan; Tombstone, Arizona; Cape Fear, North Carolina; and Kissimmee, Florida—and helped lots of people of all ages to learn about their futures so they could stop the bad stuff from happening.

"Then, when the carnival went out of business, I moved to Summerdale. You ever hear about that place? No? Well, if, I mean *when*, we survive this thing, you should definitely visit. I'll even take you there myself. It's a small village of psychics in Ohio. I had to pass a test and everything for them to accept me, which I did with flying colors, and they welcomed me with open arms. I lived there for several decades. I was so happy there!

"Here, you must try one of my peanut-butter cookies." Moira reached a nonexistent cookie across the table and placed it on the edge of her guest's flower-patterned, porcelain saucer. "It's one of Momma's recipes." She proceeded to lift her mask and nibble on one herself.

"I also helped the police—back when you could trust authorities like that—solve a few missing persons' cases, and a few robbery cases," Moira continued. "And even a murder case once—you may have heard about it: a young Native-American woman was found strangled by a river not far from Summerdale.

"Turns out a no-good drug dealer and trafficker from the area killed her after she tried to escape from him. Not long after that, I started having visions about this Covid pandemic, and I just knew I had to head back to the farm here where I'd be safe!

"Which all brings me to today." Moira lifted her N95 mask again for another sip of tea that wasn't there.

"I know, it's a lot, but like Momma always told me, 'Knowledge is power.' I saw it all: a virus—that in my visions looks like plump, spiky-and-snotty boogers— would spread across the world unstopped, invading and murdering millions. I can see them floating in the air outside and even being sucked into people's noses and mouths. And contrary to what anybody says, once they're inside you, they never leave! There's no treatment or shot they can ever give you to stop it.

"I know, it's terrifying, but it's best you know the full truth."

10:37 AM

A knock on the front door caused Moira to jump in her chair. She put her forefinger to her mask-covered mouth in a *Shhhh!* gesture. "Keep quiet," she whispered. "I bet it's one of them again. I'll take care of it, you stay here."

Moira slowly stood, made sure her mask still formed a tight seal around her nose and mouth, and crept to the front door. Through the locked and laminated front windows, and the panes in the front door, she could see one of them disguised as a young deliveryman—a pretend man—they were good at disguises and pretending. Just off the porch behind him, she could see the blood-red-pointy booger germs dancing in the air.

Eye-to-eye now with the man via the laminated panes in the door, Moira ordered, "Stand back!"

"What?" she heard him say in return, his voice muffled on the other side of glass and plastic.

"*I said step back to the end of the porch!*" she yelled. She intended to nip this shit in the bud right away.

The man looked confused, but backstepped to the top of the six wooden steps.

Moira unbolted the door, opened it just enough for her thin frame to slip out and so no viruses could slip in, and stepped onto the porch.

"What do you want?" she asked flatly, eyeing the figure top to bottom. She had no time for games. This battle was now well underway.

"I have a certified letter that needs your signature," the deliveryman replied, extending an envelope and clipboard with the form to be signed. The word "PLAGUE" burned from inside out across his face, and she could hear the scalding sizzle of flesh.

"Stop! That's far enough," Moira said, raising her hand to keep him at least arm's length from her. The Covid bugs were attaching to his hair and shoulders with their red spikes like ravenous parasites. "Set the letter and clipboard on the porch and go down the steps. Then I'll sign it."

The man rolled his eyes, set the letter and clipboard on the porch, raised his arms in a playful surrender, and then turned around to walk down the steps. Gathering microorganisms parted as he walked through them, only to curl back around to dig into the full length of his body like boobalice.

Moira had seen enough.

As the deliveryman was midstride between the fourth and fifth steps, she drove the rusty pitchfork tines through his back, the tips popping through the front of his tan uniform unleashing a spray of red rain.

The viruses held on to him for dear life, their barbs fastened firmly to his dying flesh and clothing. The man made a brutal grunt from the impact, then went silent. He remained standing—a stuck pig—for a moment, just long enough for the large blue jay—its twisted head emphasizing the dried-scarlet scabbing on its fractured neck—to perch on a middle tine, then take-off again.

The deliveryman's corpse dropped straight down, his bones cracking, his right tibia and fibula snapping and hacking through hairy skin and fabric. Moira let go of the pitchfork handle so he wouldn't take her down with him.

She quickly scrubbed herself down just outside the front door, then hurried inside to get what she needed. Time was of the essence.

Arms full of supplies, she told her guest in the kitchen, "I'm so sorry to make you wait again, but I have to clean up a mess someone made. Please make yourself at home and have as many of Momma's peanut-butter cookies as you want."

For the next two hours, Moira meticulously sanitized the deliveryman's body, the inside of his truck, and the inside of the blue Subaru with her bottle of Clorox and antibacterial wipes. She then loaded the man—along with the unopened letter and clipboard—into the passenger seat of his delivery truck and proceeded to drive it to the bank that overlooked a large, deep pond on her property.

Leaving the truck in DRIVE, Moira climbed onto an ancient, rusted plow that scratched and groaned to life. She steered the growling plow behind the truck and nudged it over and down the bank, where it splashed into the water and sink. She then did the same with her guest's Subaru.

"My apologies again," Moira said to her houseguest, after having scrubbed herself from head to toe just outside the front door, then rushing in and sitting back down at the table. "Now where was I?

"Oh, yes: I saw the whole Covid massacre coming, and now here we are, and it's just the beginning. No one would believe me. I called the White House and wrote letters to the president and first lady, and the vice president and second lady.

"I called the place, I forget what it's named, where that short little doctor and the lady doctor who always wears scarves work at and I wrote them letters, too. I wrote to the U.S. Senators and Congresspeople, and our governor and state representatives. I even wrote to the mayors, commissioners, and police chiefs in the towns around here. And nothing. Which is when I realized they were all in on it!"

Moira placed another invisible peanut-butter cookie on her guest's plate. "I'm glad to see you're enjoying my fresh-baked cookies! There's plenty more where these came from, so eat up."

She then ate another one herself.

"Since nobody would believe me," she continued, "all I could do was protect myself. So here we are: the safest place on earth. At least for now. But I've already seen in my visions what's coming next. You know those two people who came to my house this morning—I mean, our house now that you're here? They ain't human, I mean, not anymore. In my vision I saw armies more just like them— sort of like zombies, but worse, more intelligent, more conniving, more vicious, but no longer human, that's for sure."

1:13 PM

Moira glanced at the plastic-covered window above her kitchen sink. The view was distorted, but sure enough, there was another one of them in the distance! No, *two of them!* She motioned to her guest to be quiet, then hunched over and tiptoed to the laminated window for a better look.

About thirty feet from the house, a woman—twenty-or-thirty-something, goth-style with blue hair, piercings, black tank top barely covering multiple rolls around her waist, shredded skin-tight black jeans bulging over thighs, and splatter-painted knee-high boots—was clomping through the high weeds and wildflowers.

Just behind her was a man—also goth-style with a scrawny build, shaved head, piercings, similar tank, jeans, and boots, and puffing on a vape.

Moira looked back at her guest. "Now they're coming pretending to be damn tourists," she said in a hushed tone, "but they ain't going to fool me, *nosiree*."

She then tiptoed back to the table. "You see, this house is kind of famous, tragic famous you might say," she told her guest. "Back in the 1970s, an author learned about my daddy being ground up by that plow, and how my little brother and sister—they were twins—had also died in similar ways here when they were just babies, and he wrote a fictionalized version of the story titled *The Corn Wept Blood*. It was a cheap, novelized rip-off of Capote's *In Cold Blood*. In it, the tragedies were blamed on a made-up version of my momma.

"Then in the 1980s, some movie folks exaggerated the story even more and made a movie called *The Bloody Cornfield*. In the movie, a scarecrow—possessed by the dead farm wife who once lived on the farm—does the killing of the new family who moves into the house. There was even a *Bloody Cornfield 2*.

"When readers and later the moviegoers heard this farm inspired the book and movie, they started trespassing here. And my poor momma had to put up with all those invaders all on her own until all the hoopla died down.

"It was only when I started having the visions about the pandemic that I moved back here because I knew I'd be safe. By then, Momma had been dead for years—she drowned when we were swimming in the lake at Summerdale while she was visiting. But this is the first I saw fans coming here again after all this time. I thought maybe they forgot about that stupid book and the movies, which is why I know those two out there ain't up to no good."

Moira walked over to her guest at the table—fifty-something Julie Clark, an attractive, mid-level executive who arrived yesterday after getting lost on her way to a conference, in a lavender pantsuit, shoulder-length blonde hair, eyes wide open, and with a brownish, crusted-over bullet hole in the direct center of her forehead.

"You'll have to excuse me again," Moira told her, making sure her guest's N95 mask was still on tight. "I promise it's for our own good."

She then ran her hand over Julie's hair. "I used to have pretty hair this same color when I was younger," she said. "You're lucky, I don't see any gray yet. By the time I was fifty-five, I was a silver fox. Okay then, I promise I'll be right back."

Ten minutes later, Moira was standing stealthily fifteen feet behind the couple who were on the bank staring down into the pond. A cloud of ravenous Covid boogers hovered around them and coated their bodies, the barbs burrowing in like deer ticks.

"You have something that belongs to me!" Moira said from behind her N95 mask, causing the couple to jump and nearly lose their balance as they twisted around, inciting the cloud of microorganisms to swish and swirl. Immediately, she also saw cockroaches and maggots mingling in their scalps.

"Fuck, you scared us! *Wait*, are you , , , *Paramoira*?" the goth woman asked excitedly. "We thought you were dead. We heard somewhere you died by suicide a few years ago."

"I'm not the dead one here," Moira spat back, now seeing an undulating lump on the side of the guy's head and a long-nailed paw covered in bloody, yellow chunks of wax reach out from his left ear, flip her the bird, then jerk back in.

"We're glad you're not, you know, dead!" the goth guy said, taking a puff from his vape. "Can we get a selfie with you?"

"No," Moira said, touching her mask to reinforce its airtight seal. "Now hand over what you stole."

The man and woman both looked down at the objects they were holding. She had a weathered board. He held a length of rusted chain.

"We're huge fans of yours," the guy said, "and of the *Bloody Cornfield* movies. They're classics! We just wanted to visit and get a . . ."

"I had nothing to do with those movies, or that trash book," Moira clarified, even though she was aware the final girl in the two movies had been named after her, as was one of the children in the novel.

Tributes she did not appreciate. Nor did she appreciate trespassers who had clearly been sent here to shut her up, lest someone finally believe her visions about the pandemic and what was coming next—something even worse and something her unwanted visitors today confirmed had already been set in motion.

In addition to the spiky, yolk-yellow-and-gray booger viruses she saw in the air, covering the couple and invading their mouths and nostrils, Moira saw the new addition of larger, elongated germs—these resembled darkened toenail clippings covered in a chunky-greenish fungus.

"Hey, is that the plow used by the scarecrow in the movies?" the guy asked, pointing to the ancient, nearby machine Moira had used earlier to shove the deliveryman and his truck, and Julie's Subaru, into the pond.

This time, Moira smelled the odor of burning flesh first. Her gaze then followed the red-hot flame as it carved "DO" from inside out on the man's tattooed sleeve and 'OM' on the woman's inked arm.

"No," Moira said flatly while observing the diseased toenail clippings entering and emerging freely from the couple's oily, engorged pores. Just as her previous visions had shown her. These new bugs weren't viruses or even bacteria per say, but something far more sinister and deadly.

"We've also followed your career as a psychic since we were teenagers living near Summerdale in Ohio," the goth woman said. "We even saw you a few times in Summerdale, but then we heard you moved away and had died, but obviously you didn't. Hey, would it be possible to get a reading from you while we're here?"

Sure as she was standing there, puce-colored worms with bulbous heads slithered from the woman's mouth, dropping to the ground where they scattered away amidst a growing swarm of the infectious, toenail-clipping pathogens. The large blue jay flew down nabbing a worm midair with its beak that was somehow still functional atop its deformed neck.

"Nice try, coming here and trying to trick me like this," Moira said with a scowl.

"What do you mean?" the goth guy asked.

As he spoke, both of his eyeballs rolled to the side and cockroaches smiled and waved at her from inside the gooey sockets that were backlit in a green glow, while hair-thin, pus worms slithered over his face and neck.

Moira had had enough. By way of responding, she raised a gun and rapid-fired two blasts—one through each of their faces. The impact caused the couple to topple back and tumble down into the pond.

Before pushing their bodies—both crawling with the Covid and rotted toenail parasites—out a little further with a stick so they'd sink, Moira reclaimed the piece of wood and chain the couple thought they could steal as souvenirs.

She then located the motorcycle they had arrived on, which was parked halfway down her long, dirt driveway. It was no small effort to push that fucker all the way back to the pond and sink it as well.

Returning to her front porch, Moira scrubbed down with Clorox and antibacterial wipes. Once back inside, Moira popped her head into the kitchen.

"I'm going to wash up some more and then I'll fix us some supper later," she told her guest. "Just keep making yourself at home. *Mi casa es su casa!*"

3:33 PM

Moira bounded merrily into the kitchen, squeaky clean and wearing a crisp, new, lavender-and-white striped sundress and her N95 mask.

"Now where were we?" she asked Julie. "Oh, right, so I'll now tell you what comes next . . ."

A car horn blared outside.

Moira stopped cold, shaking her head to let her guest know to remain dead silent once more.

She then stood, patted down her sundress, checked her

N95 mask, and walked to a front window. Through the plastic and glass, Moira saw it was that counselor, Becky or Betsy, or whatever her name was, who had been there that morning.

The fungus-coated-toenail-clipping germs seemed to be gathering around the woman in the afternoon sunlight like moths to an illuminated bulb.

Moira took a deep breath behind her mask, fastened it even tighter, and then cracked open the front door to cautiously squeeze out.

"Hi, Miss Bent," Betsy said, waving.

"I told you once to get off my property, I ain't telling you again," Moira sad angrily from the top of the front porch steps.

Betsy took a step, but stopped when Moira raised her hand.

"Miss Bent, I forgot to ask you something this morning," Betsy said.

The jagged, fungal-infused toenail clippings coated the woman like barnacles on a whale.

"What's that?" Moira asked suspiciously.

"What is today's date?" Betsy asked.

"Do you take me for a fool, young lady?" Moira replied.

Betsy smiled. "No, Miss Bent, certainly not, but please humor me. What is today's date?"

After a moment, Moira decided to indeed humor the woman before putting an end to this once and for all. "It's Friday the thirteenth, of course."

"What's the full date?" Betsy pressed on.

"You're wearing on my last nerve, lady!" Moira said. "It's Friday, March the thirteenth."

"What year?" Betsy asked.

Moira groaned from behind her mask. "The year, young lady, is twenty-twenty."

Betsey slumped her shoulders as a sad expression grew on her face. "That's what I thought you'd say," she said. "Miss Bent, today is Friday, JUNE the thirteenth, and the year is TWENTY-TWENTY-FIVE."

Moira smirked. "I knew I'd catch you in a blatant lie!"

"I'm not . . .," Betsy started.

"*Liar!*" Moira screamed.

"Miss Bent, please calm down," Betsy said, stepping forward.

Another raised hand from Moira stopped her cold in her tracks.

"Miss Bent, you have a condition where every day you wake up you think it's March thirteenth, twenty-twenty," Betsy told her. "It's a condition called . . ."

"*Fuck you!*" Moira screeched. "That's what it's called!" Somewhere in the distance, the large blue jay cried out in response, and in solidarity. "I want you off my farm right now!"

"I can't leave this time," Betsy said, starting again to approach the steps. "DEATH" burned from inside out across her eyes like an engulfed, avant-garde pair of sunglasses.

Moira raised her gun and blasted multiple rounds into the woman's neck, knocking her back like an invisible fist was repeatedly sucker-punching her. By the time Betsy collapsed, her head was barely left clinging to her body.

All the green, toenail-clipping microbes raced into the woman's body as if like metal shavings to a giant magnet.

"Another mess to clean up," Moira said. But as she turned back to her front door, a rumble came down her driveway.

It was a muddy-green, military-style truck with a large, boxy storage trailer attached, leaving a raging stream of dust in its wake.

Moira leaned outward and squinted to get a clearer

look. This hadn't ever been in one of her visions. The moment was cut short when a sack of some kind was forced over her head, and everything went black.

4:02 PM

"Yes, affirmative, the subject has no pulse," a familiar male voice said. "No heartbeat, no breathing, nothing, just as we expected."

Moira's hearing sharpened in on what was being said around her.

Another male voice—clearly over walkie-talkie—said, "Proceed as planned."

"Will do, sir," the original male voice said.

"Okay, let's get this over with," a familiar woman's voice instructed.

"Great, remove the hood," the man said. "I want to look into her eyes as we do this."

The cloth sack was removed from Moira's head. She could immediately tell that her N95 mask had also been removed. She frantically attempted to raise her hands to her mouth and nose for some protective coverage, but her arms and legs were fastened down with restraints.

She assumed she was in the trailer she had seen attached to the military truck coming down her driveway. It was like the back of an ambulance, only larger and with more screens on the walls.

Moira looked at the people hunched around her, staring at her like she was some carnival-sideshow freak. There were five—each of them was attired in a sleek, fitted, silvery biohazard suit with a clear-domed helmet.

This was never in any vision she had, either. What was happening?

She was too afraid to open her mouth. But she instantly recognized the individuals under the protective shields—the deliveryman from that morning, the goth couple who had trespassed on her land, Betsy the counselor, and . . . but it couldn't be, could it? Julie, her guest whom she had welcomed into her home for safe keeping, and for tea and for her Momma's peanut-butter cookies. The guest a vision had told her was safe, was someone with whom she could ride out this epidemic.

All of them were very much alive.

"Congratulations, Miss Bent," the deliveryman said— the same man whom she had driven her Daddy's pitchfork through that morning. "You are Patient Zero for what we have named in your honor: *Moira-00* . . . Don't look so surprised, you deserve it!"

Moira swiveled her head side to side. *No, no, no.*

"Ah, but, yes, yes, yes, Miss Bent," the man said. "You see, Covid was just a test run, and we learned a lot from it, particularly from the folks who remained locked away even once all the danger lifted. Folks like you, Miss Bent, for whom the pandemic never truly ended, at least not in your minds."

The woman she knew as Betsy—whose head she had nearly decapitated only minutes ago—leaned in, fully intact. "As we studied folks who remained in a self-quarantine, like you, we discovered something fantastic," she explained excitedly. "When any of you would die by suicide, your DNA did something extraordinary. It literally developed a new enzyme that enabled you to come back to life. Well, conscious and functioning, anyway."

"Liar," Moira now whispered. None of this was in any of her visions, and her visions were never wrong.

Betsy smiled. "No, not lies at all," she said. "And it's all thanks to you that we initially discovered this revolutionary way to reanimate dead tissue. While we had you under surveillance as you self-quarantined, our team saw you hang yourself in the kitchen of your house here. They went in, cut you down, and laid you on your bed, intending to go back the next day to retrieve your body.

"But after waiting overnight, when they went in to retrieve your body the next day so we could do an autopsy and study it, there you were, awake and scrubbing down your floorboards. That was the exact moment we knew something special had occurred. A new discovery—the greatest of all time, in fact—that would change human history."

"No," Moira said. According to her visions, Covid would never go away after Friday, March 13, 2020, and would continue to grow and evolve and kill more and more and more people around the world until only she and Julie were the last two souls left on earth—all thanks to the rigid precautions she was taking.

"Yes," the male half of the goth duo corrected her— the man whose face Moira had shot off a few hours ago. "In fact, if we took an x-ray right now, you'd see your neck is still broken and your larynx is crushed. Your head is actually positioned crookedly because of it.

"We decided to leave you be here alone on your farm to see how this progressed, and here we are two years later. Meanwhile, when we then saw other shut-ins kill themselves—no matter the method, even the really messy ones—we'd immediately collect their bodies and take them to various facilities around the world where we studied them as they came back to life."

The goth woman—whose face was also just blown away—chimed in, "Which is how we discovered the evolutionary development in enzymes that only happens in self-quarantined individuals. A dynamic mutation of sorts. It was a combination of isolated immune systems morphing and mixing with a new, unprecedented level of frenetic stress and chronic fear on the brain that produced revolutionary new chemicals in support of self-preservation.

"Unfortunately for subjects like you, you're rendered

more or less a zombie, albeit an advanced zombie—no heartbeat or breathing, but still some brain activity, and you can come off as more or less normal for short bursts of time, and you can even feel pain.

"However, this discovery, with the few, small tweaks we were able to facilitate in the lab, miraculously makes the healthy reanimation of destroyed or dead tissue possible when administered to the living. Well, possible for some of us anyway, moving forward. But we're having to act fast so no one discovers what we have and uses it for nefarious purposes!"

"What? I don't understand," Moira said. None of this made sense. Did they really just say she had killed herself? She then noticed that inside this trailer there were no spiked-booger Covid viruses or any of the pathogens that looked like chunky, fungal-stained toenail clippings.

"During the past few years, we've harvested enough of the enzymes to now replicate and grow them in our labs," Julie—Moira's houseguest whom she had shot in the forehead at point-blank range just the day before— explained. "Now we don't need any of you anymore. With a few tweaks to the life-sustaining enzyme, we were also able to reverse-engineer and construct the deadliest virus ever known to humankind. Its only antidote is the original enzyme that, as you can see with us, heals and regenerates life. All of us have been injected with it, and will now live forever no matter what happens to us."

"Liar," Moira spat at her former houseguest.

Julie smiled. "You didn't even realize you were feeding me, and yourself, invisible peanut-butter cookies and tea," she said. "Nor did you realize you've been scrubbing your house with the same empty Clorox bottle and filthy, dry-rotted antibacterial wipes for the past two years. Even more disgusting, your N95 masks that you think you're replacing each day are the same crusty, rotting, putrid masks . . . essentially overridden Petri dishes at this point . . . that you've been using for years."

Betsy jumped in, further revealing, "Last year, we began to exterminate everyone like you—those people who opted for self-induced quarantine despite zero proof of any viable danger left from the Covid pandemic. It was so easy since you all had shut out the world, and quite frankly the world forgot about you, too, so no one noticed or even suspected you all were dying from anything other than loneliness and isolation.

"Though the only surefire method by which we had to exterminate people like you—who technically couldn't die so to speak—did pose some . . . let's just say, some visually-challenging issues, but we were able to solve that with some cosmetic ingenuity and pay-offs so family and friends were none the wiser."

"And you, Miss Bent—our glorious Patient Zero," the deliveryman said with a big, admiring smile, "you are our final elimination. We purposely saved that honor for you. In the near future, we will unleash the new virus—this one engineered to target the world's crops and water supplies—that we estimate will exterminate everyone on the planet within a couple years, everyone, that is, except for the few thousand of us who will remain to repopulate earth into a much better, happier, more peaceful place."

"But you, Miss Bent, will always be a hero to us," the goth guy said. "Without you, who knows how long it would have taken to connect the necessary scientific dots."

"Statues will be erected to you," the goth woman said with wide, starstruck eyes. "And history books will note your selfless contribution to the ultimate survival of the human race and the peaceful, loving world we'll create. I bet movies will even be made about you—telling your real, heroic story, not like those cheesy *Bloody Cornfield* flicks or that stupid *Crying Corn* novel or whatever it was called.

You deserve so much better than that, and we'll make sure you get it!"

Moira was about to speak, but the deliveryman placed a piece of electrical tape over her mouth. "I assure you this is going to hurt us more than it hurts you, Miss Bent, because we've actually grown quite fond of you," he said. "But we really don't like to hear screaming. It's so unsettling, especially when you're dedicated to world peace like we are."

"I promise I'll make this as quick as possible," Julie said. "We decided since you were so hospitable to me, it was only right that I have the honor of doing this."

The woman raised a shiny hacksaw, its silver fangs glistening.

"Thank you, Miss Bent, and Godspeed," she said.

Moira could feel the penetration, rip, tear, and back-and-forth chew of every razor-sharp tooth along the hacksaw as the blade was working its way roughly through the thin layer of skin on her neck, then slicing her throat, next fileting muscles, slashing arteries, and finally a few more forceful, crunching thrusts dismembered her spinal column just below the base of her brainstem.

The relief was welcomed.

But before everything went black, she could faintly hear someone yelling what sounded like, "WAKE UP!"

The Jumping-off Point
J Louis Messina

Weathering the gust that swept my hair and clothes back, as if in a wind tunnel, as if hands to push me away from danger, I swayed woozily atop the ledge of the Roxy Hotel, breathed in the faint stench of death below, and, compelled to jump a sheer eight stories down, peered over the roof.

Why was I there?

Because I have an impulse to leap into the void. Doctors said I'd grow out of it, but I never have. Nothing to worry about, they said. You need a hobby, a career, get laid. But all I could think about was jumping.

I'd had the condition since childhood. Ruined my life. Wherever, whoever I was with, I found a place to jump off, and there'd go my job, my date, my friends. They have a name for it, because they have a name for everything. High Place Phenomenon (HPP). A sudden and unexplainable urge to jump from a high place. No one who has it acts on it. But that all changed months ago.

While I mused on my imminent sacrifice, the familiar rush of feet raced behind me; not to entreat me *not* to jump, that you have *everything to live for*, but the urgent clatter of people who had lost their will, who had a craving, a sickness, a burning fever, and before I could shout at them to stop—for I knew it was a useless plea—a man and a woman flashed by me and sprung off the roof to their deaths, silently, without regrets, like cannonballing into a pool. They plummeted gleefully, relishing the big splash to come.

When they splattered like a watermelon, other people looked up, spotted me, and pointed, but they didn't say 'don't jump' as one would expect, but cried the unexpected 'Why isn't he jumping? Is that the carrier? The spreader of the disease?'

To be honest, I hadn't thought anyone was left alive in the city.

I'd been in therapy for my condition for quite some time. This had been in a hot New York August that melted bodies and minds like butter left on a stove. My analyst, having reached a decade in my lack of progress, suggested I act on my impulse.

"We've delved into your childhood for quite some time," my therapist, Dr. Brady, a cipher of man in a heavy, green sweater as relaxed as him, said. "And neither your mother, father, or siblings, or any inciting incident has been found, other than you've isolated yourself from others. We've established your fear of being close to anyone, but we have come no closer to a solution. It's time, then, you face your problem head on."

"How so?" I said, slouched in the cushy leather chair. I stared out his office window on the tenth floor, longing to dive off. "It's hot in here. Why don't you open the window?"

"We've been through this before. Not going to

happen." He flipped his notepad over. "I think, Mr. Simms, you should jump out of a plane."

"Nice. Most people tell me to jump off a cliff. Getting tired of me already? Are you suggesting suicide?"

"Heavens no!" He hesitated, as if he'd considered the notion. People weary quickly of my smart mouth cracks. "That'd be unprofessional. Learn to skydive. Go safely to your death. When you alight, your compulsion to jump will have been satisfied, and you'll no longer feel the need."

"The ironic thing is I'm scared of heights. Isn't that a laugh?"

"We'll work out that enigma later. By far, this is the more pressing issue. You might even bond with them, make a friend."

"Highly unlikely. I like being alone. That's why I work on cars."

I figured that if I leapt out of a plane and could pull a cord, spread my wings and fly, my desire would evaporate like water at high altitudes. That is, if I didn't wet myself on the way down.

Somewhat reluctantly, I enrolled in the Long Island Skydiving Center. There were predominantly large, thrill-seeking men and women who looked like they could kick your ass, totally opposite of me. I felt like a lollipop amongst a box of expensive Cuban cigars.

My first experience would be tandem skydiving. Tethered to an experienced instructor, we'd jump together. But my fear of heights got the better of my compulsion to jump, and, after a month of classes, I backed out.

Even when I explained my fear of heights, they encouraged me. Instead of laughter and ridicule, they were surprisingly sympathetic.

"You're not the first skydiver to have that fear," Tyrone said, posing like a Navy Seal action figure and waving me off. "I've had it myself. Took me ten tries to jump. You need gradual exposure. We'll help you through it. Once I did, piece of cake."

"Peter," Gus the instructor said, clamping my shoulder, as if we were old buddies. "Although you can't jump yet, you've paid your fee. Fly in the plane with us until you're comfortable enough to skydive. Then come back and finish the class. Let the others inspire you."

Overcoming my fear of heights for my desire to jump, I accepted.

The afternoon blazed as we took off. The plane was like a cocoon you had to birth from. Having been in the outside world, I preferred the cocoon. Once we reached 20,000 feet, the skydivers opened the door, checked their equipment, and prepared to jump. My desire took control, and I drifted to the opening, like you would to a lady with nothing on but a smile and open arms. Freud would've had a field day.

"Get back!" Tyrone said, snapping his head around. "You don't have a parachute. You might fall out."

"Yes, I might." Holding onto the sides, wind whipping my face, I gazed down into the finite sky, down to the distant patch of Earth that would mark my broken body's grave. The only thing that kept me rooted was my fear of heights. "But I won't."

From the cockpit, the pilot and copilot shouted in alarm.

"What the hell is that?"

"Damn! I think it's a falling meteor."

"With some kind of glowing mist. Hold on back there! We're going to fly around it."

The Cessna 182 rocked, dove, and climbed. While I clutched onto the doorway, the skydivers tumbled to the floor, rolled backward, and grabbed the bottom of chairs.

"What're you two doing in there?" Gus hollered over to the cockpit. "Trying to get us killed?"

Like a leviathan, the mist swallowed the plane, and for a minute, the air sizzled, sparked, and darkened, and the Cessna quaked and jangled, caught in turbulence. I thought bolts and screws would pop off and the plane fall apart.

The strange mist covered me from head to foot. My skin electrified. I wheezed and coughed, almost lost my grip, and fell forward. Imagining the fall, it was both horrifying and exhilarating. The mist seeped into my body.

My head throbbed. A group groan raked through us, a collected despair that trumpeted doom. If the plane were to crash, I decided the better way to die was to leap sans parachute than be crushed in crumpled metal and fire. I preferred a fun ride down to a quick death.

The shaking stopped. Everyone gasped like steam to release pressure. The plane righted itself; the mist had vanished. Seconds later, the meteor struck the terrain. Debris spewed upward and left a crater a mile wide.

My body tingled and burned, my head feverish, and my hands glowed green then faded. I reeled over to the group and held out my hand to help them up.

"You guys okay?" I asked, taking the instructor's arm and yanking him to his feet.

"Yeah," Gus said, tottering. "Wait until I give those pilots a piece of my mind."

"Did you see that weird mist?"

"Nope. Too busy holding on for dear life."

"I suppose we should go back. Do this another day."

"Probably a good idea," Tyrone said, nodding in agreement. "Everyone's shook up."

Alice and Derrick nodded, too. With a sudden, unexplainable action, and to my amazement, the four of them trooped to the open door, and one-by-one, without a word, they sailed out. I figured they were such diehard skydivers that they couldn't resist not jumping. They had it worse than me.

Pitching over to watch them fall, I waited and waited for the parachutes to open. Even with my little training, I knew they had reached a point they had to deploy the chutes, but they kept falling and falling until they became dots and in succession hit land.

Blinking rapidly, it took me a bit to realize what had happened; even then, I refused to accept it. My eyes had played tricks on me. They were seasoned vets. Not all the chutes could've malfunctioned. It was as if they wanted to leap to their deaths.

Like me.

As the impossible horror of it sunk in, I staggered to the cockpit to inform the crew. I didn't think they'd believe me; hell, I didn't believe it.

"The others jumped," I said, poking my head in. "They're all gone."

"Doesn't surprise me," the pilot said. "Nothing fazes them. They'd skydive through a hurricane."

"You don't understand. They didn't open their chutes. They jumped to their deaths."

"You been drinking?" the copilot said, frowning at me.

"No. But I wish I had. Got anything?"

"That's some sick joke," the pilot said.

"You better report it. It's true."

My breath came in spurts. I felt weak in the knees and confused everywhere else, and the pit of my stomach churned like a speeding cement mixer. They stared back at me a long time, as if I was haunting the place.

"I think he's in shock," the copilot said.

"Might be telling the truth," the pilot said. "Let's look. If this is a gag, you're going to be in big trouble."

"You can't see anyone now," I said. "Try to contact somebody."

"Gus, this is Mike," the pilot said into the com. "Report back."

When no answer came, the pilot put the plane on auto. They unbuckled and marched to the door and peered out.

"There's nothing to see," I said, exasperated. "Land the plane and send out the paramedics and a steam shovel to scoop them up."

It was like watching a pedestrian walk straight into a bus for no apparent reason. Together they jumped. No parachutes. They spiraled down. Not a peep. It wasn't long before they thumped the earth. If I wasn't in shock before, I sure had it bad now. My skin had turned cool and clammy. My jaw had dropped like a skydiver. I'd just lost the pilots.

What the fuck do I do now?

I raced to the cockpit and sat. Fumbling with the intercom, I pressed the button, and my words spilled out like jigsaw pieces dumped onto the floor.

"Up in plane! Pilots dead, need help, can't fly, if anyone is there, please answer, don't know how long before I crash."

The com crackled, then someone spoke.

"This is the control tower. Say again?"

I said it again. They asked me to check their pulse to make sure they were dead. I said I can't, they jumped from the plane. Why? they asked. Damned if I know, but I must land this plane.

"We'll talk you through it."

Like in every plane disaster movie, they gave me step-by-step instructions. Sweat streamed down my face and pits. My body stunk. As I approached the landing, the closer the cement loomed, the more my fear rose, but so did my concentration, for every fiber of my being strained to do it right. The plane touched down, bounced several times, and before long, I'd landed safely. I think I did wet myself.

"Do you need help?" someone called from outside.

Prying myself from the controls, I wobbled to the jumping-off point. They'd placed stairs there, and my feet tumbled down the steps and missed a few. They caught me at the bottom, stuffed me into an ambulance, checked my vitals, and sped me to an office in the tower.

There, two guys in Walmart suits interrogated me. I told them the whole absurd story. They looked puzzled and doubtful, but I repeated the story verbatim. Implying murder, they asked if I had been the one who got rid of them.

I said I'm not that persuasive a fellow. I didn't have a weapon and can't even get you to believe me. I couldn't throw a wet towel overboard. Without a word, as if they'd had enough of me, which I couldn't blame them, they turned and walked out the door and left me there. I waited twenty minutes.

Had they gone for the police? A bathroom break? A round of gin rummy?

Tired of waiting, I opened the door and peeked inside. The place was empty. I paraded through, calling out for anyone, but no one answered. From outside the windows, from every direction, bodies rained down around me. Dumbfounded, I ran out of there and to the parking lot just in time to see my interrogators make a crash landing. People leapt from the tower like happy lemmings.

Had the whole world gone mad?

I had to get out of there and called for a cab. While I waited, I contacted my therapist.

"Doctor Brady!" I said on my phone, breathless. "I've got to see you now. Just got back from skydiving. Something horrible is happening. I'm having a mental breakdown, and I don't know what to do."

"Settle down. If this can't wait until your next appointment, I can squeeze you in for thirty minutes at three PM today."

"I'm leaving now."

Once the cab let me off in front of the doctor's

building, the cab driver got out, too, and left his door open. As I hurried into my doc's building, he toddled into another.

Rushing to the elevator, I pressed ten. I few more people piled in before we lifted off. The doors opened and closed on floors below mine, ones that had been pressed, but no one got off. Fingers reached over and punched twelve, as if everyone had changed their minds.

When I got off at ten, they looked like bowling pins ready to be bowled over. Their faces were in a trance. It wasn't the first time I saw that look. The doors closed, and they rattled to the top.

Sprinting down the hallway, I flew into Dr. Brady's waiting room with a few minutes to spare. I pounded on his door. A crazy theory from out of a science fiction horror plot had invaded my thoughts.

I had caused the people to jump to their deaths. That strange mist from the meteor had transferred my impulse to jump like a disease, a pandemic that spread by my mere presence. Crazy was too tame a word for it. This ought to keep me in therapy for another decade or two, or locked away in an asylum.

"Come in," Dr. Brady said.

I fell inside, as if being chased, slammed the door shut, as if to keep a monster out, and braced my back against it, as if to barricade myself in. My chest rose and fell in waves. Across from me was a mirror. I looked a fright and scared myself. The man in the mirror was the one I was running from.

"Things are getting out of hand," I said. "I went to skydive, as you said, went up in the plane, just to get used to it, but I wasn't going to jump, but they all did, and now their dead, and I had to land the plane, and now they're dead, and I think I killed them."

"Mr. Simms, take a seat. Have a glass of water and calm yourself. You're babbling. I can't help you until you do."

I nodded over to the chair and flung myself down. The room spun. I took a sip of water and splashed some on my face. My breathing slowed. Everything would be alright. The doctor would help me. I'd explain what happened from the beginning, and he'd tell me I'm imagining things. All in my head, brought on by my compulsion, and we'll work it out, and my life would go back to normal.

"I'm better now," I said, resting in the chair. "Once I tell you what happened, what I think happened, and you tell me what really happened, I'll be okay."

"Very good. Now we can begin."

Strutting to the window, he jerked it up, climbed out onto the ledge, and stepped off. I sat there for a minute, took another sip, waited for him to return, thrummed my fingers on the armrests, rose, sauntered to the window, and peered down. As I did, bodies fell from the rooftop like fleshy bombs dropping from the sky. I looked upward. People lined up, as if waiting for a carnival ride to death.

Shutting the window, I laughed hysterically; not because I'd found it funny, but because I'd lost my sanity, and the mirth released my utter terror. Tears spilled down my face. I took the box of tissues next to the chair, wiped my eyes, blew my nose, looked back to the window as more bodies fell, giggled, snorted, cackled out the door, and traipse to the elevator, where I entered, pressed number one, and guffawed to the bottom.

When the doors opened, I lurched out and people flooded in. Crowds waited for the other elevators, zombies seeking death, and as I shuffled out the exit, more people moseyed in. My laughter morphed into cries.

Cars and streets were abandoned. People everywhere filed into buildings, and as I ambled along like a day sleepwalker, bodies thudded the pavement. I had to dance out their way or get crushed. I had become a mass germ of destruction.

Could scientists discover a vaccine? Does it spread by touch, sneezing, saliva? Is it viral or bacterial? Could they study it and contain it? Could they eliminate the disease from the source and stop it cold? If I stood six feet apart, would everyone be safe? Wear four masks? Can they quarantine me without contracting the sickness?

If it's spread by something impossible, through the mind, transferred, it's mental. How do you stop a mental disease? Is it mass hysteria? Like those Salem witch trials? What if it acts the same as a virus? A type of mind virus. Let it run its course? The only way to eliminate it is to kill it. Which meant I had to die.

Never had I felt so alone. I wished for human contact more than ever. Someone to talk with. But anyone I encountered would jump. Doesn't make for a lasting relationship.

People were jumping from all over, from every building in sight. And New York was a smorgasbord. The Empire State building was getting a vigorous workout. The broken windows on the crown of the Statue of Liberty wept humanity. It spread like a virus wildfire; which meant, once you had it, you could spread it to others.

How far would it go? To other cities, other states?

That week, I slept and ate in the best hotels and restaurants until there was no one left in the city. On the TV, they showed more people jumping in more states, Pennsylvania, New Jersey, Vermont. Even the cameraman jumped. If this kept up, there wouldn't be a soul left on Earth.

Wandering around and over bodies, I arrived at the Roxy Hotel with its glitzy brick and iron façade, except for the corpses that littered the entrance. I'd always wanted to go there but thought it too expensive. The lounge and bar were empty. I poured myself a shot of their best whiskey and knocked it down. Two more, and I was ready to go.

Humming and tapping my toe to the tune "Meet Me at the Roxy" in my head, I proceeded up the elevator, walked off, and trekked the stairs to the roof. The only way I could end this was to kill myself.

I plodded to the jumping-off point. Would this really stop the disease? If others had it and spread it, wouldn't it keep going? Although, if they died, that would stop the spread. Everywhere I traveled, it'd start over. That is, if they had a place to jump off. But every place had buildings.

After the man and woman leaped off, and the few people below finally vaulted, I stood there deliberating for hours whether to jump or not to jump. Hamlet had nothing on me. When my legs got tired, I stepped back onto the roof.

#

"Of course, you didn't jump," the fat man said, leaning against his Chevy, wiping sweat with a cloth across his flushed brow. The sun was blistering. "Or else you wouldn't be here."

"Very astute. No, not when it occurred to me to go to the flattest place I could find with no buildings."

"The desert." His eyes rolled up, as if recalling a fond memory. "When I visited the Grand Canyon, I'd had that same impulse to jump. I wanted to leap off, but I couldn't do it, either." Blocking the sun with his hand, he squinted in the distance. "What about the mountains over yonder?"

"I'm living so far away, anyone who walked there would die first. And if they did make it, there'd be no one around to spread it to."

"Why'd you stop to help me?"

"Loneliness. Being a hermit drove me to need human contact. When your car broke down, I saw my opportunity. Lucky for you I was a mechanic. Cars don't come by here too often."

"Couldn't get anyone on my cell." Seeking coolness, he fluffed his Hawaiian shirt away from his sticky chest. "Don't have water or food. Thought I'd die here."

"So, do you believe me?"

"Everyone's heard of the jumping madness disease that swept through the East Coast. No one knows how it started or why it ended." He crinkled his mostly agreeable sunburnt face. "I suppose it's as good as any explanation. A virus from outer space. Ha! Effin wild. Wait till I tell my friends this story in California."

As he took off, I wondered if he'd drive into the desert to the mountains miles away and throw himself off, but he kept riding down the desolate highway and disappeared. For a while, I thought he'd been a mirage.

It'd been four months since the Roxy. I guess, at last, the mysterious mist sickness had worn off. I dreamed about going back to civilization. Although it didn't pick up stations well, I had my high-powered radio to keep me company, but the desert wasn't much of a home.

After a few more weeks arguing the pros and cons, I decided it was time. I couldn't take the solitude any longer. Leaving my tent behind, I packed my belongings to see if I could hitch a ride to the next city and start over. A car would come by every hour or so and might pick me up. When it got dark, I'd try again the next day.

Standing by the road, I turned on the radio. The news played. As dusk descended over the sand, I listened intently, grabbed my satchel, and crawled back into my tent.

People in California were jumping to their deaths, and it had spread throughout the West Coast. That man had brought the virus with him. Probably was a carrier like me. No one would be coming.

Writing a lengthy letter, I stuffed it in my pocket, took

a swig of bourbon, and, knowing I could never return, snuggled into my sleeping bag.

#

At the crack of dawn, with a full canteen, I hiked to the mountains.
END

The Hiding Ugly on The Train
Carl Bluesy

The train's horn howled, silencing the stomps of passengers. I cowered in a ball behind suitcases on a luggage cart. Sweat soaked my favorite Minnie Mouse T-shirt. Not being able to hear the kidnapper's footsteps was terrifying.

Mom and Dad were home when he took me. They did nothing to stop him. Why? Moms and dads are supposed to protect their kids. It was the scariest thing ever when he burst into my room. I tried to scream, but no sound came out.

He stepped on my Mad Lib book, ripping the pages. He pushed me and I landed on my fairy-doll Wendy, breaking her arm. The pain brought my voice back, but it didn't matter. I screamed for help as he dragged me by my feet through my house. Mom and Dad just watched from the living room, holding each other.

The bad man took me further from home than I'd been

in my whole life. He stuffed me in a dark storage compartment after the train left the station. It was like we were playing a game of hide and seek. Not that I could play games since getting sick. So much bad stuff, all because my skin became gooey and made me ugly.

When the train horn stopped, I put my listening ears on for the man's footsteps. I would never allow him to sneak up on me again.

Not ever.

I moved slowly and tried my best to stop my body from shaking. It wasn't from being cold; it was the shiver I had when I first slept without a night light. I pressed my face against the suitcases that hid me and peered through the tiny gap. The bag must have been full of dirty clothes. It was smelly and made my nose itch.

The train's changing speed jerked me around. I slapped my hand against a blue bag to stop from falling. The back of my hand drooped like melted cheese. I pulled away, knocking the bag over the cart's edge. Despite doing my best to hold it in, I slipped out a scream when the luggage crashed against the floor.

The man said I'd suffer consequences for disobedience, but he never said how he'd punish me. That part he left to my imagination. Such an old, adult trick. Except he was no regular adult. What if he hit me? Grown-ups aren't supposed to hurt kids, but they're not supposed to take them from their moms and dads, either.

It didn't matter what he did. After the millionth doctor appointment, it was obvious the worst was coming, no matter what. It started with arm wrinkles and bags under my eyes. They said I was a new case and a unique sickness. Nobody had seen bones turning to mush.

On my last visit to the hospital, I overheard the doctor talking to Mom. Even if I didn't fully understand, the point he made was clear. The doctor said it was only a matter of time before I lost enough bone mass to stop me from walking, and that my skull would deteriorate, and without a skull's protection, the inevitable pressure on my brain would cause spasms.

The long car ride home after was the worst. There was so much I wished my mom had said. That I'd be okay, and the people who stared were wrong. I wanted to say stuff too, but I was too scared to ask what spasms were, so we both sat and said nothing the entire ride.

My legs still worked, and the man couldn't do anything if he couldn't find me. It was a small jump off the luggage cart, but I landed with a loud bang that jiggled my legs. The hallway had a metal floor, and I forgot how noisy they were. At home, the Disney rug beside my bed made for a soft landing. Standing in the middle of the walkway was the only lit spot.

There was nothing scary, just side carts filled with bags, each a unique color, as though the room was dressed in hippy shirts. Still, the man's presence lurked in every corner, making it difficult to take a step. My muscles fought against me, like a warning, "Don't do that, or you'll be sorry."

On a different baggage cart, I moved bags to create a new hiding spot. Underneath, tucked into the netted side pocket of a backpack, I found a long neck dinosaur. The toy reminded me of Wendy. Weird 'cuz she's a pretty fairy, not a blue dinosaur. It was wrong to steal, but I needed something to listen to me, even when I didn't talk out loud.

Dylan, yeah, that sounded right; he looked like a Dylan. "Hi Dylan, I'm Mindy."

Dylan didn't answer, no surprise. He wasn't a talking toy. He would speak once I found the right voice.

Thud, Thud. Zip.

He's back.

My heart dropped and my stomach spun. What would

he do if he caught me? Fear poured from head to toe, making my feet heavy. I made myself stuff the bags back and rushed to the old spot. The one *he* put me in. With the sound of him putting his suit on, I hopped on the train cart, my heart racing. The door would open any second and he'd…

It was a struggle to lift the suitcase. So heavy, so full. My arm shook as I pulled. Dad always told me, "Put your back into it." Well, I was. My back, legs, arms, even my face. When the door slid open, my heart dropped, and the luggage followed.

I didn't dare glance up, afraid of the rage behind the bird mask. Instead, I stared at his black rubber boots and the matching gloves gripping a square Tupperware.

The man took slow steps toward the luggage cart, where I curled into a tiny ball. His breathing caused a weird wheeze inside the mask. In school, I'd seen pictures of that mask during medieval week. Mrs. Evans said it was what doctors wore in ancient times. I thought it looked like a creepy bird costume with goggles. I knew it would give me nightmares forever.

"Going somewhere, are we?" His voice muffled by the mask.

I squeezed my lips tight.

"You were told to stay hidden. What don't you understand about a simple direction?"

"I want to go home."

"No. You're too sick. That's why—"

"I want to go home!"

The man sighed, letting the silence stretch out.

"Please, mister, I miss my mom and dad." Unable to resist the urge to peek. Fog covered his round goggles around the edges with each breath.

"What you want is irrelevant."

I shot forward, slapping the edge of the cart, and a

chunk of hair broke loose from my head, brushing against my cheek as it fell. "Why?"

"The wishes of the terminally ill hold little weight—"

"I'm not sick!"

I squeezed my hands into fists, making my nails dig into my palms. The man leaned over, covering me in his shadow, and set a plastic container beside me. Before standing, he swiped the hair off his boot.

He held out the strand of blonde hair as proof. "Look, you're falling apart."

The man dropped the hair onto my lap, and I began twisting it between my fingertips. It felt dirty knowing that *he* had touched it.

"Why did you take me?"

The man pinched the loose skin on my arm, stretching it like silly putty.

"You may be sick, but that doesn't mean you're not useful. Now eat, and this time, stay put."

He shoved the bag I had failed to lift in front of me, and with one push, the bag pressed against my legs and forced me to the end of the cart.

"Not like ya' be hard to find. You'd leave a trail of hair and skin behind."

I flinched at each thud of his heavy boots until he shut the door. The room grew colder, surrounded by the chill of darkness. "It's okay," I said, my body shaking as I squeezed my dinosaur friend. "The bad man's gone."

Tears fell from my cheeks and covered Dylan's face, making him cry, too. "Why am I so ugly?"

Dylan stared at me with warmth. He didn't need to utter a word to get his point across. He was so kind. I wiped my tears off Dylan's face with the bottom of my T-shirt. "Why can't things be like they used to be?"

I kicked the bag off the edge of the cart, sending it crashing to the ground. I hated everything, my mom and dad, for not protecting me, my body for getting sick, most of all, the man for… for… for everything. "Stupid masked man can't make me follow his rules."

I grabbed and chucked the container of food. The lid flipped off the Tupperware when it struck a suitcase on the cart. Potatoes splattered everywhere.

"Stupid luggage."

A big kick sent the chicken sliding underneath the bottom of the bag compartment. I grabbed a fistful of mashed potatoes and rocketed them across the room, not caring how loud I was.

Let the man hear. *I hoped he did.*

Clothes, toothbrushes, and floss flew out of the bags. It wouldn't be possible to hide behind luggage when they're scattered. The weird stuff grown-ups packed covered the floor. A bag of coffee beans, books, and some CD disks, like the one Dad kept in the garage. They might be mad when they saw what I did, but that's their problem. I'm not cleaning it up.

The meat of my hand shifted when I grabbed a backpack strap. It moved around the boat in a gross, unnatural way. I let the strap slip from my grip. With opposite my thumb and finger I pinched my left pinky and cringed as it spun around the bone like jelly until the nail was where the fingerprint part belonged.

That should've hurt. Why was this happening? What happens when there's no bone left to hold me together? When I'm nothing but a mush puddle?

Light shone over me when the door opened. My shoulders sagged and my head hung low, waiting for the footsteps.

"What did you do?"

I squeezed myself tighter.

"Answer me." The door slammed shut.

"Go away."

"Why? Why did you do this?"

The wheeze from his mask filled the air.

"Answer me, you little brat."

"I don't want to be here. Why did you take me?"

"You think you're the only one? There's more to this sickness than your pity party."

He pulled out a syringe with something green inside and lowered it to my squishy skin. "You should be happy. I eavesdropped on the doctor talking to your mother in the hallway. Now you play a part in saving others' lives before yours comes to a short end.

"Get away from me." My cheeks burned, replacing my tears. I jerked up, my legs numb as I shot forward. Within three steps, I tripped over a bag and smashed my face against the floor.

I crawled toward the door. My muscles may have been working, but they wiggled, making balancing, even on my hands and knees, very hard. He grabbed my ankle, tripping me. After I smacked my head on the ground, he hoisted me up with a grunt and shaky legs. Dylan was close enough for me to snatch as I dangled upside down.

"You're too much trouble." The rage in his voice fogged his goggles. "Now you're going to stay hidden and quiet. If I have to hogtie you to ensure this, I won't hesitate."

"Leave me alone."

"Just… shut up, kid. God, why does it have to be a fucking kid?"

I watched the man's feet. Once I memorized the rhythm of his steps, I dropped Dylan in front of him. The long neck snapped, taking the man's balance. His grip loosened, and I fell on the floor beside him. The door shone as though Heaven was on the other side. Fast to my feet, I ran toward the light and freedom.

I passed through a second baggage car; a large open

duffle bag lay open in the center. This must have been where he changed into the bird-man costume. No way was I staying there. Next was a passenger car. Light flooded the cart through the windows, seats filled with adults eating baked goods. The sweet scent of muffins replaced the stink of the prison room.

Dozens of eyes fixed on me with disgust the moment I entered.

"What is that?"

"A kid in a costume?"

Their words stabbed my heart, each insult cutting deeper. I rushed to the closest woman to tell her I was a regular kid and needed help, but only a high-pitched squeak escaped.

"God, get away from me," said the woman, pressing up against the window, a horrified stare glued to her stupid face.

"What the fuck is that?" said another passenger, pointing behind me.

The man who stole me still wore the bird mask, although the beak had a zig-zagging crack.

Good.

I sprinted to the end of the train car. The door didn't budge when I pulled, only the red pulley beside the doors shook from my effort. His gloved hands snatched me away. My bones shifted as the man pulled me back toward the storage car. We inched in slow jerks as he stepped with one foot and dragged the other.

"Is this for real?" a passenger asked.

"This must be a show. Those are costumes. Look, the kid's makeup is falling apart."

With my skin jiggling, the idea of sliding out of his grasp seemed doable. I flailed around, trying to break his grip, but the rubber gloves stuck to my flesh. He stopped at the end of the car to slide the door open, exposing his wrist.

My stomach churned at the thought, but I knew it needed to be done.

I drove my teeth into his flesh and pulled. His skin stretched and tore as I bit into him. Blood gushed past my gums, replacing the salt taste with an overpowering metallic taste and flavor of raw meat.

Unseen hands grabbed me. The view of the room spun when someone ripped me off the man. He screamed as I flew across the train car, bits of skin stuck in between my teeth, keeping his pork-like flavor in my mouth. After the room stopped spinning, I reached up, expecting someone to help me. Instead, they gave hate-filled glares.

I needed to look at something, anything other than the cruel train people, or I'd cry. Big girls don't cry. Beside the door, I noticed a lever on the wall. What did the sign say?

Emeeer. Emerg barks. Emergency brakes.

Perfect.

I dove for the pull handle. The moment my fingers grabbed hold, there was an ear-piercing shriek. Everyone flew forward, bouncing off the seats. One woman even somersaulted onto the aisle floor.

I rushed to the outside door before the train people got up. With a final breath, I leapt off, landed on the rocky surface and rolled. My body splattered on the stones, warping and reforming around the jagged points. A disturbing but helpful feature of my condition.

The crunching gravel behind told me the masked man was close. He ran with a limp, I guess tripping him helped more than I thought. I sped across the field, my skin rippling against the wind. Despite how hard it was to run, keeping out of his reach was no problem.

I hadn't a clue how long I had been running, thirty, forty minutes. The moment I slowed my pace, a wave of tiredness hit me and I collapsed at the top of a hill. My heart pounded and sweat-drenched my shirt. The pain in my legs helped distract me from the fear of the man, who was out of sight. Nothing remained except trees from a nearby forest.

Alone again.

I sat on the hilltop, hugging my knees as the sun set. When night came and the moon shone, my stomach hurt from not eating. I tried to focus on the sounds of crickets. Nature always made me feel better.

The man in the mask trudged up the hill, coming into view. Instead of running, I waited for him. Soon we were face to mask. The air grew colder from his presence. It felt like caterpillars were crawling all over my body.

"Why won't you leave me alone?"

"Your condition may be useful. Even though you're terminal, that doesn't mean everyone who acquires this disease has to die."

"Nuh-uh, there's no cure. The doctor said so."

"Yes, I've heard similar things from so-called medical professionals who lack imagination, or the will to push moral boundaries."

"I don't… What are you saying?"

The man sat on the wet grass beside me. I shifted so our bodies never touched.

"You're one of two carriers of this new disease. I've conducted my own research." The man paused and took several deep breaths. "Look kid, I have yet to understand this disease fully. It behaves similar to a fibro dysplasia ossificans progressiva, only in reverse." He paused, studying me. "You can't comprehend a word of this, can you?"

I shook my head, and the man sighed.

"Fucking kids. It's bone turning into muscle instead of the other way around." He paused, catching his breath. "Not enough is known to develop a reliable cure, but I have a theory. Because you're young and still growing, your developing nervous system naturally creates more mass. It may be the key to restoring bone structure."

His speech didn't help me understand, not even a bit.

"What if I refuse to go with you?"

The man adjusted the mask, straightening it. "How's that going for ya? Remember the passengers on the train? Wouldn't you prefer walking into a room without your face making people recoil in disgust?"

He was right. People's stares stung more than the real pain.

"No." I got to my feet and backed away. "I don't care what you say. You took me from my mom and dad. I will never help you."

"Ha, your parents didn't have a choice. What makes you think you do?"

I turned to face him. "What about my—"

He jerked forward and grabbed me around my neck. On reflex, I pulled at the man's glove. With his free hand, he slid out a syringe, the one from the train. I kicked against his legs and scratched at his arm as he lowered the needle to my temple.

"It's my life, not yours!"

I grabbed hold of the beak of his mask and pulled it, slipping it off with ease. Stunned, I let the mask drop. Bags sagged under his eyes to the bottom of his lips, the only visible skin past his nose. Never seeing his face, I assumed the beak was empty, but it was the perfect size to conceal his witchy-long nose.

"Bitch. You broke it."

The man released his grip, and I slipped onto the wet grass. He grasped at his precious mask.

"You're sicker than me." I sprang forward, clawing away before he got his icky hands on me.

"Stop," said the man. "Or we both die."

The man ran close behind me as I burst past the tree

line. Branches scratched my cheeks and soon his footsteps were gone. This time, I paced myself and hid behind a bush. He hadn't gotten used to weak bones from how loud he stumbled around, cracking so many sticks.

I covered my mouth to squash my will to scream when the man came into sight. The skin broke. The blood wasn't yucky anymore. He was going to find me. How could he not? This is a good hiding spot when playing hide and seek with someone my age. But this was no game. Grown-ups always find kids.

He stopped so close I could touch him if I stretched my arm out. This was the end. After he checked left and right, he limped on, never giving a second glance at my hiding bush. I waited until my breathing returned to normal and my heart stopped racing before I left my hiding spot.

The sun had peeked out by the time I discovered a stream. Outside water may not be good for you, but I was past worrying. I ran too much to care. The ice-cold water was so refreshing. As long as I kept my eyes shut to avoid seeing my ugly reflection. That first sip was the tastiest drink imaginable.

I sat by the water the whole day, listening to the birds chirping and the fish splashing. It had been forever since I'd been this calm. The stream was my favorite place in the woods. Maybe the best spot in the world. No, home was still the best. Except that house had become the place where my parents lived, instead of where I belonged.

How could I let the man trick me into thinking I lost my parents' love? Or that they gave me to that monster by choice. They always protected me and taught me what to do when things went wrong. Dad told me that if I got lost, to stay where I was and they'd find me. So that's what I did. I sat, and I waited.

I left the stream twice a day for food. The acorns were hard to break into, but once the shell cracked, the inside tasted sweet. Small nuts were never enough to stop my tummy from growling. There must be something bigger to eat.

On the sixth day, I found the man when returning from one of my searches for nuts. He laid face down in the stream; the mask clutched in his dead grip. The top layer of skin had melted away and his head pancake flat, but the meat underneath was fresh. It looked like an uncooked steak and reminded me of the flavor that stuck in between my teeth when I bit him on the train. I wondered how long he would keep before making me sick, or if I could build a campfire.

Either way, he'd last longer than nuts. Since I knew he didn't care what happened to my body, I felt no guilt about my plans for him while waiting for Mom and Dad to find me.

The man was hard to drag. With each heave, I only moved him an inch. When his glove slipped off, I fell on my bum, splashing water everywhere. When I tried standing up, I accidentally looked at the stream and caught my reflection in the water, and everything became clear.

I stopped caring what others said. If people didn't want me part of their world, that was their loss. I'm fine here. The stream showed my beauty. It didn't matter that I was alone, this would be my new home. I'd love myself even if no one else did.

END

Pheromones

Devin James Leonard

You used to think you'd die if you ever went near a girl or had to talk to one, but these days, that's a high probability. Ever since the sky exploded, made the strange mist drizzle down to the earth, and triggered a murderous rage virus, you steer clear of everyone and talk to no one but yourself.

It's the thirty-third day of your solitary existence when you run out of chickens to slaughter and you've got to leave your isolated farmhouse to search for food. You should have kept the hens alive, Bobby, and you'd have had eggs to feed you, but oh well.

Vehicles are safer than houses to stick your head inside, so you walk three miles to the ditch you drove your dad's pickup into that day you were coming back from the supermarket. It's been over a month since the roads got choked up with accidents, and people snapped into a rage and started killing each other. Most of the food in the grocery bags will have spoiled, but the canned stuff ought to be fine as long as no one has scavenged them yet.

The truck is right where you left it, but the passenger door is open, and you just know those brown bags you left on the seat are gone and you've spent over an hour hoofing it under the hot afternoon sun for nothing.

You won't travel much further. The cows back home need you to protect and tend them, and these days, their milk is worth more than gold and as precious as shelter and bullets. You can search the abandoned cars on the return trip, but you know damn well there won't be any supplies or apocalypse packs of any kind.

The sun-bloated, festering carcasses of the men, women, and children in the roadway? They were just as unprepared as you were. There was no warning and, therefore, no time to stockpile survival items in their trunks. Unlike these dead families, you're alive because you were lucky enough to be alone when it happened.

On your way back, you catch sight of a sun and dirt-stricken lady scrounging through vehicles. She's a hundred yards away, and you whistle at her, only to make your position known. Never in your life—your life before, that is—would you think to call out to a woman in such a way.

That was bad etiquette in the past, but now it's for both your safety. Once she notices you, you flash an affable wave, which she doesn't return. That would have been embarrassing in a different situation, but not so much now.

You keep your distance, traveling toward her at a wide berth, and once you've gone past, and she's behind you, you look over your shoulder to keep your eyes on her. No matter how harmless they appear, there is no telling who is capable of shooting you in the back. You haven't wandered outside your home much since the clouds flashed those strange colors, but one thing you know for sure is everybody is a potential threat.

It's not only the people you can see that are dangerous, or even the ones you stumble upon by accident and bump into while turning a corner. It's the vultures lying in wait, the scavengers who want what you've got.

Will kill you for it. Walk down this road in plain sight with a jug of water or a gun slung over your shoulder, you best believe someone's waiting to pick you off to take what you possess. That's why you left the rifle at home; you don't wanna be caught holding something worth getting killed for.

With no such luck finding sustenance in vehicles, you decide it is time to man up and search a house. Choose the next place you come across. This one is a two-story ranch not a mile from your farm. You know who lives there, a cute girl named Alice you went to school with and were too shy to talk to. You're twenty-four years old now, but now it's too late to chat her up. Either she's dead, like so many others, or she'll kill you or you'll kill her if you get too close.

First thing you do when you reach the house is bang on the door and shout to see if Alice or anybody else is home. If there is, you'll leave. You're no thief, killer, or plunderer.

After several knocks and no response and determining the home vacant, you unsheathe your hunting knife, crack the door, and step inside. You enter a dusty hallway, dark from all the shaded windows and no electricity. You move into the living room, where everything is neat and organized. Nothing out of place. No messes to suggest any rumblings have gone down under this roof. No corpses, either. At least not in *this* room.

The kitchen is in one piece, too. The only sign life once lived here is the coffee mugs on the table and the stale, half-eaten breakfast on plates. You check the cabinets and find boxes upon boxes of dried pasta and several cans of soup.

The soups are of the creamed variety—potato, mushroom, clam chowder—which you hate, but will make do in a pinch, which this is. The refrigerator stinks of rotten meat, but at least there's a pitcher of filtered water half full, and just enough to top off your canteen after taking half a dozen gulps first.

From the window above the sink, you see a backyard cluttered with various children's toys and playthings. Little rolling cars lying on their sides like a morbid, miniature reenactment of the real cars out on the highway. You step out the backdoor to get a better look but think better of it once you land on the deck. Your foot is on what once was a puddle of blood but has now dried into a dark splotch of red. It makes the porch look like a paint job left unfinished.

What's at the end of this trail of blood? There is a white dress lying in the overgrown grass. Looks like a piece of laundry that fell off the line, except this blouse has a person in it, a slender woman of shriveled flesh, the skin of a sundried tomato.

You don't need to get any closer to see how she died. Her face will be a shredded mess. Eyes gouged out. Throat clawed to bits. Like every corpse you've come across, she will resemble a person who has taken a nosedive into the blades of a running lawnmower.

That's enough exploring. With all the kid's toys out there, the last thing you want to see is dead children. Once you're back inside, you inspect the downstairs bathroom and find a twelve-pack of toilet paper, half a tube of toothpaste, and an unopened half-gallon jug of hand soap.

You locate a luggage bag to carry your items, and once you've packed it all away, you wheel it down the hall and set it by the front entrance.

It's time to check the second floor, and as you climb the steps, there's a knock at the door behind you, and a woman's voice that sounds just like your mother's—tough and stubborn—hollers, "I know you're in there. I've been watching you for a while."

You try not to move, but you tremble and shake as if

by reflex. Where is your knife, Bobby? It's not on your person. You had it in your hand when you first came in. You must have set it down in the kitchen.

"Tell me you're hearing me," the woman says, her voice rising with a challenging cadence, "cause I will not repeat myself."

"I—" You swallow a dry lump, unable to find the words or the courage to speak. Then you clear your throat and try again. "I can hear you," you croak, and once again, louder, "I can hear you."

"Good," the woman says. Her voice lowers a touch but maintains its sharpness. "Now, listen. I don't want us to hurt each other, so I'll make you a deal where we both come out of this alive. Say yes if you're still listening."

"Yeah."

"Get yourself a bag and load it up with half of whatever you found in there. Now, I'm not greedy, but I am hungry. I also don't want to see you starve, so I'm not asking for everything. Just give me half, toss it outside, and after that, I'll leave."

You take a deep breath, shake away your fears, and find a modicum of bravery to yell, "How about I step outside with my rifle and be done with you?"

The woman cackles with hearty amusement. "You don't have any weapons, kid. I told you, I've been watching you."

Well, she's half-right. You've got a knife, but, being that it's in the kitchen, it might as well be in the next county.

"Maybe I found a gun in here," you say.

"Tell you what," the woman says. "If you got a gun, cock it, rack it, or shoot it, whatever you gotta do to prove it. If you do that, I'll leave."

A few seconds of silence pass, and the woman's smug confidence seeps through the door as she says, "That's what I thought."

"If I hand over this food," you shout, "I'll starve to death."

"I'm not asking for all of it. Just a portion. And to correct myself—I'm *not* asking. So, there's your deal, and here are your options. One—you comply, and the transaction will be over. If you refuse, I'll kick this door in and maybe you'll get the jump on me. But we both know what happens if we catch a whiff of one another.

We'll both snap, and only one of us will come out of that snap alive. I'm just a tired old thing, so I would appreciate it if you passed on that option. The other option is I wait out here with this pistol I swiped off a cop and blow your head off the second you walk out the door. I don't want to do it, but I will."

You remain silent, debating.

"If you doubt I have a gun," the woman says, "here comes your proof."

The gunshot report, even though outside, is deafening and terrifying. The bullet tears through the door and you bounce away, hugging the wall, with your hands raised.

"Okay, okay, you made your point, lady!" you screech. "Just give me a minute to collect some things. Please, don't shoot."

"Don't skimp on the good stuff," she says, almost sounding amused by the shakiness of your voice. "I want the cream of the crop. Got it?"

Cream of the crop?

All right.

Though you're losing a partial amount of your food supply, gaining nothing but your life in return, you place all the creamed soups into a plastic bag with good, gleeful riddance, feeling that you somehow won out in this debacle. You tell the lady to get away from the door. You're about to toss the bag outside.

A moment later, you listen to the sound of her footsteps scuffling through the grass, and you rush to the living room window, hoping to glimpse her before she leaves your sight, but you miss her. You didn't get a clear shot of her face, only seeing a wisp of grayish hair and the brown collar of a shirt. There is no telling whether it's the same woman you saw on the roadway and whistled to. Fact is, you can't recall what the woman looked like anyhow, so what's it matter?

With a bandana wrapped around your face, covering your mouth and nose, and tied off at the back, you open the door, fling the bag of soup out and onto the dirt drive, and shut the door once more. Hidden from your view, and from a greater distance away, the woman shouts, "I'll be back for that later, for obvious reasons."

"Now what?" you ask.

"Count to a hundred before you leave. Understood?"

"Loud and clear."

You start counting, and you keep counting while you hide the remaining supplies in your luggage bag. You can't leave with it now. The woman might shoot you for it.

By the time you exit the house to head home empty-handed, you're still quaking in your shoes and you've counted far past one hundred, damn close to a thousand.

***

You wake up hot and starving. Last night you pushed through the stomach cramps of hunger, and though you thought sleep would do you wonders, it was scorching in the house, so you brought a pillow and blanket outside and made yourself a comfortable perch in the open hayloft, where the night air was cool and the chirping crickets would help ease you to sleep.

You tried to not think about the woman, tried to not let

the ridicule interfere with your rest. You were embarrassed and angry at yourself, but, hey, you're still alive, and you can always go back to the house for the supplies you stashed. Told yourself you'd be ready the next time you're followed.

You're sluggish today because it's early morning and already the sun is blistering your skin as though it's got a personal grudge against you. You may have an unlimited supply of clean water from the well, but dammit, you're hungry. Sleep had not come easy because the loft floor was hard on your back, and you couldn't shake the woman from your thoughts.

Counting to a thousand was easier than tallying how long it had been since you talked to a woman, and it's just your luck, Bobby Crowder, that the first one you came across in all this mess stole your food and threatened to kill you.

There is a large townhouse common beyond the field where your cows graze and the stream you fish, an apartment complex where most of the people live—*lived*—in this barren hellhole you call a town. You've never gone over there, but, hey, remember how often you fantasized about making your way to the stream? Meeting a pretty girl your age sitting on the opposite bank? It never happened, but, hey, it still could.

Those townhouses might have stashes of food, but from where you're standing, those buildings resemble a desert island and, depending on how many survivors there are, could be stocked full of savage killers. You ought to work the creek instead. Bring your pole and fish up some trout.

That's what you do. First, you milk your six cows, which takes up too much of your morning, and then you slap on some waders, grab your pole and a bucket, and tramp through the sunbaked field grass until you reach the deepest part of the stream where you and your father would always go. You hear splashing sounds over the rippling water. You walk toward the bend in the creek, against the current, and your heart stops with a nervous shock.

My God, you can't believe it. Your fantasy has come true. Seated in a waist-deep pool, bathing herself, is a young woman. Her skin is pale in places and sunburned in others—tan lines from where clothes would protect her from the sun.

Only she isn't wearing a lick of clothing right at this moment. She is stark naked, with her bare breasts hovering over the current. Her face is bent close to the water as if she's searching for her reflection in it.

Now, you're frozen and petrified, and you don't know what to do. Faculties malfunctioned. You've lost the ability to blink or breathe. She doesn't see you. She seems to be in her own world, serene, unhurried, not a care in all the land.

You don't want to interrupt her, but now she sits up straight, exposing more of herself, and splashes water on her face, running her hands over her chin-length blonde hair, and slicks it back until it's soaked and turns brown. Droplets of water fall down her face, her chest, and her buxom breasts.

You clear your throat, making it loud. "*Mm-hmm!*"

The woman snaps her face downstream, locks onto you, and you avert your gaze, raising your face to the sky. "Just wanted to make my presence known," you say while squinting at the sun. "Didn't want to spook you."

"I'm not spooked," she says, "but with the air tunneling through here, you might be standing in the wrong direction."

You look, but only to gauge her alarm and to assess her threat level. She straightens with minor tension, relaxes her shoulders, and resumes her lounging position. She doesn't bother covering herself.

"Come over this way," she says, pointing straight across from her.

You shuffle through the water and climb the bank opposite her, and once you're up there, you place your back to her and say, "Is that better?"

"Better," she says.

"I just came to fish," you say. "I'll just—" You start to walk away.

"Catch any?" the young woman says, and you halt.

"Not yet." You can hear the soft splashes of water as she cleans herself.

"You got a name?"

"Bobby Crowder."

"It's okay to look at me, Bobby Crowder. Kind of awkward talking to someone who won't face you."

Keeping your eyes averted, you snicker. "I couldn't help but notice you're naked."

"I'd be more worried if you *didn't* notice I was naked."

You turn your face in a slow, dreadful motion, and when your eyes meet hers, she smirks. She must find your timidness enduring.

"Would you like to know my name?" she says.

"Uh, yeah."

"It's Margaret," she says, and since your voice has clogged your throat and you're gaping at her like a horny caveman, she adds, "Did you come from the farm over there?" You nod, and she says, "Must have plenty of livestock…stocked."

"Just some cows." You nudge your chin at the townhouses. "You're from over there?"

"Mm-hmm," she says, her hand feathering the water.

"Are you alone?"

"We're all alone now—technically."

"I mean—"

You can't help but stammer and, for Christ's sake, who

can blame you? It's not every day you converse with an attractive girl who's not only buck naked but doesn't seem the least bit concerned that you're looking.

"Family," you stutter. "Do—or did—you have family?"

"You mean, are they dead?" Margaret says. "It was just me and my mom. Before and now. She moved—for lack of a better word—to the house next door."

"How come you're not afraid of me?"

"Should I be?"

"You're the first person I ran into who didn't run in the opposite direction."

"Well, Bobby Crowder," Margaret says, "if there's anything me and my mom have learned so far is that you can have a conversation with someone as long as you keep your distance."

"Where is she now?"

"Searching for essentials." She snorts and shakes her head with disapproval. "It's so dangerous to go anywhere, but my mom, she could never sit still for long. Can't tell her anything, no matter how hard I try."

You wonder if her mother is the gray-haired bitch who robbed you of your soups.

"Do you have anyone to talk to?" Margaret asks.

"I'm on my own," you say.

"Then come back tomorrow. I'm here every day. I'll even keep my clothes on, so you're not so nervous."

"I'm not nervous," you say—nervously.

Margaret winks and giggles. "Tell it to the fishes, Bobby Crowder."

***

Next morning, you're back on the grind, milking the cows, only, unlike every other morning, you've got some pep in your step. Also different today, you save the milk instead of squirting it straight on the ground, bottling as many as a dozen mason jars. You place the containers into a plastic milk cart, plus you fill another half a dozen jars with water from your well pump alongside the barn and lug it to the stream, submerging it in a shallow spot on Margaret's side. The stream, cold as it is, will keep the liquids fresh and, more importantly, will rinse the items of your fingerprints, smells, oils, and whatever else might send Margaret into the proverbial freakout.

It's midmorning when you return home, whistling and skipping, and as you approach the front porch, you stop dead in your tracks. The front door is wide open.

What was that quip your father used to say? "You may have been raised near a barn, but not in one." Never in your life have you forgotten to shut the door, any door, and you most certainly did not leave it open today. Doesn't matter how giddy you've been while daydreaming about Margaret all morning. You were not so absentminded to—

Yeah, you were, Bobby. You forgot something. Look at your hands. What's in them? That's right. Nothing! You were so distracted with delivering refreshments to Margaret—you fucking milkman—that you left your rifle and your knife in the house. You ventured out completely unarmed. The only weapon nearby is the shovel lying in the grass a few yards away, right where you chucked it a month ago after you buried your mother and father.

You scoop up your weapon and ascend the porch, tiptoeing, though no matter how quietly you try to move, the wooden deck creaks with every step. Whoever's in your house is not aware of the noise. They are far back in the kitchen, and cannot hear you over the racket they're making. Cabinet doors are slamming shut, shoes stomping on the floor your mother used to clean multiple times a day.

You clear the doorway, your eyes on the kitchen at the

back of the house, where the commotion is coming from. You can't see the intruder, but already you feel a change of pressure in the air and static electricity channeling through your body. The hairs on your neck prickle, gooseflesh bristling on your arms.

Your head fills with congestion as a lightheaded sensation of superhuman awareness whooshes through you. Your consciousness begins to swirl, transforming into a black hole of violent thoughts. Heart, body, and soul flooding with piping rage.

It's like fighting to stay awake when you've reached peak exhaustion. The change is happening; you can feel it. It's happening far too soon. The rabid possession is taking over before you've claimed sight of the intruder. You've caught the other person's scent, their smell, their pheromones, whatever it is.

You look down at the shovel, your hands gripping it so tight your knuckles have turned white. It's the last thing you see before the blackness of that hateful black hole swallows your vision and devours your mind.

You fade out.

***

Your mouth is filled with drool, and when you gasp back into consciousness, you inhale some of it and choke. You hack, spit, and cough until you've calmed your breathing, and see that it's blood instead of saliva you were choking on.

As you hold your trembling, blood-soaked hands in front of your face, you grunt in breathless pants and tell yourself, over and over, that you are okay, you are alive.

From head to toe, you're a wet mess of gore, but other than a tightness in your jaw, you don't believe you're injured. You see nor feel any wounds. Aside from the soreness in your mouth from clenching, snarling, and biting, you're okay.

You are in your kitchen. Beside you lies a body. Your opponent's head is a pile of mush, a splattered crater of blood, brain, and bone. A sledgehammer taken to a watermelon couldn't make such a mess as this.

It's a woman you've killed.

The only way you are certain is the protruding breasts beneath her shirt, the thin feminine frame, and the small delicate hands. Her skin, wrinkled and freckled, tells you she is much older than you, and so do the chunks of gray hair on the head of your shovel lying on the tiled floor, dripping with brain matter.

Her body convulses, and her headless neck gargles and spits like a leaky hose, as if the woman is still trying to breathe. You have only a vague recollection of what you've done, and you're okay with that. You couldn't control what happened, so why agonize over it?

You wash yourself at the well pump, change your clothes, and wander back to the ranch house where you stashed the luggage container yesterday. Though you are tired beyond repair and can hardly walk, you're famished.

The pasta you stored away is the only lead you have for food, and you have got to eat. The walk will also help shake off the side effects of the possession, the strange feeling of coming out of it. That feeling like you've been violated. Like your body has been returned to you after someone else has used it to commit terrible acts.

This time, you remember to bring your rifle, but as luck has it, you see no one on this trip. You're pretty damn certain the woman you just killed is the same woman who threatcned you yesterday and forced you to hand over your creamed soups.

When you're back home, you light the gas stove with a match, heat a pot of water, and while it boils, you drag the dead lady outside, dig a hole, bury her, scrub the kitchen, wash yourself at the well once more, and by the time your food is cooked and you've eaten, you are far too lethargic to meet Margaret by the stream.

You'll try tomorrow.

***

Another rinse and repeat morning, only today your body aches from the exertion of murder. You wait until the sun is at its peak to hike through the field and approach the stream. Margaret isn't there, but the milk crate is, and unbothered. Either she feared touching it yesterday, or she hasn't been back to see it.

A few yards upstream, you stand in the water and cast your fishing line, your eyes drifting downstream, to Margaret's pool, waiting for her to show.

Casting and casting. Catching nothing. Looking and waiting. Waiting and watching. No Margaret. You'll stay as long as you can. You've got nothing else to do all day but survive, and you can do that anywhere.

Tired of standing and heat-sick from the sun breathing down your neck, you take a rest and sit on the bank, your waders submerged in the water from the waist down, and you shut your eyes. Time passes, though you don't know how much.

You are jolted awake by a sudden splash. Downstream, with her legs crossed and head bowed, Margaret sits atop the bank, tossing pebbles into the stream.

After you sit up, call to her, and wave, you wander over and plop to the ground on your side of the creek, across from her.

"How goes the fishing?" she asks, resuming her rock-tossing and looking down at the water.

With a shake of your head, you underhand lob a small

stone into the water. "Thinking I'm gonna slaughter one of my cows," you say. "I hate to do it, but food's getting scarce and they're a pain in the ass to milk every morning."

"You still milk them?"

"Have to, else they'll die."

"What happens if you don't?" Margaret says. "Do they get too full of milk and explode?"

You chuckle. "They have to be milked, or they'll get what's called mastitis. It's a painful infection, and I've seen enough death to know I don't need to see my animals go through it, too."

"Bright side, I guess," Margaret says, "is you have an endless supply of milk."

You nudge your chin at the milk crate in the water. "That's why I'm hoping you and your mother will have that empty come tomorrow."

"My mom used to drink milk with every meal. You'll be her new best friend if—" She stops, peers down, and sighs.

"If what?"

"If she comes back."

"Where'd she go?"

Margaret spreads her palms. "Out looking for food. She always comes back before dark, though. Last night, she didn't."

Images of the woman you killed flash in the dark recesses of your mind where you've tried to forget it, leave it behind. Pictures of a lady with gray hair and a face that's no more than chunks of mush project inside your memory like a grim slideshow, and your face flushes. Your heart picks up the pace, and your throat dries. Your testicles retreat inside you, and you're overcome with the sudden urge to urinate and vomit.

"I hope she's all right," you say, almost choking on the words. "So, she loves milk, huh? What about you?"

"Tell you the truth," she says, shaking her head, "I'm lactose intolerant."

"Well, ain't that a bitch?"

"Indeed, it is. But I've heard raw milk's easier on the stomach than pasteurized."

"That's a misconception," you say. "It'll shoot through you just the same."

"And toilet paper's in short supply these days," Margaret quips.

"Wanna know what else is a bitch? I hate milk."

"Really? You? A farm boy?"

"Hey, I can stomach it. I just don't like it. Never been a fan of dairy."

"Not even ice cream?"

"Nope."

"Bobby Crowder," Margaret says, "you are weird."

"Well, this weirdo is hoping you and your mom aren't vegetarians. I slaughter a cow, I'll be coming into so much meat, most will go to waste without refrigeration."

"I don't want to take everything you've got."

"It's not taking if I'm offering," you say.

"Hey, I won't say no to a steak."

"No promises what the cuts will be, but—"

"Beggars can't be choosers."

"That's right."

"You're sweet, Bobby."

You pull your legs up from the bank and stand, slapping the dirt off your waders, readying to go, when Margaret speaks but stops herself short, peering down at her feet.

"What is it?"

"I—" She squints at you, pondering some thought. Then, she shakes her head and says, "Never mind."

"Hey, your mom's going to come back. She'll be fine."

"I know, I know," she says. "It's just—yesterday was

the first time she hasn't come back. And tonight will be the first time I go to bed alone, not having my mom on the other side of the wall to talk to me." She pauses. "I was going to say I wish you could stay with me, but—"

"But you forgot we'd kill each other."

"I just like your company, Bobby. I like talking to you."

"I like your company, too, Margaret."

"It sucks, you know? Not being able to get close to someone anymore. Can't hold them. Touch them. Kiss them."

"Did you have a—" You trail off.

"Did I, what? Have a boyfriend before?"

"It's none of my business," you say. You bashful bastard.

"It's okay. And no, I didn't. Did you have anyone?"

"No."

"I like you, Bobby," Margaret says with a genuine smile. "And I think I'd have liked you even before all this."

You cross your fingers and hold them out. "Here's to hoping somebody finds a cure."

"Here's to hoping. Plus, you've seen me naked. It'd only be fair if we were even."

A loud snort escapes you, and you chuckle. "We don't need a cure for you to see me in my birthday suit. All you have to do is ask."

"You little tease," Margaret giggles.

"Hey, you're one to talk."

***

At dusk you sit on the porch, in your dad's rocking chair, and stare at the fresh mound of earth beside your parents' graves, telling yourself it isn't Margaret's mother. There is no way of knowing. Unless her mom comes back.

Or doesn't. Anyway, you're pretty certain the woman you killed is the scavenger who took your soup.

But who says the women can't be the same person? Margaret said her mom goes out every day searching for food. What are the chances of that? Well, here's the thing, Bobby: you're in a small town that had a low population before. The numbers are down to almost nothing now. The same day you murder a woman is the same day Margaret's mother doesn't come home? Coincidence?

The question now is, do you tell Margaret about it, or do you wait?

***

You head on over to the stream, but you don't bother with the fishing pole. The only thing you've managed to catch out of the water is a damn crush, and it's making you nauseous to think about what you must do next.

You wait on your side, and you hear the faint scuffling of feet on the grass as Margaret makes her approach. You pray she comes bearing good news, that her mother has returned, but from first glance, as she comes into your view with her head so low that her chin is touching her chest, and her arms hang slack at her sides, it doesn't look promising. When she sees you sitting there, she drops to the ground, dangles her legs over the edge of the bank, and shakes her head. Your heart jumps up into your throat.

"Margaret," you say.

"Bobby," she says.

"I have something to tell you."

You work up the courage to explain what you've done. You keep in mind that she cannot lash out at you, and it makes it easy for you to tell her. "I have no idea who the woman was," you say, "but I wanted you to know it happened. That there is a chance it could've been your mother."

Margaret listens in silence, and when you're finished, she bites her lip, shakes her head furiously, and says, "No," either in denial or distress, or both.

She cries.

"What did she look like?" she asks. Her voice trembles and croaks, every word a struggle to speak.

You give her the gruesome details, how her face was undiscernible after what you did to her.

"She had gray hair. That's all I can tell you."

Margaret jerks her face away, grimacing, heaving, and sobbing. Snot runs down her nose.

Other than your heart pounding and your hands quivering, you remain stock still and quiet and remind yourself to breathe.

Margaret hyperventilates. Her chest rises and settles with heavy, frantic breaths, and it looks precisely the same as when the possession takes over. What the mist from those strange clouds causes everybody to do when you get too close to somebody. Margaret looks ready for violence.

From across the stream, she looks at you with a hateful snarl and hisses like a violent lunatic. She clutches a rock as she launches to her feet, and with a sharp grunt, she pitches it toward you. You raise your arms to shield your face, and you feel the sting as it smacks your elbow. You fall back, roll over, and jump up with your hands raised in surrender.

"Margaret, please—"

"You son of a bitch!" she screeches and chucks another rock at your face.

"Stop!" you shout. "We don't know if it's—"

You duck as another rock whizzes past your head.

Margaret jumps and crashes into the water. Quaking with rage, eyes wide, her breath heaving in maniacal gasps, she screams, "I'll kill you!"

She stumbles through the water, tripping while treading, groaning, and baring her teeth with wrathful anger.

Run, Bobby. It's the only way to save you both. She's out of her mind. Just—

A rock hits you square between the eyes, and you fall backward. Your forehead throbs and pulses. It hurts so bad, that all you can hear is a ringing in your ears. She's knocked your block off, and now she's crawling on top of you, ready to bite and claw what's left of it to death.

Margaret drops onto your midsection and your breath leaves you. She clasps her hands around your neck and squeezes, pressing down on your windpipe. She isn't even possessed yet, and she's delivering superhuman rage-strength. Her face twists with madness. She is crazed. You can't breathe at all, and now your vision begins to leave you. You're drifting away from consciousness, sinking, far, far away, as if drowning in quicksand.

You're okay with this. Let her kill you before your scent, your smells, your pheromones entwine. If anybody deserves to die, it's—

***

You come back from it with a rushing gasp of humid air that scorches your throat and chest. Facedown on the ground, you cough and spit the dirt you've just inhaled. The front of your shirt is wet and warm from lying in what you can only presume to be a mud puddle. The hard ground pokes you in all the wrong places. It feels as if you've taken a nap on a stiff mound of bones.

Every muscle and joint aches. Even your mouth is sore, and you brush your tongue along the columns of your teeth to ensure they're all there. When you swallow, you taste copper.

Dead field grass flutters against your face and tickles your cheek. Only it's not grass, but hair. Not your hair. Blonde hair. You smell defecation, and you are not lying in a mud puddle, but a pool of blood. Not your blood.

When you sit up, you cannot bring yourself to look. You turn away while you stand, and as you stumble toward home, treading through the fields where your cows once grazed, you never look back. Not even when you hear the wind carrying a lady's voice toward you, a woman worriedly calling out Margaret's name, wondering where she is. The voice telling Daughter that Mother has made it home safe and sound.

Deus In Absentia
Fay Jekyll

1348.

That was the year carved into the archway of the church I approached; the very same year as right in this moment, while I stepped over the bodies of the dead in the street. The new church I had been summoned to in the heart of London now saw to an unanticipated purpose. A hospital of sorts, a spillway for the masses of infected.

I stepped over the dead, only to examine the dying. I was halted in my tracks when a corpse moved; a thin, pustule-riddled arm grabbed me by the ankle, the sheer chill of his hands sent a frightful shock to my system. All at once, I cried for God, then cursed his name in my blasphemous mind for the doctors who'd had the sense to flee from here. While they still could.

The boy, weak and feverish lay face down in the waste of animals and humans which lined these streets, lacking strength do to anything else *but*—and there I was, concerned for the cleanliness of my boots.

"Please, Doctor," he croaked. When the child spoke, blood oozed around the gums in his mouth. Though late for my meeting with the bishop, I stayed with him. The symptoms he displayed, I diagnosed silently, meant his death was imminent. "Please, Doctor."

"Yes, child?" I asked softly, trying not to meet that horrific glaze in his yellowed eyes, nor breathe in the toxic miasma that surely surrounded his house.

"Please…why has God forsaken me?"

His hand was still outstretched for my ankle when he fell face down again, this time lifeless, into the muck of another street eradicated by this foul plague that crept upon our shores not a month prior.

In a small way, I thought it a mercy the child had died, to be in the arms of God and to end his suffering. But mostly, because I would not have been able to provide him with an answer.

The tears that begged to fall from my face, I withheld, for if I was to cry for this child, then I would be duty bound to shed all the lost a tear, and my soul would be bled dry.

Already, before the child's body had cooled, great black rats were upon him, cleaning blood and puss from their whiskers, nibbling on the corpse. I grit my teeth, funneling the overwhelming sadness that loomed and lingered like a sickness of its own, into anger.

"Away, foul things," I spat, whipping my coat in their direction. They scattered, into upturned barrels, into houses and through windows, their squeaks of protestation the only sound to break through the bleak and frigid air.

"Doctor!" a voice called to me, clear and bright, from someone who was evidently sound of body.

I whipped my head around then, eager to rest my weary eyes upon living flesh, to the bishop who stood upon the steps of his church, his body halfway through the door. One hand was extended warmly to my direction, and I made haste to ensure his gesture would not be shown in vain.

I took his hand with a firm grip. It was warm, but not feverish.

"I am so relieved you have made it," the bishop said, wasting no further time with pleasantries, and he shut the door fast behind us, closed off to the smell of corpses in the street, and the chaos of a ruined city beyond.

Yet even inside, the rattling coughs of the infected rang about the high ceilings of the inner sanctum. I turned my feet in their direction automatically but could not help furrowing my brow in confusion when the bishop led me past the multitude of cries for help.

"You called for a doctor, Bishop?" I clarified, while he ascended the narrow stone staircase of a bell tower.

"Indeed," he said solemnly, "the best doctor in town," he flattered me, but with no further clarification. At least, not until we were upon the roof of his dominion.

"Do you not wish for me to help those people?" I asked him, placing my travelling bag of ointments upon the tiles—unchipped and unweathered. It began to dawn on me that the medicine was unnecessary in this house of worship.

The bishop stopped on the roof, his hands outstretched across the small balcony as if he was making an attempt to embrace the town and spoke slowly, methodically, as if he had planned what to say but dare not utter it aloud.

"Look out there, my son. What do you notice?"

Fires. Death. Destruction. Sickness. Loss. Tragedy beyond human comprehension.

"A plague," I stated simply, as if those words might encompass what consumed our land. Our minds. Even now, I could hear the cries of the infected upon the wind, screeching in pain. I knew now what I did not know a month ago, the subtle difference of anguish over a loved one's suffering to one's own.

"A plague," he repeated, with venom. Usual for a bishop, then again, a bishop calling me to his aid in this manner was entirely peculiar, but unprecedented times called for such things. "You might have thought that for all your supposed advancements in medicine, your lot might have learned something from the *last* one."

"Did you call me here to mock my profession? Because I can assure you, God and medicine can co-ex—"

He cut me off with a wave of his hand, not in a way that was dismissive, more…frustrated.

"Chaos. Chaos is what I see out there. Chaos is what we need a cure for."

"I would have thought people turn to God in a time of crisis, for order and direction," I stated dully, as if I had not cursed His very name moments ago. Even now, I was sure the dark stain upon the ground a hundred yards before me was the child who had since met our maker, his lifeless body merely rat food.

"The devout do," he sighed. Then, he seemed to awaken from his musings and turned his back to the dying world only to face me. I thought him quite a young man for the game, but his face haggard, like one who had not slept. Much like my own. I noted the sleeves of his religious garb were stained with yellow and crusted chunks. There was a sour, rancid smell the breeze released from the entrapment of the fabric. I had lanced enough of those rancid red pustules to know from whence it came.

This was a man who had tried to step in where my colleagues fleeing to the countryside had failed him—at least the ones who had the same theories as myself.

"Do you know what else is contagious, Doctor?"

"Pray, tell," I asked bluntly. My empathy for his pain was running short, and the bag by my feet burned a hole in my consciousness, begging to be picked up, begging to provide assistance to the sick no matter how futile. Alas, he continued with these riddles.

"Fear. There are rumors that the Devil is amongst us…or that God has forsaken us. There is a divide and unrest out there, so that half the world is dead or dying and the other half wants something to blame." He cast his eyes outward again, his gaze mighty and dark, toward the shouts of outrage and fires that burned between empty houses and mounds of unclaimed corpses.

I saw what he had his wary eye upon just then: a mob in the distance, a haze of blazing torches and indistinguishable ravings of anger.

"They can blame the Devil," I said, but he seemed displeased with this lack of effort on my part. Regardless, my duty called to me, despite his status and insistence. "Perhaps, while we discuss matters, I might ease the suffering of your burdened flock. Your *devout* ones, I presume?" I asked, reaching for my bag. Inside, the vials of lotions and herbs I had acquired clinked together with the unmistakable chime of hollow glass, reminding me how depleted my resources truly were.

However, he'd considered my request and bowed reverently, giving me permission to descend away from the clean air.

We entered the chapel, which was enclosed by another set of doors, keeping the draughts at bay, locking the stagnant air into this repugnant room which reeked of clammy death, a wave of which rolled into my mouth and nose.

The thick wood closed behind us, and not a head turned to welcome our arrival. I doubted they had the energy. In the absence of judgmental eyes, I donned something that had been given to me a week ago, by a doctor who had fled for a quiet northern coast. It was a mask of sorts, that one might mistake for a costume, and I forgave the bishop his incredulous glance, for I, myself, had laughed upon the first sighting of the cloth that now smothered my face.

The herbs and flowers in its beak-like appendage over my nose kept the stench of sickness quietly at bay, masking it with a perfume that would make my time here tolerable. There were holes for my eyes, but I was thankful the gauze hid the warm flush of embarrassment that crept to my sallow cheeks.

"Do you really have to be wearing that mask?" the bishop clearly could not help but ask.

"It's a precaution," I said quickly, smoothing over the fact I had not yet evidence to point to either use or uselessness.

Then again, everything was new here so I could not be to blame if it *was* folly. The plague was new. The cure unfound. Curses, even the *cause* unfound.

I reached the nearest woman, and with no protestation she allowed the rising sores upon her neck to be examined, and though she was not yet ravaged by the disease, something else entirely consumed her, and she was the dead inhabiting a living body.

"Who did you lose?" I asked her softly.

Though her eyes glassy and vacant, she allowed herself the luxury of crying that my profession could not afford.

"Everyone," she whispered. Then, she slid back down to lay upon the pew.

My medicine could not help her.

It was to those openly sobbing, keen to catch my gaze that I flew to. Despite my limited vision in the mask, I felt the bishop's presence behind me, watching, ready to add another riddle, but still I tended to a good lady's wounds with vinegar. She winced and wailed frightfully so, while the little remedies I had worked to clear the decaying black flesh upon her fingers.

While this symptom was new to me and brought great fascination, her screams of anguish displayed to me that she found no fascination at all in her dying, only fear. It was in the rasp of her voice and the heaving of her chest, fear in the wide whites of her sunken eyes.

Her cries nearly swallowed the racket of the restless undevout outside and my head whipped up from the patient I was attending. The bishop heard them, too—the approach of the rabble.

It was blasphemy they were crying. Curses and blasphemy.

We shared a knowing glance, the bishop and I. Wordlessly, he swept to the doorway, and I heard the telltale *clunk* of a heavy bolt sliding across, keeping them out.

Or, more disconcertingly, trapping us in.

Before he could close the door to the chapel, I sprang to my feet and caught him by the arm, muttering so as to share a private word.

"You've been watching them burn down the churches, haven't you?" I muttered, keeping the rising bile that threatened to overspill into my mouth down with only the one thought: the innocents in this chapel who were blissfully unaware of our plight, to the mob who had circled around this way.

The bishop wrung his hands and avoided my accusatory glare.

"Believe me, Doctor, I did not know they would be at our door on this day. But yes, it is part of the reason I asked you here."

There was a banging at the door that interrupted the fragility of this conversation. Someone was trying the lock, with no such luck. I made a point of not flinching. The dying around us had not yet stirred, not acknowledged what was yet amiss.

I did not speak, waiting impatiently for the bishop to explain, and his shoulders slumped while he sighed with a weary resignation.

"The *fear* of this plague is contagious. It has caused two factions," he said, waving a gentle, open palm to those who lay about us. "Those who have turned to God in these trying times, and those who—"

This time it was his words that were cut off by further banging on the door, but I understood his implication.

"I have called for many doctors now, for one reason. We need to bring the people together with a good enemy," he said, merging two palms together with interlocked fingers. "One that the less devout can see, can *blame*." Those hands were released and instead clutched furiously to my lapels, desperately in fact. "Doctor…I am seeking your advice. There must be something tangible we can blame."

Something to blame that wasn't the church.

"I have my theories," I said, "but you shan't like them."

"Please, I am all ears. Only God can overhear you here."

I pursed my lips, debating this conversation thoroughly. While he had been so kind as to flatter me earlier, it was still the truth that I was the *only* doctor in town, my expertise limited.

While I thought on, the doors rattled furiously now, with the vigor of someone trying to break through. Even the sleeping awoke from deathlike slumbers to murmur concern.

Yet, the bishop was unphased, unmoving. Only I surmised it was because there was no other way out, for if there was, he might have suggested it.

"Very well," I agreed slowly, for the sole reason that talking might calm my nerves before the inevitable assault.

I took off my mask, removing the sweet smell of dried herbs from my nose. There would be no more helping the living dead now, for I was surely one of them.

"It has been suggested to me that the air itself is infectious, a miasma. Where there is bad air, the plague will follow."

The bishop furrowed his brow and wrinkled his nose, further displeased.

"I cannot tell the people to blame the air," he cried. "That would turn them further from God. That would only heighten the fear, the death toll."

I considered it then, for the first time. How many might have died of sheer fright. Even now, my own heart was pounding with a sickening rate that threatened unconsciousness, and I clutched it. While wanting no part in creating false enemies, even in clearing the name of God, the protection of lives was a promise that defined me.

"This plague has spread so swiftly," I mused, speaking louder now, for it was obvious our assailants had broken through the first doorway. I braced my shoulders flat against the door before which we stood, the flimsy barrier between us and them, between order and chaos.

The bishop followed suit and so did the sick who could yet stand.

"Only the wind could fly as fast as the rate of spread," I dismayed, wracking my brain for anything that might spread as fast as a plague, faster than the contagion of fear.

"Birds," the bishop grunted. He was straining now with the impact of ten men pushing against straining wood.

My eyes flew wide, and I almost released the door, forgetting myself, but the false hope was crushed by my rational thinking and by what I had observed.

"Birds cannot explain how the sickness has spread inside of homes, to those who have been isolated from the skies above," I said. My thoughts went to the boy in the street, how he had died inches from the threshold of his barren home. How those great black rats had made such a meal of him…

"Rats," I said. The word fell out of my mouth before I could catch it.

"What did you say?"

I coughed then, clearing my throat from the dry lump of nerves which tangled themselves in knots.

"Rats," I mumbled. "It is possible," I considered, weighing the implication of my words, "it's not implausible that rats have carried this disease to us. If you think about it, they—"

"They get into our homes!" the bishop said quickly, for conversation would be shortly impossible. "They get into our food. Into the streets and aboard the ships. Rats can spread disease!" he said loudly, his voice ringing in the high ceiling like a psalm, alive with a kind of joy that had not been heard in this room for weeks. It was then I noticed movement from the near-dead, awoken from deathlike slumbers by the outburst.

"Rats?" I heard mutters of confusion, and then further of contempt.

"Rats!"

The chorus echoed, a new truth solidifying itself as a growing seed in the minds of the angry sick. The holy man was right, one moment ago they were laid down with resignation, ready to succumb to their Lord's will, and now anger charged a spark of life in their weakened hearts.

"Burn all the rats!" The infected person beside me screamed. He was riddled with buboes, his clothes grubby and alive with ticks and bugs that made my very eyes feel itchy. Before I could dissuade him from such a course of rashness, I cried out from an alarming sting of pain.

"Ah! Something bit me," I muttered, wiping the small insect off my hand. Common lice, I knew.

"Never mind that, you fool," the bishop wheezed. "Hold the door closed! Keep the barricade!"

Slam. Slam.

The mob outside rattled against the door with such force that my very bones shook on impact.

Slam. Crrrack!

The wood had begun to splinter inward. My back would never have anticipated the shard of wood, the one that bent inward to the chapel to impale me.

I always suspected the plague might take me, but not quite like this.

Warm blood pooled in my hands. My own, for once. I heard the scrabble of hands clawing through the hole to get in and wondered briefly if they knew their efforts were killing me.

"I think we were both wrong, Bishop," I spluttered, wheezing heavily. My internal organs were shutting down, my chest cavity betraying the final thoughts the fresh clarity of my mind had yet to share.

"I know what spreads faster than disease, than fear," I said.

"What?"

"Burn all the rats!" I heard the rallying cry echo, moving outward from our chapel of death to fresh ears.

With my dying breath, despite the blood pooling out of my mouth from my ruptured lungs, I croaked, "Misinformation."

Texas (When I Die)
Iphigenia Strangeworth

The first time I tried to kill myself, Momma slapped me the minute I got out of the hospital, told me I didn't understand what death was, asked if I thought I'd just wake up again. "Death is *permanent*," she screamed, gripping my wrist so tight it hurt. I was fifteen then. Last week, I succeeded, and now, lying in a casket with an overpowering hunger building deep within me, I guess Momma was wrong.

I put a hand to my chest, feeling for my heartbeat, but there's nothing. My *swollen* hand, I notice fretfully, touching my stomach to find it actually *bloated*, after all the work I put into keeping a perfect, flat tummy. I was still overweight when I died, 96 pounds, Momma wanted me to get down to 90—*you're only 5'2, you could really manage 85 I think*—but my stomach was *flat*.

I'm so hungry I don't bother to think about that right now, though, and just pound my fist against the top of the casket, deliberately inhale to scream, and gag, aware of an awful odor. There's some kind of fluid on my face, coming from my mouth and nose, actually, and I decide to just stop breathing.

I don't feel any stronger than I did when I died, but by God I'm getting out of here. I don't even feel claustrophobic, don't care I've been buried alive, I can barely think of anything except eating, I'm so hungry I don't worry about counting calories.

Distantly, The bones in my hand break, and finally, I dislodge the lid, dirt raining down onto my face. It takes hours, but eventually there's enough room to actually dig, biting at the dirt and trying to spit it out when I decide it's not what I want.

My hands break free first, the little taste of cool night air energizes me and in minutes I've clawed free. I'm clambering out of my grave, gazing up at the full blood moon, stretching jerkily and getting to my feet, shaking with hunger. I've always avoided food, panicked at the thought of eating, bought my clothes too small until I reached size zero, but right now I think I'd eat *anything,* even fast food.

It doesn't really sink in that I was dead and buried until I see my name etched into a headstone, *Delta Dawn Carver*, my birthday, my deathday, a brief epitaph, *beloved by all.* It's shiny. I touch the smooth surface, and jolt back when I see the state of my hand; it looks *melted.*

The skin is sliding off, it's a horrible grayish color, and the nails are all ripped out, my fingertips shredded down to bone in my desperation to escape; everything broken, protruding at odd angles beneath the gray, too-soft skin. I poke the back of one hand cautiously, push at it with an exposed bone until the skin splits easily, reveals some part of my skeleton shattered and sticking out. I don't think it's supposed to do that.

There's no time to think about it, though, barely time to mourn the gorgeous, obviously expensive gown they buried me in, completely shredded and covered in soft, sweet-smelling grave dirt. I need to eat, like, *yesterday.*

I don't recognize this cemetery, I've got no idea how to get out, so I pick a random direction and run, kicking off my heels. It's freeing to run around barefoot. I haven't done it since I was a little girl, before practice took up all my time. Distantly, I feel the bottoms of my feet split; running puts too much pressure on them, but it doesn't matter, whatever gets me out of here the fastest.

The other graves are dug up, too, I realize, and as I reach a path, I almost run right into some awful monster in the dark, something with mottled, bluish skin, maggots burrowing into their empty eye sockets, but I don't have time to question it—figure it must be Halloween or something. It wasn't October when I hung myself, but I only *think* it was last week, I don't know for certain. Could have been longer. Need to eat *now.*

This is Glenwood Cemetery, I see as I sprint down a winding path, past an old woman whose wrinkled skin is starting to slough off the bone; it must have been hard to get a lot here. I always fucking hated Houston. Of *course* Momma would make sure I stayed here, of-fucking-course. Someone bumps into me, a bloated, moaning man running the same way I am—an awkward, shambling gait, bits of flesh catching on the ground behind him.

I wonder how fast they updated my Wikipedia page. I always thought it was crazy, the way people changed celebrity Wikipedia's so fast after they died, had a sort of morbid fascination with it, actually. I liked to look at my own page, too; sometimes wanted to go in and edit it, *Delta Dawn Carver (born February 14, 1992) is an American country singer who's failed at everything else she ever tried, has no real-life friends, and was not hospitalized for anxiety or stomach ulcers or whatever else Momma said but for attempted suicide and a cocaine problem...*

Kitty and I sometimes guessed how celebrities were going to die. "Overdose," she said when yet another teenybopper Disney star was caught with heroin, "suicide." When comedians were hospitalized for depression, "anorexia" when actors lost massive amounts of weight for Oscar-winning roles.

She never knew my real name, and I sent her photos of my cousin when she asked what I looked like. Delta Dawn Carver was her favorite singer. Won't Kitty be glad I'm back? If I could get ahold of a phone after I eat, I can reach out and tell her I'm okay, sorry I was gone a bit, my hands are shattered but I can't feel anything, and I can move them just fine. Maybe I'll even tell her who I really am.

Finally, I'm at the gate—along with a couple dozen other people. Some stumble, one dragging himself along— no legs. On second glance, his guts are trailing behind him. Most are sprinting full-tilt, everyone animated with the same frenzied, starved energy.

I hear car alarms, gunshots, screaming in the streets, and I wonder what's going on for a second before I see a woman with no lower jaw climb onto a car trapped in a traffic pile-up, punch through the windshield and throw herself inside, ripping the driver's face off.

We might be the source of the problem.

When I woke up, I was just thinking about eating, you know, *normal* food, but now nothing has ever looked more appetizing than the twitching, dying driver. I can't control my body; I'm breaking through the window and ripping his arm off, tearing at it with my teeth, swallowing without bothering to chew, and it's *not enough,* it doesn't do *anything.*

I eat faster trying to ease the hunger pang coming from somewhere deep in my soul, not even my stomach at this point.

I scream in frustration, and then the jawless woman

hooks her fingers into his eye sockets, cracks his skull in two, and tears his brain out. He twitches once more, violently, then goes still, and she takes a fistful of gray matter and shove it down her throat, not letting the lack of a lower jaw stop her.

She relaxes instantly, a blissful expression lighting up what's left of her face, so I grab at the chunks of brain left clinging to the jagged edges of his skull and shove them in my mouth. "*Ohhh,*" I moan, relaxing, smiling stupidly at the jawless woman.

For a split second, the hunger *stops*. Momma used to say you couldn't understand true joy if you'd never felt pain, and just the absence of that awful, all-consuming hunger is the most powerful euphoria I've ever felt, better than any drug.

But just as suddenly, it returns in a hideous, crashing wave, and I sob, tearing his head in half, hoping to scrape the inside of his skull for more.

There's nothing.

I can't even be mad at the jawless woman for taking most of it, I'd have done the same, so I turn and run, searching for someone else, someone alive, the living dead all around me don't distract me, don't set off the eagerness the man inspired.

Glenwood's right on Buffalo Bayou, if I remember correctly. Before the voice lessons, guitar practices, endless touring concerts, autographs and talk shows, I used to ask Momma why it was called a bayou, and she'd drawl *'cause it's by you, bah-you* in an exaggerated Southern accent.

Fans were always surprised by my lack of an accent in person when I had such a twangy singing voice, put the country girl act on for interviews, and I wanted to tell them I'm from fucking *Houston,* fourth biggest city in the country. I never rode a horse in my life until they put me on one for a music video last year.

A date told me I was *exotic* once, looked offended when I laughed. He was from Los Angeles, an up-and-coming actor almost exactly my age, born the same month, squeaky-clean reputation, no possible scandal there.

"Exotic?" I giggled, pushing chicken around my plate. "'Cause I'm from Texas?"

"Well, yeah. I mean, you probably grew up on a farm and everything," he said sheepishly. I was a little offended he hadn't bothered to check my Wikipedia page; I'd read *his*, thoroughly, cyberstalked him before our date, in fact.

"Trust me, I'm far from exotic." Momma hated anything *exotic,* mistrusted foreigners on principle, fretted over growing LGBT+ acceptance, worried about violence in movies and sex in books. She whined that it would rot my brain, all this deviance, complained about celebrities with "ethnic names."

"He oughta change it," she huffed, reading an article about the recasting of Doctor Who and trying to figure out how "Ncuti Gatwa" was pronounced. "I mean, it would only be *polite* to change it. No one can say it!"

"Rwandan. People can say it," I pointed out.

"Oh, don't give me that PC shit, you've got to appeal to a wider audience than just a few minorities. He really *needs* to change it if he wants a career."

I wonder how he's doing now. Ahead of me, someone whose arm is broken in five places rips an old man's head off, and I shove past them to the lady wailing in the doorway, lunge at her and shatter her skull before she can react, tearing her wrinkled flesh away like tissue paper, and cracking the skull to rip her brain out. I sink my teeth into it immediately, and *finally* feel peace.

I sigh, go still for a moment, slowly savor every bite, the beautiful lack of hunger washing over me in waves. She's wearing a modest pink nightgown, like my grandmother used to wear, and for a brief moment I realize what I'm doing, gag, open my mouth to scream— the hunger's back and I forget again, swallow the last of her brain and sigh, relieved, basking in the afterglow until the pain returns and I jump back up.

The jawless woman is back, tottering after me as I follow the sound of screaming farther into the city. I wonder if she recognizes me; she looks about my age, maybe a little older. I must look awful, though. If I wasn't so hungry I'd want a mirror, and as we run awkwardly along, I poke my face curiously, find it swollen and liable to burst if I keep messing with it, so I stare at my arms instead, see that they're covered in scratches with little chunks of flesh ripped out from so much digging.

I can't call my new friend 'the jawless woman', it's terribly rude. She's really not so bad; she has such pretty… something, surely. I glance back over at her, take in her bloodshot, sickly yellow eyes—surely *my* eyes aren't that ugly yellow now?—and her discolored flesh, more rotted than mine.

The dress they buried her in looks like it used to be nice—designer maybe—but it's so torn up now. Can't tell what color her hair was when it's matted with so much dirt, half her scalp gone, exposing her skull. Well, she must have a nice personality; that's what they say about ugly girls. I decide to call her Puppy, because her tongue lolls out like a dog's.

When I try to inhale, all I smell is my own slow decomposition, but I can see better than ever, my hearing painfully clear. There's a flash of movement in the window of a house we're running past, so I smack Puppy's shoulder to get her attention and point at it before sprinting to the door, moaning in agony at the intense, all-consuming hunger pain.

What was left of my skin bursts when I slam my fist against it, leaving it hanging by the wrist. All the broken bones in my hand are now exposed, but I can still use it so who gives a shit. Puppy kicks the door, slams her shoulder against it, and it swings inward; she nearly falls but I catch her. I make sure to shut it behind me as we run in, up the stairs on all fours, leaving deep gouges in the wood.

She takes one room and I take the other, find it empty but throw myself on the floor to check under the bed. Then I hear her wail, a long, low sound like a banshee. I run toward the noise and she's crouched over a woman's spasming corpse, cracking her skull in half, but she takes the time to point at the closet.

I break the door down effortlessly, find a little boy curled up in the corner and realize this is a child's bedroom as I slam his head against the wall until it splits open and I can tear his brain out which I eat in two bites.

I sigh, leaning back in the brief, peaceful stillness. Stepping out of the closet, I see a room decorated with *Winnie the Pooh* wall stickers, plushies, even furniture— the lamp has Piglet and Pooh sitting at the base.

There are still rails around his tiny bed. I loved *Winnie the Pooh* when I was his age, demanded Momma read me the old stories endlessly, wouldn't settle for just watching the Disney movies. I spent hours in the backyard, pretending I was in the Hundred Acre Wood, until Momma called me in to say the vocal coach was there.

Puppy stands, arms wet and red to the elbows, meets my gaze then groans. I don't think I could speak if I tried, and I *know* she can't, so I take that to mean what I'm already thinking: we should find more food.

Until we're not hungry anymore.

An aching exhaustion has started to settle over my mind, but it's overwhelmed by the hunger which outweighs *everything*. I crave food even more, praying that if I just eat enough I'll be able to rest again. Death was so, so peaceful.

There's no one else in the house, or at least we don't

find anyone else, so we go back to the street, past a boy with a huge chunk of broken glass stuck in his face and an infant's headless corpse in his arms, like a baby doll. Momma told me babies are buried together in cemeteries so they have friends in Heaven, or at least that's what the Victorians thought.

I remember a child's headstone with a fairy carved into it above the words *to die will be an awfully big adventure.* I wonder if the kid buried there is back now.

Several gunshots ring out in quick succession, and I figure there must be someone still alive in that direction, since it's not like we need guns for anything. If I shot someone in the head, it'd just explode everywhere, I'd be scraping up their brain off the floor—*ugh.*

Puppy must have the same idea, because she stalks faster in the direction of the gunshots, until we're in somebody's yard—a man with a shotgun who's just run out of bullets. Someone's dead on the ground, someone who looks like they should have been dead for a while, so we run forward and I get there first; Puppy keeps going on into the house. I tear the man's skull open.

His face looks sort of like a bizarre, red flower, split in half like that, I reflect as I bite into his brain. As I eat and bask in the brief, simple joy, I hope Puppy's found herself something to eat inside. It's nice to have a friend in real life, not just someone online who idolizes you, who'd be scared of you if she knew who you were.

That's the way fans acted around me: giggly and nervous, wanting a photo or autograph or video or something, like I was a fucking zoo exhibit. I was terrified to tell Kitty who I really was.

Just a week before I killed myself, I performed in Dallas, the last concert of my career, though nobody knew it but me, and I saw people online speculating about how my voice wavered as I sang a cover of *"Texas (When I*

Die)", wondering if something was wrong, if I'd lost a loved one. Why was Delta Dawn Carver crying as she belted out the last lines of a song she'd sung a million times, sung at every concert in Texas.

Momma always said suicide was a sin, the one sin you can never repent from, and I always thought that was ridiculous. The *only* unforgivable sin? Murderers and child rapists go to Heaven if they feel really bad, that's fine, but not me? Still, I worried when I tightened the noose, couldn't help but laugh at the last song I'd ever sung live, and I prayed for anything else *but* my home state. *Lord, just get me out of Texas.*

Maybe Momma was right, maybe suicide really is a mortal sin and this is my punishment, but surely not *everyone* crawling out of the grave killed themselves, something else is wrong. Besides, I swear I was at peace before and I just want to be at peace again, away from Momma, away from the crowds, away from the cameras, away from fucking Texas where I'll rot when the sun rises it's so goddamn humid here.

How long can I last like this, anyway?

I imagine rotting to nothing and running all the while, never resting, never sleeping, just like before: awake for days on end, hyped up on cocaine and codeine and amphetamines, writing for hours and realizing it was just gibberish, until I passed out. Momma just told the press I had some anxiety issues but I was fine, really, I was a good girl who went to church every Sunday, never drank, never dreamed of touching drugs, God bless.

Puppy comes back out, burial gown splattered with fresh gore, raises her hand in a lazy wave, and tilts her head to the side; I follow without question. I went to the Downtown Aquarium with my Girl Scout troop in second grade, before Momma started homeschooling me, and I'd really like to go again.

I hum tunelessly as we walk, trying to remember an old song. *I'll fix your feet till you can't walk, I'll lock your jaw till you can't talk,* and Puppy makes a deeply uncomfortable buzzing noise from somewhere in the back of her exposed throat, apparently singing along.

Someone crashes a car into the side of a building and we run forward, a group of others following us, breaking through the glass to reach whoever's inside—a whole *lot* of people, it turns out—college kids, I think. Puppy manages to grab one and wrestle her out, and while she screams *no no no, God please, no no no, God,* I dig my fingers into one of her eyes.

Puppy does the same on her side and we pull her head in half, split her brain as evenly as possible given the circumstances and share our meal in contented silence. They have white tigers at the Downtown Aquarium; I wonder if anyone's taking care of them now.

Puppy's got her arm stuck down her throat, so I carefully pull it out, pat the side of her face. She gurgles at me, squeezes my wrist before we stand up, the hunger returning in waves. I wonder how she died. I suppose it must have been a car accident or something.

I had a long list of DUI's by the time I killed myself, had often thought about just driving off a bridge but never did it—too scary, too much like some kind of awful, fatal roller coaster. I wonder what Puppy looked like before she died, if she was pretty. I can't even tell by the top half of her face, all the skin's gone gray, wrinkled up, peeling off in places.

I'm still bent over the dead college girl, pawing curiously at the base of her skull where it meets her spine, hoping to find some piece of her brain left over, when a shot rings out across the street and we all peer up. Everyone's finished eating. As one, we follow the sound to an old house.

There aren't a lot of old houses in Houston, nice that they've held onto it; I bet there's a million real estate companies trying to buy it. Like vultures, Momma used to say, swooping in the minute someone died to try and buy their house from a grieving relative, tear it down, then build a modern monstrosity. We lived in River Oaks; how long would it take to walk there?

Everyone swarms the man standing in the front yard, crushing the poor bastard crumpled on the ground before him, head destroyed, and a few people fall from shotgun blasts, but then he runs out of bullets and he's dead in an instant.

Puppy and I are too far away to share the food, so I grab her arm and tug her away. I want to go to River Oaks. First and foremost, I'm fucking starving and nobody in River Oaks can run. They've all got personal trainers but they just make you look good—aesthetic Instagram muscles that aren't much help in a situation like this. Second, I bet Momma's at home, locked in the mansion I paid for, not making a noise.

It takes well over two hours to get there, allowing for frequent meal breaks. I never ate this much in my life; I can't believe I'm so hungry, can't believe I still have room to eat. Being dead burns calories, I guess.

Puppy stays with me the whole time, and though we can't really communicate, I'm glad she's here. I hope Kitty's well, wherever she is. This hunger is unbearable, and hopefully she's either hiding or dead. It's a fast, painless death, having your head ripped off or torn open, and they're not coming back.

Kitty and I talked over the phone, never video called. I told her my camera was broken. She liked apocalypse movies, had plans for every possible movie apocalypse, but she always admitted she'd probably just die in the first five minutes.

"No, see, it's about *capitalism*," she said around a mouthful of dry Froot Loops, *Snowpiercer* playing in the background. "The poor people at the back of the train and the rich people up front, and they have to eat ground-up roaches in the back. And it's by the guy who made *Parasite*."

"I thought it was just about the world ending," I giggled nervously. Kitty thought I was stupid; I knew that, but she liked me, anyway.

"It *is,* but it's also about capitalism. So's *Parasite*."

"And… *Contagion*?"

"No, *Contagion's* about a virus and washing your hands."

"Right," I said, nodding even though she couldn't see me. "Sorry, I just… haven't seen those. You know how my mom is."

"Crazy bitch," Kitty said agreeably. "So, how would you survive *28 Days Later*?"

The sun is rising by the time we get to River Oaks. I recognize the streets, recognize the woman running toward us as my neighbor Barbara, so I'm careful to rip her head off as fast as possible, completely painless.

I moan in relief as I rip her brain in two, half for Puppy and half for me, trying to remember the difference between left and right. One side of your brain is logical and the other side's creative, isn't that what they say? Maybe Puppy was some kind of STEM nerd before she died—and her fist is stuck in her neck again.

My house is just up this way, not much bigger than the house I grew up in. Grandpa made his money in the stock market and I made Momma's money on the stage. I touch Puppy's shoulder and point her in the right direction, grunting in a way I hope conveys *food*, and she seems to get the gist, claps her ruined hands together a few times.

The day I died, I spent all day in my room, bleeding

through maxi pads. The doctors promised the heavy bleeding would stop after twenty-four hours, and I finally got up late in the afternoon, swaying, to demand Momma call them again. I found her in the kitchen, drinking a strawberry margarita.

"Need a doctor," I mumbled, sweating profusely. "I'm still—"

"It's the drugs," she said stiffly. "You're *coming down.*"

"They got rehab for that."

"No. You've got a concert in Austin next week."

"Cancel it."

"No."

"Fucking *cancel it!*"

Momma slammed her hand down on the table, nearly knocking her drink over. "I won't let you ruin your career over this! Women miscarry all the time and they don't go crazy over it. You didn't give a damn about the baby when you went on another fucking coke binge—"

"I didn't *know!* How the hell was I supposed to know I could even *get* knocked up when I barely get my period."

"You shouldn't be on that shit, anyway!"

"*Cancel the goddamn concert!*"

"Go to your room!"

I wished the kitchen had a door to slam, but it didn't, so I just went upstairs without fanfare and threw myself onto my bed, sobbing. I'd already been planning on doing it, intended to have one last good time before ending everything, I really *hadn't* known I was pregnant.

It could have been anyone's, really; maybe the Marvel actor or that guy who used to be in a boyband or my dealer or Barbara's husband or my gynecologist. Momma slapped me when she found out, screamed that she spent all day every day keeping me out of the tabloids, and I hit her right back, told her I'd stay out of the tabloids if she'd just let me out of the fucking spotlight.

I was getting the belt ready when Momma knocked on my door, and I froze. "Momma?" I asked hopefully. *If she comes in, if she hugs me, if she just smiles at me, maybe I could...*

"Charles called to say he's decided on your dress for Austin," she said.

Just as I expected, both of Momma's cars are in the driveway, the front door intact. Someone I don't know crawls past, missing the bottom half of her leg, and we step around her to approach my house. Puppy throws herself against the door until it breaks, splitting her skin further, and walks inside hopefully, tongue flopping around as she turns her head every which way. There are a lot more possible directions to turn her head now.

Momma's going to be in either her room or mine; she's nothing if not a creature of habit. I go toward hers first, irritated by the sheer size of our stupid house. It feels like my stomach has teeth, like it's trying to eat me from the inside out. I just need to sate it for a *second*. Her bedroom door is closed, locked, and pressing my ear to it, I hear her breathing inside, pause to high-five Puppy and ram my shoulder against it, just twice before it falls in.

And there she is, curled up in the corner, whimpering, lips moving in a silent prayer, a rosary clenched in her fists—except she's not Catholic, so I've no idea where she got it or why.

It takes a second for her to recognize me, and I see it in her face when she does. For just a second, the thrill of her panic overrides my hunger, and I actually slow as I approach her, let it really sink in. My face was swollen when I woke up, but half of it burst and caved in on itself somewhere around 2 AM, so I think she recognizes my dress and hair more than anything, but she definitely *knows*.

"Delta Dawn," she whispers. "Baby—"

Puppy jumps on her before she can finish whatever she was going to say, hooks her fingers into her eye sockets and neatly rips her skull in two. I join her on the floor, and we savor my mother's brain over her broken corpse, the warmth of the rising sun washing over us, blood pooling around our knees. For a second, the hunger is gone; for a second, I pray Kitty is safe or dead; for a second, we lock eyes and I see the disgust in hers, but then the hunger wins out and we finish eating in companionable silence.

THE STAIN
Norman Goodman

PART ONE

Everyone was leaving work—just one more marketing agency housed in the Belgrade Palace— when Marina caught the elevator door and slipped her emaciated frame inside. The chatter fell silent, abruptly. A few seconds later, her coworkers resumed talking, but the tension lingered like static in the air. Marina felt it, too. She slid her wireless earbuds into place but didn't play a single track. No music. No radio.

When the elevator reached the parking level, everyone surged out, brushing past her on all sides. She was left alone in the lift. With a deep breath, she stepped out and made her way toward her car. A Volvo V40. Safety first, she recalled his ironic tone. She was digging through her purse for the keys when something touched her shoulder. She nearly screamed. Her heart thundered violently.

"Oh—shit. I'm sorry. I didn't mean to scare you, did I?" It was one of her colleagues from the elevator. He looked at her, intrigued. He thought her vulnerability was something deeply woven into her being—something she wore like a too-tight shirt stretched across a solid frame.

Did he come back *just* to talk to me? The thought flickered through her mind, alien and unwelcome. "No, you didn't," she said, though her body trembled in a way that made it clear: this was one of those transparent, obligatory lies. "Did you want something?"

Marko. One of the younger members of the market analysis department, the same department she belonged to. She'd heard the gossip: "that cocky little guy is way too ambitious," and "he's already gunning for a higher position," without caring about the senior colleagues who were more deserving. With her, though, he was always pleasant. She figured it was because he didn't see her as a threat. As competition.

And maybe he was right. She wasn't ambitious anymore. Not really.

She studied him more closely. Marko had thick hair, often slightly messy in a way that somehow worked, and a neatly trimmed beard. His body clearly showed signs of regular training—people would call that kind of build "lanky but athletic." He dressed well, stylish but never flashy. Still, it wasn't his looks that caught Marina's attention.

It was a stain.

A tiny speck of ketchup on the lapel of his blazer. So small, yet somehow, impossibly loud.

Obscene.

Offensive.

"Yeah, so…" he faltered for a moment. She looked into his eyes, then glanced away. That gave him back his confidence. He smiled. "I was just wondering if you'd like to grab a drink."

It took effort to return her gaze to his too-friendly teeth—and that damned red blotch.

"A bunch of us from work are going out. Thought you might want to join." His smile widened. He touched her forearm.

His hand was cold.

A pack.

"Thanks for the invite," she managed a weak smile and turned her back on him. "But I'm just… too tired."

"Oh, come on!" His face tightened, then quickly returned to its predatory grin. And in that fraction of a second, Marina learned more about him than she had in two years of working together. "I mean, I get it…" His hand again, uninvited, on her. She imagined the stain crawling down his fingers and onto her jacket sleeve. She shivered. "How long has it been? A year?"

Now *that* surprised her. No one had dared to be so blunt before. That topic had been off-limits. She pursed her lips and looked at him like he was a piece of rotting meat—or worse, like he was Nothing. Then she got in her car.

He didn't want to be Nothing. He wanted to be Someone.

She closed the door just as he stormed off—back to his pack.

Eight months, she thought, as her Volvo slid silently toward the exit. *Eight months, three days, and seven hours.* As she drove, she kept thinking. What drove women insane wasn't all that macho posturing or the need to dominate. No. It was that **awful demand for rationality**. What does he know about how long it's been—what it *means* to me?

Her house—a well-kept two-story in Senjak[1]—greeted

---

[1] Senjak is a settlement in Belgrade, located on a hill. It belongs to the municipality of Savski Venac. Like Dedinje, Senjak belongs to the wealthier neighborhoods of Belgrade. After 1945, it had a similar development as Dedinje: when the communists took over, they declared the

her with silence and darkness. She leaned against the door and, now safely on her own ground, exhaled loudly. She was exhausted. This week had been hellish.

Then again, weren't they all lately?

She kicked off her shoes and collapsed onto the sofa. She didn't turn on the lights. She knew exactly what she was suffering from—***depression*** and ***grief trauma***—but wasn't that completely normal? Why did people expect her to be different? To *act* different?

She poured a drink from a glass bottle in the cabinet and downed it in one go. It was Macallan, his favorite. She sank back into the couch. Something nudged her to think about her life. The truth was, she was still young. Just turned thirty-five. She had a home, a car, a decently paying job.

"You can crawl out of this," she whispered aloud. Her voice was thin, unconvincing. "You *can*," she shrieked—then burst into tears. She could… but did she want to? Since he left, the world had bled out its color. Nothing touched her anymore. She didn't feel sadness, or joy, or pity, or fear. All emotion had been burned away. She found people disgusting.

Eventually, she turned on a lamp.

And that's when she saw it.

The ***stain***.

It loomed in the upper corner of the ceiling, near the bookshelf—right at the junction of two walls and the ceiling. It took up just a sliver of space on all three surfaces. Roughly the size of a human fist. Or a tennis ball. In that half-light, it looked completely black. But also… strangely

---

previous residents enemies of the state, kicked them out of their (large and luxurious) houses sto that new communist political and military elite could move in.

pliable. Like it shimmered slightly. Or was made of rubber. Suddenly, a chill passed through her. Something wasn't right. Like she'd stepped into a parallel world. It had to be an optical illusion. But the filthy blotch was real.

"What the hell? Where did *you* come from?" She stood. It looked like mold, but she wasn't sure. It would've been a first. She'd never had mold problems in this house. She'd repainted everything just a few months ago. *Eight months*, a voice whispered. *Eight months and—*

Enough.

Shut up.

She moved closer, pressing her face to the freshly painted surface, which still held the faint chemical scent of paint and dispersion. That smell always reminded her of semen. Now the stain was directly above her. Larger than she'd thought. It touched all three planes.

The core, deep in the crux where ceiling met wall, was pitch black. A ***tar-black*** that absorbed light instead of reflecting it. The edges faded to lighter shades of black, like bruises healing outward. The perimeter was… cobwebbed. And there was something else. It glittered. Not brightly— but in that strange, evasive way stars glint in the night sky. The next moment, the shimmer was gone. No matter where she shifted, the dark substance refused to glint again.

"Wonderful," she muttered. "Exactly what I needed— mold."

She'd have to get some cleaner. Handle it this weekend. Mold wasn't healthy. And once it took hold—

That night, Marina barely slept. All night long, she dreamed of the stain. There was something in it. Something dark. Something that **was calling her name.** She was unable to fall asleep until morning.

PART TWO

Davor was a striking man in his early thirties. He owned a small PVC window frame manufacturing company in Voždovac[2]. It wasn't a big operation—just him and three other workers handling the core assembly tasks. When things got really busy, he'd hire a couple of extra hands through a student agency. That made him the purchasing manager, lead installer, driver, and quality control all rolled into one.

Still, he was content with the life he had built. The business had grown steadily, year by year, and the three full-time workers were more than employees, they were friends. Practically family.

That Friday, Davor was handling a delivery himself—frames for a private law office out in Višnjica[3]. He loaded the materials into the back of his Renault Express and climbed behind the wheel.

Beyond work, his private life was stable, too. After a turbulent decade of chaotic relationships and misfires, things had finally settled. He'd married two years ago. They had two daughters. A home. A routine.

But was this the life he truly wanted?

He found himself reflecting on that as he drove. The thought passed the time. His mind wandered—uninvited—

---

[2] Voždovac is a large Belgrade municipality in the south part of the city area. It is known for its football clubs (the two largest Serbian clubs – Partizan FC and Red Star - have their stadiums in the immediate vicinity of the municipality) and for the organized crime clans that were powerful and dangerous organizations during the 1990s and early 2000s.
[3] Višnjica is located on the right bank of the Danube, and stretches for almost 5 kilometers, from Rukavac and Ada Huja, all the way to Bela Stena, an ada in the Danube, very popular and visited place during the summer.

back to the girls he'd dated in college. (He'd never actually finished college.) Each person who enters your life leaves a stain on your soul, he thought. Sometimes that stain is light. Sometimes it's dark. Back then, he couldn't keep anything steady. Relationship after relationship crumbled like dry plaster. Just like the one with Marina. *Why the hell did I remember her?* he asked himself, uneasy.

There hadn't been anything *special* about that girl. Nothing to set her apart. He'd had deeper loves. Wilder ones. But then that voice inside him whispered: *Except for the incident.*

Shut up.

It was nothing. Nothing at all.

He was approaching Autokomanda[4]. Time to focus. Not drift into those masochistic daydreams. Yes, this was the life he wanted. He was happy. And yet... that day, he didn't feel quite right.

As he drove past the Belgrade theological college, he worried it might be the flu. That would suck. He'd promised Jovana and the girls a weekend at "the village." It wasn't a real village, just a weedy patch of inherited land near Ritopek[5], where they could escape to the quiet along the banks of the Danube. No, it wasn't the flu.

------

[4] Autokomanda is a city district in Belgrade, and also a interchange on the highway that passes through Belgrade. It is located on the three borders of the city municipalities of Voždovac, Savski venac and Vračar. It is named after the barracks of the JNA car unit that used to be located there.

[5] Ritopek is a suburban settlement of Belgrade, Serbia. It is located in the municipality of Grocka, 20 km east of Belgrade and 19 km west of the municipal seat, on the right bank of the Danube, across from the village of Ivanovo in Banat region of the Vojvodina province.

It was something else. A discomfort. A mild, crawling ache… That's when he realized: it was his right hand. His fingers. They hurt. That's why working the machine that morning had felt like pushing through tar. When he finally reached the client's address, he examined his hand.

That's when he saw it. ***The stain.***

It had bloomed on the pad of his index finger—dark, almost like a fast-growing mole. He could've sworn it wasn't there the night before. Yet somehow, all day, he'd felt a dull agitation, like a buzzing fly in the corner of his mind. But he hadn't connected it to the blotch.

He put on protective gloves and unloaded the frames. His hand felt slower. Less responsive. He noticed a reduction in mobility, but it wasn't alarming. Maybe he'd injured it somehow—pinched it on the machine, maybe, without realizing.

Driving back, he wiped down his right hand with a moist towelette. Every finger. The index, too. The ache subsided slightly. But the stain remained. Was it… larger now? He reached for the touchscreen on his GPS, and that's when it struck him—he couldn't feel the tip of his finger.

He pinched it. Nothing. He grabbed his key and pressed the metal tip into the very center of the dark patch.

Hard. No pain. That's what worried him.

Still, he forgot all about the stain the moment he pulled into his driveway and saw his little girls rushing out to greet him, their faces lit with joy.

PART THREE

She woke up and looked at the clock. Half past twelve. *Half past twelve!*

She bolted upright. Could it be? She rubbed her eyes and checked the numbers again. She couldn't remember the last time she'd slept that long—maybe back in high school, after rave nights. That former life—wild, exciting, but carefree—felt so far removed from the one she'd lived the last five or six years; it was as if she'd dreamed it.

Still, she had slept through the entire morning. And for the first time in ages—she felt rested. That feeling, now so alien and unexpected, actually scared her.

Stop tormenting yourself, she thought as she emptied her bladder. *Are you seriously upset because something good happened—because you finally got a decent night's sleep?*

But… I feel good. Really good. Full of energy.

What was I supposed to do today?

Then she remembered. The stain. Like a punch to the gut. She walked to the living room and raised the blinds, and nearly collapsed. Overnight, the stain had tripled in size. In daylight, it looked even more grotesque—*oily,* threaded with some kind of…

"Fucking hell!" she yelled. "What is this shit? What the actual fuck is that!"

There was no answer. Not without a closer look. She felt like she'd been shoved into a waking nightmare. *Told you so,* whispered the voice in her head. *That deep sleep? A harbinger.* She staggered to the utility closet. There it was—the tool she needed. A putty knife with a long handle. The grip was still crusted with lime from past repairs, and the blade showed tiny rust spots. Her heart picked up speed.

Darling… you should've thrown this thing out.

She remembered it clearly—eight months ago (yes, yes, *eight*), she'd sealed the fireplace herself, filled it with concrete, then smoothed and painted the wall. She was proud of that accomplishment—her first hands-on repair job. The wall still looked innocent. It *would* have, if not for that abomination oozing from the ceiling like some cosmic infection from a second-rate sci-fi flick. She dragged over a chair from the dining room and climbed on top.

That's when she could *smell* it.

The stain.

It gave off a faint chemical odor—acetone, ether, or something in that family. Her stomach knotted. The scent wasn't overpowering, but once inhaled, it lingered in her nostrils like a ghost. She shivered at the thought of what might be floating in that toxic air. Could she *see* them? Black particles. Like spores. Drifting.

Enough. It's bad enough without your neurotic breakdowns.

She raised her trembling hand and touched the mottled zone with the scraper. It wasn't a stain anymore. It was a kind of *tumor*. A wall cancer. How deep did it go? Fascinated and horrified, she watched as the fine hairs on its surface twitched in unison—then curled inward like petals, trying to *grab* the scraper's edge.

A brittle fragment broke loose—powdery, ashen, speckled like iron filings. The flecks danced wildly in the air, as if they had a will of their own. A surge of fear clamped down on her. What if one of those fragments landed on her skin? Or worse—what if she inhaled it? She recoiled and fell.

"Aah!" she cried, crashing to the floor. Bruised, but nothing broken.

Still, she felt more helpless than ever. This was a slow-motion collapse. A train to nervous breakdown, with just a few scenic stops along the way. She tried to return to the familiar oceans of her depression—but the bitter comfort it once gave her was gone now.

That ritual… had sailed far out of reach. "Come on. Pull yourself together," she told herself in the calmest voice she could muster. "It's just mold. Fucking *mold*. And I'm going to deal with it."

She limped toward the door. Time to gear up. That was a declaration of war.

She went to the big home-supply market where she'd shopped before and stocked up: five kilograms of "**Bimold**"—a product advertised as *"concentrated disinfectant and whitening formula for removing mold, moss, algae, soap scum, and other deep-rooted organic contaminants."*

She also bought a few bottles of sodium hypochlorite cleaner, some sprays, and a good old-fashioned jug of bleach. The smell of chlorine brought back unpleasant memories. Still… she felt better. That sense of control nearly evaporated by the time she returned home.

"I'm going to fix you, bitch," she muttered to the stain, which pulsated gently at the edge of her vision.

She prepped the area—covered the parquet and wardrobe with old newspapers, pulled on her "Green Barrier" gloves (acid and base resistant, with that weird talc feel), and laid out rags. Then she attacked. With a full-force splash, she threw the Bimold onto the wall—aiming high, toward the ceiling.

Grayish streams ran down like oil on a corpse. The stain began to dissolve under the chemical flood. She climbed the chair again, scrubbing with fury. Then came the hypochlorite. Then the mold spray. A triple assault. She stepped back to admire her work. The cleaned area looked brighter than the rest, but that could be fixed later—with stain-blocking primer and a new coat of paint.

She could hear it. The chemicals reacting—hissing. The sound made her skin crawl.

Now in the zone, she kept cleaning. It felt *good*. Physical. Grounding. God knew the house needed it. She hadn't vacuumed in weeks. The apathy was gone now.

Just… gone.

While sorting the closet, she found his shirt. And sweatpants. The moment her fingers touched the fabric, she recoiled like she'd been burned. She carried the clothes to the kitchen and tossed them into the metal trash bin. Then she burned them.

Done. That chapter, closed.

It was only around 9 PM that she remembered to check the wall. The site of the original stain. What she saw made her sit, and bite into her forearm until she bled. The black substance was still there. And *how*. Despite all the bleach, the poison, the scrubbing—the **thing** had come back. Worse than before.

It looked… proud. The obscene form framed by the stark contrast of the spotless wall. Larger. Defiant. It was growing. Growing at a steady, purposeful rate. Unafraid of any weapon Marina had thrown at it. The black filaments—now longer—swayed in patterns.

Hypnotic. Calling. Drawing her in.

She stepped closer, spellbound. There was a sound coming from it. She could *swear* there was a sound. She blinked. And the hairs—those whispering tentacles of cosmic desecration—were gone.

Vanished.

That's because they were never there, said the voice. *They never existed. Just your mind, sweetie. Those hairs. The stain. But look at it now…*

"Enough!" she shouted.

The filthy growth froze, then melted into a tar-black mirror. A perfect lake of meaninglessness.

How is this possible? Her vision blurred. Strength left her limbs. This, this was the real world now. No joy. No light. No future. Just the stare. The wait. The knowing that nothing comes next. Not even fear. Fear is for people who still have something to lose.

On the oil-slick surface, concentric circles began to ripple as if something from behind, from *within*, was pressing forward. And then she saw it. A *face*. Eyes closed.

She froze. Her mouth hung open. Saliva dripped from her lips.

Then—

The eyes opened.

PART FOUR

They were just leaving Belgrade, somewhere near old Kaluđerica[6]. Davor always took the Smederevo road to reach their weekend cottage by the Danube, but this time—it felt like a mistake. The traffic was dense. The air, choked with exhaust. He rolled the window up and switched on the AC. His fingers wouldn't respond. Again. He glanced at them. The blackness had spread.

"For God's sake, Davor—what did you do to your hand?" Jovana asked. She'd noticed his index and middle fingers, swollen and bruised. No. Not bruised. Black. Hardened. Like two burnt twigs tossed into a fire.

"Can I just—"

"Don't touch it!" he snapped, yanking his hand back and shoving it into his pocket.

She flinched. "Does it hurt?"

"No. That's the thing. It came out of nowhere. I don't know what it is. I can't feel anything in those fingers. And it… it feels like it's spreading. I think I need to see a doctor."

"Okay. But what's going on with *you*?" she asked

---

[6] Kaluđerica is the westernmost settlement in the municipality of Grocka. It is located 6 kilometers east of central Belgrade and stretches in two fork-like urban formations between the road of Smederevski put to the north and the Belgrade-Niš highway to the south. It is said that Kaludjerica is the largest illegal settlement in Europe because it was not built according to any urban plan.

softly, gently touching the back of his hand.

He hated being touched while driving.

"Nothing. Why?" His tone was sharper than he meant. He caught himself. "Sorry, babe."

She was right, and he knew it. He turned to kiss her. But she leaned away, still smiling. He could tell she was hurt. Fine, then. *I can pout, too,* he thought.

"Not toward me, silly. Toward them." She tilted her head toward the back seat. The kids. They were bickering now, fighting over a toy. A rubber duck. A yellow one. The kind that squeaks when you squeeze it. And they *kept squeezing it.* Over and over. High-pitched. Repetitive. Squeal. Squeal. Squeal. Then came the shrieking, each trying to rip the toy from the other's grip. It grated on him. He felt like his skull might split.

"I'm not being distant," he muttered. "It's just… the noise. It's too much. Can you calm them down a little?"

"They're just kids. Let them be. What's *wrong* with you?"

"There's nothing fucking wrong with me; it's those spoiled little—could you, for just *one* goddamn second—" Both kids screamed at the same time. "—*SHUT UP!*"

Silence.

Anja's blue eyes went wide with confusion. For baby Andrej, it was too much. He burst into tears. "Look what you've done now!" Jovana snapped, just as the traffic cleared and Davor slammed the gas pedal down.

"*Me?*" he shot back, turning toward her, ready to fight this to the bitter end. "What did *I* do? They're the ones—"

"*Look out!*" she screamed.

He whipped his eyes back to the road—and saw it. Their car had drifted into the opposite lane. And barreling toward them, a massive truck. Lead-gray. Merciless. Davor hissed and grabbed the wheel—but his right-hand fingers wouldn't move. Wouldn't grip. His palm slid off the steering wheel. In a last desperate lurch, he seized it with his left hand and yanked them back into their lane.

The truck thundered past. A rumble of death, barely missed.

Jovana sobbed—then began to scream at him. "You could've *killed us*! What the fuck is wrong with you! Do you even think about the kids? WHAT. THE. FUCK. IS. WRONG. WITH. YOU?!"

He pulled over a hundred meters down the road. Sat still. Breathed deep. His vision dotted red. His chest ached. His blood pressure was volcanic. Then he turned and hit her.

Hard.

She cried out and curled into herself. The kids started crying again. Softly this time. Like mice.

"I'm sorry… I… just… I'm sorry."

PART FIVE

As for the diseased fingers—his index, where it had started, and the middle one it had spread to—the doctors had done their part. They rubbed them with some kind of ointment designed to prevent further drying of the epidermis, then wrapped them in thick layers of gauze.

The fingers were immobilized. He had no sensation in the index finger at all, and the middle one only faintly at the base, but even there the feeling was fading. What was going on deeper inside the hand—within the muscles, the bones, the blood vessels—no one could say for sure.

Or maybe they just don't want to tell me, he thought bitterly.

Then someone made the decision to transfer him to the Infectious Disease ward. Access restricted. No visitors. That didn't stop them from gathering in the hallway. He could hear them arguing. Could catch pieces of words like "basocellular," "anemic necrosis," "immunosuppression," and "vasculopathy"—each one sending a shiver down his spine, feeding new nightmares. And the nightmares had been growing stronger, more senseless by the night.

The doctors left him waiting, pending "further testing." No one knew what it was. What illness had taken hold. That was the phrase they repeated like a prayer: "Further analysis is required." He raised his trembling hand and stared at it. Whatever it was—it was spreading, he thought, and his body quivered. He had lost sensation in his entire arm just hours ago.

He picked up the fork from his dinner tray and stabbed it into his forearm. Nothing. Not a trace of feeling. He wondered if the blackness had reached his brain. Was he still perceiving the world rationally? Was he still sane? But then again, mental health is a stretchy concept, isn't it?

He unwrapped the gauze. With his other hand, he touched the finger—knowing full well he shouldn't. A flake came off. Just a tiny one. Then the entire finger crumbled. Disintegrated. Into dust. Davor screamed. "No! No! Noo...!"

***

Sandra worked as a nurse in the ER, in the maternity ward. She had just finished her third consecutive night shift when she heard the scream. It came from upstairs—the Infectious Disease ward.

Not unusual. People got jumpy when locked in isolation. She headed for the staff room to wash and change. She always showered before heading home—who knew what germs floated through those corridors? But tonight, she didn't have the strength. She just wanted to crawl to her apartment and disappear.

In the hallway, she noticed a stir among the night staff.

A doctor ran upstairs, still wearing a surgical mask. There were muffled, anxious voices. Then sobbing. Several voices.

What the hell is going on?

Truthfully—she didn't want to know. Her shift was over. Any emergency could mean staying longer. She planned to slip out of the building before anyone noticed. She forced herself to wash her face and hands thoroughly.

That's when she noticed it. The stain. Just a speck, tucked into the corner of her eye. As small as a poppy seed. She was sure it hadn't been there the night before while doing her makeup. It had to be mascara. She tried to rub it off while keeping her eye open, fighting the instinct to flinch or blink.

But it wouldn't come off. That pitch-black fleck stayed put. Dear God, what is this now? Her heart picked up pace. A burst blood vessel? No, it didn't look like that. She closed her eye. Opened it again. Vision normal. No discomfort. Hm… what was that word... macula? As far as she could tell, there were no symptoms. So, what the hell was it?

Tomorrow, I'll go see an ophthalmologist, she decided. *But not now. Now, I need rest.*

She felt vulnerable. And in that state, she missed him the most—the man she'd loved. Who loved me back? Was that even true? She still thought of him. Every day, almost. To leave me like that, without a word, without a message… for no reason.

That bastard.

Deep in her bones, though, she felt something was wrong. He loved her. He wouldn't just walk away. At least, that's what he always said. What did she expect? He had cheated on his wife. Why did she think he wouldn't cheat on her, too? But after days without a single message or reply, she'd gone looking for him.

His coworkers delivered the shock: Mladen Stanković

hadn't shown up to work in five days. The exact same number of days he'd been silent with her. No one knew where he was. His wife had officially reported him missing.

The only logical conclusion? He'd run away. She'd read about it—people abandoning their lives, cutting all ties. She found that behavior disgusting. He'd always said he would leave that frigid psycho bitch. But Sandra had never imagined he'd dump both of them. She wondered where he was now—what city, what country.

You bastard. You had no right to do that to me.

Lost in these thoughts, she made it home and stepped straight into the shower. She closed her eyes when the shampoo ran down her face. Wrapped her hair in a towel. Stood in front of the mirror. Looked at herself.

Her right eye was completely black. Her vision—blurred to hell. The left had started to show flecks.

PART SIX

It was Monday, though Marina neither knew nor cared. She hadn't gone to work. Her mind no longer recognized obligations or social expectations. In fact, there was barely anything left of what could be called learned human behavior. Reality, as she perceived it, had collapsed into an abyss—an immense, trembling chasm like a tear in the ocean floor. She felt like a tiny, trembling rock surrounded by a pitiless void, bathed in the beam of some unimaginable spotlight, and that light fell only on her.

The house had changed. The doors had become jaws, the staircase a gullet, and the empty rooms now bristled with invisible traps. She wandered in a fever dream, trapped in a well of blackness where, now and then, she caught glimpses of what might have once been her home.

She discovered a hole in her head—so deep she imagined dropping things into it and never hearing a splash.

That inner well was connected to the stain, the one spreading across her ceiling, like a Klein bottle looping itself through space and mind.

The filth had spread further now, infecting much of the wall and ceiling. From it grew trembling hairs of dark slime, shivering to the beat of her pulse. Sometimes, the mass took on the shape of a mirror—swelling, warping, and calling to her.

Worse still, it showed her things. Memories. The kind she had buried deep. Her and her first boyfriend in a tiny student apartment—Davor. She remembered his name. How could she forget? He wasn't just a passing figure. No one is. Everyone leaves a scar—sometimes a scratch, sometimes a bruise, sometimes a stain so deep it burrows into the soul. They had been together for months.

And she had ignored the signs. His temper. His control. Until one day, he locked the door and told her to lie down. He shoved two fingers inside her while she begged him to stop, climbed on top of her, ignored her protests, slapped her when she resisted, and forced himself into her again and again. She had been so ashamed she told no one. She buried it. Buried him. In the stain.

Eventually, she recovered, enough to trust again. Mladen had seemed like the opposite of Davor—gentle, attentive, kind. Their marriage had been the best thing that ever happened to her. But after he hurt his back playing tennis and spent time in the hospital, he began to change. He left the house more often, always claiming it was "for work."

He started showering twice a day. Switched cologne. She didn't want to believe it, but something inside her already knew. One night, while he slept soundly beside her, she went through his phone. It was locked—a new habit. She unlocked it using his finger. Inside, on one of his messaging apps, she found the truth.

And more than that. Her name was Sandra. A nurse. She'd been the one to approach him. She'd made the first move. But that didn't absolve him, not in Marina's eyes. It didn't save him from what was coming.

Now the stain—the mirror—showed his face. His shocked expression when she told him. His face bulged and twisted, swelling out of the wall, spiraling into nonsense like dark icing smeared across a slab of black glass. She knelt before it, eyes wide, hands clasped as if in prayer. She could feel it—soon, the time would come. Soon, she and the essence behind the stain would become one.

PART SEVEN

Inspectors Obradović and Konstantinović sat in the shared office of the Belgrade Police Department, on Despot Stefan Boulevard 12. The mood was grim. Everyone was whispering about some strange skin disease spreading through the city—some were calling it the "Black Plague of the New Age."

"Still working that case?" asked the older inspector, glancing over his colleague's shoulder at the pile of documents stacked across the desk.

"Of course. Did you think I'd leave something unfinished?" Obradović replied without looking up. "I've had a few unsolved cases in my career, and every single one still haunts me. I swore this one wouldn't be added to that list." His voice softened slightly, and he finally raised his eyes. "Besides, it helps keep my mind off the thing everyone's obsessed with—that damned sickness.

I overheard two officers from the third shift talking in the parking lot this morning. Even against my will, the details keep slipping into my ears, into my brain. Did you know there are already *hundreds* infected?"

"Jesus Christ," hissed Konstantinović, dropping his

weight into one of the squeaky rolling chairs. He had no desire to talk about the outbreak, but as the hours passed, it became harder to avoid. There were too many tear-streaked faces around the station.

Every few minutes someone answered a personal phone call in a panic or ran to the nearest TV for updates. In a strange way, Konstantinović almost felt lucky. He had no children—his marriage to Marija had been barren on several levels—so there weren't many people left for him to worry about. Just Marija, himself, and a few close friends. And the disturbing truth was, he wasn't even sure how much he still cared about them.

"This so-called epidemic actually opened my eyes," Obradović continued. "I took a second look at the medical file of our missing person, Mladen Stanković. A few weeks before he disappeared, he was admitted to "Dragiša Mišović" Hospital. Gastrointestinal issues. But that's not all—he had black patches on his skin. It all suggests poisoning."

"Okay… so maybe he ate something bad? Or drank something spoiled?"

Obradović shook his head. "I don't think so. I spoke off the record with one of the doctors who treated him. He's fairly certain it was a reaction to a large dose of pharmaceuticals—specifically, antidepressants. Now guess who those drugs were prescribed to?"

"His wife? You still haven't taken your eyes off her, huh?"

"You know it's the most logical place to look. These kinds of crimes usually come from someone close. Spouse. Family. Friends."

"Sure. But you're still missing motive. And a body. If she really abducted her husband, where'd she hide him? In the basement? We already checked. There's nothing there."

"You're close but listen to this: Three days before he

went missing, Marina Stanković bought a large quantity of cement at a supply yard called Vanas, out on the Obrenovac road. She paid in cash and requested a third party to handle the delivery—even though delivery is normally included in the price.

The only reason we caught this detail is because we reviewed her car's GPS history. That was the only unusual trip she made during that period. On the day of the disappearance, she went to a supermarket and a hairdresser. Totally routine. Which means she didn't drive him out to the woods. Or to a river."

"I remember that. But she explained the cement purchase as part of some home repairs—something about a burst pipe, right? Isn't it more likely the guy just ran off? Abandoned her? God knows the thought's crossed *my* mind more than once."

"We believed her at first, yeah. But I did the math again. No one buys that much cement to fix a pipe. That's the kind of load you use when you want to seal something off. Permanently." Obradović looked directly at him.

"Oh my God." Detectives's eyes widened. "You think she… what, buried him?"

"I've heard stranger things. In this line of work, you learn fast—people are capable of anything. There are no limits to human depravity."

Konstantinović sighed. "That much, unfortunately, is true."

Just then, a scream pierced the station just a few offices away.

"No, no, no! God, what's happening to me? Get it off me!" someone shrieked in abject panic.

Obradović stood. "Let's go. Time to pay Mrs. Stanković another visit."

PART EIGHT

They arrived at the Stanković house around noon. It was Tuesday—the third day of the outbreak that the media had begun to call "the ash blight." They rang the bell, but there was no answer. Inspector Obradović dialed Mrs. Stanković's private number, which he'd had written down for some time. The message came back immediately: the number was disconnected.

"So, what now?" asked Konstantinović, already uncomfortable. He didn't like the way his partner handled the case—too much was based on gut feeling and instinct. Then again, Obradović's instincts had proven disturbingly accurate in the past.

Instead of answering, Obradović smashed the glass on the front door. "Didn't you hear the sounds coming from inside? That's probable cause." He reached in, unlocked the door, and stepped inside.

Older detective sighed and followed.

They knew the moment they crossed the threshold something was wrong. The house was cloaked in unnatural darkness. The air was thick—overwhelming—with a smell that defied easy description. A heavy mix of moisture and rot, touched with the sharpness of ozone, like the aftermath of lightning striking a barn full of wet hay.

"Mrs. Stanković? Police! If you're inside, please respond!"

"I don't think she's home."

"Her car's in the driveway."

"That doesn't mean—" Konstantinović stopped midsentence. Something inside him buckled, like a support beam giving way deep within his psyche. That moment when the structure of coherent thought begins to slip toward a pit of unreason. Something was moving across the floor. It took a second for their eyes to adjust to the dark. Then they saw her.

Marina Stanković was home. But she was no longer "home" in the head. She was naked, crawling toward the wall, her face slick and splattered with thick, white saliva. Her tongue hung from her mouth. Her eyes were open, and for a moment, Krsman could swear there was a writhing mass of malignant life behind her eyelids. Then, nothing. The windows of her soul went blank. Her mind had moved out.

The wall was smeared with filth. Human waste—and something else. Something oily and dark they couldn't yet identify.

"Dear God. She's completely lost it."

"Marina… can you hear me? Help me lift her—watch out!"

The woman struggled wildly. Whatever had taken over tried to bite at their legs.

"What do you think happened to her?"

"I won't speculate… but guilt can do this to a person. I'm calling for an ambulance. Keep an eye on her."

Why not switch roles? Detective thought grimly. He didn't want to stay in that house for another second—not that he could explain exactly why. There was something in the air. Floating. Waiting.

Obradović made the call and then began exploring the house. "Come look at this. Help me move this wardrobe."

"Look at this wall. Someone patched it up badly."

"Yeah. There used to be a fireplace here—I'd swear to it. Why would anyone seal off a fireplace?"

"And more importantly… Hey, buddy… what do you think *that* is?"

For the first time, they truly looked at it. That enormous, obscenely dark blotch. It was vicious—like a two-meter smoker's lung regurgitated onto drywall.

"Hell, if I know. Mold. What else could it be? Best not

to touch it. I heard about a guy who poisoned himself trying to scrape mold off his wall."

Obradović contacted headquarters and requested a forensic team. He was fairly certain of what they'd find behind that wall. The ambulance didn't arrive for nearly half an hour. The city was in chaos. Entire families were showing up at hospitals with black marks on their bodies. The TV was full of warnings. The newspapers brimming with hysteria.

"They don't know how it spreads," one of the grim-faced med techs told them. "But I'm not going near anyone without gloves and a mask. Hell, there are thousands now. Hospitals are out of beds. I'm not showing up to work tomorrow. No way."

PART NINE

That evening, inspectors Obradović and Konstantinović stopped by for a drink each at a mutual friend's place—a former policeman who ran a bar on Ada Ciganlija[7]. They enjoyed getting away from the city's hustle and the sound of ambulance sirens. At the city police headquarters, three people were already sick with ash

---

[7] Ada Ciganlija, colloquially shortened to Ada, is a river island that has artificially been turned into a peninsula, located in the Sava River's course through central Belgrade, Serbia. The name can also refer to the adjoining artificial Lake Sava and its beach. To take advantage of its central location, over the past few decades, it was turned into an immensely popular recreational zone, most notable for its beaches and sports facilities, which, during summer seasons, can have over 100,000 visitors daily and up to 300,000 visitors over the weekend.

blight.

The doctors still didn't know what it was or have a cure. The Ministry of Health was holding an emergency meeting where the declaration of a state of emergency in Belgrade was expected.

Isn't that strange? Why is it localized only to the capital? Obradović thought. There was no evidence ash blight symptoms appeared outside the wider city area. Besides, such a disease was unknown to the global medical community. The Serbs were once again gambling with fate.

"Why the long face? Don't tell me you're scared of this infection? It'll pass. Nothing will happen to you or Andrijana…"

"It's not that. I haven't told you one more thing I discovered about the case."

"Listen to him. The world is falling apart and he's still talking about the case."

Obradović seemed to sober up, then. "The world is falling apart, yeah… It's connected to the disease. Our case."

"Excuse me? How so?"

"These days, the media is showing the faces and names of the zero patients. Those in whom, supposedly, the first symptoms of ash blight were observed. Those names, those people…" Detective had to stop and lick his lips, "appear in the case of the disappearance of Mladen Stanković. A case I'm increasingly sure is actually a premeditated murder.

"Davor Ilić, a small entrepreneur—a man with only a few hours of life left, as doctors predict — studied at the Faculty of Economics at the same time as Mladen's wife, Marina Stanković. Moreover, there are witness statements that they were in a relationship that ended abruptly. Soon after that, Davor dropped out of the faculty, and Marina became a withdrawn girl prone to depression and panic attacks.

"As for the second patient, a certain Sandra Panić—she works at the Emergency Center where the sick Ilić was first brought. However, she was not in contact with the patient. In fact, she worked in a different department. She doesn't know the patient. On the other hand, she knows the missing Mladen Stanković. Or rather, she knew him. I don't believe we'll find that man alive and well. It seems they were secretly involved. Mladen was planning to leave Marina, get a divorce, and start living with a nurse."

"So, what happened, then?"

"Mrs. Stanković found out, killed her husband, and walled him up in the fireplace. The punishment, however, didn't come only for the adulterer but also for the girl who had an eye on her husband."

"I don't understand it. How is that possible?"

"Fuck me if I know. But everything revolves around Marina, don't you see?"

PART TEN

Marina felt heavy and hungover, like a stone at the bottom of a barrel. Her head was swollen, and her tongue— a glove of inverted skin. Her face had that limp, vacant look of stunned emptiness. It was the effect of the medication, of course, but also the final realization that it was over. If any part of her mind had been preserved, she would have known she had been admitted to the Special Hospital for Psychiatric Diseases in Kovin.

There, she would be kept until an assessment of her mental state and a possible trial. The forensic team had found the remains of her husband in the wall, but that was currently put aside. The entire nation was fighting an epidemic of a necrotizing disease. Twenty percent of the capital's population was infected, with no signs of decline.

Moreover, there was no cure or help for the infected. The human body was, part by part, being consumed by tissue death.

The sick people were dying in the most terrible agony. Finally, the inevitable happened—the disease spread to the rest of Serbia. The state was in chaos, and the world medical community was in panic, just like the regional political elite.

Marina was pulled from peaceful dreams by the sounds of screaming. In the special hospital, they were not uncommon, but these carried an extra layer of despair and pain.

"No! My legs! My legs have rotted away!" Ash blight had reached Kovin and was claiming its first victims.

Marina experienced a change in her head. It was as if someone had suddenly plunged a hot knife into her temple. She raised her eyes. Then she saw it.

A stain.

On one of the virginally white walls appeared a pulsating darkness. You can only recognize what you observe. And you can only observe what is already in consciousness. Did Marina create the stain, or did the stain create Marina as she was?

It spread and opened—a passage into nothingness. Behind the syrupy mirror lay a cosmic void that carried comfort and peace. Marina's bladder was the first to give out. Then came the scream. She opened her mouth and shouted into the vortex as the darkness in the room grew and grew, an anthem in praise of paradox.

Once she gave in to that weakness, she could no longer stop. She screamed until she lost her voice, until her vocal cords hurt and refused to vibrate any longer. The silence that followed was even more terrifying than the noise; the remnants of the scream hovered in the air like droplets of black ink in zero gravity.

While the infection outside sowed death and suffering, Marina stepped through and crossed over to the other side.

Meat
Ross S. Simon

Britain, 1349.

The era of the Bubonic Plague: the Black Death.

Throughout Europe, in this horrible age before scientific medicines and rational theories were in evidence, pestilence and biological chaos had been going on, without much mind, for quite a while. Eventually, from rats in the alleyways as well as their accompanying vermin, in many cities upon and around the Continent, an entirely new and incurable disease arose. It was in the food the people ate and the water they washed themselves with; it was in the very air they breathed.

The result was long, slow, painful, natural genocide. One was considered blessed by God, in this period, not to come down with the internally and externally destructive Plague. Rather than educated doctors and competent surgeons, Europeans had only priests and brides of the Lord to rely upon to protect them, via blessings, from the flesh-eating, brain-poisoning effects of this pandemic.

Moreover, if they could not save you—which they

never at all could—your loved ones, as soon as you were dead (which was very soon, indeed), relied on lowly rejects of men, at the bottom of Europe's invisible caste system, to properly dispose of your rotting, mutilated corpse. These filthy, lonely men were known as drivers of the meat wagons.

They were considered untouchable to those still living—who were hopefully not infected with the Death—and lived every moment in mortal danger of catching it themselves, which they very often ended up doing as the destiny of their short, miserable lives.

Most of the time, these men were cleverly chosen by kings and lords as former criminals or lawbreakers, those defiant of royal decree, or even as such undesirable types as homosexuals, or perhaps such heretical groups as Jews. They were released from dungeons or pardoned out of execution expressly for the purpose of loading decaying bodies, still rife with Black Death, into open carts with their bare hands, and then hauling them away to be buried, in a short trip they might not even have survived.

By many who had such a job, it was considered a worse fate even than life imprisonment, or execution, or to some even than being tortured to death.

However, it wasn't so to one man. This man, out every miserable, grim morning in 1349 in the just-outside-Londonshire village of Wakendside, in fact, enjoyed his job for a certain reason. He was a hideous little toad of a man—secretly not totally intelligent; autism had not yet been named—yet he proved very competent at doing the labor for which he had been commissioned. The man's name was Ulvin Grumpelt.

His close friends called him, simply, "Ulv."

Yes, you have misread nothing. Ulvin Grumpelt, driver of the meat wagon in the age of the Black Death, had close friends...at least, of a sort.

That bleak, gray morning in Wakendside, Grumpelt, up with the rooster's crow and out with his wagon, stopped his horse at the entrance to each of the poverty-gripped village streets, which stretched for about forty feet with linings of crumbling, dismal shacks full of sad-minded families, detailed by the Royal tax collectors on a list each meat-wagon driver was given, and almost all of whom, whether they had the Plague yet or not, were surely doomed.

The filthy and twisted Grumpelt strolled along the street in a slow zigzag formation, banging the bottom of an otherwise unusable iron kettle with a large spoon, to alert the victims of the Plague he was here again, to take about half of them away for good.

"Bring oot th'deaaad!" he called among the houses, in a gurgling voice. "Bring oot th'deaaad!"

Laboriously, heartbrokenly, the citizens of Wakendside carried or dragged the corpses of their loved ones, whom they would soon join in death, to the little cart, and paid Grumpelt ten pence. Then they staggered back into their homes, weeping, not even knowing if the tears should rightly have flowed for their just-lost family…or for their own selves.

At ten of the clock, Grumpelt's shift in Wakendside was over. He then drove his wagon to the freshest available graveyard, taking the long route there…for a whimsical little reason.

For fifteen minutes into the hills around Wakendside, well out of earshot of the still-dying villagers, Grumpelt had kept driving.

Behind him, in the wagon's bed, the legless torso of an emaciated young man, who had developed patches of exposed muscular tissue and lost one eye and most teeth after death, stirred and propped itself up on one dirty, raw elbow.

The torso looked at Grumpelt.

"So then, Ulv," mumbled the half-corpse with its near-toothless mouth, "'Ow go the rounds, this proper day?"

Ulvin Grumpelt looked behind him and smiled. "Oh, just biz as usually is done, Marvin," he said calmly. "Pity your old lady had to get rid of you."

"Ah, well, doubtless she'll be done wi' afore too long, 'erself," spoke up the near-skeletal dead body of a middle-aged woman in the cart. "'Appened to know them's rats nearby Marvin-lad's and 'er home."

"Hm, indeed, it can't be helped none, Mrs. Leavendridge," the torso named Marvin said to the skeleton. "I's sure your husband did the best job what he could."

"That's right, Miz L.," Grumpelt commented. "You were the rat-catcher's wife for the street, what?"

"Amazed the old man and I scraped by long as we done," said Mrs. Leavendridge. "Tell 'im I done said 'ello, soon as he has 'is turn on this 'ere wagon."

"I'll be sure, ma'am," said Grumpelt.

From among the cart's remains, up popped the corpse of a young girl now, half her skullcap having fallen off and much of the brain matter having softly dribbled out. She looked toward Grumpelt, curiously.

"Mistah G., suh," she said with a smile, "where are we headed, might ye know?"

"To a glorious place called Heaven," said Grumpelt with a large smile. "Better by far than this humble Earth. You've been chosen as angels, all of you, by the Good—"

"Er, no, suh," cut in the open-skulled girl. "I mean, where, exactly, might you, suh, be dropping us off?" She glanced at the other dead remnants of people around her; Mrs. Leavendridge smiled, and it tore her emaciated oral flesh a little.

"Oh. Well, that's up to the gravediggers, then,"

explained Ulv. "We're giving you folks back to the earth, we is. Ashes to Ashes, Dust to Dust and all such stuff. It's part of your new position in Heaven."

"Oh." The lass seemed puzzled. "Funny thing, being buried in the ground in order to get to Heaven."

"'S a certain thing about it," Grumpelt explained, with a confident face. "Your earthly body and your divine soul need to go in different directions, and…" He leaned in close to the girl's gutted head and whispered. "Don't tell no one I said this. None still alive yet, I means. Your spirit and your flesh 'aven't parted ways just quite yet. Just as soon as ye're given back to the earth in meat…the Good Lord'll be ready for ye." He smiled wider.

The girl smiled, herself. A bit or two of brain matter that had remained, softer than mush, leaked mostly bloodily out from between her teeth.

It was now the turn of an old man's body, covered with blisters and sores throughout like the Biblical character of Job had once been, to prop itself up and whisper at Grumpelt.

"Yew and yer bloody versions of what the Lord has written," he hissed sourly into Grumpelt's ear. "You act as though all've us are Heaven-bound. Weren't it His wrath that brought this terrible Death upon England?"

Grumpelt sighed. "He works in somewhat inexplicable ways, Mr. Haroldson," he said. "Just 'live your death' the same way ye've lived your life. One day before another."

Haroldson almost spat out another reprimand, which would have been accompanied by pus from his inner oral sores, but citing Ulv's convictions, the old man decided to stay mum from there. During this silence, Ulvin stared ahead at the road, in thought.

What he didn't tell them about, was some ideas he had concerning the Plague. Ulvin had decided to himself that he'd explain them to those more willing to listen, after he'd developed these ideas somewhat.

#

The next morning, Grumpelt's wagon was on another impoverished street, and the man himself was strolling around, banging his kettle. "Bring oot th'deaaad! Bring oot th'deaaad!"

An adolescent brother and sister emerged from one hut, carrying in tandem the corpse of their not-yet-forty-year-old father. They seemed numb, inured, to the miseries of ubiquitous death, to the Plague's malevolence. Obviously, because they had lost too many other family members before Dad, it had enough thus inured them as only two young people could be, rendered them willing, more or less, to live out each day with few or no tears.

Ulvin recognized the man they shoved onto the cart as they handed him his pair of shillings; his name was Henry Betterman, a peasant on Grumpelt's list who'd held a conversation with him (at arm's length) during a stop on one of his meat-wagon rounds just a few days earlier. He'd helped the bodies of his wife and his baby daughter onto the cart (careful not to touch him) before talking with Grumpelt in a tone of gloom about Henry's crumbling life. Although he said it was the Lord's work, the Plague was decimating his family and those of hundreds of thousands more within the British Isles alone.

Indeed, three close ones gone, one after another, would have been what it took to jade his young son and daughter of the last of their compassion…and of their hope in life.

Ulvin, however, would see this as a mere opportunity to speak with Betterman again.

Once his cart had progressed through Wakendside, en route to the graveyard, Ulvin and Henry Betterman struck up their second conversation.

"So, Mr. B.," said Ulvin. "'Ow feels it to be free, once and for all?"

Betterman, his flesh peeling from his face and neck, lay back in the meat cart and flicked from side to side his yellowed, bleeding eyes. A bit of pus splattered out from them.

"I…suppose me worries are over, Grumpelt," he admitted. "I'll at least have a chance to see my wife again, and little baby Coline."

The corpse of a nine-year-old boy sat up, his skin all pockmarked and gnarled. He said, "So what? So many of us are dying. This wasn't the way it was supposed to be!"

"Now, now, Reginald," coaxed Ulvin. "I know there are those of us unhappy with death, and I've been considering my impending own too. In fact…"

Ulvin glanced around, and then looked in close to Betterman and Reginald. "Confidentially, just before falling asleep in my hovel last night, I was pondering what makes this Plague a plague. Now, it's been conjectured durin' the Classical Age—and I's hoping the Church don't get wind of this—that matter is made up of indivisible particles, wot? So…I get the idea there's a plan the Lord made up for us…pertainin' to these particles. We ain't just made up from dust. This dust would perhaps transform into certain bits. Hence, the lots of little bits that make up you or me, living or dead."

Henry Betterman and Reginald listened closely, curious about this. Reginald was more genuinely so.

"Furthermore, the Plague itself is made up of little, nasty bits that clash with ours, that so kill. We can't sees 'em, they're so small, and yet they're everywhere. In the water, in the air. We can't avoid these little Plague bits. Now, I got the idea, further still, that there be a third kind of little, invisible, and indivisible bits yet."

"Oh boy," muttered Betterman.

"Seriously," said Ulvin. "This third kind of bits is a kind we haven't found yet. It destroys the Plague bits the way the Plague bits destroy us…or close to it. Maybe it's found in some kind o plants, some kind o animals, wherever. Even still, the important thing to know—however surprising—is that the nature o the Plague isn't exactly divine. It's earthly…and what's more, we can probably start fighting it by keeping our indivisible bits away from its indivisible bits."

"Rubbish!" barked the now-angered Betterman, spewing bloody bits of meat.

At this point, up sat a young woman, exactly half of whose skin had rotted away and fell off her bones. "No, sir," she said. "I think Ulv has a point, at least about staying away from the Plague bits."

"I does indeed, Adriana," beamed Ulvin.

"Silence, both of you," snarled Betterman, suddenly a preacher. "The Lord does what the Lord knows is best. If He wishes to punish us with this Death, so be it. What Grumpelt purports is anathema, pure and simple. The fact that you haven't yet died from the Plague, Grumpelt, is stupefying!"

"All right, then, Mr. B., I'm sorry I shared my conjecture with you," said Ulvin, turning back around and staring ahead indifferently. "I didn't know you wouldn't take it well."

"Not take it well!" Betterman was livid, even in death. "You ought to know Who 'doesn't take it well,' Grumpelt, since He set it on England in the first—"

"Right, right, right. I'll pray for His forgiveness, sir, you have my word."

There were those, Haroldson, Betterman or whoever, who were hard to cope with about their side of the Black Death.

#

Ulvin was fortunately at least partly literate, so that night, before going to bed in his hovel, he used a charred wood stick on a spare cloth shirt to make a diagram, however crude, of his theory of the Plague coming from "indivisible bits." It showed a few small circles labeled as plagg bitz following arrows to "attack" smaller dots around a stick figure, dots shown as mann'z bitz. Five words were underlined beneath the diagram: Stai uwai frumm plagg bitz.

Of this, he was exceptionally proud.

Grumpelt carried this diagram in his pocket to Wakendside's village the next morning. After the usual routine of banging his pot, yelling "Bring oot th'deaaad!" and collecting bodies, he drove the meat wagon toward the graveyard, and about halfway there, looked over at the day's bodies.

"Top've the morniiing!" said Grumpelt, cheerfully.

Up sat twin four-year-old boys, a matronly woman, and a man in his early fifties, all with decayed, festering bodies.

"Guess wot, me friends," chirped Grumpelt. "I have a surprise for you all."

"A surprise?" said one of the boys.

"I've figured out this Plague somewhat," said Grumpelt, beaming with accomplishment.

"I thought it already had been figured out," said the woman with a shredded-skinned scowl. "The Lord's wrath brought—"

"No, no, I mean besides that," said Grumpelt. "I've come to know, through thinkin', what makes the Plague a plague--which I told others I'd figure out, and how we can overcome it. It's simple thinkin', but more 'vanced thinkin' on it in the future—not only in England, but throughout

Europe and prob'ly the whole world—could start a new age of science and reason, just like the ancient Greeks and Romans used to have."

"No fooling," said the man.

"It's all marked down on this swath of cloth I've got in me pocket, here," said Grumpelt. "Just give me a mo to dig it out—"

Grumpelt froze. He just sat there, staring ahead for about a minute. The cart rolled on, but after a few seconds, he dropped the reins.

His eyes bulged, and his teeth grit. Veins started clearly showing, boldly black, in his face and neck. He reared back.

"Oh, no," said the twin boys, in unison.

Clutching his own throat, foaming at the mouth, Ulvin Grumpelt toppled off the driver's seat of the meat wagon, into the mud below.

Within a few minutes, up came a pair of gravediggers.

"Huh. Bugger," one said. "Another wagon driver down, just like the rest of the Death victim haulers."

"Only a matter o time, it was," said the other, "just like all the rest."

"This one wasn't like the rest, not quite," commented the first, looking at the Plague victims strewn across the wagon's carrying space. "D'you see him talking out loud to himself...thinking 'e was talking to the dead,'ve all bleedin' daft notions?"

The two diggers laughed and laughed. "Plague must've gotten to his head, first," one said between mocking laughs. "What else? The Black Death works in ways ye can't explain. Just like the Lord."

They drove the wagon the rest of the way to the graveyard, then proceeded to bury Grumpelt and all the rest who were on it. They didn't bother to change the clothes or even empty the pockets on the bodies, as the sooner plague victims were in the ground, the swifter their judgment for

Heaven would be.

MIND SPORE
Iris M. Winter

1

Annie scrambled to her feet, desperate to escape the confines of the enduring flight. Retrieving the case he always carried, Hutton followed her out into the unwelcoming embrace of the jungle.

A distinctive man stood head and shoulders above the locals. He smiled and walked toward them.

"Welcome to Papua New Guinea. You must be Dr. Annabel Burgess?"

"Please call me Annie, Professor Kent."

Stepping forward, Hutton shook the eminent Professor's hand. "Your picture doesn't look much like you." He held up a book, comparing the fly-leaf photograph with the real thing.

"Ah, publicity shots and field work rarely mix, Dr Hutton."

Several of the natives busied themselves unpacking the aircraft. A number of large metal trunks appeared, followed by tenting equipment and supplies. Last to be unloaded were the numerous Gerry-cans of fuel and a portable generator.

Kent shepherded the new arrivals toward two narrow motorized canoes.

Annie climbed into the first seemingly inadequate vessel. The craft sat low in the gray-green water. Lush verdant canopies hung above her head concealing, she guessed, a variety of tree snakes. A porter sat at the head of the canoe, staring doggedly ahead.

The water rippled a few feet from the bank as a scaly tail disappeared. Annie sent out a secret prayer that researcher would not be on the menu. The second canoe filled with equipment, the first with bodies. Both sank even lower toward the murky water, dank heat rising, slowing in its wake.

Hutton stowed his case safely at his feet while Kent shouted over the noise of the motorized canoes: "Thanks, both for agreeing to assist with this research. I believe some local flora and fauna possess powerful medical applications."

Hutton grinned broadly.

"Please keep your hands inside the canoe at all times. Pacu fish have powerful jaws designed to crack nut shells, with teeth uncannily similar to our own. They have been known to take a chunk out of a fisherman's foot or leg."

Annie folded her arms defensively, the canoe bobbing only inches from the dangerous waters. The two vessels chugged rapidly down the darkly swirling river toward their base camp.

"Your book outlines potential uses of relatively unknown animal and plant sources." Hutton looked uncomfortable in saying any more than that.

"Indeed! Fig wood tea, for example, has very powerful effects. A combination with .1cc of epinephrine can occasionally cause fatal cardiac arrest."

Hutton became animated. "I can't wait to discover more. Annie, did you know the castor oil plant contains ricin – five hundred times more poisonous than cyanine?"

"Yes. My medical training *did* cover the basics of poisons." The insult hung like the gauzy curtain of mosquitoes they were passing through. She checked her exposed flesh for bites.

"I'm sure you both have much to offer," Kent said diplomatically. "Using practical research and fieldwork, the aim is to determine medicinal uses of native plant species."

Annie spotted a small clearing with a welcoming party not far upriver – a heavy-set man and a rather willowy female. They had almost reached base camp. She doubted the availability of a hot shower – it would be necessary to rough it for as long as was needed for the sake of science.

2

Annie shot awake after a restless and sticky night involving a chorus of unfamiliar noises. Emerging from her overly-hot tent, a bright blue parrot with a black beak and yellow rimmed eyes stared from a tree, its head cocked questioningly to one side.

Numerous insects hovered low in the moist air and the sound of voices could be heard in the distance. With haste, she headed toward the noise, rucksack slung over one shoulder.

"Good morning, Dr. Burgess. I trust you slept well?"

Professor Kent was already unpacking equipment with the eager assistance of Mark Hutton. The students were also present and Annie was keen to get acquainted.

"Annie, can I introduce you to my final year PhD students who'll be working with us on this project? This is

Tokie and this is Richard."

The willowy Japanese girl smiled shyly. The thick-set, florid academic raised a pudgy hand in greeting, sweat already permeating his T-shirt.

"It's good to meet you both properly. Now, what can I do to help?"

"Nothing left but to get to the site. Then you can help set up the experiments," Hutton said, appearing to take great pleasure in issuing orders.

Annie bristled, remaining silent. Inter-team rivalry was not a good thing on a small project like this, but the man seemed determined to point-score.

Kent spoke measuredly: "I'd like you to take some samples when we arrive, Annie. Insect life and vegetation. I'd like the others to make a wider search of the area, set up some traps and take photographs. We'll share ideas and finds later today." The canoe swayed dangerously in the swirling Sepik River as the team climbed in. "That reminds me, I've brought breakfast to have en-route," Kent added, unpacking a cooler box.

Choosing a bottle of water and some fruit, Annie found that they sped through the water like a new scalpel through turgid flesh. But she couldn't relax enough to forget the ever-present Pacu, attracted to the splashing of the two canoes as they headed onward.

She glanced across at Kent, who appeared lost in thought. Hutton examined his fingernails rather than make embarrassing eye contact with her. Tokie sat huddled at the back of the canoe, quiet and undemanding. Richard had spread his bulk like a gas filling all available space, his blue T-shirted stomach vying with the canoe's inner sides. A porter steered them toward a suitable drop-off point.

Arriving at a quiet stretch of river to disembark, giant water lilies delicately wafted in

the calm area of water. Their number appeared a solid

floor, tempting the new arrivals to walk across the white-pink carpet.

Annie keenly took charge of the first-aid case and her own small trunk containing Petri dishes, tweezers, and specimen bottles. She hopped from the lurching canoe, scaling the bank to Pacu-free ground. The others followed while two porters expertly brought the second canoe into shore.

She was met by an enticing perfume exuding from orchids vying for insect pollination. Further still, she encountered an array of vivid blue, orange, purple, and pink Heliconia. Their leaves resembled a lobster's grasping claw, the flowers accessible to only the most specialized birds and insects.

"Oh, it is so good to be back!" Kent had evidently followed closely behind, also admiring the colorful display. "We should get samples," he indicated the Heliconia. "Such a marvelous feeling to be unveiling a new shroud of mystery."

He trotted off, happy in his work.

"Found anything good?" Hutton asked, apparently now happy to converse with her.

She shook her head. "Nothing unusual. Only just started really."

Hutton gripped his case, knuckles white in the sweltering heat.

Annie nodded toward the accessory, observing, "You two seem very attached."

He glanced down at his cramped hand, swiftly changing the subject.

"Isn't this such a great place?" Feeling hyped in unfamiliar surroundings, Hutton was fighting it. There was a lot hanging on this trip.

Kent called for his colleagues and Hutton responded like a Pavlovian hound. Tokie and Richard arrived in the clearing, the young girl handing Annie a bottle of water. Richard gave

a perfunctory nod before joining the others, leaving Annie alone in her work.

The setting was a sensual overload of colors, scents, and sounds. Delicately preparing to extract pollen from a neon-orange Heliconia, she sensed company but felt strangely unthreatened. Her gaze met that of an inquisitive spider monkey, dangling by its long tail just a few feet away.

"Well, hello. Have you come to see what I'm doing on your patch?"

The monkey stared, ready to make a quick escape when necessary.

"It's OK, I won't hurt you."

The animal looked as though this was seriously in doubt, skittering away with lightning speed through the tree canopy without a backward glance.

3

It was barely light, night song still hanging in the humid air. Richard Travis fought his way through a densely canopied area of rainforest, the richest and most diverse ecosystem.

He swiped at his moist brow, the pungent odor of unwashed body hitting him as if that of a stranger. Richard saw he was being observed by an unhurried sloth hugging a nearby branch, its long, hooked claws viable enough to disembowel a man if only the sluggish animal could muster the enthusiasm.

Craning back his head in an attempt to peer further into the dense canopy the student over-balanced and suddenly, his world view was that of a prone man struggling to right himself. Among the fallen fruit carcasses left by monkeys and resident sloths, Richard spotted an insect that made him look twice.

It was familiar, yet not so. About a foot from his face sat a giant ant, an unusual protrusion like a plant shoot emerging just above its empty dead eyes.

He had a plastic specimen container zipped in the pocket of his shorts. Musing the consequences of his insect find—for it was his—Travis quickly decided not to share the discovery with commandeering colleagues. His doctoral examination was a few months away. With a discovery like this, anything was possible and he stood to make a name for himself.

Container in hand, Richard carefully unscrewed the lid. How to go about this? Sitting up may disturb the floor covering, burying the precious find. Rolling away might lose its position. He stared anew at his prize then looked up. A sprinkling of white spores floated down toward him from the branch above.

The effect was captivating and he gasped in awe.

Springing impressively to his feet for a habitually non-athletic, sturdy individual, Richard headed back to camp. The heat had increased measurably, but his mind was otherwise occupied. Nearing camp, Mark Hutton stretched outside his tent, although Richard pretended not to have seen him. The other man was reptilian, with glassy pale eyes to accompany his almost albino skin and blond hair.

"What are you up to, eh?"

The insipid eyes glinted in jest, but Travis only heard it as accusation. Clammy fingers caressed the container in his pocket. Hot beads of sweat joined with others, trickling slowly down the back of his neck to pool in the cleft of his back.

"Right. Well, I expect Professor Kent wants us to collect more samples. You can never have enough examples to check out. That's something you should always remember." He gave a knowing, authoritative look.

Travis nodded, stooping to enter his tent. There was definitely something about the man he didn't like, but Richard wasn't quite sure what it was.

Curiosity drew the container out again for one last look. He unscrewed the tightly-fitting cap. There was now a tiny split visible in the insect's protuberance that had not been there before. Had he damaged the carcass in transit?

Richard leaned in for a closer examination, his face only inches away. There appeared to be something moving inside. He pulled away, shuddering. His chest suddenly felt tight, head muzzy. Coughing and wheezing, he wondered if he was starting a cold.

He quickly replaced the lid, hiding the container in his rucksack. Richard wiped his nose and eyes on his sleeve and prepared to join his colleagues. He exited the tent.

"OK? You look a bit spooked."

Hutton's insipid eyes held the question in a prolonged stare and Richard Travis nodded a little too vigorously, instantly regretting it.

"You seem like the sort who can keep a secret and not blabber about it."

The man was in his face again, challenging for an answer to the statement. Richard squeezed himself into a camp chair, his head swimming.

"You see, I'm here with an ulterior motive," Hutton explained quickly, waiting to see if the student gave any hint of a reaction to his disclosure.

He didn't.

With a proud grin, Hutton whispered: "I'm actually doing research into chemical warfare, potential applications of biological weapons for the military. After all, we're always facing new and deadly enemies..."

A scintillation of white light shot behind Richard's eyes. The growing pressure in his head suddenly went stratospheric. "Wow!"

Hutton peered conspiratorially around the empty camp. "Exactly. Maybe you could help me find some kind of neurotoxin in this place. But whatever you do, don't tell the others."

4

Back beneath the canopy where he had found the stricken giant ant, Richard stared up as the

fluffy white spores periodically rained down from above. Transfixed anew by the sight, he was unaware of Kent striding over with Tokie to observe the phenomenon.

"I'll get a container to catch some of this stuff," she suggested.

Richard Travis was wearing a cotton sun hat pulled right down over his eyes. He nodded in response, his mind fighting for normality.

Kent squinted at the receptacle and said, "Watch yourself with that, don't breathe it in. That fungus has a rather sinister tale behind it. Let me tell you the horror story…"

He gave a ghastly and contorted smile.

"As they fall, the spores target the giant ant. The ant breathes them in and the spores spread. They send the ant mad as its brain is slowly liquefied. Whilst this is going on, the ant is compelled to climb the tree from which the spores fell.

"As it does so, the fungus grows outward from its brain, resulting in a protrusion that forms with an opening like a shoot. When the ant is forced by madness to the top of the tree, the protrusion opens to rain down more fungal spores. Ants below then inhale them and the whole process begins again. Pretty gruesome, eh?"

Tokie pointed. "Look! There's a dead monkey up there

in the branches…"

"Can I have your binoculars a moment?" Kent asked, lifting them to his eyes while the cord remained around Tokie's slender neck.

"What does this mean?" Richard asked, already exactly aware of the consequences.

"It means fungal spores have mutated from giant ants to monkeys," Kent confirmed.

"The body has dropped into a hammock of leaves and branches. You can just see the shoot protruding from its forehead.

Hutton appeared from nowhere. "Did I hear right, Professor? Just think, only one step away from mutating into a fungus that could kill a human." Rather than being horrified by the prospect, Hutton appeared to positively relish the idea.

"Dr Hutton, we must first explore the circumstances and possible outcomes before acting."

"Sure. All I'm saying is, this could have huge biological potential..."

Annie arrived through the trees. "What's going on?"

Hutton looked irritated, then replied: "We've found something, but the Professor has advised caution. Probably just best to leave it."

"Not exactly what I implied. What we've discovered, Dr. Burgess, is that spores which infect the giant ant appear to have migrated to a species of monkey – a cross-species hybrid mutation."

"Do we take samples to study the mutation back home, or continue here with our intended research?" Annie asked.

"I vote we get out," Richard said, grimacing.

"There are arguments for both options, I agree. Whatever we do, we must handle it carefully."

Hutton interjected: "We get the monkey down from the canopy, treat it as a bio-hazard and take it home with us.

Better facilities. No humid conditions accelerating decay. We can continue collecting samples then leave by the end of the week. Sound like a plan?"

His face appeared child-like, convincing.

The party looked from one to the other. Kent had the deciding vote.

"I think Dr. Hutton is right. We should retrieve the body and refrigerate it. We have plenty of samples and now something potentially exciting – perhaps as an application in pest control. We'll stay the night and pack up tomorrow."

Annie was disappointed, having just acclimatized to her work here.

"I'll get suited up, get the thing down," Hutton said, delving into his mysterious case to pull out a bio-suit.

"You came well prepared," Kent said, intrigued.

Hutton addressed the enquiry head on: "I brought several in case there were poisonous plants, snake venom, that sort of thing. Here, take these to put in the equipment trunk."

He scaled the tree with relative ease. Gently agitating the branch, a rigid arm swung free from the leaf bundle. Hutton could see the protuberance that emitted fungal spores. Four inches long, it resembled a shoot growing from a potato.

The monkey's long tail anchored it in position. With a firm shake, Hutton caught the corpse as it dropped into a sheet of plastic, securing the edges of the bundle tightly in one fist as he held on with the other.

Hutton unveiled the rigid animal, spreading the plastic sheet on the ground. One paw pointed pitifully toward the branch where it had met its fate. Aside from the protuberance, the body appeared normal.

Annie put a protective arm around Tokie's shoulders, escorting her away from the drama. Rooted to the spot, Richard was brought back to reality when Hutton dug him sharply in the ribs, sealing their conspiratorial bond.

5

Tokie lay restless on her hot sleeping bag. It would do her career good to be in on this discovery, maybe even get mentioned in a scientific paper or two. It was after all she who had first seen the monkey. The unfortunate creature would just have rotted away in the trees, or been eaten by scavengers.

A shadow passed the tent, someone moving about outside. There was certainly no possibility of anyone prowling around the camp: any visitor would have to come by

boat. Perhaps it was someone heading for the camp toilet. Tokie closed her eyes, calming her breathing.

Without warning, a figure suddenly blundered into the tent and rolled on top of the shy Japanese girl before she had time to react. Tokie emitted a muffled cry, establishing from the weight and smell that the attacker was a man.

She fought hard, but the physical weight was no match for her slight frame. A sharp pinch

pierced her neck, followed by an intense jagged pain as what felt like a tube was inserted. She struggled desperately, becoming weaker. Eventually her kicks and cries abated, her limp body a fragile china doll beneath a hammer blow.

By morning the camp had packed, ready to leave. The porters ran to and from the motorized canoes following Kent's urgent instruction that they needed to go, pronto.

Annie grabbed her rucksack and headed over to Tokie's tent, bending to speak softly outside the canvas.

"Hey, I'm just grabbing some fruit for breakfast. Can I get you anything?"

There was no response.

Kent approached, raising a hand in greeting.

Annie asked, "Have you seen Tokie today? Her tent's half open."

"Perhaps she's at the waterfall, having a last dip?"

She shook her head.

The air inside the tent was fetid and musty, the devastating scene horrific. Annie gagged loudly, a hand over her mouth.

"Doctor Burgess?"

"I need one of Hutton's bio-suits!"

"Whatever's the matter?" With a sense of foreboding, Kent entered the tent.

The girl—if you could call the desiccated, mold-ridden form a girl—lay rigid on top of her sleeping bag. The grossly swollen head hung heavily to one side, a gaping neck wound oozing copious pink froth. A bulging forehead and hugely bloated cheeks had compressed the eyes to mere slits.

The canvas was sprayed with an array of blood, tissue, and gray, spongy material. With a cry, Kent recognized it as brain matter.

"We need to leave, now! Can you bear to collect what remains in a preservation bag? I'll tell the others."

Annie nodded slowly and automatically.

She worked quickly to rid herself of the sight. The form was almost potato-like. A mold-infested, shriveled vegetable left too long in a dark, dank cupboard. The specimen bag sealed the shapeless blob safely away. White spores rose from the stained sleeping bag where Tokie had once lain.

Shouts and quickening footfalls suggested the others knew the oriental girl's fate.

Annie met them outside.

"What the hell's happened? Kent says Tokie's dead from some mysterious cause?"

Hutton's insipid, waxy face was a mixture of incredulity and intrigue. His pale eyes glinted as she nodded.

Shock and disbelief rippled through her body.

"It's something I've never seen before. She looks almost mummified, but her head is swollen and spongy. There's a nasty tear on her neck that looks like a point of entry for some type of stinger or proboscis. Perhaps some species of insect – although it would have to be a pretty large predator to attack a sleeping human and make a wound like that. Oh, and there were those fluffy white spores floating around. Completely inconsistent with any known blood-sucker."

Richard Travis gave a short, sharp ejection of a word, almost exhaled as a breath: "Spores."

He clamped his mouth shut. Beads of sweat ran down to meet the neck of his T-shirt. In the heat of the day, under extreme stress, no one noticed the large man – sweating profusely – was incoherent.

6

Wisps of black smoke still rose, testament to the burning of the Japanese student's tent and possessions. Her body encased in a specimen bag was now inside a metal trunk to prevent any seepage.

Guarding the corpses of the monkey and the girl, superstition enveloped the two porters in the second canoe. Their frightened native tongues chattered endlessly.

Rounding a bend in the river, the motor of the first canoe gave a loud belch and the craft fell silent. Annie looked about her as they drifted to the center of the murky Sepik. A reptile on the opposite bank eyed the opportunity, barely leaving the surface water disturbed with its sleek entry.

The second canoe drew up, a porter quickly throwing a rope for them to attach. Kent waved his arms against the idea.

"The motor will probably burn out if we're towed along. We'll have to make camp here for the night."

"It'll take days to get back without a motor!" Hutton yelled, clutching his case tightly.

Richard stared at nothing in particular. His forehead itched terribly and now a lump had formed. His ears rang as white noise pumped through his brain. Incapable of clear thought, he couldn't even remember how he had got here.

No. There was nothing.

Expertly rowing the canoe, the porter sweated in the midday heat. As the expanse of water widened, the currents changed and the boat and its occupants jerked like puppets. The two men in the second canoe were terrified of losing their charges over the side. Or worse, the temporary coffins bursting open…

Kent suggested the porter should rest. Hutton rose slowly and edged forward, his case firmly locked in one hand.

"Leave that behind! You'll need both hands free to row."

"Sorry, Professor. I'm worried it might go over." Hutton grabbed the oars, case safely stowed at his feet. The canoe soon regained some pace.

They pulled into an area free from creepers and low branches. The porter at the rear of the craft eyed the specimen containers in the second canoe.

"Can't we leave those things on the boat?" Hutton asked.

"A little more respect, Dr Hutton. Yes, we don't want the spores becoming unnecessarily agitated."

7

Hutton wanted to get his hands on the monkey. How to play it with the bumbling Professor and the ever-vigilant Dr. Burgess? Richard wasn't a problem – they had an understanding. The fat student seemed subdued anyway, the heat obviously zapping someone so large and unfit.

He mumbled something about looking for a clean water source, case clutched close to his body for security.

Getting here had indeed been difficult. Nonetheless, he'd arranged it so he was the only researcher from his university department available to take up Kent's offer.

Although he'd suffered a few nasty bruises and a hefty insurance claim, that car accident had put Dr. Walker out of action. But what was a written-off car? A mere inconvenience when compared with what the military had offered him in exchange for finding a viable biological weapon.

Hutton heard the rustle of leaves behind him. Shaken from his daydream, he spun around with a sharp cry: "What do you want?"

Annie stood only feet away, shocked by the ferocity of his response.

"I'm s-sorry. Kent sent me to see if there was any water we could boil for tea."

"As you can see, there isn't," Hutton snapped, raising his free hand in a wide circle.

"OK, I'll leave you to it. Whatever *it* is."

Hutton's thoughts were immediately consumed by finding a unique method of killing.

Suddenly, Richard Travis lurched into view.

Heading through the hanging creepers and closely packed trees, Annie stopped dead. She could hear a hushed monologue and listened avidly. From her vantage point, she saw Hutton standing conspiratorially with Travis.

"I'll find a way of rewarding you. But only if you

agree, mind."

Annie studied Richard through the trees. Expression unreadable, his large body appeared uncoordinated in the heat. She strolled into camp a few moments later, slipping inside her tent. So, Hutton was trying to strike up a deal with the student. What was Hutton's big secret?

8

As evening fell, Richard's forehead itched furiously and pain shot through his tender nerve endings. His shaving mirror reflection showed an angry red lump. He tentatively probed, finding the mound squishy and yielding. Squeezing cautiously, he expected an ooze of plasma or pus. Instead, his thin skin split to reveal a white bulge pushing through the hole in his forehead.

The protuberance wriggled slightly. Richard dropped the mirror in repulsion; it landed on his sleeping bag. Mustering courage, he felt the tip of the writhing bulge. It appeared to move freely under his fingertips, responding to his touch like a sucking mouth. Bile rose, saliva dripping between his gritted teeth and down his chin.

Richard trod clumsily, stumbling outside the canvas confines. Alone in camp, he grabbed a bottle of water from the cooler. Drinking it down, he wiped his bile-drenched mouth on the back of his hand.

The protrusion twitched again. He felt the thing—for it was a living creature—push its way further out of his skull as it tested the night air. The invader now occupied a generous proportion of his brain, stunting coordination and reasoning. He fell onto his knees in the dry earth, his actions directed by the trespasser upon its yielding host.

Inside his tent, Hutton heard the thud as Richard went down. His mouth drew tight as a knife slash, wondering what they were doing about food. A colleague dying was one thing, but there were other priorities and life went on.

Richard Travis gingerly opened his eyes to find he was on his back. His head ached terribly, stocky legs lacking coordination, body like clammy jelly. A neon rainbow now played on his retinas.

Managing somehow to stand upright, he possessed no sense of direction. Richard propelled himself toward the nearest tent.

The prone occupant lay in the evening heat, dreaming of elsewhere. It was only a matter of time before things would start to change – big time. A noise outside brought Hutton to his senses.

The tent suddenly caved as Richard lurched through the back. Eyes black and dead, his huge frame filled the entire space. Hutton lay frozen in shock, the speed of the disruption impossible to process.

"What the Hell? Do you want to talk about our deal?"

Zombified, Travis projected himself onto the prone body. Hutton struggled briefly and tried to shout out, but Richard's weight crushed his chest. He kicked out as his carotid artery was punctured by the probing white stalk. Oozing froth cascaded from the gaping neck wound.

Richard crawled on his belly like an invertebrate, unable to raise his bulk upright. Outside the tent, the slug-like form came to rest in the undergrowth. The porters moved unawares nearby, shouting that dinner was ready if anyone wanted it. Tonight, there seemed few takers.

"I'm surprised Richard wasn't waiting by the cooking pots, as usual. Perhaps the heat has gotten to the poor boy," Kent said.

Annie swallowed her forkful of food. Suspicious of the absentees—Hutton predominantly—she wanted to find out more before saying something she might regret.

"Have you worked with Mark before?"

"No. The invitation was for a Dr. Walker to join our

research party, but the poor man was in a nasty car accident. Of course, there is no way he could be here up to his hip in plaster."

"We're lucky Dr. Hutton could step in at the very last minute."

"I'm sure he'll be a great asset."

9

Richard's body lay nearly-dead in a clump of trees at the camp entrance, the occupant of his bloated form guiding every thought since the spores took residence.

Annie reluctantly walked over to Hutton's tent, venturing: "Mark? We're thinking of making a start."

There was no response.

Convinced Hutton was ignoring her, Annie stomped angrily over to Kent.

"Perhaps he took a sleeping tablet last night. I'll see if I can open the tent. These zippers have a habit of not going quite to the top so one can work a finger in and open the flap."

A moment later, Kent's head and shoulders disappeared into Hutton's tent. They reappeared quickly, as if scalded by hot liquid.

"Oh, dear Lord…"

Annie stole herself to take a peek, already knowing the inevitable before it was confirmed. Mark Hutton lay bloated and mold-ridden, neck cranked to one side weeping a familiar pink froth.

She rushed to retrieve a bio-suit, Kent stumbling into a chair to stare unblinkingly ahead.

Sweat poured from her forehead. Annie raised an arm to try and wipe it away, clumsily catching the strip holding the face mask in place. She quickly righted it, but not fast enough to avoid a few rising spores in the enclosed tent.

In panic, she pushed her way outside, grabbing Hutton's briefcase. The partially-closed clasp suddenly sprang open, spilling the contents close to where Kent sat.

"What's this he's been carrying?"

Kent pointed at a satellite phone and modem link that bounced into the range of his left foot. There was also a small computer and a brown envelope.

Annie ignored the CONFIDENTIAL warning, pulling out a passport.

"This isn't him! He's an imposter!"

Kent took it gingerly. The photograph was familiar, but the passport holder was Byron Ellis – a man clearly posing as Mark Hutton.

"So, who is Hutton and why would someone pose as him to come on my research trip?"

Annie pulled the small computer closer. It was password protected with typical Hutton/Ellis secrecy.

Kent cradled his head in his hands.

"Try the word 'Byron'– a reminder he was lying and none of us knew."

Access denied.

"What about 'Papua New Guinea'?"

Annie typed and the computer opened up like an Aladdin's cave. A recent file contained a letter marked 'KENT'.

"It's from the military!" She read rapidly. "He was looking for new biological weapons, for which they have offered a great deal of money."

The professor gave a look of disgust, shaking his head.

"We have to take his body home – even though he wasn't here for the right reasons. Hold on, I've had an idea!" He scooped up the machine, accessing the Internet. Moments later, his eyebrows shot toward his hairline.

"I've just searched the university staff profiles. There's a person calling himself Mark Hutton in the same

Department as Walker, having worked there for a year."

"That means he planned all this months ago. You don't think he deliberately engineered the accident so Walker was out of action?"

Kent shook his head.

"Who knows what lengths he was prepared to go to. I prefer to think that the car crash was an unhappy misfortune. The alternative explanation is too sinister to contemplate."

"His body is bagged up. I'm sure if I persuade them, the porters will make space for another metal trunk on the second canoe."

Kent looked up briefly to meet her glance.

"Oh, what a tangled web we weave..."

10

The tent burned like a funeral pyre for the nightmare. There was no sign of Richard Travis and the porters were looking restless, ready to leave.

"I can't believe this is how it ends – in regret and betrayal," Annie said, reflecting Kent's morose expression. She sniffed. "We should find Richard and get out of here. The whole place has too many bad memories."

With the words barely spoken, she caught a glimpse of movement. Suddenly, the mold-ridden form lurched straight for one of the terrified porters. At the sight of the huge, sweating slug the agile man automatically dodged aside. But somehow, Richard's uncoordinated brain still managed to comprehend, swerving his pungent, squelching body into the man's path.

The porter let out a yelp of fear, stumbling and tripping over his own feet. The clumsiness allowed Travis to make a lunge for the porter's flailing right arm. He cried out, desperately pulling his body from that of the blinded form used to accommodate its new owner.

Tugging desperately at his captured limb, the man swung his body around in order to free himself. The motion caused Richard to pitch forward, releasing the terrified porter as Travis careered head-first into the camp fire.

The rank smell of burning flesh and human hair pervaded the air and Annie put her arm over her nose and mouth to escape its pungency. What remained of the zombified man struggled against his own lack of coordination in the flames, a gurgling sound bubbling from his throat.

Without warning the porter grabbed a Gerry-can of petrol, splashing the liquid over the slowly-cremating, writhing body. It was then that the piteous form gave an inhuman, guttural roar.

The obese, now silent mass continued to burn for hours, excessive body fat causing the flames to spit violently like a hog roast. Eventually the fire died. Only a blackened consolidate remained, piles of gray ash floating upward, mocking the spores that had escaped the other bodies.

Annie watched the porters burn Richard's tent and possessions before loading the last of the equipment into the second canoe. She wanted to escape, return to normality. Her hair and clothes smelt of scorched flesh. The smell would remain in her nostrils long after she had showered the residue away.

The metal trunks containing the bodies of Tokie, Hutton/Ellis and the dead monkey were carefully placed in the back of a battered old truck. The smaller container was treated with less respect, its grisly and potentially deadly cargo known only to Kent and Annie. The truck pulled to a slow stop near to where the little Cessna waited.

Annie tried to force away thoughts of when she and Hutton—who had turned out to be Byron Ellis—had arrived in the same aircraft the week before, meeting Kent for the first time. She desperately wished things had been different, knowing she must learn to accept the horrifying and macabre nature of this ill-fated research trip.

On the home-bound jet, she splashed her face with cool water from the small hand basin then gazed at her reflection in the mirror. Jungle humidity had done her no favors and straggly dark hair framed her florid complexion. Overnight, what looked like an angry red mosquito bite had appeared in the center of her forehead.

Annie gently ran a finger over the mound and found it yielded to her touch. Perhaps a botfly larva, moving around in there. It itched furiously in response to her probing and she scratched tentatively with her nail.

She arranged her hair to cover the area and took another look at herself. It was definitely an improvement, although the irritation remained.

Back in her seat, Annie whispered to Kent:

"It's so good to be getting back to the city."

Nights of the New Dead
DW Milton

Auntie Sarah stood facing the water with a vacant look in her clouded eyes as the wind kicked up, moving her thin, stringy hair. The flaps of her filthy robe undulated in the breeze. Somewhere deep in her cortex, a frayed neuron misfired.

During her thirty-three years, six months, and ten days of life, she loved this spot. The crash of the waves on the rocks. The call of the gulls accompanied by the occasional foghorn of a ship as it safely passed the lighthouse. Yet, in the days following her death, there was only a sagging recognition.

The young girl came up behind her auntie. Her salvaging completed for the day, Linny's shoulders sagged and she barely noticed the beautiful blazing maroon sunset. She wanted to get the woman inside before the new moon crowded the sky.

As twilight retreated into the darkness, Linny took her elder's hand. It was cold because no blood flowed through the vessels. Auntie Sarah's heart ceased beating a fortnight ago, yet, unlike Linny's mom and dad, Sarah was not *the before dead.* She was the new dead, the kind of dead born of the new moon.

Sarah did not acknowledge Linny's touch, not directly. Misaligned synapses encased in her cranium spazzed then faded. Linny gently guided her only surviving family member back to the cover of the tunnel. Linny could see the sickly scarlet glow of the newest body in the earth's orbit grow over the horizon. Sarah's jaw clicked as she ground her teeth.

#

Once secure deep inside the storm drain, Linny left Sarah and headed back to the grate. The youth needed to barricade them inside as she had every night since they moved here from their last hideout.

With effort, Linny shoved the warped wood pallet to the hole she had made in the fence but, before she could lean it back, the large rectangle slipped from her grasp and smashed to the ground with a loud crack. Wood splinters flew. Rusty nails stripped from the rotten wood like naked thorns.

Linny managed to jump back in time but not before her sleeve caught and a jagged metal tip tore across her arm. Warm blood flowed. Biting her tongue, she swallowed a scream. It was dangerous to make any noises at night because outside, the two moons congested the sky and the Carriers were crawling out of their holes, hungry.

She needed to hurry. Linny had learned soon after that night that it was safe to leave Auntie Sarah alone during the day, however nighttime was different. As the new dead did, Sarah tended to wander when the sun slept. Clever, Linny discovered a solution for that; what Linny could not control was keeping the others out.

Two weeks ago, their insulated world collapsed. Sarah's secluded home burnt down in a fire set by Carriers. Although Sarah prepared them as best as she could for this inevitability yet the unexpected happened – a Carrier bit Sarah. Linny was devastated.

Before the plague, the island avoided the notice of most except for the ships that traversed the nearby reefs. Once the plague took hold, many fled the mainland. As with any scourge, it only took one Carrier to poison the rest. Sarah and Linny together survived for almost eight years. Linny could not imagine life without her auntie and therefore she could not leave her.

The hurt girl wiped her tears from her eyes. She had anticipated the wood was rot so she devised a backup plan just like her Auntie had taught her to do. Over the last few days, she collected stones from the shore and placed them in deserted crab traps left at the nearby dock.

She dragged the last rock-filled crab trap in front of the opening and then the exhausted girl headed back down the damp concrete passageway to the ledge. From there she climbed onto the shelf where she pulled the rope to lift the makeshift stairs. With access into the cave denied, Linny set down her bags and sighed. She lit the small candle with a match. As usual, Auntie Sarah stayed where Linny had left her, legs crossed in a lotus position.

The young girl plopped down across from the woman. "How are you this evening, Auntie? Are you hungry? I found some blueberries near Mrs. Jansen's old place."

Auntie Sarah did not reply. She had not said a word since that night yet Linny refused to give up.

"Your studio was not completely destroyed." Sarah's niece reached into a large burlap sack and retrieved a delicate glazed terracotta bird. The Utak was her aunt's favorite piece. The girl took one of Sarah's hands and placed the figurine in the palm. Linny then guided the artist's other hand to the ornament making a little nest. "I found this."

Auntie Sarah remained mute.

Linny yawned. It was getting late and she needed to secure her aunt. She hated to do it, but she discovered the first night after Auntie Sarah had been attacked that the infected are most active when the crimson moon was high.

Linny remembered the initial news reports before the radio stopped broadcasting. Experts described something about the red moon's reflected light that activated an unnatural hunger in the sick. Supposedly, if infected were kept away from the unnatural moonshine, scientists claimed the infected did not exhibit the heightened aggression the Carriers did. Instead, they lingered in a sort of restlessness. However, all bets were off once the ill ate.

Sarah had not eaten since being infected.

The hungry girl munched on some of the blueberries while she watched her auntie. The dim glow of the candle threw shadows that flickered against the damp concrete walls but her aunt remained motionless. Linny removed the thick leather belt she had retrieved from the ruins of their home.

"Do you remember when the birds flew over the house and you grabbed your camera?"

While speaking, she carefully slid the belt around Sarah's waist and secured it to the metal pipes running behind her aunt. "You said it was a good sign and would bring us luck." The girl smiled at the memory.

With her Auntie secure, Linny wrapped a charred blanket around Sarah's shoulders. She then crawled back to her spot and curled up on the singed quilt, the same quilt she brought with her to Auntie Sarah's home the night of her parent's car accident.

Linny laid her head down on her arm staring at the small bird huddled in her Auntie Sarah's hands. Pulling the quit tighter, "I could not find any of your photographs. I really wanted the one you took of Mom and Dad on their wedding day. You know the one in that pretty silver frame." She yawned again, her eyes heavy, "They looked so happy."

Linny's arm throbbed where she scraped it earlier. Tomorrow she would trek down to the shore and clean it in the salt water. She tucked her ragged sleeve around the laceration, which quelled the pain a little, just enough to drift off into a fitful sleep.

#

Without a working clock or watch, Linny had no idea what time it was when she awoke. Sarah stood at the cave opening, like a pet needing to go outside. Linny rolled over on the bedding. Her injured arm burned like fire. She tried to stand, but fell back dizzy. Slowly, she crawled around the cave to collect what she would need for the day.

When ready, Linny directed her auntie down the ledge and out the drain tunnel. Linny hugged the wall as they moved through the passage. Her head swam and her muscles were weak. The girl strained to move the rock filled crab traps and her wounded arm ached afterward.

Linny knew she would have to search extra hard for rations. She was sure once the stone laden traps were in place that night, it might be a few days before she would be able to move them again.

#

The sun was high and the wind carried the spray from the water. Outside, Auntie Sarah, due to either muscle memory or a few remaining synapse connections, meandered to the lighthouse on her own to wait. At the cliff,

Sarah's blank stare failed to acknowledge the small boat or the single figure in it heading toward the shore at the far end of the bay.

#

Despite her best efforts, Linny's scavenging did not provide the couple of days of food she sought. She cursed herself for not keeping up with Mrs. Jansen's garden. It needed tending. The young girl looked at the antique sundial at the edge of the plot. She did not have the energy or time for the task today. Instead, she crept into Mrs. Jansen's cellar to collect the last of the before-dead neighbor's canned goods.

With only a few hours left in the day, her sack only half-full and her body aching terribly, she still needed to wash her wound like her Auntie taught her. Although the cut had stopped bleeding, a red puffiness had set in and her hand looked swollen. In addition, despite the cool breeze off the ocean, Linny was sweating and was very thirsty.

Unable to make it to the shore, her next best option was Mrs. Jansen's well. Using her uninjured arm, Linny pumped the handle freeing a gush of water. First, she drank as much of the cool liquid as her belly could take. Too tender to touch, she could only rinse the cut. Before leaving, she filled her two canteens.

The girl was crouched next to the pump, when the stranger snuck up behind her.

#

She had been groaning for over an hour. The young girl was conscious but delirious with fever. Many times, she cried out for a family member named Sarah.

The stranger did not look up from his meal. At first, he

worried she would be able to untie herself but that was a while ago. Convinced she could not get loose, he had resumed eating the rations he had pilfered from her burlap sacks.

He slurped the rest of the water from the canteen and exhaled a large belch. Leaning against the cool rock wall of the cellar, he relaxed. A refugee on the water for seven days, he had not eaten in the last two.

When things had gone south on the ship, he managed to kill his way to the raft with Sutter and Jeffrey. Then things got bad on the raft so he did again what he needed to do. Finally, his luck had improved when he saw the lighthouse. Once on shore, he thought he had won the lottery when he discovered the old house, its cellar and (he leered at) the girl.

Tired, the survivor dozed as the new moon hit its zenith.

#

Outside, the Carriers bathed in the crimson radiance of the new moon. For the first time since being bitten, Auntie Sarah wandered with them until she reached Mrs. Jansen's property. The exposure to the alien moonbeams reawakened something deep in Sarah's mind.

It was a tender memory of the summer that Linny came to live with her. Sarah and Linny visited Mrs. Jansen to deliver a strawberry rhubarb pie. The fruit came from Mrs. Jansen's garden and Sarah wanted to repay the generosity. Now years later, inside Sarah's new dead brain, synapses slowly awakened, buzzed and sizzled. Lost in the faded memory, she stood outside the abandoned house.

In her mental haze, Sarah cried out even though her brain was full of pathogen eaten holes. As a result, only unintelligible noises escaped her mouth. Caught in an organic loop, Sarah circled the house. She followed the same path for hours, calling out in her garbled speech until her voice cracked. Finally, as the night seeped into day, the woman halted in front of the cellar door and waited.

Linny's auntie had spent the night retracing steps taken years ago with simply her muscle memory carrying her. Although she could feel a budding awareness, it was fleeting yet throbbing within the faint recollection.

Underneath, there was something else. An itch that needed scratching. Since her contact with the ruby moonlight, a new primal sensation flooded her. She needed to eat.

#

Inside the basement, Linny lay bound and breathing heavy, her body fighting the bacterial infection from her laceration. Across from her, the stranger stirred.

Like a shot, the man startled awake, gasping and shaking, unsure of where he was. He jerked his head around. Once he saw the girl, the empty canning jars and the thin stream of weak daylight filtering through the slanted doors, he calmed. Everything was all right, he reassured himself. Although, he could have sworn he had heard something like a groan or maybe a hoarse voice speaking nonsense.

All he knew for sure was that he was famished.

The man stole a quick glance at the unconscious child in the corner. She would stay put. He grabbed Linny's empty sacks and climbed the stone stairs. Touching the wall to steady himself, he removed the boards he had wedged against the doors to secure them during the night. With a grunt, he pushed with all his might.

A blazing morning sun greeted his unready eyes, blinding him. He blocked the light with his hand and in that one gesture, he left himself open for attack.

#

Not a violent person in her former life, Sarah's hunger drove her. A starved beast, she threw herself on the unsuspecting man. Although three times her size, the stranger was no match for the infected woman. Nails tore at his eyes, popping one of the globes. Vitreous ran down his surprised face, pooling in his open screaming mouth. Teeth mashed at his lips and ripped out his tongue in a homicidal kiss.

He fought to no avail. A sick black ooze of coagulated blood tricked down his abraded knuckles as he punched and kicked at his assailant. Only once did he have the advantage when he rolled on top of the woman, pinning her arms but a quick knee to his groin sealed his fate.

Whimpering, half-blind and mute, the man crawled away, attempting to return to the safety of the cellar. The ravenous woman would not allow it.

She pounced like a ferocious tiger, grinding his legs into the earth halting his progress to the door. She seized his head by his hair and pounded his skull into the ground, stunning him. With blackened and torn nails, she savagely ripped open his scalp. Blood sprayed from the ruined vessels, coating her. Licking her lips, she gorged on the gore.

The poor man screamed and gurgled as he choked on his own blood and mutilated tongue.

Auntie Sarah dug in deep for the real meal but it eluded her, encased inside bone. She beat her fists at the skull's surface, screaming in frustration, an addict denied a fix. She scratched and bit at the cranial bone while the man slowly became unconscious from blood loss.

Furious she could not access the food she so

desperately craved, she jumped up and screamed at the limp form. She howled in his ears. In a manic rage, she kicked him in the ribs, rolling and pushing him down the basement stairs. At the bottom step, she heard a sickening crack as his head collided with the stone floor. Fresh blood flowed, pooling around his head.

Uncoordinated, Sarah tripped down the steps and landed next to the stranger's body. Desperate, she grabbed his head again and slammed it against the stone floor. With the blows, the thick skull cracked like an egg, exposing the sweet meat underneath.

#

Now satiated, Auntie Sarah's missing myelin sheaths and corrupted neurons that had been previously ravaged by the infectious pathogens began to regenerate. Occasionally, her hand jerked or her eyelid twitched as the silent electrochemical connections returned.

Reborn, Auntie Sarah stood. As the neural networks reformed and imprisoned neurotransmitters released, her face softened. In the shaded sunlight, the cellar became familiar. A look of recognition crossed her face. The lost memory came into full focus. Mrs. Jansen was gone but a small form lay curled in the corner.

Auntie Sarah took the bird figurine out of her robe pocket and rubbed it, caressing the grooves, tracing the markings. Slowly, the vacant look disappeared as her brain tissue healed. Her eyes cleared. She moved toward the girl and bent down. With a cold, new dead hand, she gently touched the child's feverish forehead then her flushed cheeks.

The woman leaned in and sniffed at her niece. She stopped at the torn sleeve. With loving care, Auntie Sarah slid back the clothing. Under the ripped fabric, the wound festered, dark with gangrene. Linny's auntie smelled the sickly sweet rot of Linny's flesh, salivating. She licked it and then nibbled at the skin and underlying muscle.

Linny groaned and attempted to roll away but her auntie held her tight. Too ill to fight back, the young girl whimpered.

Auntie Sarah glanced over at the stranger's body. She had only eaten half the brain. Auntie Sarah raised her niece's arm like a drumstick and took a massive bite, chomping the infected flesh to the bone. The woman chewed and swallowed. She took another huge chunk of the vile meat and consumed that as well.

Linny's auntie stopped when pink tissue emerged and fresh blood flowed. Transferred through Sarah's bite, the pathogen swam in Linny's blood. Her first death was inevitable, however, once Linny sat in the blush of the new moon and fed on the rest of the man's brain, she, like her auntie, would recover.

Sarah sat next to her niece and caressed her forehead. As the New Dead, they could live and not worry about the Carriers attacking them anymore. Although it was far from an ideal existence, they could still be together as a family.

All Auntie Sarah needed to do now was wait for the night.

The Sorrow
Jen Janet

My name is Tyler Sullivan and today is my birthday! I'm seven now. In the morning, Mommy baked me a cake and we ate it after lunch, with mountains of ice cream! It's summertime, so the ice cream got all melty on my plate, but then Mommy turned on the air conditioner, so it got colder inside our house. I already ate most of the ice cream though. It's chocolate, and that's my favorite.

Mommy and I are in the living room now. She's sitting on the couch watching TV, and I'm playing with Legos on the floor. I'm making a big spaceship from Star Wars. When it's done, I'll show it to Mommy, and maybe I'll even get to show it to Daddy next month when I see him. He likes Legos, too. Daddy doesn't live with us, but I really like visiting him because he sometimes takes me to the movies. He lets me eat all the popcorn I want, and sometimes he buys me Skittles. They're my favorite.

I look toward the couch, and I notice Mommy's mouth is in a big frown, like she's angry or sad. Her eyes are on the TV screen and she looks worried. She's been acting kind of weird lately. Mommy said she'd play with me, but she stares at the TV even more.

Tonight on the news the bald man talks about the new pandemonium. Mommy says it's called a *pandemic*, but I think kids at school were saying it funny. Mommy notices me watching the TV and she says, "Don't worry, Tyler, it only affects grown-ups. You'll be alright."

I don't think she believes that, because her eyes look sad now, all watery. I get up and sit on the couch next to her. I wrap her into a big hug. I don't remember Mommy crying very much, but now it seems like she cries every day. I'm worried about her. She's the best Mommy in the whole world, and I don't want her to be sad.

Her shoulders shake a little bit, and I lay my cheek against her arm. The fabric of her shirt feels itchy on my skin, so I move away. The sound of her sniffling is louder than the whir of the big air conditioner in our window.

"Don't cry, Mommy."

She's dabbing at her eyes now with a tissue. I wish I knew what made her so sad these days. She's been forgetting things, too. Yesterday, Mommy forgot to wash the dishes after all of our meals and it left a big smelly pile in the sink. The trash bin in the kitchen is overflowing, too. I can smell rotten things in there.

"Maybe you should go outside and play, sweetie. Just stay where I can see you," she says. I look up at her to see if she's still crying, but she's heading into the bathroom now and her back is turned away from me.

When she comes back, she has a little bottle of medicine in her hand. The kind she told me never to play with. She said they can make me sick. But when I asked her why they make her feel better, she just told me they're only for grown-ups. They look like white candies.

I watch as she pops two of them into her mouth. She

sees me watching her.

"Don't you want to ride your bike outside?" she asks. "You should go play. I'll call you when dinner's ready."

I'm outside now. Mommy isn't here with me. I'm alone, and that actually feels really weird, because she doesn't usually let me go outside by myself for very long. Even when I wanted to ride my bike with Ben from down the street, who's four years older than me, she still told me I couldn't. I wasn't allowed. Ben is really cool, and there's a huge swimming pool in his backyard. I got to jump in and do a belly flop once.

It's really hot outside and my hands are getting all sweaty. I wonder if it's possible for my fingers to go pruney out here like they do in the bath. Just from being outside. My Mommy said it's from the hoo-mid-it-ee.

Humidity, I think that's how you say it.

I'm not sure what humidity is, but I think it has something to do with water. All I know is, it makes me really sweaty and gross after. I think I want to go back inside.

I'll wait for Mommy to wake up. I can see her through the window, lying on the couch with her eyes closed. She should be awake by now. It's almost dinnertime, and she always makes me dinner on Saturday nights. Mommy didn't take naps before. But lately she's been sleeping for a while in the middle of the day. She must be really tired.

I walk over to my bike. It's leaning against the shed out in the backyard. But I don't really feel like riding my bike today. We have a long driveway where I can ride it, and lots of trees around our house. Mommy says I'm not supposed to go into the woods alone. She says there might be coyotes in there, and they're like big dogs that aren't very friendly.

Then I see something move at the edge of the woods. The leaves are still rustling a little from the movement. At first I thought it was an animal, but now I don't think so. I only saw it for a second. But it looked like a man—a really really tall man—with skinny legs and arms. I keep staring at the same spot where I first saw him. But I don't see anything anymore.

I think he's gone.

Mommy told me not to talk to strangers and I'm pretty sure he's not supposed to be in our yard. Sometimes the neighbors walk through the woods on our side, but this feels different. I'm not sure why.. I think about running inside and telling Mommy. I don't think I should try to follow him because it could be a bad man.

I decide to tell her about it and see what she says. When I get to the living room, the TV is still on but the volume is low. The bald man on the news is still talking about how all the adults are getting sick. But I don't understand it, because they're not getting sick like normal. When I got sick last year, I had a fever of one hundred and two degrees, and Mommy said that was pretty serious. I had to eat soup and stay in bed for a long time. I stayed home and didn't go to school.

It seems like the adults are a different type of sick. They don't have a fever, but sometimes they won't get out of bed. They stay sad all day until eventually, they die. Mommy didn't tell me how. Right now the bald man on the screen is talking about a whole group of grown-ups who jumped off the roof of a big office building downtown. He said there were forty-two grown-ups who did it.

I turn back to Mommy. She's still asleep on the couch, but at least she doesn't look too sad anymore. I reach for the TV remote on the coffee table, but notice the orange bottle of medicine. It's empty. Three of the little white pills have tumbled out of the medicine bottle. But the rest are gone. There's also a glass bottle on top of the coffee table I've never seen before. I reach for it and sniff the top.

Gross! I put it back down. It smells kind of like

Mommy's nail polish remover. Why would anyone want to drink that?

I don't want to wake her up because she's been really sad lately. Maybe she just needs time to relax. Sometimes Mommy says she needs to recharge, like a battery.

I go back outside. I can see into our next-door neighbor's yard. They have a big swing set and a trampoline in the back. Sometimes I play with the girl who lives there. She's seven too, just like me now. Her name is Priti and she has dark curly hair, and her favorite color is pink.

I head toward Priti's house when I see her walking toward me from the side door. As she gets closer, I notice she looks scared. I've never seen her looking like that.

"What's wrong?"

"My dad won't wake up," Priti answers. Her eyes are all red. I think she's been crying too, just like Mommy.

"That's weird," I say. "My Mommy is sleeping, too. But she takes naps a lot now. Maybe your dad is just tired?"

Priti doesn't seem to believe me. But I want to help make her feel better.

"Hey, I have an idea."

"What?" she asks.

"It's dinnertime, right?"

"Yeah… My dad was supposed to make pasta tonight."

"I'm getting hungry. Are you?" I ask her.

"Yeah."

"Then it looks like we can eat whatever we want," I grin at her. "It's my birthday today! Mommy made me a cake. We ate it all, but we still have a lot of ice cream. And I know how much you like Oreos. Want to come over?"

Priti smiles a little bit. "I guess so."

"Come with me," I say, glancing back to make sure she's following. We go into my house, and head into the kitchen. She's been to my house before, and knows where we keep the snacks. But this time, Mommy isn't going to tell us not to eat too much sugar. I tell my friend to stay very, very quiet so we won't wake up Mommy.

Priti grabs the package of Oreos and eats one at the kitchen table. I fling open the freezer door and stand on my tip toes to reach the tub of ice cream. It's really cold and it hurts to touch it for too long. I take down the container and plop it onto the kitchen table beside Priti. Then I get two spoons from the kitchen counter, and we eat the ice cream straight from the tub.

I'm excited. If Mommy found out, she'd scold me and maybe even Priti would get in trouble. But I'm really hungry. I think Mommy was supposed to make dinner ages ago.

Once all the ice cream is gone, Priti announces that she has a stomach ache. I feel fine, but I know you're not supposed to eat a whole tub of ice cream. Mommy told me it's bad for your health. Most of the Oreos are gone now, too.

"Let's go to my house," Priti says. "I want to check on my dad again."

After we're out the door, I gaze up at the sky. It's not as bright outside anymore. The clouds are big and fluffy, colored orange and pink, like cotton candy. I know it will be dark soon.

We see two girls on the lawn at the house across the street. I recognize them because they both go to my school. The tall blonde one is Olivia. Last summer, I saw her do a backflip off the diving board in Ben's pool. It was really cool. She's older than me—eleven years old. She looks really worried. Her younger sister's name is Jess, and she's eight years old. I used to play with her sometimes. I think our mommies are friends.

Jess yells to us from across the street. "Hey, come over!"

Priti and I run down the driveway, but we stop when we get to the street. Mommy told me to be very careful when crossing the road. I look both ways, and Priti does, too. Something feels funny. I notice I haven't heard any cars going down the street today.

"Priti, have you seen any cars today?" I ask.

She thinks for a second. "No."

"Don't you think that's weird?"

She shrugs, and moves to cross the street, so I follow her. As soon as we go into the neighbors' yard, Olivia comes forward and tells us that their parents never came home.

"They're not answering their phones," Jess adds.

Olivia says, "The baby won't stop crying. I don't know what to do." She has a panicked look on her face, and she asks us to follow her. I've only been inside their house once, so I don't remember where everything is.

Olivia and Jess run upstairs and we follow them. We enter their baby brother's room; it's painted blue and white. There's a cradle in the corner, and I can hear a baby wailing. It's really loud, and I don't feel so good. I'm nervous. Something is wrong.

"I think he's hungry," Olivia says, staring at the baby inside the cradle. "I don't know how to feed him. Mom and Dad always do that."

Priti says, "We have more ice cream at my house. Can he eat that?"

Olivia glances down at Priti and rolls her eyes. She seems a little frustrated. "No, babies can only eat special things. Babies can't eat ice cream."

"Where did your parents go?" I ask Jess. I have to speak a bit louder now, because their brother is still crying. Olivia leans over and tries to tuck a blanket around him, but I think it makes him uncomfortable. He wiggles a lot from side to side.

Jess looks at me. She has big blue eyes and they look worried. "Mom said she was going to the grocery store this morning. Then Dad went to look for her when she didn't come back. We don't know what to do."

I think Priti is getting nervous too, because she says, "Let's go check on my dad. Will you come with me?"

I nod, and we tell the girls we'll be back afterward. Once we leave the room, I feel much better. I don't like hearing the sound of their baby brother crying. I want to help, but I don't know what to do.

Priti and I go back outside, and we cross the street again back into her yard. But before we can go inside Priti's house, a boy runs toward us. I recognize him too. It's Ben from down the street, the boy I tried to ride my bike with.

I think the sisters saw him running, because now Jess and Olivia are outside again. They're crossing the street, too. We're all in Priti's front yard, staring at each other. Ben is pale and has a lot of freckles, but today his face looks whiter than I've ever seen it. It's like a ghost from a scary movie.

He looks sick.

I expect him to talk to me, but instead he turns to Olivia. I guess that makes sense because they're around the same age. The older kids always seem to prefer hanging out with each other. Maybe he thinks I'm too babyish.

Ben says, "Something happened to my parents."

"Our mom and dad didn't come back yet today," Olivia adds, looking at him.

Ben asks us to follow him. He leads us up the street toward his place. It's about five houses down from mine. He brings us upstairs, but all the bedroom doors are closed. Ben stops in front of one of them. I think it's his parents' room.

He reaches out, putting his hand on the door handle. He stops for a moment. He's thinking about something. Ben turns to Olivia and says something I can't hear. She looks really scared now.

When he finally pushes open the door, Olivia goes inside. Priti, Jess, and I move to look in, but Ben stops us. He's blocking the door with his body now. He doesn't want us to see. Why is he letting Olivia see instead?

A second later, Olivia rushes out of the bedroom. Her back is against the wall, and she starts to sob. Ben slams the door shut, and it makes a loud noise. He looks at Olivia, and he starts to cry, too. I've never seen Ben cry before, and it makes me a little scared.

"You should call 911," Olivia says to him.

"What is it?" Jess asks, tugging on the bottom of Olivia's shirt. "What's in there?"

Her sister won't answer.

Ben jumps up and runs out of the hallway. He moves down the stairs, and his footsteps are loud and clunky. Olivia follows after him.

"Wait up!" she calls.

Ben hasn't stopped running. We're all outside now. Ben crosses the street without looking for cars first. I still haven't seen any drive by. He's in the backyard at my house now, all of us are following him, sprinting across the grass.

Ben stops and falls to his knees right next to the shed. He's shaking. Olivia catches up with him first, and she puts her arm around him.

He's crying.

"It's the sorrow," Olivia says quietly, turning back to us. Her face is stained with tears. She's sitting on the ground with Ben, and his head is low, his hands covering his face. "It's just like they said on TV. They call it the sorrow."

"Where's Mom and Dad?" Jess asks her sister. She's afraid. I can hear it in her voice.

Olivia looks like she wants to say something to her, but

then we hear a rustle in the trees. I turn to look at the woods.

We watch as four people emerge from the trees. I call them people because I don't know what else to call them.

They're not like us.

Their faces look like ours, but otherwise they look different. The not-people are very tall and skinny, even taller than Mommy and Daddy. They all wear strange black clothing. It looks hard, like it's made from plastic or something. It doesn't look very comfortable.

The not-people walk closer to us. Priti is next to me and she takes a step back.

I'm scared.

They don't have any hair on their heads, so they remind me of the bald man on TV talking about the news. Their eyes are like ours, but black. There's no white inside them at all. There's only black. I can't tell if they're girls or boys, either.

Ben scrambles to his feet and clings to Olivia. Jess tries to take a step back but she falls over onto the ground. I can't believe this is happening on my birthday. It feels like the cake and ice cream with Mommy happened so long ago.

I have a really bad feeling about the not-people. I'm wondering if I should run away. But they might be faster than us. I don't know what to do. I wish Mommy was awake. She would know what to do. Maybe if I scream really loud, she'll hear me.

Before I can do that, I hear a voice in my head. All of the not-people are staring at us. I'm not sure how I know that, because their eyes are all black so I can't tell exactly where they are looking but somehow, I know they are staring right at me.

Do not fear us, the voice says. *We want to help you.*

It sounds pretty, like how I would imagine a prince or princess in a storybook would speak. I know the not-people are talking, but their lips aren't moving.

"D-do you hear that?" Ben whispers.

I nod, and so does Olivia. I think the not-people are talking to all of us inside our heads.

I hear the voice say, *Our home is very far away, and we've traveled for a long time. There is something wrong with our home, and it's dying. We are looking for a new home. Do you understand what we mean?*

They wait. Slowly, I turn to look at my friends. Olivia and Ben nod.

Good, the voice says. *Your home is much better, but it is dying, too. It's dying because of what the older ones have done to it. Do you know what they are doing to your world?*

We all look at each other. Priti and Jess seem like they are about to cry, and Ben and Olivia look terrified. Ben is even more pale than he was before. He's the color of the white sheets on Mommy's bed. I don't know what to say.

But the voice continues, *We noticed the young can be taught how to take care of this world. The old ones stopped caring about preserving your home. We don't understand why. But if we allowed them to continue, your world would die long before we would all be able to live here, too. And so, we created the sorrow.*

I see a tear run down Olivia's cheek. Ben is crying again, too.

Come with us. There is nothing to fear. Together, we will rebuild your world. We will teach you how to preserve it. Everything will be much better for all of us afterward.

The not-people step closer to us, and I see the leaves on the trees behind them shake. I think there's more of them in the woods. A moment later, two other not-people come forward from between the trees. Then three more. Then another. And another.

We are your parents now.

The Man Who Sold the World
Ricardo D. Rebelo

I sat on the train heading to Fall River, Massachusetts from Boston. Massachusetts residents refer to it as "The T." I take this train and this route every day. Even though I work at New World Bio Labs, I still don't make enough money to live in the city proper.

It was hard looking at all the faces of the people I was going to kill on the way home. My only consolation is them not knowing I have killed them yet. They had a little while left.

At least they had that.

"You're gonna be OK," the woman on my left said.

"I'm sorry?"

"I said you're gonna be OK. You're crying, whatever it is you're gonna be OK."

I reached up and wiped the tears in my eyes.

"She hurt you real bad, huh?"

Her? She thought it was a woman. The old woman in the yoga clothing thought I had a broken heart over a woman.

She was right.

"Yeah, a woman," I said and finished drying my face. My hands shook while doing so. She reached over and took them into hers.

"Whatever she did. You are going to be OK. You're young, and there are plenty of fish in the sea."

"Fish, yes," I said.

I'm going to kill all the fish.

Every… single… one.

I stared at the older woman's hands. They were the hands of a woman who had lived her entire life with privilege. Perhaps not filthy rich because she was riding the train but from the Lulu Lemon outfit and Patagonia down puffy jacket and headband I would say she didn't spend a lot of days eating instant ramen.

Her death would affect a lot of people.

Once she grabbed my hands the door closed on her life, even if she didn't hear it.

"What's her name?" she asked.

I chuckled knowing the name would make her chuckle. "Medusa."

"Medusa," she said and cupped her hand over her mouth to stifle a laugh. She was doomed now. I felt like a bastard knowing that.

Medusa was a project we had been working on with the Department of Defense. It was a bioweapon that would cause all the muscles in the human body to become completely rigid including the heart. It was intended to use against populations of people who opposed the current government in foreign countries. The goal was to code it to a specific genetic pattern so you could customize who would be affected by it.

They never met the goal.

Last week, while working on a particular strain, Marty Smith—a biologist I worked with—was exposed to the virus in its raw form unbeknownst to him. When it began to kick in, Marty began to sweat profusely and then suffered from a type of mania.

He grabbed Carol Jones his lab tech by the neck and bit into the back of her head right below the skull and tore a chunk of flesh out with his teeth. Carol initially ran from Marty but not far. She collapsed on the polished tile floor and bled out from her wound. Marty went back over to her and dug his fingers into the wound he created.

I was frozen in fear during the entirety of this ordeal. It took a while and a lot of reflection to understand what I was seeing but being a man of science with good skills of deduction I was able to figure it out.

Marty was infected. The infection had caused his body temperature to soar to what I would guess was somewhere in the 107- or 108-degree range and had cooked his brain. That was when the mania kicked in. It must have set off an urge to sate itself by consuming the pineal gland in another person, sadly that was Carol.

I bolted from the lab, slipping in Carol's blood. The hallway should've been empty. Instead, it looked like a war zone. Bill Wilder was—God help me—beating Sadie Hawkins with a water cooler tank. Marty had always been an extrovert and probably shook hands and told jokes to everyone in the building on any given day.

It looked like the entire staff of New World Bio was trying out for a gladiatorial tournament. People were hitting each other with chairs, phones, desk blotters, anything they could grab.

Those who had defeated their enemies were doing what Marty had. They were biting or digging into the backs of their foes' heads.

It must be the pineal gland they were after.

At that angle it would be the fastest way to it. It was a craving that was consuming them.

But the big question for me as I witnessed all this carnage was… Why wasn't I sick? It must be something in my genetics that I did not share with my colleagues.

Jimmy Rogers, our IT guy, had finished dispatching our custodian when he turned to me. I could see the vessels in his eyes had burst and painted his corneas an impossible shade of bright red.

That's when I just ran…ran until I got to the T- Station, until I got on this train. I didn't think about the repercussions until it was too late. My desire to survive surpassed the awareness of what it would cost others – cost everyone.

Now, looking at the old woman's face, knowing what comes next, the truth sat in my gut like a stone.

A trickle of sweat formed and beaded on her forehead.

Could it be happening that fast?

I had to think of a plan. There wasn't any contingency set up yet for Medusa, no antivirus, we hadn't gotten that far.

All I could do was run…until… when? Where?

I would hide in my apartment at the Artificer until this blew over. It was an old mill building they converted into apartments.

It would be strong. Lots of good places to hide…I think.

Then when things blew over I could steal an abandoned car from one of the victims and hide in an abandoned house on the Cape. I love the Cape. It would be so quiet after everyone killed each other or turned to stone.

A little girl sitting across from the old woman coughed.

Shit, I killed this little kid.

She was just sitting there watching YouTube videos on her mother's phone. Her mom, still in her nurse uniform was taking a nap. I hope the video was something she really enjoyed.

It would be her last, after all.

Should I just kill her now and get it over with? Would she suffer less If I just throttle her in front of her mother and the old lady. They would probably think I'm crazy.

Maybe they would be right?

How do I know Medusa is not in my brain right now giving a head full of dark intrusive thoughts?

Maybe I should just try to kill as many of these people as I can here and now before they are at each other's throats. At least if I did that I would be taking ownership of what I did or am doing. Not sure what tense is appropriate here.

But they should know this is all my fault and if they rip me to shreds wouldn't I deserve it? Would being beaten to death on the south bound T Train be an appropriate penance for unleashing an apocalyptic virus on the world be adequate penance?

Fuck.

Why am I being so philosophical?

A sneeze from the end of the compartment blew me out of my introspection. It was a guy in his thirties wearing a shirt that seemed three sizes too small for him. You could tell he spent every free moment at the gym doing arm and chest workouts. Every inch of flesh that was exposed looked vascular. I bet if I asked him he could tell me his body fat percentage precisely. He probably carried a fat caliper in his pocket.

I could imagine his hands around my neck if he knew I already killed him. The veins in his face pulsing with testosterone enhanced energy looking to cut the oxygen from my body. With his strength he could probably tear my head from the shoulders and rip out my pineal gland like he was getting the meat out of a pistachio.

If things suddenly went south in this compartment he would look like a juicy meal to the infected. That may be my only hope for survival. His arteries laid out like a topographical map on his synthetically tanned skin. A superhighway for the infected to travel.

Despite it all, he sneezed.

He must be furious about that.

How could his fine well-tuned body have a flaw in it? He worked so damn hard to be in tip top shape and…he sneezed again. This time he had the speed and temerity to lift his forearm and sneeze into that. He was at least being considerate to the other passengers.

Unlike me.

The train PA whistled and then announced.

Next stop Freetown, all passengers looking to depart, Freetown.

Normally I would have no interest in Freetown. There was nothing there, but a forest filled with Pukwudgies and satanists. At least those were the legends people told of the dark strip of woods known locally as the Bridgewater Triangle. But maybe, just maybe that would be a suitable place to hide until this all blew over.

Whatever this turned out to be.

Maybe I would be wrong. Maybe someone did develop an antidote or will develop one quickly.

Who's to say?

The little girl coughed again.

Shit.

The old woman took out a monogrammed handkerchief and wiped her forehead with a clean end of it.

Double shit.

The muscle head sneezed again. This time it came too fast for him to catch, and I could see a strip of mucus come out of his nose and connect to his tank top.

Fuck!

It was like I was watching a shitty action movie where they do a split screen between the hero and the timer on the bomb and your heart would beat in anticipation to see if he would save everyone in the stadium, or bus, or whatever was going to blow up.

Except here I couldn't see how much time was left and there was no blue wire for me to cut and save the day. My attention now bounced between the old woman, the young girl, and the muscle head. Which one of them would snap first? Who would succumb to the mania?

I can't do this. I got to get off in Freetown. I covered my face with my hands in hopes of masking the horrors I might have to see.

"Sir, would you like a tissue?" a voice said.

I must have been crying again. Fuck, these were nice people. I know in the surrounding New England states people often referred to us as Mass holes, but I always thought that was overblown.

I began to pull my hands down and said, "Thank," and before I could add, "you," I could see that it was someone offering a tissue to the muscle head. Mucus was coming out of him now in a river of filth. The blood vessels in his eyes were starting to grow wider and redder with the threat of exploding.

I had to watch the whole thing unfold and take the blast head on. It was too much to handle so I decided to confess to the old lady.

"Look, I need to tell you something," I said to her.

"Yes," she said as another bead of sweat marched down her forehead.

I felt a shudder coming from deep inside of me. My soul felt like an engine about to rattle to pieces. The old woman looked like she was not faring much better than me. The corners of her eyes were tight as well as the edges of her mouth. Her jaw was moving, clenched but grinding. There was a war going on inside of her. She had decided to fight it alone and she was paying a price for it.

"I work for this company, you probably have never

heard of it, it's called New World Bio labs it…" I trailed off because the grinding of her teeth had become so intense I could hear them push back and forth over each other. Her pupils had shrunk to pin pricks, and I could swear she was looking through me more than at me.

"Go on, you were saying," she said through a mouth full of gritted teeth. There was a tinge of red in those teeth – blood red.

"I was saying that I work for this company called New World Bio Labs and the government gave us some money – a lot of money to…

Blood was now trickling out of the corner of her mouth as the grinding intensified. This woman wasn't going to make it to the end of my confession.

"Mommy, my head hurts," the little girl across from us said, still staring at the phone screen. Beads of sweat were dropping from her forehead and landing on the screen. This was agitating her and affecting her enjoyment of the music video she was watching.

"You'll be fine, honey," her mother said without opening her eyes.

The song, *"Bring Your Daughter to the Slaughter"* from Iron Maiden started playing in my subconscious.

"You were saying," the old woman said reminding me I was in the middle of confessing to genocide before the little girl won my attention. I turned back to her and could see that her entire chin was now coated in blood and bile.

The train bounced on the track a bit and took everyone's attention away. The driver engaged the brakes, and the commuter train slowed before it stopped in Freetown.

The muscle head stood and roared like the Incredible Hulk. He even stretched his arms back and flexed into a Hulk pose. Almost on cue his shirt, which had been two sizes too tight tore at his biceps and chest to add to the effect. All the vessels in his eyes had finally burst, giving him a demonic look on top of all the other theatrics he had brought to the commuters.

The old woman, not to be out done, stood and pointed directly at the muscle head as if to acknowledge that he was either a teammate or the enemy and let out a screech which came with a tsunami of not just blood from her mouth but the entrails that had once held her together.

The train compartment now looked and smelled like an abattoir. The other commuters would have been terrified if they had still been in their right minds but alas they were not.

The little girl now spat out her entrails over my shoes and turned to her mother and bit her on the neck almost as revenge for neglect.

But I knew better.

I knew what they were all looking for.

The train jolted as it came to the stop. I wondered if the commuters in the other compartments had any clue what was going on in ours?

They would find out soon enough.

The doors slid open, and I threw myself out of the train car. I landed on the cement platform with a thud. I turned to look back at the car out of instinct. The old woman was on the muscle head's back now. She clung to his back like a second spine, tearing through his neck. She had already bitten off one of his ears.

There were people on the platform watching this in horror. They were screaming for help. They yelled for someone, anyone to call the police.

An older man who looked like a college professor long since retired came to check on me.

"Hey, buddy, are you OK?" he asked.

I didn't have the strength to respond.

He was already dead, and he didn't know it.

My involuntary killing spree had only just begun.

The Burning of Our Souls
Hannah Baxter

He'd seen hundreds of fires before but never one that erupted from a man's chest.

It had started off as another ordinary day, as much as it got for Garrick. At the warning trill of the bell, he'd spiralled down the bronze fireman's pole and lugged on his heavy mustard-colored overalls. No matter how scuffed and mud-encrusted his old boots got, the intense routine always made him feel alive.

Despite the severity of their calls, Garrick couldn't restrain the childlike joy that flared in his chest when the guzzling engine roared to life and the light bar flashed out. It was his eight-year-old self's dream come to life; the wind tearing through his scalp through the open window. The top ladder rattled down on them on the roof atop its heavy telescopic boom.

The fire had been called in at seven that morning, a Code 3, which required the most rapid response possible. Garrick's rubbered metacarpals creaked with each preparatory flex. It had only been a twenty-minute drive down from their station, which even with the morning traffic influx of honking commuters, their ETA would be about 7:52, give or take. In this business, every second counted.

Garrick sat in pensive silence. Ronnie Black was two seats away from him, leaning back with his arms folded behind his back as if they were headed out on a leisure trip. Tufts of rusty red hair peeked out from under his switched off safety lamp, his uniform inflated around his lanky frame like a circus tent.

His spry limbs could maneuver him through tight spaces, that the much stockier Garrick could only dream of entering. As if gifted with some kind of extrasensory perception, Ronnie picked up on Garrick's removed staring. He turned around and gave him a devilish grin, which paired with his already oversized helmet, made him look far younger than he already was.

"This sure beats the office, huh?" he chuckled.

Why Ronnie had even bothered with him in the first place still baffled Garrick. Garrick was a wallflower, growing in the faint cracks, with a tendency for long, uncomfortable silences, which coupled with his size, made people even more uneasy around him. For this reason, he preferred to watch around corners rather than interact.

Ronnie, on the other hand, threw himself into social situations at any given opportunity. He had a magnetic personality that drew those around him in, regardless of their temperaments. Before the day that they had first met was even over, Garrick found himself sitting on the neighboring stool beside Ronnie's at the local bar, clinking pints together.

Ronnie was a certified adrenaline junkie, having sat Garrick through a slideshow of life-risking activities, such as climbing to the first base of Mt. Kilimanjaro or grinning out from a cramped tunnel in Mammoth Cave National Park in Kentucky, hundreds of miles under the ground. Like any addict, Ronnie was always in search of his next fix, which was when he had found firefighting. He was endangering himself again, only this time he was getting paid. That was his reasoning for it.

Garrick envied and pitied Ronnie's blitheness, how he was able to stumble through every situation with only a smile on his face afterward, as if he kept a four-leaved clover tucked inside his front pocket. Garrick shook his head. Every time they made it through unscathed couldn't erase others' losses.

The house was already engulfed by the time they got there, the fierce flames burning it down to bare wooden bones. A woman in rollers with messy mascara streaming down her middle-aged jowls wailed on the front lawn. Garrick was certain some kind of accelerant could only make the combustion this ferocious, concluding it was a clear-cut case of arson. But he kept that conclusion to himself, at least until the paperwork had been filed out.

The battalion chief was 'Big' Bill Tillery, a man whose very name made even the most jovial among them straighten their backs. He was a stern man with a gunmetal gray moustache. Garrick was no slouch in the height department, but he was eclipsed by the meteoric Bill. He was a true veteran of the force, having been in active service since '83. He'd extended his services in 2001 to New York, where he'd pulled survivors out of the asbestos-choked rubble of the World Trade Center. Since then, he had smiled only once in a blue moon.

"Eyes up," he barked, guttural yet restrained, like a trained rottweiler.

As he and the rest of the team had begun to set up a safety zone, the woman's arm vined around him, her absurdly long garish cream-tipped fake nails skimming over his shin.

"Please!" she cried, "Please, you have to go inside, my

husband's in there!"

Her ragged pink dressing gown flapped open in the wind, the lapping straps catching the floating embers, all that remained of her life. Forgetting the immediacy of his duties, Garrick bent down.

"Don't worry, ma'am," he assured, "we've got this."

It was the standard reassurance people in the service paid to civilians on-scene to prevent them from interfering. But Garrick was determined to make it a reality.

He smashed through what remained of the door with his axe, searching around the room which was rendered unrecognizable by the ravenous flames. The curtains had been eaten away by the overwhelming heat, which clogged the visor of Garrick's mask with heat and soot, forcing him to squint through. The ceilings were oriental standard board. Tough and common, cost-effective material used in a frightening number of buildings, it became a death trap when a naked flame was applied. Garrick was surprised that the building had stood for that long without incident.

The flank of the fire, flaking molten plaster down was enclosing in on him. As well as that, the thought of backdraft never left his mind. The room was stuffy to an unbearable degree, even with two weighty oxygen cylinders connected to Garrick's breathing apparatus. The lack of ventilation meant that an array of combustible gases was building up, swirling into a ball ready to hatch out into an inferno. Backdraft had taken out more than a few good men in his experience there. He had to find the man now, before it was too late.

"Hello?" he called out over the roar of the fire, "anyone in here?"

A ghostly moan echoed out from down the hallway. The thermal imaging camera on the temple of his helmet picked up on a vivid heat signature. His heart leapt with hope. Garrick chased after it, weaving his way through a shower of debris from the collapsing upstairs.

"It's okay! I'm—"

Garrick's throat dried up into silence. For a few baffling moments, he forgot

he was standing in the middle of a burning house. He blinked, wondering if what was in front of him was real or smudged into being by his condensation-smudged visor.

A paunchy, middle-aged man with a receding curly black hairline sat in a flaming brown leather Winchester reclining chair, the footrest still up. He stared at the disintegrating wall with a glassy, doll-eyed stare, dressed in only a pair of graying Y-front underwear.

Garrick had seen people burn alive in front of him. The agonized spasms as they flapped at their combusting bodies, the uncontrolled blaze eating away their flesh and melting their muscles was not a sight that was easily forgotten. The man was unconcerned by the tongues of fire licking their way from his feet up. From the languorous but visible shutter of his eyelids, he was completely conscious but lacked the motivation for any self-preservation.

"Sir? Hello?"

A heavy joist dislodged from the ceiling and rocketed down like a downed satellite from the night sky, tailing flame rising to join the others marching across the floorboards. Garrick strained out a gloved hand toward the man.

"Come on!" he cried.

The man stood. He shambled toward Garrick, a charring cape draping his bare hairy back. He stopped just a few feet away from him. Then, the man opened his mouth, wider than should have been humanly possible. The revolver crack of his dislocating jaw echoed in Garrick's mind long after.

The superficial veins lining his forearms bulged through the skin like a colony of scarlet tubeworms through wet, translucent soil. He vomited out a torrent of pure flame, like an expert fire eater regurgitating a lit, twirling baton. A miniature jet ruptured from his sternum, like an even more hellish interpretation of the wriggling chest burster from *Alien*. Garrick recalled squirming at the scene as a child through the half-open spaces of his fingers while his brother cackled, shovelling popcorn into his mouth. Now, the nightmare was real.

Garrick gaped on in mute horror as twin jets erupted from the man's orbital sockets, sizzling away his reddened sclera like egg yolks abandoned to blacken on a hot stove. The force of the blasts forced him back. Garrick raised a hand to his eyes to shield them from the explosion of unearthly bright light that consumed the front room.

It was Ronnie who'd saved him. He had dragged him out, dazed from the cindering interior wall that had fallen on top of him in his cindering limbs. When Garrick regained his senses, they had descended the towering inferno and were on the ground, staring up with breathless, soiled smiles at the overwhelming blue of the sky.

The welcoming breeze combed through their helmet-ruffled hair. Both men soaked in an aurous ocean of sunlight, grateful to have survived another day. It was the only lucid part of that day. The rest had been a blur of flashing lights and overlapping voices. All the while, Garrick kept his head to the ground, trying to understand what had happened.

In the aftermath of the incident, the consensus had been that an underlying sewer pipe running directly under the living room of the house had resulted in the explosion that had killed the husband. Garrick had been vindicated of any blame but was chained to his own guilt like a condemned man shuffling down the green mile. He wanted to believe the official excuse, to erase away that incident. The human body was eighty percent water. How could a person just burn up like that, without any outside source?

The absence of reaction had further raised the level of concern of those around him. He had been called into Big Bill's office. A framed photo of him shaking hands with the mayor sat adjacent on the cream-colored wall. Various medals and other appraisals glittered off the various shelves, but none were as coveted as the chipped WORLD'S GREATEST DAD mug that sat at the corner of Bill's computer keyboard. The seat creaked beneath Garrick's considerable frame. The nightmare scenario of it breaking flashed through his brain like lightning, potent enough for him to cringe. Aware of Bill's slight bemusement at his sudden facial paroxysm, he erased the expression from his face.

Bill Tillery tented his large, weathered hands that looked like they could tear a phone book in half. As he did so, the golden slip of his wedding ring tilted down his finger to the middle phalanx.

"There's no shame in taking time off. This kind of thing can eat someone alive from the inside out. You're a good man, Griffith. I just don't want to see any more go down."

Garrick had been first introduced to the concept of spontaneous human combustion at around six or seven. Somehow, along the years, the memory had slipped, like a spare set of keys down the side of the couch, so distracted by the comfortable routine of mundanity that their existence was forgotten. But like a trigger phrase awakening an undercover sleeper agent, the memory had been reignited by the burning man.

The Char Man. It was a name that had struck fear into the hearts of generations in the Ojai region. Like every good urban legend, the truth was overlaid by elaborate onion layers of eye-watering ambiguity. Some swore it all began in 1948, when a man had been cruising down the road in his gleaming new Ferrari 166 Sport when he had veered off the road and into a tree. Flames had spurted up from the crumpled hood and engulfed the man, and he had run past the good Samaritans that had assembled on the scene screaming into the dark border of woods, still enwreathed in flames.

Others held onto an even earlier variation of the story, that stretched back into settler times, where a man and his wife had lived a grueling life in a small rural log cabin. That was until the man had gone mad and set fire to the place while his wife had still been inside. It was said that he stood outside and watched her scream and claw at the glass as the fire inched ever higher behind her multi-layered petticoats.

Whatever the story, the unanimous opinion was that a living flame flickered out in those woods in the dead of night, fueled by hate and ready to turn anyone foolish enough to venture out there into its kindling. It was said the Char Man could burn up someone like a Roman Candle from ten feet across with only a wave of his skeletonized hand. One of the kids at school, a wild-eyed gap-toothed boy by the name of Bruce Peterson had sworn on his grandmother's grave that he had seen it happen with his own two eyes to a friend of a neighbor's cousin.

The tale dripped down like wax from a candle into Garrick's subconscious, solidifying into nightmares. The Char Man would chase after him in all his carbonized glory, the peeling flesh of his face melding with the tattered, burnt fabric of what was once his clothes, becoming a deathly moult.

Despite his legs being burnt down to clacking, rickety tibias that shone through in the waning moonlight like a dog's half-buried bone, he was a surprisingly fast runner. He pursued Garrick with an Olympic speed. No matter how far he tried to run, the monster would always be inches behind him. Just as his undead claws swiped down to claim

Garrick, he would awake screaming and thrashing off the soaked sheets of his own bed. It invoked a terror in him that he couldn't explain.

Following the incident, Garrick pursued spontaneous combustion with a scholarly interest and soon found out that the Char Man of his childhood night terrors wasn't an isolated case. The term had first come along in 1746, but it was only in the advent of the twentieth century that cases seemed to have occurred with alarming alacrity. There was Mary Reeser, the plump unassuming widow who was found to have been burnt down to just a shrunken skull and a single smouldering leg when her neighbors had been alerted by an intense heat that radiated from her room.

The most recent had been in 2010. One of the earliest cases, stemming from the seventeenth century, before it had even had a name, where an Italian countess had gone up in smoke, had even inspired the demise of Krook in Charles Dickens' *Bleak House*. Garrick, who had read that same book dozens of times over as a teenager in his messy, closed-off bedroom until the corners of the pages were folded-up, was stunned that he had only made that connection now.

Unable to withstand any more lithographs of burnt corpses, he had ripped himself away from his chair, leaving the extensive document that he had been compiling open on his computer. Not even bothering to put on a coat, he stormed out the front door into that day's downpour. It soaked right through his thin checkered undershirt, but Garrick stood there with his arms open, embracing it. All the guilt and confusion that had haunted him like a persistent spectre was washed away through the thin sewer grates, agglomerating with all the other detritus of society.

Garrick soon realized he'd bitten off more than he could chew with the downpour. He rushed to find the nearest shelter, a corrugated iron tin roof, the remnants of an old bus shelter that had been left to rot long before Garrick was born. The relentless rain plinked down through the time-worn holes, pinpoints of light swimming in the shadows like a flotilla of halos. In the darkness, somebody coughed. Startled by the sudden noise, Garrick jerked around. Had he really been so lost inside his own head that he hadn't noticed someone standing just a few feet away from him?

A woman leaned up against the stripped paper interior of the old bus shelter. She rinsed out a rain-soaked ringlet of hair between her index and thumb, blonde-brown tresses darkened to a near complete mahogany by the sudden unpredicted downpour. It was held back into a low ponytail by a cheap pine-green scrunchie.

She scratched at the stiff mandarin collar of the red-double-breasted, cotton twill long top she wore with fingernails dappled with chipped dueling shades of pink and deep purple. Her black slacks swished as her feet beat a rapid rhythm into the ground, as if it was against her nature to stay still. The formal wear clashed with the relaxed aura she exuded. She returned only a nonplussed look at his hitched breath.

"It's okay," she held up her hands in weak surrender, "I'm definitely not a ghoul or anything."

Neither of them knew what to say next. Engaged in a stressful social version of Russian roulette, they avoided making eye contact with one another, each dreading the inevitable next click of conversation in the revolving chamber. They stared out ahead into the light, at the pylon-stabbed hill ahead, a left over from the bronze age.

"So," she broached, "you an eighty-sixer, too?"

Garrick blinked as the woman looked him over.

"Eighty-what?" he asked.

"Eighty-sixed. You know, sacked, dumped, canned, career alternative enhancement," the last one seethed with a particular venom, "fired."

Unsure of how to respond, Garrick only gave a courteous shake of his head.

"Very much employed, I'm afraid."

The woman sighed and shook her head.

"Damn. And here I thought I'd found someone to share my misery with," she laughed at her own suggestion, "nah, no-one deserves that. Still, got to look on the bright side. We've found a roof over our heads. Do you know how long it takes for others to find that after they get the slip? Months, even."

"The roofs I'm under are usually collapsing in on me," Garrick added.

The afterimage of the man blaze sizzled through like nitrate film stock, unseen by his companion. The woman sucked her teeth.

"Wow. I'm guessing you're not an accountant."

It was the first time Garrick had laughed in months. He was at ease enough to give out a greeting to her, something he had never done before. But like a lucky charm tucked inside his pocket at a casino, something about this woman made him positive enough to place it all on red.

"Garrick," he grunted out, unsure and monosyllabic.

The woman was much smoother in the proceedings, extending out a small, doll-like hand, a golden bangle jangling around her thin wrist.

"Sally. Sally Callow." She introduced herself with the effortless confidence of a real estate agent tying to pitch him a nice two-storey with a spacious back garden. Garrick would have taken anything she sold in a heartbeat. That one name soon became his whole world.

"Garrick."

He found himself once more under that healing shade of blue, only with Sally's hand squeezed around his callused one.

"Hm?" he murmured, half-conscious.

The memory of his own name melted away. The sun kissed his brow, tempting him back into that catalepsy. It was a gentle heat, far from the baking danger of the burning houses that he entered, his faced lashed by sudor.

They lay together on that very same hill they admired from afar when they had first met, the wind blowing through the rustling grasses like pan pipes. The lacy helm of Sally's white sundress moved with it. She looked ephemeral, a mirage, ready to disappear if Garrick dared lift a finger. Her aquamarine eyes sparkled like the wide expanse of the Sargasso Sea.

"You look like you've got the whole world on your shoulders." She trailed a finger over his scarred knuckles, "Tell me what's on your mind, Atlas."

The innocuous sentence shook him to his core, reconstructing his very foundation. For as long as he could remember, Garrick had toted everyone else's problems. He had taken the drunken blows of his stepfather to protect his trembling mother and dealt out his own to those who picked on the weaker and quieter in the playground. He was a packhorse, strong and assenting. In all that time, no-one had ever asked to help him.

Without even realizing it, Garrick had become a non-entity. In a way, it suited him, shying away from attention like a vampire from light, as if the slightest exposure would destroy him. Then, Sally had come into his life. She spirited him away to restaurants, bars, and fairgrounds for dates.

"You're different," Ronnie remarked, "like you've got something else on your mind nowadays. Sorry, some*one*."

Garrick refused to give him the satisfaction of an answer.

She was his white rabbit, frisking him through Wonderland and given him the connection he had no idea he had been aching for. With her he was his own person again.

He wasn't the only one who had suffered. Sally lived a life marked by near constant misses. She'd almost died before she'd even taken her first breath, her umbilical cord crushing her neck. After being declared legally dead for three minutes, she'd snuffled back into life, surprising everyone in the delivery room. Sally nearly choked to death multiple times on baby puree. Before she was even three years old, she'd split her skull open after a fall from a faulty highchair, requiring fifteen stitches. But such incidents failed to darken her sunny disposition.

"I got this one when I was eleven," she pointed out a constellation of white pocked holes ringing her wrist, "a dog jumped out at me when I was walking home from school. Only stopped when my sister threw a whole paper mâché volcano that she'd made for science class at him."

Garrick grimaced.

"Jesus."

"Yeah," she conceded, "it is gnarly. Had to get a rabies shot and everything. But I like to think of them as pitstops in the roadmap of existence. Despite everything I made it. I survived life."

Sally turned around with a sprightly smile.

"Hey, that'd make a great epitaph!"

Garrick rolled his eyes, pecking at his dim sum with a fork.

"Can we have one dinner that doesn't revolve around our inevitable deaths?" he sighed.

Sally shrugged.

"Hey, the climax is always the best part." she salaciously winked.

Only Sally could make death so appealing. In the minefield of her life, even the slightest sliver of sun was cause for celebration. Garrick still couldn't decide whether she was the most accident-prone woman alive or the most blessed. But his life was better for having met her. She was like petrichor after a thunderstorm, earthy, enriching, and still charged with a lingering static. Garrick was inspired by her determination to live and wanted to go through all of it with her, the good and the bad.

He had no clue how bad it would get.

They called it the Phoenix Virus. The first few cases had been recorded fifteen months ago, scattered across the Henan province in China. According to traditional Chinese mythology, the phoenix or fenghuang was a symbol of luck. It was one of the primordial four beings created by Pang Gua, who were present at the birth of the universe. It soared sovereign over all other birds, the embodiment of harmony favored by royal women. In the Qin dynasty, the emperor's concubines ornamented their glossy black hair buns with fenghuang-shaped hairpins. The connection between it and the western idea of the phoenix was a weak one, but it stuck. Instead of a fiery plumage, this phoenix wore the tattered cowl of Death itself.

The index case had been traced back to a businessman in Luoyang who had been having dinner with his family when he'd sneezed and transformed into a fireball. Fearing widespread panic, the Chinese authorities had initiated a widespread cover-up as they tried to deal with the crisis themselves. It had only been through the tireless internet campaign of Li Jie Zhang, a local reporter who'd been investigating the businessman's death, that word had gotten out. He'd disappeared soon after posting his last video online.

Rumors swirled he'd been snatched up by government agents who'd been tailing him. Six months later, Zhang had resurfaced in a video shot in a white room, singing the praises of the People's Republic with a shaky smile. His deeds, coupled with the enigma surrounding him, had led to him becoming an online martyr. But the epidemic had slipped past their fingers, spreading from the villages to the cities and across the oceans. The rest of the world had idled on as the threat grew undetected, until it was far too late.

It started small, a rattling cough that wouldn't go away, a sore throat and a mild fever. People shrugged it off as a seasonal thing at first and took the doctor's advice, which was to drink plenty of water and take some aspirin. However, their body temperatures continued to climb to an unbearable degree. Those who had been rushed to the emergency room melted the cold compresses the doctors and nurses applied to their reddened bodies. The lucky ones would die of heart attacks and multiple organ failure before the worst could come.

There was nothing that could alleviate the overtaking, agonizing heat. Without warning, people would burst into human bonfires in the middle of the street and shrivel away into ashen shells. A one hundred and forty-five-pound man would become a six-pound pile of ash in under a minute. Garrick had watched shaky video recordings of such incidents for far longer than was healthy with a familiar nausea.

No matter what race or sex the unfortunate was, the only face he could see was that sad-faced man who'd exploded like a supernova in front of him months ago, a silent Cassandra who'd portended an apocalypse.

By the spring, there were over eight hundred and eighty-five thousand cases and over a million deaths worldwide. Inoculation was a distant dream, with the countries of the world racing against each other to come up with one. The government issued immediate statutes-people needed to stay in home, public gathering spaces were limited, masks were mandatory and there was an imposed distance of five feet apart. Garrick washed his hands until they were raw and throbbing.

A simple trip to get groceries became nothing short of

a military style operation, lugging on sterilized fatigues to do battle with an enemy approximately a millionth of their size. Many of the explanations for what caused the virus that the experts offered were those that Garrick had encountered before in his research on spontaneous human combustion—static electricity, stress and extreme emotional states. Women were more likely to be affected than men, especially those who were heavy drinkers.

As the virus ravaged the world and the response became more uniformed, the united consensus was that it was a viral pathogen that replicated the hyper-clocked body's metabolism, pushing it to boiling point. As well as that, it proliferated the production of phosphine gas in the gut and converted it to diphosphine P2H4. This would have an explosive chain reaction with methane and hydrogen byproducts and ignite inside the body.

As if by a sixth sense, Garrick had acted long before the quarantine had been declared and moved them both in together. His modest loft had plenty of space for each other. Until now, Garrick had never imagined himself as anything but alone in it. Noticing the glaring lack of comfort in Garrick's place, Sally had dragged in a mountain of throw pillows and a blanket from her apartment. It was the ugliest thing Garrick had ever seen in his life: a crocheted, rainbow monstrosity with more holes in it than a slab of Roquefort cheese. This, he thought, was what would drive him mad, not the toilet paper shortages or the very real threat of going up like a Catherine Wheel. But it had a persistent charm to it that eroded away his initial limestone resistance.

It had covered them as they sat next to each other in the evenings, binging their way through *The West Wing* and *The Sopranos*, a flat membrane that softly pulsed with their combined body heat. Along with that, she'd purchased a few potted hydrangeas and African masks to liven the place up. She'd placed them under the glaring view of the gaping windows.

Like millions of others, Sally and Garrick did their best to adjust to a world that had been changed forever in such a brief period. They'd held buffering Zoom calls with friends and loved ones confined inside their own houses, negotiated daily chores between each other and tried to figure out what to do now.

Bored out of her mind indoors, Sally had decided to take up baking. Every morning, Garrick would come down from his workout to find the kitchen counters snowed over with flour as she busied herself with her latest culinary creation. It had been a long and grueling process of trial and error, but she managed to make a decent banana bread, which she counted among the proudest achievements of her life. They had it for lunch, the sweet, warm sponge infused with a fruity aftertaste that danced on Garrick's mouth like molten sunbeams.

Sally had used the unexpected free time heaped onto her hands to become a Renaissance woman. She cast her die at a variety of hobbies: calligraphy, pottery and Zumba, to varying degrees of success. She'd gone along jogging with him at the crack of dawn, down the dilapidated industrial estate where there was limited chance of running into any other people. A social butterfly from the womb, Sally always had to be doing something. When stationary, she would tap her feet and snap her fingers without even realizing it. Garrick had feared that the enforced closeness would repel them away from each other.

As the world outside fell apart, theirs strengthened. Not to say that there hadn't been arguments. There had been petty squabbles over who'd left the toilet seat up and misplaced things that had sometimes ended in regrettable words and slamming doors. In the end, they'd always admitted their faults and made up. Garrick was amazed that both were still sane during all of this, let alone together.

The quarantine ticked into the six-month mark and the deaths peaked at a million, he'd decided to mark their anniversary through a karaoke night, one of Sally's favorite pastimes. A gaudy disco ball shimmered from the high ceiling. The joy that had transcended Sally's face when she'd come into the room and seen all his work would be a core memory for him, something he'd treasure for the rest of his life.

They had belted out *'Don't Stop Believing'* and flicked cashew nuts at each other until the little hours of the morning. As selfish as it was, he hoped it would never end, that it would continue to be the two of them, safe in their own self-created world. It was those little moments that helped him with the heavy burden that he had been saddled with.

When the global pandemic had been declared, the Fire Service had been uplifted into indispensable. Every fire that they attended was now a potential biohazard scene. Their uniforms were exchanged for scrub-like ones that reduced the risk of contraction. The five-foot rule was negated when an infected person came charging toward you, screaming and in flames. For this reason, all personnel were ordered to dispatch those with immediate efficiency, for the safety of those around them.

Dispatch. The word soured on Garrick's tongue like a lemon slice. It was a blustering bureaucratic substitute, hastily installed to hide its true, blunter meaning 'kill'. Never did Garrick imagine being forced to take lives. He'd joined the service so he'd never have to see anyone die in front of him again. But the killing was more than a mercy, it was a necessity. There had been a case in Wisconsin when a 'burner', as those infected had been unkindly called, had rushed around in a panic and lit a row of houses, killing sixteen people.

It weighed on some more than others. Unable to wash

away the blood on their hands, a few rookies quit the force, with only the hardiest staying on. After dousing himself in stinging sanitizer, Garrick had walked by the half-shuttered windows of Bill's office. The great man himself had been hunched over his desk with his head in his hands and a half-empty bottle of bourbon at his elbow.

Coming into work one morning, he'd found Ronnie leaning against a wall. Alarm pulsed through his body, which stiffened as he waited for Ronnie to erupt. But he had turned around to reveal red-rimmed eyes, his cheeks glistening like river rock with spilt tears.

"My sister," he choked out, "she-she went up last night, l-like a candle, took the whole house with her. Oh my God, Gar, her little boys were in there. D-Damien and Hunter. He…he just turned nine, Damien. A kid. He…didn't deserve that… none of them… Oh God, I should have been there…" Ronnie collapsed into hopeless sobs under the weight of the tragedy. Garrick abandoned stricture and braced a hand to his back, sitting beside him until he was quiet. After that, Ronnie had never been the same. He carried out his task in unsettling silence, wearing a thousand-yard stare.

Every day after was filled with the crippling uncertainty of when death would come strolling round the corner, where anyone could burst into flames like a matchstick ran over a coarse striking surface. Some couldn't take it. They flung themselves off bridges or ended it in the cool comfort of an overflowing bathtub. Rabid preachers raved from their pulpits that it was the end of days.

The only thing that got him through it all was Sally. She was what he woke up in the morning for and counted down the minutes until the workday ended and he could go back home to her. She gave his life some modicum of meaning, made him better. Garrick knew he should have known better—nothing could last.

He'd only shuffled off his scuffed boots by the front door when a frantic clattering of falling pans came from the kitchen. Garrick dashed off in the direction of the kitchen, hands already curled into antecedent fists. There had been a recent rash of burglaries around the block, looters reaping the rewards of the gradual crumbling of society. Garrick wasn't a rich man, but he was determined to protect his precious few treasures.

Sally was doubled over, leaning with her palms flat on the closed kitchen shelf door for support. Her breathing was languid and saw-edged, as if the simple act of breathing was destroying her insides. Her oversized pink sweater was saturated with sweat. Her soaked hair clung to the back of her neck like a limp rat tail, having doused herself under the still-running shower in a desperate bid to cool herself odd. When she looked at him, her eyes were rheumy, lower lids puffy and twitching.

"Sal…?"

She herded him away from afar.

"Don't," she croaked out," I don't want you to get it, too."

Garrick couldn't understand. They'd followed all the regulations, right down to a tee. Of all the people to be struck down by it, Sally was the one who deserved it the least. They had been so close to making it through, too. Just yesterday, scientists had announced they had started vaccine trials. The sheer unfairness of it all made him want to scream but he resolved on doing what was best for Sally.

A barrier of plastic tarp forming an isolation tent was erected around the sofa that had become her permanent bedrest. Garrick took it upon himself to remove all flammable substances from the apartment, to prevent either of them from waking up to find everything in cinders. It didn't stop him from lying awake at night, wondering if this would be when the door was splintered in by a battering ram and men in hazmat suits would fill the room.

He contemplated taking her to a hospital, finger hovering over the digits on his phone pad. Even though it was his job to contain people like Sally, Garrick refused to see her as anything other than the woman he loved. He knew if he handed her over, he would never see her alive again.

They lived on the edge of a knife. Garrick would intermittently enter through the zipped slit in the front in a gloves and mask to spoon her meals into her mouth or dab at her forehead. They were only two doors down from each other, but the proximity between them felt more like lightyears. He wanted to hold her, rub soothing circles into her scapula, tell her it was all going to be alright. All Garrick could do was scrub himself raw in the bathroom after every encounter.

"If I ever see the inside of another hospital again, I'll scream," she remarked.

The wet sponge Garrick was holding glided over the batonlike curve of her clavicle, that conducted the symphony of her skeleton. He hated himself for doing so, how demeaning it was for a woman who tore through life with an irrepressible, fiercely independent mania.

"I know," his voice was deadened by his face mask, "but Sal, I wish you would just—"

She fixed him a look of sweaty, trembling scepticism. Garrick's heart quivered. He was an idiot for thinking he could fool her. His heart was flattened into red construction paper.

"It's okay," she wheezed, "I'll—"

"Sally—"

"—survive."

A solid steel rod of determination upheld her faltering tone. Garrick, so used to hearing that mantra uttered jokingly, couldn't help but be unnerved.

Garrick did everything he could to ease her pain. The room was filled with the juddering clank of the three fans, all whirring about in tandem. He placed cold packs under her arms and across her clavicle. Nothing seemed to help. Day by day, she deteriorated before his very eyes.

"Let's go up the hill again," she rasped.

Her face was empurpled, afloat in a pool of her own sweat. Garrick paused, pulling away the straw she had been using to imbibe the glass of ice water.

"Sal, be serious. You're in no shape—"

"Please, Garrick."

He could never say no to her.

He laid her down on the backseat, tapered with spiderlike layers of protective plastic where Sally lay prostrate, like an entrapped fly. Garrick struggled to fit the keys into the ignition, his hands shaking to the point he couldn't even hold a pencil. This burst past the threshold of unreasonable into the void of insanity. Sally's upturned hourglass was seeping down to the last few granules. If these moments would be her last, then he wanted them to be happy, in a safe place rather than in an empty, sterilized hospital room.

He carried out the girl who had once danced circles around him on those drunken Friday nights like a baby. Sally fought against her own body to stand. She staggered up the hill on atrophied legs, like a fawn taking its first feeble strides. Garrick struggled to reconcile those cheerful memories with the wasted form that shambled up ahead of him.

The thought tore through him like a bullet. She was going to die here and there was nothing

he could do. She shuffled through, like she was walking through water, extremities weighed down by the pressure of the currents. Sally sobbed with every step she took, snot stringing from her nose. She was a woman possessed by the sole intent of making it to the summit of that gentle slope where they had spent some of the best days of their lives.

The moment she made it, Sally fell to her knees and went up, a flash in an oil-drowned pan. In the process of cremation, a human body would be burned away between one and three hours, at a maximum heat of two thousand degrees Fahrenheit. In Sally's case, it happened so fast Garrick's brain raced to process it.

The fire devoured her clothes first, down to the last lingering cotton fiber, then her skin. Garrick braced himself for the sight of bone, soon to turn to ash. Instead of crumbling into nothing, Sally stood. The bonfire around her grew higher. Garrick was rendered catatonic at the humanoid outline that rippled through the firestorm veiling. It resurrected the bogeyman that had plagued his childhood, the Char Man.

He remembered being crushed in the back of his brother Scott's truck on a midnight ghost hunt with his giggling friends. A half-empty can of beer spilled onto Garrick's shoe, the yeasty fluid soaking right into his sock. It was a rite of passage around those parts, where kids would nudge each other out into that clearing of woods where the Char Man roamed and call his name.

Scott had pulled him behind a broad ponderosa pine, pulling out a sloshing can of kerosene and an abandoned mannequin that he'd dug out of a mountain of trash and wrapped in torn strips of bedding, like a cheap Halloween mummy decoration; told him in hushed, giddy whispers how they were going to give them all a real scare that night. One none of them would ever forget. Garrick had nodded along with dumb acquiescence. He hadn't really thought further along to the risk, only wanting to be as cool as his older brother and his friends.

Spooked by the ghostly hoot of a great gray owl, he'd struck the lighter early. It had caught on the edge of Scott's fuel-soaked denim jacket, the one stickered with sewn-on band patches that their mother was always badgering on for him to wash.

Sheets of skin sloughed off the body like wrapping paper, exposing scorched flesh that bore the faint indentation of zippers and buttons that had been fused to his body by the intense heat. Steam poured from the meaty open wounds that covered nearly all his brother's body. Garrick did nothing, too terrified to act. His nightmare was alive. It called him by his first name, pleading for him for help.

A tragic accident, they called it. Their father had never forgiven him for it. Scott had been his firstborn, his golden boy, the measuring stick that he had used to emphasize Garrick's own faults. That night, Garrick's life had taken a swift detour into Hell.

The memory of his dead brother clung to him like a parasitic twin, subsisting on his will to live for nutrients, growing in guilt over the years. He was convinced his shame was visible to everyone and had retreated from life. Then Sally had come along and made him want to live again.

Unlike Scott and so many others, Sally didn't burn away. She rose like a pyre, a being of pure, faceless flame. She was Jean Grey, surging forth from the white-outlined comic book panel in all her radiant terror. *Hear me, X-Men! No longer am I the woman you knew! I am fire and life incarnate!*

Along with terror, Garrick was overcome by a strange, revenant solemnity. As if he had been granted a glimpse of the face of God. Garrick wondered how she saw him through those absent eyes, a bleached face staring up at her amidst the autumnal inferno, frail and mortal. Did she regard him with pity? Or had all emotions been incinerated with her human appearance, leaving behind a blank burning slate?

The woman he loved had been ripped apart and reassembled in front of his very eyes, molecule by molecule, into something unrecognizable. She held up her arms, a shroud of flames growing down. Garrick did his best to squint through the ultraviolet light. No, not a shroud, but wings. Golden scales extended down from her ulna, past her radius until it surpassed the length of her body. A crest of feathery flame tumbled down her back.

She soared up, higher than he could ever hope to see. She became a distant speck that split the sky in half with the fiery contrails that she left in her wake. She went from the scorched circle of earth she'd left behind, in breathless, singed wonder.

Only a Fever...
P.S. Traum

Family

"**I**s God Dead?"

I often stared at that question on the magazine cover—TIME magazine no less—framed on my ice cream shop's wall. April 1966. When I picked that issue up last year at the marketplace, I had been overwhelmed by emotion.

I had struggled for years to escape my zealot family's puritanical, judgmental oppression. Seeing that cover now publicly—*nationally*—voiced my long-repressed doubt felt like vindication. How could I not frame and proudly display it?

Now there we were, Springtime again. My daughter was attending an Easter party, but I wasn't worried. She has a healthy attitude toward religion... Blessed indifference! As all children should. And the party... kids playing with fuzzy bunnies, and decorating eggs they'll never eat. I'm fine with that. No proselytizing or gruesome crucifixions and spooky resurrections there. Just silly childhood playtime.

Groovy.

Anastasia had just turned eleven. Her mother Zoe was only fifteen when she fell pregnant. Hard to believe my beautiful Zoe was only four years older than our daughter is now when we conceived! Shocking, really. I was a mere adolescent myself at eighteen, but adult enough to capitalize on our good fortune and turn potential disaster into opportunity. We quickly got married, both happily free to escape the clingy clutches of our over-controlling respective parents.

I promptly sold my flashy 1958 Meteor, a four-door Rideau made in Canada and customized in deep dark blue, and we invested our meager savings in our little venture, an old-fashioned malt and soda fountain, the only such shop in our small town.

The next year we bought a new-style jukebox, and soon the teenagers were keeping us in business. The tiny shop only had two booths and two tables besides the counter, yet on average we were making three times the minimum wage of a dollar-twenty-five, so our humble family was modestly comfortable. Perhaps profits would be higher if we started making our own ice cream, but we were happy enough.

Not that we didn't have problems. Three cars in a row were lemons; we may as well have bought Edsels. We ended up with a nice new Chevy Corvair, a cozy little thing with an air-cooled six-cylinder rear engine. But the automobile fiasco drained our savings… back to square one.

Worse, Zoe got hurt a couple weeks back. She still liked to go out horseback riding, and the damn temperamental mare threw her. A cracked rib, sprained elbow, and broken left leg. With that big heavy cast weighing her down, ankle to mid-thigh, she couldn't get around or do a whole lot. Even as I mused, lost in recent reverie, she was sitting in the back toiling away on some belated bookkeeping.

I'm eternally thankful she didn't break her neck. Even so, yet another unexpected problem soon presented itself.

"Ambrose Sprague!"

The voice shouted at me outside the glass door. It was sunny outside, and there was a glare on the glass. It looked like portly old George. A retired wartime photographer. He was carrying someone, a girl.

"Anastasia!"

I ran for the door, practically tripping over myself. Sure enough it was my daughter alright, my beloved little girl. I held the door as he maneuvered her indoors. I quickly took her from him. She was limp, but warm, thank goodness. Breathing. Alive, but asleep.

"What is this, George? What the hell? What's the meaning of—"

"Ambrose?" Zoe called out, hobbling into the main room on her crutches.

"Careful, honey, you know the floor's slippery." I set Anastasia down in a booth while George went to escort my wife over to us.

"What's wrong? What happened to my baby? *What*?" Her mounting shrieking usually preceded one of her infrequent "panic attacks," as her overprotective mother called them.

"Don't worry, Mrs. Sprague, no need for hysterics, the child's fine. Just tired I suppose, a bit of a shock from the bite, most likely."

"Bite? What bite?"

George was already pulling up the sleeve of her dress and pointing at a bright white bandage wrapped around Anastasia's right forearm.

"Oh, just a little nip, a dog bite they said."

I glanced at my wife, we shared the same thoughts, the same questions, which George seemed to anticipate.

"They said it was nothing much. And the schoolteacher, Miss… Patricia? She tried calling you all but there weren't no answer, so I said I'd bring her right over. I figured you'd be here but I would've driven on to your house if you weren't."

I headed to the phone mounted on the wall.

"Lines are down, Ambrose. Lot of trouble in town, it seems."

It was a lot to dump on me. All I could think about was my poor daughter lying there, still unconscious.

"Trouble? What kind of trouble?"

"A few accidents, a couple fires… A bunch of drunks, sounds like."

Zoe carefully sat next to Anastasia and placed our daughter's head in her lap. "In the morning? It's Easter week, not New Year's Eve." She held her palm to the girl's cheek.

"Well, switchboard's overloaded, no calls going through. Firefighters all busy. Maybe we got a full moon tonight or something."

"George, a dog bite? What kind of dog? Was it a pet, or a wild dog? Goddamnit, George, was the damn thing rabid?"

Zoe went white as a sheet as her voice broke. "Oh my God."

"No, no, nothing like that."

"Did you see it? Were you there?"

"Well, no, truth be told, but Mrs. Bradbury said she cleaned it up and bandaged her up and said she was fine, and I hear her husband took care of things, and… We tried calling, but…" George grew agitated and awkwardly backed away to the door. "Sorry to sour your morning, folks. Don't you worry none. The girl will be fine, I feel it in my bones. Anyhoo, I got me some other people to check in on, there's a lot going on out there."

I went over to shake his hand. "Thank you, George. I do appreciate you rushing her over here. Even so, I think I'll go find Doc Gaines. Any idea if he's at home?"

"Sorry, no clue, friend. Good luck to you, though. You folks be careful now and keep an eye out for any spreading fires. Stay out of the mayhem." The man exited, hurried back to his pickup, and drove away.

"Ambrose, feel her forehead. Does she feel hot?"

"Maybe." I shook Anastasia gently.

"Oh my God, what if the dog did have rabies, Ambrose? Or worse. We need to take her to Doctor Gaines. Or at least a nurse, he has three now, you know. Oh God, Ambrose—"

We both gasped when Anastasia mumbled and stirred.

Zoe stroked her face. "It's okay, baby, you're home. How do you feel?"

Our daughter frowned as her eyes flickered open for a moment.

"K-k…"

"What, sweetheart?" I leaned close.

"Kyra..."

"Kyra? Your friend from Garden Club? What about her?"

Anastasia passed out again. Zoe looked up at me, worried.

I tried calling the Doc. Dead silence. I slowly dialed number after number, every rotation of that clear plastic dial felt like an eternity. Nothing. I went to the front windows. I could see smoke rising in a few spots of the town. Our ice cream shop was in the outskirts, near the old botanical gardens and children's petting zoo. A brand-new red Corvette flashed past at an unholy speed. I glanced at my wife and shook my head.

"I don't know what's going on, Zoe." I helped her up and walked her to the back parlor. We also had a simple bathroom, a small storeroom, and a walk-in freezer, all tucked away in the back. "I want you and Anastasia to stay back here. Away from the glass. I'm going to go out and find the Doc. Just to be safe. And I'll lock up behind me, okay?"

Zoe slowly nodded.

I carried Anastasia to the parlor where we had a long sofa. I brushed her long auburn hair away from her porcelain face. She was an exceptionally lovely girl, perhaps even more so than her pretty mother. I kissed her forehead. It did feel hot now.

"I'm scared, Ambrose." Zoe clutched my hand. "Should I be scared?"

I dragged the phone back there as far as the cord would allow. I wrapped a towel around some ice and handed it to Zoe. I saw Anastasia's doll—Talky Tina? No, Chatty Cathy—perched on a shelf. A Christmas gift from her grandmother last year.

I was sure she had already outgrown it. I brought it over, anyway. At home, Anastasia had also shelved her old favorite Raggedy Ann and even her new toy, the Easy-Bake Oven. Somehow it made me sad. I suppose I didn't want my sweet little girl to grow up.

"Ambrose. Dear God."

Zoe had tears in her eyes. It occurred to me we lived fairly sheltered, comfortable lives. The situation was new for us. We were unaccustomed to trouble. To fear.

"It's okay, Zoe, I really doubt we have to worry about rabies or anything like that. It's fine. Look. There's not even any blood soaking through. It can't be a very deep bite. You have everything you need back here:. water, ice, food.

"Hey, I even bought those new chips she seems to like, Doritos, and her Crunch 'n Munch, too. Just keep trying to reach someone. I'll be right back as soon as I can, okay? It'll be okay, honey. It's only a fever."

I kissed my darling wife and headed out the door, flipping over the sign from "Open" to "Closed." Zoe's lips felt cold.

###

Daddy

My car was all but surrounded. A few raggedy-looking men, and a couple women even, were pawing at my windows. Hoping for handouts? They certainly resembled the common image of hobos, and seemed to be parroting the basic gestures: reaching out, insistent, perhaps begging for scraps like dogs at a dinner table. But it was challenging mustering up any sympathy, those bums were grown adults, after all, who should know better.

A group of them blocked my path, but it didn't necessarily seem to be their intent. Indeed, they looked confused, lost. What was I supposed to do, run them down? I had heard of such things, thugs and tramps congregating in an area and pestering passersby. But in our small decent town? So many? So suddenly?

It was a strange lot. They looked dirty, unkempt... most of them looked unwashed; I was glad my windows were rolled up. Superficially they appeard similar, but upon closer inspection, there was a variety of age and sex and profession.

Very expensive clothes on one couple. The only common feature was their milky glazed eyes. Surely a sign of advanced drug use. Were these "hippies," after all? The "flower power" youth the news spoke of lately? Although, some of them were far from young. I didn't care for the idea of junkies and potheads poisoning our town with their wares, corrupting our children.

Anastasia. She needed me. Zoe. My two lovely ladies. They were depending on me. I couldn't just sit in my car and wait it out. Those tripped-out hoodlums weren't listening to my shouts and admonitions. They didn't seem to hear me at all, or certainly didn't care. I needed to help my daughter; I couldn't take a chance and leave it to fate that she'd be okay.

If there was any possibility at all that my darling Anastasia could suffer the ravages of some disease like rabies.

I opened the door roughly, pushing a distracted chubby man out of the way. He was covered in filth, as though he soiled himself and then wallowed in it, utterly disgusting. When I slammed the car door, a young woman lunged at me. She was bleeding. Or bloody, anyway.

Her blouse and slacks were so saturated they clung to her skin like paint, red and dripping. Then, the wretched woman actually tried to bite me! I backed away, only to be groped by other transients. I realized they were trying to grab me. I pushed my way out of the growing crowd. Whatever the nonsense was, I wanted no part of it.

My car was already on the right street, so I ran to old Doc Gaines's home. His front door was wide open, which didn't bode well. Neither did the smears of blood on the porch. I cautiously followed the stains and puddles down the hall until I found the Doc, or rather, what was left of him.

It looked like he had been torn apart. Severed arms on the carpet, a long strand of intestine draped over the glass coffee table. His decapitated head stared up at me forlornly from the couch.

I wasn't the sort of person to scream, even at such a

sight as extreme as that, but I fled the house, nonetheless. Another crazed mob was awaiting me in the street. This one had children. I recognized two of them as Anastasia's schoolmates. The boy was dragging something. Something still squirming. Someone.

I turned and ran.

Violent mobs? Those psychotic vagrants were attacking—no, *killing*—townspeople? And somehow corrupting even our children. How, with what, drugs? I was getting scared. I imagined my wife and daughter besieged and trapped by these insane radicals. My Corvair was still blocked, the fiends struggling with a policeman. I thought perhaps I could lend aid.

All rational thought went out the window when the man shot his aggressors pointblank. One in the chest, one in the neck, perfect shots. They were unfazed. Something very bad was happening that I couldn't grasp. Things were quickly escalating, degenerating, beyond civil unrest and chaos. It was a... I struggled to define it. Some psychological plague? An invasion?

I peered around at the town. Smoke. Distant screams. A wail of a fire engine truck. Had there been anything in the morning paper I had somehow missed? I knew there were constant military conflicts in southeast Asia, was it some wretched new chemical weapon?

I remembered the story of that nutcase up in a tower on a shooting rampage, on a Texas college campus last year. And increasing murders everywhere, in the cities, crime sprees in the badlands, an increasingly violent world. Utter madness. It was all over the country. Was the chaos happening elsewhere? There were 197 million people in America.

I ran through the streets. I knew I would have to reach our shop on foot, halfway across town. Everywhere around me, an explosion of violence and death I was powerless to stop. Invaders attacking people, clawing at them and biting them, like rabid dogs. Some fought back, sticks, rocks, pitchforks, and yet…

They weren't strangers. I realized I recognized several of them. Our own townsfolk were doing these horrible things. It was spreading. The air? The bites? And people weren't just biting.

Now I realized they were actually *eating* their fallen victims! Revolting. Monstrous. The attackers get axed, shot, run over. Some were falling apart bodily; it wasn't just some plaque! Something else was happening. You don't take a shotgun blast to the back and keep on walking like nothing happened. No one takes an ax to the face and keeps shuffling after you, ax still dangling, lodged in the skull. A child can't stroll around with her innards spilling out and dragging behind her.

No, I was witnessing something far beyond mere madness and illness. People with fatal wounds and crucial missing parts. Mutilated degradations eating people despite lacking a functioning digestive tract, or any organs at all, in some cases. Heads with all the flesh shredded off. Bloody naked bodies, skeletal… more bone than meat, and yet walking around and attacking people, right before my very eyes.

I was experiencing a living nightmare, a Hell on earth. It was an evil, pure evil. Unholy.

Occult. *Supernatural*, they call it. How else could you explain those impossible events? Those… cadavers. Shambling, cannibalistic corpses.

Mommy

"You'll be okay, baby. Your fever will break, and your

father will bring a doctor. Go ahead and sleep. You can stay home from school as long as you need to, sweetheart. You can stay in bed and I'll bring you a tray. I'll cook all your favorites. You'll be watching all your favorite shows: *Bewitched*, *The Monkees*, oh, and *Star Trek*, I like that one!"

Zoe finished washing her hands and face in the bathroom and took a deep breath. She wrung out a towel and packed some ice into it. The woman carefully made her way back to her sleeping daughter on the wobbly crutches. She held her palm to Anastasia's forehead.

"Oh! Good! Your fever broke! You're nice and cool again. Thank goodness, it seemed like—Wait." She stared at the girl's chest, then held her hand over her mouth and nose. "You're not breathing! Anastasia!" Zoe shook her hard. "*Wake up!*" She panicked and slapped her daughter. "*Anastasia!*"

The girl convulsed, and her eyes sprang open. She sat up, her upper torso bending stiffly at the waist as her jaw dropped, hanging slackly.

"Thank God!" Zoe wept as she grabbed her daughter up in a tight hug. She laughed nervously. "You scared me, honey; please don't scare Mommy!" Zoe blinked, she sniffed and caught a whiff of something she couldn't quite place—a scent of something sickly sweet. "Anastasia honey…"

Zoe shrieked as her daughter bit her. Anastasia sank her teeth into her mother's neck at the collarbone. After the second chewing motion, Zoe shoved her away.

"*Anastasia*! Why would you—"

Zoe froze when she stared at her daughter's face. Close up, Anastasia had become pale, her veins were visible through lightly translucent skin. Her big blue eyes, normally bright and watery, were milky and glazed over, with an unfocused, almost wall-eyed stare. The girl had barely broken the skin on Zoe's neck, but still had a smear of blood on her full pouty lips, which she licked hungrily.

"You're sick, really sick! You're infected or something. I think you have the rabies, baby, you—"

Zoe was interrupted when Anastasia grabbed her roughly by the hair, pulling her close as she lunged forward and chomped down on her mother's face. Zoe screamed. Anastasia jerked her head back, ripping off Zoe's upper lip and tearing her nose. Zoe screamed again and instinctively thrust her lower palms out, smacking Anastasia in the mouth.

"*Let go of me*!" She sputtered the words, lacking her upper lip.

Zoe shoved the girl hard. Her cast slid on the slick linoleum and she fell backward hard onto the floor, pulling Anastasia down with her. Zoe felt a sharp pain in her back as she twisted. The bandage on Anastasia's arm tore and came loose. The girl snapped at Zoe's face like a dog.

"Stop it! Anastasia! I don't want to hurt you!" Her speech was slurred as she tasted blood filling her mouth.

Zoe crawled backward away from her altered daughter. She was too shocked to weep, and stared wide-eyed at the vicious feral creature crawling after her, unrecognizable as her beloved child. Anastasia grabbed at her mother's cast and her leg. Zoe kicked out with her good leg, striking the girl in the left shoulder with a crunching, popping sound. Anastasia's arm dangled awkwardly, dislocated, without much effect on its grasping.

"Oh no, what's happening?" Zoe slapped her daughter. "Anastasia! Wake up!" She cried.

Zoe scrambled, crawling backward again to escape her daughter. Her legs were splayed out, the heavy cast dragging at an angle. Anastasia's hands clawed into Zoe's thighs as she tried to bite her face. Zoe lashed out, scratching the girl's face and pulling her hair. Anastasia glared at her with unblinking dead eyes as her jaw hung slack.

Zoe shuddered and made a sickly moaning sound. Anastasia lunged again. Woman and girl clung tightly to each other's dresses as Zoe kicked again, ripping their fabric apart and knocking the skinny girl back a few feet. Zoe quickly pushed backward but struck her head against the walls in the corner. Her head wavered as she slumped forward, dazed and trapped.

Anastasia's mouth opened and closed, drooling heavily and bleeding, as she slowly advanced upon Zoe's vulnerable injured legs, crawling between her bare inner thighs.

Daughter

When I reached Russo Street, I relaxed a bit. As I ran down the road, our modest little ice cream shop soon came into view. I mused that maybe we could throw a big party for Anastasia right there in our shop on her twelfth birthday. She could invite all her little classmates for one of those dance parties she loves watching on television.

As I unlocked the door, my relief and elation started to shrink away, replaced by an ominous trepidation. It may have been irrational, but the sense of fear and doom only increased when I realized there was a strange odor in the air, contradictorily mysterious and familiar.

Instead of calling out to my wife as I normally would have, I grabbed up a large wrench from behind the counter, then slowly and silently made my way to the back rooms.

As I turned the corner, I could hear faint but disturbing slurping sounds. When the source of both the inexplicable smell and sounds was revealed to me, I dropped the wrench.

I inched closer, confused and disbelieving my own eyes. My knees went weak as I beheld a nightmare. This time I did scream.

My dear wife—the love of my life —Zoe, was splayed out in the corner of the room near the bathroom. Her head lolled back with bulging eyes and a torn-open mouth. Her dress was torn too, and between her legs was a pale, blood-soaked pubescent girl, her own dress torn and hanging off her slender shoulders. It was my darling Anastasia.

My beloved daughter was eating out her mother's lower abdomen and thighs. Raw flesh hung from Anastasia's mouth as she turned toward me. Her head unnaturally rotated to glance at me indifferently, then she turned back to resume her obscene meal. My veins turn cold as my body shook.

Zoe's entire crotch and the surrounding flesh was gone. Her hollowed-out pelvis was a bloody bowl of chewed-up tissue. Her inner thighs were also eaten away, and the way her lifeblood had flowed out across the floor suggested her femoral artery had been bitten into first.

The revolting *thing* that had once been our beautiful Anastasia continued to loudly, sloppily gorge. Evidently her digestive tract was full, because the chewed-up meat simply fell out of her mouth onto the corpse of her mother. Zoe remained immobile, truly dead. Perhaps she had irreparably bled out before any inexplicable infection could take hold. The crimson bones of her pelvis, lower spine, and femurs were visible.

I felt both dizzy and nauseous, and nearly passed out from shock and despair. My legs and bladder gave way, and I collapsed onto the floor, sliding down the wall in a sitting position much like my murdered wife's. I couldn't think, let alone speak or move. I could only helplessly stare in abject horror.

Anastasia had terrible scratches on her face, as if

perhaps her mother had tried to fend her off. There were equivalent scratches on Zoe's lower thighs, and clumps of auburn hair in her hands.

There had evidently been something of a struggle, a final battle. And there, on Anastasia's forearm, the bandage had fallen away. I could see the original bite clearly. Not a dog's bite at all. Human teeth marks. A little girl's bite; presumably from her friend Kyra. I could only imagine the girl's mother was protecting her with the lie, to shield the infected daughter from exposure.

I could hear the ambient hum of machinery in the shop. The freezer, the ventilation, the lighting, the jukebox. I closed my eyes. I could almost hear the vivacious laughter of the customers, adolescents discovering love and lust, kids giggling as little boys told stupid jokes, pubescent girls like Anastasia and her friends practicing creative new dance moves they memorized from television. Our shop was a playful, peaceful, pleasant place to visit, a respite from reality, a haven.

It really was a nice little ice cream shop. Zoe called it charming. She was proud of our costly jukebox. She enjoyed selecting new records. Anastasia loved music. She particularly loved young Lesley Gore and The Shangri-Las. Anastasia must have worn those record grooves down to nothing, playing them over and over and over.

My energy was waning. My very mind was fading away. In a mere instant I had mentally documented and reiterated the day's devastating events, silently reciting them to Anastasia like a doomed narrator.

I shuffled backward and slumped down against the freezer door. Maybe I would drag my dead darling Anastasia in there with me. I could hold her in my arms, and we could simply freeze together, forever free in peaceful oblivion...

I opened my eyes. My lips twitched and my mouth

opened, and I found myself quietly singing one of Anastasia's favorite songs while I helplessly watched the pallid corrupted corpse of my beautiful daughter continue to mindlessly chew on the cooling flesh of my deceased beloved wife.

"I Can Never Go Home Anymore…"

Payday

Chris Moss

nother $9,600 to go. Then I'm free.

The African sun has barely risen above the wavering horizon, but there's already beads of sweat dripping into my eyes. My fingers twitch against the rifle, but I manage to resist the urge to wipe my face. The prickling droplets are trapped beneath my mask anyhow.

Blinking away the sting, I peer around the corner at the blocky gray warehouses near the edges of the settlement. The men around me shuffle, silent but for the crunch of gravel under our boots and the hiss of our gas masks.

Almost there. My eyes drift back over my gear, checking, rechecking, then adding up the costs of the corporate-issued gear.

Ballistic armor, factory second, $1200; Gas Mask, reconditioned, $800; Gloves, military surplus, $45; Boots, steel cap, $190; Patrol Rifle, worn, $395; Ammunition, 250 rounds, $80. Corporate inventory accounting fee, $25.

The money from this job will cover all of it and more.

Almost there. Almost. Then I can—

>*Squad Two in position?*
>*Squad Two, confirm?*

My fingers push hard against the uncomfortable rubber mask, leaking in a puff of air as I try to activate the subvocal implant in my jaw. It takes barely a thought to relay the reply.

>Squad Two, ready and in position.

The Commander's reply is terse, the tightly packed data packet bristling against my own implanted nodes.

>*I expect immediate responses, Squad Two.*

Nash Industries Cerebral Node and Mandible Subvocal Implant, Starter Model. Equipment cost, $1800; Installation - Corporate Medical fees (CorpCare), $45,000.

That was the highest start-up cost. A calculated risk. But a few more of these jobs—

>*Squad Two, you have the Ready Signal for Preliminary Objective. Squad positions marked. Target has likely turned most of the settlement. They are calculated as acceptable human asset losses.*

The salty sweat drops over my lips as they twist into a grin.

>You mean, they think they're living in Ancient Egypt?

>*Squad Two, cease pointless chatter or you will be subject to a corporate performance review. Your only concern is acquiring the Archetype variant.*

My vision blurs as the derisive snort sends a little film of steam over the inner faceplate.

"Alright boys," I call, my voice muffled through the gas mask. "Get ready for the signal. We grab the Archetype and get to the transports. I'll buy the first round when we're back stateside."

The squad perks up, rechecking their gas masks and making sure their weapons are free. Even after twelve hours on a plane and armed with whatever cheap gray scrap they can afford, they're still more than a match for whatever is out there. That's not what they have to worry about.

The Archetypes. Nash Industry's—the Corporation, to those working for them —most prized product line. All you need is a piece of someone, the quantum information embedded in their molecules or some such, and the Archetype Treatment turns it into an injectable personality. A hazy blur of memories, skills and experiences, distilled into a tiny vial. Originally it was used for military applications, but then certain groups got a different idea.

"Ahn thet-tu ghaat-ah pen maa-ah ahn aabaui!"

Why not bring back the legends long past? A world where kings, emperors, and pharaohs walked out of their tombs and back onto the battlefield—and that suits the Corporation just fine.

>Squad Two, attack. Retrieve the Archetype variant. Failure will be billed against your personal debt as an Operational Loss.

"Let's make some money, boys!"

The squad replies with a muffled grunt. As we tumble out from behind the factory wall, we're greeted with the sight of a few dozen combatants, waving improvised spears and clubs.

"Aabaui! Ahr ahn ahritu khet nebt bahnt!"

It's a weird bunch of defenders. Villagers from surrounding settlements, some men and women from the big city, holding wooden shields in front of dirt-stained business suits—even a handful of international tourists, by the look of it—screaming in unison as they charge, hollering battle cries in a language that hasn't been spoken for thousands of years.

Shame their battle tactics are just as outdated.

"Squad Two, open fire! Go! Go! Go!"

The crack of the gunfire echoes in my mask, and the familiar smell of gunpowder mixes with the sweat running down my face. The first line of defenders tumbles into the red-stained dirt, but as we advance, there's a *thwip* through the air beside me and one of the squad screams. Ollie, my 2IC, pushes me back and waves toward a nearby warehouse.

"Cap! Shooter on the roof!"

There's barely time to squint through the ill-fitting mask before another squad member goes down. There—there he is! A flash of muzzle fire from a distant roof, the black-robed blob pulling himself up and—

The second crack of gunfire sends my guts clenching, but the enemy shooter just slumps over, a shapeless dark blob tumbling off the warehouse roof. I spin around, but there's no other shooters in sight. No way my boys could have made that shot, nor those stuck-up bastards in Squad One.

"VOC?" yells Ollie, slapping a field bandage over a puncture in his gray armor and staring up at me in astonishment.

My only reply is a shrug, as I motion my gun toward the remaining defenders, stumbling over their dead to try and blockade the warehouse doors.

"Squad Two! Get that door open!"

"I'm telling you man, it's the VOC!"

"Shuddup and clear out the rest of the trash. If it *is* the VOC you'd better pray they don't get to the Archetype before we do."

The faceless man nods and raises his gun toward the screaming crowd. The group of European tourists make a screaming last charge at our line, but my mind is barely on them as the squad mows them down.

VOC. The Corporation's special forces. Corporate raiders that the rest of us just whisper about.

If they're here, then it must be serious. A few years ago, there were rumours that Eglinton Pharmaceuticals was trying to develop a diabetes cure in South America, one that would wipe out the demand for the Corporation's insulin products. VOC was never officially involved, but Eglington's entire R&D team died in very public 'accidents,' and any witnesses to the lab fires died soon after.

Now, somewhere in that warehouse, someone has released an Archetype virus. Not the single dose, highly profitable pay-per-use Archetypes sold by the Corporation, but an infectious disease that rewrites the personalities of an entire population.

For free.

It's enough to make a grown man weep. Grunts like us bust our goddamn balls to make some dough, enough to get out of debt and buy a few luxuries. I ain't asking for much, nothing greedy, just a nice housing unit, a fridge full of beer and not needing to worry about other people's problems; then some *bastard* comes along and does something like this.

Zealots and damn prophets. The *only* thing worth fighting for is a payday.

A pale, bloodstained face howls up at me as I reach the warehouse doors. My muscles work on autopilot, smacking the former tourist back into the dirt. The rifle barrel finds its mark. Squeeze, not pull. Beneath the gas mask, salty lips twist up into a snarl.

"Ollie! Why aren't these goddamn doors open yet?"

"On it, boss!" yips an armored gray figure. Ollie's the closest thing our little squad can get to a tech specialist, his heavy gloves fumbling against the electronic keypad. My heart is still thrumming as the doors whine, then slowly open. Peering inside, it takes a moment to squint past the fog in my mask. There's movement, a figure, running; he's winding up his arm, he's throwing—

"Everyone back!"

I throw myself sideways. Squad Two trips over themselves trying to scramble away, but it's already too late. A little silver cylinder falls into the mess of limbs and I don't need to look hard to see the pin had already been pulled, an oily stream of pale smoke spewing out the top.

"Check your seals!"

Don't know who yelled it—probably me. We claw our way over the bleeding defenders to put distance between us and the belching white smoke. Then as quick as it started, the thick white cloud clears, leaving a circle of thrashing arms wildly waving the gas away.

We aren't trained solders. Not really. We're mercs at best. Despite everything, we all lie there for a second, blinking stupidly as we suck on our gas masks.

"Sound off!" I bark. "We all good?"

It takes the men a few moments to reply, the gray figures awkwardly pulling themselves up.

"We're good, Cap!"

"You sure?" I snarl. "Anyone here feel like building a pyramid? No?"

The men's laughter is nervous, but it's enough to get them moving again. It's just as well, because the doors are still opening, and the men inside taking up positions behind heavy machinery, don't look like the villagers and tourists we just liquidated. The orders are already bursting out of me as Squad Two rushes through the doors and looks for cover.

"Get moving! Flank and pin them down! *Watch for more gas attacks!*"

They don't need to be told twice. They're nervy now, I can see it in the way they're ducking their heads and fumbling their reloads. I understand why.

There's a bitter, oily taste clinging the back of my throat like a bad cigarette.

The warehouse echoes with the rattling scream of

gunfire, as I scurry behind an industrial loader.

Goddamn cheap corporate rats, they knew the mask seals weren't compliant. *"Oh, it'll be fine, just make sure you shave and put some Vaseline along the seal edge."* And you went and fell for it, didn't you? You just had to cheap out on that one. You should've paid the extra $250 for a fresh mask.

Something sparks off the silent machine and ricochets past my head like an angry hornet.

Dammit, *focus*. The ones out the front were just the cannon fodder. The real fight begins here. My fingers are still trembling as they fumble along my jaw.

>Squad One, we are pinned down within the warehouse. We need your support!

>Squad One, copy!

>Squad One?

Damn it, damn it, damn it! My mouth still tastes like smoke as I take a deep breath to yell over the gunfire.

"Squad Two, we're on our own! Seal the door behind us!"

Damn cheap bastards, leaving us to do all the hard work. The bitterness sucks all the way into my lungs, dark and oily as I snarl and return a volley at the robed men and women huddling behind the industrial plant.

I motion to the two men beside me and we crouch down beneath the bullets, looking for a position to create a crossfire. My eyes dart over the warehouse floor, looking for something—anything—we can take cover behind.

Industrial stamp press, probably recycled, paint flaking off the sides, worth about $12,000?

Metal shaper and roller, cutting attachment at the rear, ain't seen one of those since my mine site days. Surprisingly new, $8,000.

Generator, reconditioned. Looks like one of the old diesel types with a diamond battery integrated into the side.

Way too much power for a small factory like this. Looks a bit like the ones from the mine at Swenett. If I close my eyes, I can almost feel the sun on my back as I gaze out across the great Iteru River, watching the noble ibis fly toward the granite quarries beyond.

What? No. It wasn't like that. I mined coal for the Corporation up out of Hobet in West Virginia.

Where the *hell* is Swenett?

Thwip.

The next bullet almost takes my face off. My arms and legs must've decided they've had enough of my brain because they're already moving, ducking and rolling behind a stack of thick metal pipes. A dark-robed shape flashes across my vision, but the rifle comes up and it leaves a satisfying splatter of red across the factory wall as whoever it was limps back into cover.

A hatchway, there, up against the back wall! That's what they're guarding! Looks serious, perhaps it used to be a bomb shelter? Basement storage for the factory?

Despite everything, there's a happy little rhythm to the next few shots squeezed out of my rifle.

"Ollie, we've got them pinned! Get around and flank them, you yellow-belled bastards!"

A cluster of three men hesitate from behind a blocky green lathe.

"Cap, are you sure? Ain't got but six of us left—"

"Then there's less of us to divide the payout. Get out there, you snivelling little shit, before I come over and push you out myself!"

That gets them going, the lazy little bastards. Can't blame them overmuch – they're good men when things are in their favor, but the moment the transaction looks like it's going south, they bail quicker than them Nubians at the battle of Kerma. My sword smote them well that day, I—

No, wait…Kerma?

It's not important right now, just keep moving.

"Cap! Are you with us? Wake up!"

Squad Two's shouts bring me back into the battle. Three more shots, and two more of the defenders tumble, the black robes already spilling red across the concrete.

"Keep firing!" I yell as the remaining robed figures try to retreat. They can see we've got them now, even if there's only a handful of us left. The last two try and make a break for it, and my hands are trembling so much they almost don't make the shot.

We need to get through that hatch. The payday's there, she's waiting for me.

There's five of us left, as we huddle around the hatchway set into the concrete. Ollie touches the side of his jaw and puts his other hand over the thumbprint lock.

"How long?"

My voice comes out as a rasp, it's all I can do not to cover the mouth of my gas mask as if it'd somehow hide what happened.

Focus. No-one has to know. Just get to the objective. Everything will be OK after that.

"It'll take me a few minutes, Cap," murmurs Ollie, his eye rolling up into his head behind the cheap plastic mask. "This one's tougher than the front door."

The sudden *bang* makes us all jump. It's coming from outside.

"Squad One?" whispers Ollie, his hand still pressed up against the touch pad. My response is a growl as I raise the rifle toward the sound.

"Wouldn't bet on it, Ollie. Squad Two, form up! Ollie, you got less than a minute, d'y'hear?"

The hammering grows louder. The warehouse doors groan, then a crack appears as they roll an inch apart.

"Ollie!"

"Almost there, Cap! We've got to get to her! Gotta

keep her safe!"

What?

The hammering increases, and the crack in the warehouse doors shudders farther open. Can't see much of what lies beyond, but there's a pile of bodies shuffling against the glare.

"Aabaui! Aabaui!"

"Open fire, boys, we just need to hold them off a bit longer!"

The gunfire rattles the air around me, and my hands itch as I resist the urge to tear off the oily-smelling mask. As the yells beyond the doors meld into screams, my gaze turns back to the man bent over the hatch. He's muttering, rocking back and forth as his implants work the touch pad. Can't make out more than a few snatches through the gunfire.

"Gotta get to her. My love. Gotta see her…"

Slowly, almost on its own, my rifle drifts toward the crouching man.

"What did you say there, Ollie?"

There's an electronic *beep* and the dull metal for the hatch shifts aside. Ollie looks up at me triumphantly. There isn't much I can make out through the steam huffing up his gas mask, but there's something wild in his eyes.

"I gotta get to her, Cap. She needs me, see? *Sekhet netert unen-ah em pet…*"

The rifle kicks against the side of my ribs as the *crack* of the gunfire shakes through me. Ollie collapses back, pulling off his mask and clawing desperately to bring his rifle round.

Crack. Crack.

The remaining squad—three now, the other gray-armoured bodies are sprawled over an industrial lathe—pause and turn to me. Their guns are still on the dirty suits clawing their way through the gap, but the muzzles wobble toward me for a mite longer than makes me comfortable.

"Squad Two, get in the hatch!" I bellow. *"Move! Move! Move!"*

My rifle keeps barking as the remains of Squad Two scamper down the hatchway. The figures pressed up against the crack in the warehouse door are falling back, but I am not taking my eyes off them—don't want to look down at the blood-stained heap that used to be Ollie.

There's a sudden sharp boom and the warehouse doors rattle in their tracks. Grenades, maybe. Or something just as dangerous.

Squad One?

No, they aren't carrying firepower like that.

Ollie's blank mask stares daggers into my back as I clamber down the metal ladder and pull the hatch back over my head. Around us is a low room with thick cables slung overhead, probably started as a storeroom, but the cables are leading into a tunnel cut through the concrete.

"What was up there, Cap?" asks one of the men. He's trembling now – this job ain't turned out the way any of us expected. My response is to snap and jerk my muzzle toward the narrow tunnel.

"Keep moving!"

The men respond without a word. Don't matter. We're almost there, and it isn't going to be Ollie, or Squad One or even the VOC who'll get there first.

She's waiting for me.

Only me.

The tunnel turns as it dives into the earth, opening up into low rooms lined with alcoves. The air is stuffy even through the oily mask, and the panting of the remaining squad bounces off the assortment of items lining the walls.

Water recycler, reconditioned, probably $450. Refrigeration chest, $600 each. That's a – no idea. Lab equipment? Centrifuge looks expensive as hell. Gas tank, *expensive, probably. Above that; statue, gold, Goddess Sekhmet, Daughter of Re, Great One of Healing, Giver of Ecstasies...*

"Cap? Cap! You right there?"

Takes all I have to tear my gaze away from such beauty, and my response turns into a bitter snarl.

"Keep your guard up. We're almost—"

The arrow comes outta nowhere. It's suddenly *there*, spouting from the man's neck in a spray of bright blood. The remaining pair rush forward as the man goes down in a tangle, but my rifle is already swinging around, as I stare into the shadows of the tunnel ahead. A song erupts from the darkness, the words unfolding within me.

"Ahu-nah re-ah, t'etu-ah,"

May it be to my mouth that I may speak,

"Retah, er shent,"

My two legs to walk.

"Aaui-ah, er sekher kheft-ah!"

My two hands and arms to overthrow my enemy!

The priest steps out of the shadows, the muscles across his chest clenching as he raises his arm and he steadies the bow. Girded in white linen, his feet are bare as he steps forward, still singing.

An emissary of the Great Gods. Yet he seeks to bar my way.

This false priest seeks to bar *my* way!

My rifle is already up, my fingers on the trigger. The priest snaps an order as he turns toward me but the rifle barks and kicks against my shoulder. The reply drips from my lips, thick and oily with contempt

"En sen sefet embah aa neteru apu!"

It's only after they overflow that I see the two remaining men's guns jerk toward me.

"It's nothing," I snap. "We're there. Let's just... let's... grab the payday and..."

Feels prudent to let them take the lead as we step over the body of the priest and continue downward. It ain't just because I want them to take the brunt of whatever's ahead.

The sweat is pouring down my face, trailing over my eyes and cheeks, despite the cold stone. They don't understand. They can't. They haven't been through what I've been through. The mines of Swenett, the years fighting in the army of Hatshepsut, then a life serving *her*, just as she in turn serves the Ruler of the Two Lands. She's waiting for me.

No! No, that isn't it. That isn't it at all. I'm… *me*, I am. No damn virus or whatever is going to change me. I'm gonna, gonna collect my payday and then I'm free, right?

She's waiting for me, my love.

"Shut up!"

"Cap?"

"I mean, shut up and keep moving. Eyes forward!"

The tunnel finally levels out, and it's hard not to shield my eyes as the golden light shines forth from the gloom. The remains of Squad Two flinch and bring up their weapons, looking for a defensive position. My heart clenches; it's all too much. It's…

Stone walls, carved and painted with the likeness of Amun-Ra, the Hidden One, King of the Gods. Mighty are the spells and prayers of the Great One. Around the room, lanterns of alabaster, stone lotuses flicking with life.

At the center, the granite altar, beside it the table of cedar wood inlaid with gold, to hold the ritual knives of copper and ivory. Cunning and fine work by the artisans of Thebes. I can almost smell the markets as the throng clears a path for my mistress.

And then, suddenly, *she's* there. Tall, dark haired, the white robe and golden bracelets adorning skin the color of rich copper.

My love.

No, she's not. She's just the payday. Grab her. Grab the archetype samples. The gray-armored men turn to me, the orders are there, *there,* right on my lips, but the words won't come.

But she's stretching out her hands toward me. Her song, so soothing, always so soothing, the balm to my *ba* and *ka.*

"Rekh-ah em aab-ah,"

No! Shoot her!

"Sekhem-ah em ahrit, merert ka-ah,"

Shoot her now!

"Ahn khenah-tu ba-ah er khat-ah."

"Cap? What's going on?"

The rifle muzzle moves.

Crack. Crack.

My lady gazes at me with familiar warmth as I step over the bodies of the intruders and kneel at her feet. The priestess Meresankh, my love, the Chantress who serves Hatshepsut the Pharaoh. Trembling fingers rip the ridiculous mask from my face to breath in the sweet incense of her perfume. The tears flow, unashamed, for we are finally reunited.

"Not shall my soul be imprisoned at the gates of Amenta," I whisper, staring up into her smile. "My entrance shall be in peace, *pert em hetep.*"

Crack.

The pain feels cold, at first, then blossoms into bright red as my legs collapse from under me. My fingers scrabble for the weapon, but everything is sluggish. My mouth opens, peering up at my love, but there's hot liquid in my throat.

I can't breathe.

Meresankh's smile freezes, flickering with uncertainty before the priestess collapses in a twitching heap beside me. Somewhere behind me comes the sound of boots.

"Operations, Primary Objective has been acquired."

My love reaches out, trying to mouth something, as her fingertip graze my tear-stained cheek. The voices… they seem… familiar.

"Status of Squads One and Two? Liquidated."

No, I can't lose her. I can't, I—

"Tell the professor we have her prize. Yes, affirmative, only tazered. We'll burn the rest."

There's something hot and wet pooling against my cheek, but my body shivers with cold. I had to—had to do something. Important. What was it again?

"Ahn khenah-ten ba-ah, ahn saa-ten khaibit-ah…"

Do not shut in my soul. I *will* be free.

The words are still draining from me as they drag her away.

END

Skin Hunger
Mark Pariselli

Lucas Pemberton's bony hand trembled as he poured chilled vodka into a glass. He almost dropped the frosted bottle returning it to the freezer's lower shelf. It wasn't the cold making him shaky.

Or his advanced age.

As he took a long swig, Lucas admitted he was afraid. He tried to savor the smoothness of the premium liquor as it slipped down his throat, saved for a special occasion such as this.

Well, not quite like this.

Six months ago, Lucas would never have believed he was capable of this perilous mission. But six months ago, the world was a very different place.

Carrying his glass, Lucas walked to the floor length windows overlooking the city. From the twenty-seventh story of The Eden luxury condos, he peered down into darkness. Inured to the sight by now, Lucas remembered how strange it was at first to observe the city devoid of activity by sunset.

Silent and still.

No vehicles speeding across town, no illuminated neon signage and eeriest of all, no people. No well-dressed couples linking arms on date night, no fitness-crazed joggers – not even those experiencing homelessness.

The government had swiftly forced the unhoused into shelters or jails. The gas mask wearing Special Task Force violently ensured adherence to the strict curfew. Lucas took another drink. The classical record playing softly from the living room was supposed to calm his nerves. Instead, it jarringly contrasted with the desolate panorama below.

Lucas gazed into the few lit apartments visible to him. There weren't many people left at home. Maybe there weren't many people left at all. Some evenings Lucas would lose track of time watching the muscular young man a few floors down. Keeping his own lights off, Lucas remained undetected; a ghostly voyeur.

Most nights, the young man carried on as if the pandemic had never started—riding his stationary bike and watching sitcom reruns before going to bed at a reasonable hour. This pacified Lucas. The nights when the young man exploded into bouts of rage, punching walls and throwing plates, disturbed Lucas enough that he turned away for a few weeks.

But the urge to feast his eyes on another live human being, especially such a prime specimen, always returned with the gnawing loneliness in his gut. Lucas had been alone since his wife Helena died, writhing on the floor. The passing of his only child decades ago was now considered a blessing. At least Charlie had been spared the outbreak and subsequent societal collapse.

In an apartment to the left, a family gathered around the dinner table. Lucas averted his eyes, unable to stomach the sight. Glimpses of their happy, candlelit normalcy, even if it was mostly performative, hurt too much. At least they had each other.

Incapable of sleeping in the bed once shared with his wife, Lucas now occupied the guest room. He tried to keep the condo tidy, but his negligence was evident in the scuffs and stains and piles of dirty clothes. Helena would have admonished him.

She surprised them both by willingly embracing the role of homemaker. Shortly after she became pregnant, they moved into their refuge in the country. Tall trees shaded the yard where they envisioned their son would play.

After the accident that killed Charlie, his bedroom was sealed. Lucas and Helena tried maintaining the rest of the house in his honor but this only papered over the cracks forming in their marriage. Helena remained in bed later each morning while Lucas drank more each night.

Neglecting the property, they let weeds choke the garden to death. Vegetables rotted in untended soil. Cobwebs billowed gently in desiccated rooms. Their sanctuary became a mausoleum. So, they abandoned it. Everything was sold at an estate auction in an attempt to expunge Charlie from their memories.

They needed a fresh start. The Eden, a tower of steel and glass, was the antithesis of their country home and they hoped the bustle and noise of the city would drown out Charlie's cries.

As night fell, The Black Fog descended, entirely obscuring Lucas's view of the cityscape. The thick cloud would remain until the sun's first rays, then dissolve, only to return the following evening. At first, the government accused foreign adversaries of chemical or biological warfare. When the poisonous fog was reported globally, even in the most remote locations, other theories emerged. Was it extraterrestrial? Paranormal?

Speculations about its origin ceased to matter as its

lethal toxicity became horrifyingly apparent. The world plunged into chaos. Days after inhaling the noxious fumes, looters and rioters were bulldozed into mass graves. Stray dogs and housewives clawed at their bleeding eyes. Interior organs liquefied, oozing out of ruined bodies.

While overturned cars smoldered in the dirty streets, survivors retreated into their homes, barricading any openings with scrap material. Scarves and swathes of ripped fabric were worn over mouths and noses for protection, but The Black Fog still penetrated. Seeping through cracks and into holes, it infected people with what was eventually called The Sickness. Yet, some, like Lucas, were immune…at least for now, craving more than mere human connection.

As Lucas turned away from the windows to refill his glass, the kitchen lights flickered. The record skipped. Struck by vertigo, he paused at the white marble island and gripped the ledge until the lights and music steadied. With his pension from the university, Lucas was wealthy enough to afford electricity, now powered by a backup generator in the bowels of The Eden.

But it was fading.

Lucas assumed it would soon completely fail, taking away what miniscule conveniences and pleasures remained. Wi-Fi subsisted after the outbreak and Lucas avidly followed the snippets of news reports he could access. He cringed, watching shaky videos live-streamed from illegal warehouse raves.

Neon painted revelers were savagely beaten and dragged off-screen by the Special Task Force. Much to his liking, most social media influencers went quiet. They were replaced by masked content creators anonymously documenting and sharing survival techniques, like how to cook raccoon meat.

As a lifelong vegetarian, these particular

demonstrations repulsed Lucas. Now, even those posts had ceased. The internet was barren. Except for the murkiest corners of the dark web. This is where Lucas had lurked, searching for a way to satiate a new appetite. Then he discovered the message board. Slowly and secretly, tonight's plan was devised in the shadows.

Swaying slightly, Lucas set his empty glass down in the sink. That was enough alcohol for now. The rest of the night required his faculties and fortitude. He tried to ignore the now familiar ache in his abdomen, a sensation akin to hunger pangs. According to the antique watch dangling on his thin wrist, it was time to leave.

Lucas pulled the needle from the record, cutting the music completely. In the foyer mirror, he scrutinized his gaunt appearance. Age had crept up on Lucas before the outbreak, but the last six months had hollowed him out, turning him into a frail, old man. He pulled a black mask up over his mouth and nose, partially concealing stark evidence of the accumulated years. He donned a black trench coat and snatched a hand-scrawled map off the entryway table.

Finally, he unlocked the series of bolts and latches on the front door. It swung open with a groan.

The hallway was markedly colder than the interior of Lucas's condo. Overhead lights blinked intermittently. Since the elevator crashed into the basement, the stairs were now the only exit. Twenty-seven floors down. Then Lucas had to traverse a maze of crisscrossing alleyways by foot while evading the roving Special Task Force to reach his destination. He hesitated. Was it worth the risk? Would this quell his desire? Lucas had to find out.

Breathing heavily after the descent to ground level, Lucas retrieved a set of night vision glasses from his coat pocket and put them on. His sight improved dramatically in the gloom of The Eden's lobby. Lucas sidestepped overturned desk chairs and smashed security monitors as he wound his way to the back of the building.

He approached the rear door. Lucas leaned against the blood-stained metal and listened. The only discernable sound was the low drone of The Black Fog gusting on the other side. Grunting, he knocked over the wooden plank blocking the door. Lucas crossed the threshold and was swallowed by darkness.

Dense and suffocating, The Black Fog enveloped Lucas like a body bag. Even through his mask, Lucas was hit by an acrid stench of decomposing meat, tinged with a stagnant, burnt odor. The smothering silence was unnerving as The Black Fog muted and distorted sounds into faint echoes of their natural sources. Lucas snaked around charred cars and piles of rubble obstructing his path to the mouth of the nearest alleyway.

The distinctive siren of a Special Task Force vehicle shrieked in the distance. Muffled gunfire erupted. Lucas quickly slipped between two buildings, following graffiti scarred brick walls to the first right turn. As he rushed onward, something else became audible.

Lucas slowed. It couldn't be.

But as he proceeded, the sound rose in volume, becoming unmistakably clear – the cries of a child. Lucas sped around the corner and froze. In the center of the next alleyway, his young son lay on his back, naked. Charlie, who had been dead for decades. His small arms swung at a mangy vulture perched on his chest.

Clinging tightly with gnarled talons, it flapped greasy wings. Lucas shouted and clapped his hands. The vulture raised its beady black eyes. Trying to clear the nightmarish scene from his vision, Lucas blinked and shook his head. When he looked back, it was still there. The vulture returned its attention to Charlie.

It thrust its sharp beak at Charlie's throat, piercing his

tender skin. Charlie wailed and feebly kicked his little feet against the ash covered pavement. Lucas ran forward, plumes of black dust rising around him. Charlie's final scream reverberated into the night as the vulture ripped the exterior jugular vein from his neck. Lucas slid into the spot where Charlie should be but found it empty, except for smears in the soot. Above him, Lucas heard the beating of filthy wings.

Dazed yet determined, Lucas pressed on, putting distance between himself and what he hoped was merely a Black Fog induced hallucination. His stomach spasmed painfully. Tears streaked down his cheeks as he shuffled forward.

He squinted at the crinkled map clutched in his fist, surprised to be closer to this journey's end than he thought. As he forged ahead, the buildings around him grew progressively more dilapidated. Destitute before the outbreak, the district Lucas entered was now crumbling to pieces. He tried to remember if he had ever passed or even entered the structure he was approaching.

Thinking back felt like peering into a swirling void. He didn't believe he had ever set foot in the building. He was not a religious man.

Exhausted, Lucas came to a stop and gazed up at his final destination – a derelict church. The once proud edifice now slumped like a skeleton under the oppressive pall of The Black Fog. The granite exterior was cracked, and the roof had largely collapsed, exposing jagged beams.

Shards of shattered stained-glass windows pierced the insidious air, their vibrant colors dulled by the toxic haze. The steeple remained, yet its cross was corroded. The warped front doors hung loosely on their creaking hinges. Lucas climbed broken cement stairs and entered.

It was warm and dank inside. The stink of The Black Fog dissipated, overtaken by musty traces of damp stone and rotten wood. Obscene graffiti desecrated sacred art on the walls. The altar, barely standing, was coated in grime. As Lucas proceeded, his boot slipped on the debris-strewn marble floor.

He recovered and took a moment to catch his breath. Scattered amidst the detritus, a few black feathers caught his eye. In its debased condition, the church should have felt more deserted or haunted. But Lucas knew better. Now, it was a different kind of temple.

Obeying commands from the message board, Lucas crept around the altar. A thick wooden door came into view. As promised, it was unlocked. Lucas pushed it open, revealing stone steps. A red neon glow summoned him from below. If this was a trap, and Lucas was prey, he decided he would willingly surrender to the hunter.

As Lucas descended, the red light grew bright enough for him to remove his night vision glasses. He reached the bottom and shambled into a large vault or crypt. A congregation of emaciated disciples knelt on either side of an open aisle.

Some rocked back and forth while others whispered vile prayers. Located at the head of the chamber was a shrine of dark devotion. Tormented human forms were sculpted out of junk metal and waste. Anguished faces of twisted chrome screamed silently. From behind this grotesque display emerged a voluptuous figure dressed in a ceremonial silk robe.

She stood in front of the shrine and locked eyes with Lucas. Long sleeves draping to the floor, she slowly raised her arms in a beckoning gesture. The murmured invocations faded into reverential silence.

Lucas advanced.

The faithful watched with voracious hunger. Lucas reached the end of the aisle and halted in front of the looming figure. Gracefully, she untied the sash at her waist and slipped out of her robe, exposing a tapestry of transgression. Bruises of violent purple and green flowered around lacerations. Patches of skin had been surgically excised or raggedly torn. While older wounds had putrefied, scabs crusted over fresh incisions.

The figure reached out with long nails sharpened into claws and directed Lucas to his knees. Trembling, Lucas genuflected and lowered his mask. He salivated. This yearning had become all-consuming. The figure guided Lucas's mouth to her thigh. Ravenous, he sunk his teeth into her flesh. The figure gasped, enraptured. As blood spurted into Lucas' throat, he tasted salvation.

END

Zombie Hooker: A Love Story

James H Longmore

ONE

The fat, dead guy ambled along the sidewalk, his uneven gait rolling his ample body from side to side like a badly laden truck. His face bore the unmistakable gray pallor of death, his skin mottled and peeling. The man's feet – one bare, one sporting a black patent slip-on – shuffled and scraped the ground as he made his way along the familiar route to the office where he'd once worked.

He swung a battered tan, leather briefcase in his right hand; it had fallen open months ago and spilled its cargo of paperwork out along the street and now it flapped empty. In the guy's left hand was a TV remote, which he held to his ear as if in the midst of an important telephone conversation. His cell phone, one could presume, was back at home lying atop a TV set that had not received a transmission since the emergency broadcasts had ceased. Of course, the man was dead and incapable of making a call, even if the cell towers had not stopped working when the whole world went to hell and back.

The corpse shuffled onwards, driven by an inane instinct that condemned him to repeat his old routine *ad infinitum*. His eyes stared straight ahead, blinking occasionally, with only his peripheral vision to prevent him from stumbling into his surroundings.

He didn't acknowledge the girl who stood on the street corner, he never had. Her skin was the same hue as his, her eyes almost as dead. She wore a tiny skirt that had ridden up to exhibit her soft, sensual folds where thigh met buttock, and a skimpy halter-top that exposed her decaying, pallid flesh.

The girl watched the dead businessman in his derelict thousand-dollar suit as he staggered by. She recognized that he walked this way every day at this same time, on his way to an extinct job in a ruined downtown office block. In the deepest recesses of her decaying brain, she remembered him; this was the guy who had walked by her every day when his suit had looked like a thousand dollars and his briefcase had been firmly shut.

The girl waited on the street corner that she'd called her own for almost two years. She had staked her claim to the prime piece of hooker real estate after its previous incumbent had vanished. She'd turned up eventually, in a services area on Interstate Ten, wearing a garish off-cut of rolled-up carpet. They'd never found the woman's head – or uterus, liver and heart for that matter.

Prior to her premature death during the outbreak six months ago, the hooker on the corner had been a real, natural beauty. But now, her copper-red hair lay plastered to her head, her pretty face was swollen, drab and lifeless save for fading blue eyes that somehow still managed to sparkle.

She dressed as she always did, her curvaceous figure squeezed into a stretch mini-skirt that showed off slender legs adorned with spiked heels, and metallic top that displayed her ample breasts and a firm belly from which dangled a long diamante belly ring, now hanging precariously from a sliver of rotten skin.

In the Before Time, out on *her* corner for the twelve 'till three lunchtime shift, it had never ceased to amaze just how many office workers needed to fuck in the middle of their working day. Still, it was all good business, especially on alternate Fridays.

When three o'clock came around, the hooker's ingrained routine would drive her back home to her less than salubrious apartment above the Smoke Shop to prepare for regular clients and in-calls.

Even though the Johns didn't seem to come by anymore.

Sure, cars still drove by, but nowhere near the number that used to crawl past in the old days. Back then, there'd been the regulars, the new and the voyeuristic out to catch a glimpse of forbidden flesh with all of the frisson of Victorians espying a well-turned ankle. Cars that did happen by now all maintained a steady speed and had their windows firmly closed; their occupants peering out at the hooker with frightened eyes. And she would faithfully wait out her three-hour shift, no longer caring if anyone was going to stop and ask if she was *doing business*. Things were different now.

One car – silver, German – still happened by every now and then. It would slow down, and she would dip her knees the best she could to catch the driver's gaze. All to no avail as the car would simply race away like a timid animal. Somewhere in the back of the hooker's mind, she *knew* this particular vehicle. It was from the Before Time, but her decaying mind couldn't quite place it.

The reverberating crack of a gun shot barely registered a reaction with the hooker and as she watched with her blank expression, the suited man slumped without ceremony to the sidewalk. Half of his head was gone and the gray-green muck of putrescent brain matter dribbled out of the yawning hole in his skull. He lay there oozing and twitching in a spreading pool of his own slop.

The hooker slunk around the corner and pushed herself hard against the cold, gray brick of the building that had once been a popular nightclub. Experience had taught her that where there were gunshots, there were cops.

And those, she hid from because some things never changed.

A garish red Challenger crawled by. There was a buzz-cut redneck type hanging out of the window with a rifle clutched in his scrawny hands.

"I got him, Olden!" he shouted with undisguised glee to his driver. "Blew his fuckin' brains out first shot! Yeee-ha!" He hollered his war cry as he pumped another couple of bullets into the fat guy's corpse by means of celebration. "One less of them dead fucks to worry about – they should give me a fuckin' medal or sumpthin'!" He flipped off his victim, pulled his denim-clad torso back into the car and his partner floored the gas.

The Challenger was barely a small red spot on the horizon when a blue-and-white cruised by. The uniforms within peered out through the safety of wire-clad windows like curious carrion birds at a kill. Satisfied that the fat guy was well and truly deceased, they sped away. Soon, a black mortuary van would swing by and pick up the businessman's corpse for incineration.

The hooker skulked in the shadows until the cop car was gone. She knew that she couldn't afford to be seen by the Exterminators or the cops otherwise she, too, would end her days oozing gunk onto the sidewalk.

Being a prostitute *and* being one of the undead was definitely not a good combination in these troubled times.

With the suit guy already forgotten, the girl crept out

from the shadows and began walking.

It was three PM – time to go home.

TWO

August S Phillips adjusted his silver-plate cufflinks a third time, twisted the crisp, white shirt sleeve around his thick wrist. He paced back and forth in his cramped living room and studied his reflection in the faux-Viennese mirror that hung above the mantel. He'd been presented with the cuff-links two years ago in recognition of twenty years' loyal service to the United States Postal Service; they'd even put on a champagne reception with an array of nibbles, some of which he'd never even heard of.

That had been a proud day.

A mailman's life suited August to a tee. He was a man who enjoyed his own company and he got to work pretty much alone. He had the chance to play the extrovert on his route with a nod and a smile and the occasional light banter to those he had gotten to know over the years. Then he could retreat back to the sanctuary of his tiny home and go back to avoiding the social contact that had always made him feel awkward.

It wasn't that he didn't like his colleagues at the USPS. They were a friendly bunch and some of them had even called around to the house, back in the Before Times. Mom had still been alive then, and she did fuss so when they called him *Augie*. She hated that nickname, said it made him sound like a fucking retard. And she'd pronounce it *reeeeeetard* in her inimitable Southern drawl.

Always a quick one with the expletives was Mother. A pure heart and a foul mouth, the Reverend had described her when they'd laid her to rest; her final words on God's Green Earth as a coronary destroyed her heart had been '*motherfucking cocksucker*'.

The mail service was only just starting to get back on track after the terrifying events of six months ago. The USPS had paid August for all the time he'd been hunkered down at home with only a shotgun and the emergency radio service for company. August figured that people still needed to get their mail, even through a zombie apocalypse.

That's what they were – *zombies* – and that's what they called them. Call a spade a spade, Mom had always said, and she was never shy when it came to spade-calling. August had always been amused at the folk in those old zombie films who referred to the shuffling antagonists as *those things*, like they didn't know what the dead people who were trying to eat them actually were. Had none of them ever *seen* a zombie film before?

From Day One, they had referred to the reanimated dead as *zombies*; no point beating about the bush in a global crisis, August reckoned. Call them what you will – Walking Dead, Living Dead, the fucking Dead Dead if you prefer – they were just regular people who wouldn't – or *couldn't* – lie down and stay down. Something cruel and unnatural kept them going, driving their putrefying bodies with an irrepressible urge to feed on the living. So far, no explanation had been offered as to what had caused the unholy plague, although the supermarket tabloids and conspiracy theorists had had plenty to say.

From what August had gleaned, it had all been pretty much Obama's fault.

The whole thing had been a surreal nightmare filled with groaning, decaying people that stank to high heaven and would sink their teeth into your flesh as soon as look at you. No amount of horror movies could have prepared the population for the disgusting reality of the dead preying on the living, it was all too much like some nasty dream.

But it *had* actually happened and August – along with a significant number of others – had gotten through it. And, as they say, life goes on.

What a terribly appropriate phrase that had turned out to be.

August fussed at himself once again. Was the tie right for this shirt? Was this the right shirt for this tie? Did the pants make his ass look fat? Was his hair too shaggy? He stared at himself in the mirror and studied the middle-aged man who stared back at him. It had seemed a mere blink of an eye since he straightened the black bow-tie that he'd proudly tied himself as the finishing flourish to the hired prom suit as he waited for his Limo ride to Haley Johnstone's house to show.

Those had been years brimming with hope, with endless possibilities of the vast world beyond the suburbs of the spreading city. August and his recently graduated classmates had stood with their toes on the threshold of the fantastic adventure that was *LIFE*, poised to embrace and devour everything that it had to offer.

And then college had happened. For everyone except August. Dad was long-gone and Mom was working herself in to an early grave with two jobs just to make the mortgage payments and put food on the table.

And somebody had to take care of Davey.

August glanced at the faux-oak framed photograph of Mom that sat on the mantel below the mirror. Her prematurely aged face smiled out from behind the UV-proofed glass, her brown, twinkling eyes surrounded by heavily lined skin. Her frail, liver-spotted scalp was clearly visible through the fine wisps of frost-white hair that looked windswept no matter how much she brushed it.

Next to the photograph was Mom's matt black, ceramic urn. It was decorated with gold-leaf angels and on its lid perched the engagement ring Dad had brought back from a business trip to Amsterdam. Dad had not been able to afford a proper ring when he proposed, so he'd surprised her many years later with a belated white gold and diamond ring along with a particularly virulent strain of *Chlamydia* that had almost put paid to her fertility and which she claimed to her dying day was responsible for Davey's *condition*.

Davey was what Mom had called *special*.

Davey was the eldest of the two boys, by three years and change and was so *special* that he'd eat his own shit and scream blue murder all night long like the Devil himself was sticking it up his ass. He'd tear off his clothes and run off down the street and the police would bring him back with sympathetic smiles and platitudes and then Davey would smash up the house and try eating the silverware.

There'd been the days when Davey was catatonic, it brought some welcome peace to the house even though August and his mother had to take turns to wipe the kid's ass when his bowels let go. August struggled to see how not being able to wipe your own goddamned ass was deemed *special*, but there you had it.

August had been nominated Carer-in-Chief the minute he'd graduated high-school. Mom couldn't afford home care for Davey and she would be damned – *God-fucking-damned* – if she was going to stick her eldest son in a state facility.

Haley Johnstone had gone to MIT to do something sciency, and all her promises of keeping in touch and coming home for *every* vacation went quickly by the wayside once she tasted freedom. The handful of friends August had managed to make in school also spread their wings and left the city as quickly as they could – and Ronnie Labouchardiere had travelled to England to major in something scientific under Professor Stephen Hawking.

And there's another special person who couldn't wipe his own ass.

Naturally, August had never married, never allowed

himself close enough to anyone again after Haley's correspondences had dried up. He'd tell everyone – including himself – that he was waiting for the right girl to come along. In reality he knew in his heart that the right girl had already been and gone.

August had put Davey in a private nursing home the day after their mother had passed.

He'd also ignored the old girl's wishes to be buried and gone ahead and had her body cremated; in August's opinion, there was far too much inner city land taken up to accommodate dead folk. And what a marvel that hindsight had been; he would have hated the thought of Mom up and walking around like the rest of the corpses.

He'd paid for Davey's sanatorium out of his own wages, and visited his brother once a month to assuage his guilt at palming off his own flesh and blood to complete strangers.

Davey wasn't a problem anymore. August reminded himself on occasion that he really ought to feel guilty about what had become of his brother, but the harsh truth was that what he did feel was relief. When the dead had resurrected and the fragile fabric that held society together began to shred, Davey, along with life's other unfortunates were rounded up and disposed of in hastily-built incineration units around the city. For many of them, it had been a mercy.

Paying for Davey's care had put a large hole in August's finances, effectively tying him to the small house in which he had grown up and inherited. It also meant that he had to watch every penny and save wisely to pay for the companionship that he craved.

Again, with little guilt, August had built himself a cosy routine of saving for his once a month treat – twice when he got his bonus – of female company.

He'd met Danielle, *his* Danielle only a few months

before the world as he – as *everyone* – knew it had changed for ever.

August took out his wallet, fished out the picture he had of the two of them together. They'd had it taken in the photo booth next to their favorite coffee shop. They'd fallen into it giggling like a pair of love-struck teenagers and Danielle had sat on his knee. Danielle's happy smile shone out from the small photograph and they looked for all the world like lovers.

August had been feeling extra lonely recently, ever since they had taken Martha-May away. That flea-bitten tortoiseshell cat with the torn ears and one eye had been older than dirt and was the final legacy from his mother. The cat had smelled bad, was cantankerous and a little too quick with her razor claws for his liking, but he missed her. There was always comfort in having another living thing to come home to.

Hot on the heels of the dead folk climbing out of their coffins, all mammalian pets were rounded up and destroyed; cats, dogs, mice, hamsters, rats – even though there had been not a single instance of anything other than humans *turning* and no evidence from what was left of the scientific community that they could, or ever would.

August had considered arguing that point with the people who came to take Martha-May to the incinerators, right up until the soldiers in biohazard suits had pointed ludicrously big, black semi-automatics at his face.

He *had* made a cursory protest, but the soldiers had advised him in calm, gas-mask muffled voices that they really didn't have the time for his bullshit and that they would be more than happy to shoot him should the need arise. There'd been no alternative but to take them at their word on that one, considering the circumstances.

Gazing at the photograph of his happier self, August realized that never in his life had he felt so desperately, utterly alone.

There had been occasions in the recent weeks on which he'd found himself making an excuse to drive by the street corner where he had first met her, although he told himself that it was only to check that she was alright. He'd drive slowly by, heart racing, hoping against hope that she had survived the madness and would still be there. He'd circle the block as slowly as he dared, taking in his old route by the abandoned office buildings, the litter-strewn streets and *their* coffee shop.

The coffee shop was a wreck now; windows smashed, chairs and tables spilled out onto the sidewalk like innards from a gutted carcass. Next to it, the photo booth was just a burned-out shell. It saddened August to see it like that; it had been their special place, where pretence became real – if only by the hour. There had been days he'd paid Danielle just to sit, drink the overpriced coffee and talk like he imagined a real girlfriend would. There'd be no sex on those occasions, just companionship and at least the façade of affection.

As he spent more time with Danielle, August had become convinced that he saw something in those liquid blue eyes that hinted at something more than just a business transaction. And that had made him incredibly happy.

In his heart, Danielle had been his constant companion throughout the mayhem and chaos and inescapable presence of death. His memories of her had buoyed up his spirits in even the darkest of hours and given him the motivation he needed to stay alive through the hellish carnage. And he missed her so much that it physically hurt.

August had been rewarded with a glimpse or two of Danielle on his latest sorties. She'd been in her usual place on the corner of the street and he'd slowed his car down to a crawl, still too afraid to roll down the dark-tinted windows on his Mercedes, let alone stop. His heart had skipped a beat or two as she bent her knees to peep into his car, and he imagined that their eyes had met for the briefest of moments.

He'd seen enough of her sickly countenance to know the condition she was in, but her eyes were still alive and they sparkled for him.

And then he'd driven on.

August fiddled absently with his car keys and ruminated on the decision he'd finally made; today would be the day.

The city streets were pretty much cleared of zombies now. The cops and licensed exterminator gangs were still out and about shooting the few remaining dead folk on sight but it had been a couple of months since the city had seen a zombie-related death. August thought it would be fun if they put one of those '*xx days with no Zombie killings*' boards up – one with interchangeable numbers.

He'd heard that the dead were becoming less aggressive and that the Government were planning to use the lesser decayed zombies to replace the tradesmen who were gone now. That was good news for sure; you just couldn't get a plumber for love nor money these days and August's garbage disposal had been all screwed up since the electricity came back on and now it barfed chewed crud back up into the sink whenever the dishwasher drained.

Snorting down his nose at the thought of calling in a zombie plumber, August plucked the ring from his mother's urn and headed out.

THREE

The hooker pushed her apartment door. It swung open. No need for locks these days; very little to steal, no one to steal it.

Out of habit, she closed it firmly behind her.

The three flights of concrete stairs that made her apartment block look and echo like some crumbling mental institution had taken their toll on her atrophied legs and she was exhausted; it had taken a full hour and a half to climb them today. And that was a half hour longer than it had taken her yesterday.

The hooker shuffled across the tiny room, her head lolling slightly to the left and arms swinging loosely by her sides. She aimed for the bathroom, missed and stumbled into the nursery in which stood a cheap pinewood crib. The room was no bigger than a walk-in closet, but before she'd died, the hooker had made it nice by painting it eggshell-blue and adhering Disney character stickers to the walls.

Inside the crib, nestled amongst the glassy eyed, stuffed animals lay the remains of her child, its head crushed by the silver stiletto shoe that was embedded in its soft skull.

Her baby boy – Jethro – had been eleven months old when he'd taken ill. He'd been bitten by one of his playmates at the day care center and the incident had been dismissed as nothing more serious than *it's what babies do* and a write-up in the *Boo-Boo Book*. But that was in the time before things really turned to shit.

She'd instinctively known that there was something seriously wrong with her baby, but by then the hospitals had been stretched beyond capacity, the streets too dangerous for her to venture out. She'd watched helplessly on her TV the events unfolding in the City, and then mirrored all over the country as the dead took to walking around and biting chunks out of people.

When, finally the TV played only static as the networks closed down, the hooker had known that her baby was going to die. And even worse than that, she had known that dying wasn't the worse thing that was about to happen to her offspring.

So she'd taken off her shoe and put the mite out of his misery.

The tiny corpse had finished rotting. The last of its fluids had drained out, congealed and dried on the hardwood floor beneath the crib. All that was left now were dried up, mummified remains that looked nothing like the pink, squealing bundle of life that she'd nurtured at her breast.

Before he'd died, little Jethro had bitten a lump out of his mother's cheek.

The hooker's stiff fingers crept up to touch the suppurating hole in her cheek as a vestige of memory maintained the connection between the wound and the tiny corpse in the crib. She made her way out of the grim nursery by homing in on the harsh sunlight that bullied its way through the narrow, filthy window next to her bed.

Instinct buried in the deepest recesses of the hooker's subconscious informed her that now was the time to prepare for the afternoon clientele, although she wasn't quite cognitive enough to register that said clients never actually came calling any more.

She wriggled out of her mini skirt and peeled the halter off over her head. As she did so, she pulled her right nipple away from its sagging mound and it plopped to the floor. She stood in front of her mirror in black panties and heels and contemplated.

Her body was still firm, her breasts remained full if somewhat downward facing, and the left one was still adorned with a large, dark pink nipple. Her stomach was flat and the outline of toned abs descended towards her pussy, interrupted by the thin, white smile of her caesarean scar. She had a few stretch marks here and there from her pregnancy but those were largely masked by the grey pallor of the decaying muscle beneath her skin.

The hooker peered hard at her own face as if trying to

recognise it. Her clumsy hands reached for the cluttered array of make-up scattered over the dresser and she padded a soft foundation brush over her face. She grimaced as the bristles sank through the wound on her cheek and tickled her tongue. She pulled the brush out and it made a faint sucking sound as it squelched from face, the bristles glistening wet and clumped together with rot.

Eye shadow next, daubed on in haphazard fashion with poorly coordinated movements and, as hard as she tried, more went onto her forehead than her eyelids. Finally, the lipstick. She picked out a bright red, glossy color that accentuated the scabbed remains of her lips and spread it around her mouth the best she could, and over onto her shallow cheeks.

Satisfied with her makeup, the hooker stepped away from the mirror. She dropped to her knees and they let out a sharp report as tendons snapped. She scrabbled around under the metal-framed bed and her thin, brittle fingers pulled out a half dozen shoe boxes, each one labelled in teen-girlish red sharpie. She picked up the box that read 'A.S.P' and placed it on the bed.

She'd used the boxes to store the gifts that her regular Johns bought for her, kept deliberately separate so she'd know which one was from which guy. In reality, the gifts tended to be more for the client's benefit than for hers, typically outfits that they paid her to wear. There was fetish stuff – leather, latex, cheap PVC mostly, clichéd, role-play outfits (French maid, Catwoman, schoolgirl – the practically ubiquitous Princess Leia gold bikini), and bizarrely shaped sex toys of all shapes and sizes.

Some of her more thoughtful clients bought her dresses and outfits that were not fetish although they did tend towards the shorter, revealing styles; as expensive as modest wages would allow, clothes they couldn't get their wives to wear.

The box that she tugged open had a rough-edged heart drawn onto the lid in baby pink lipstick, an echo of happier times. She pulled out a small, black dress, struggled to her feet and pulled it on. The soft fabric of the dress scuffed away small clumps of her scalp, which then clung to the shimmering fabric.

The dress clung to the hooker's every curve and accentuated her body with sensual lines. It came to an abrupt end at the curve of her pert bottom, tucking into that sexy crease between thigh and ass. The collar was high and fastened by a small zip at the nape of her neck and the back was simply non-existent; the flimsy material scooped low to expose her entire back and just the slightest hint of buttock cleft.

She had dim, distant memories associated with the dress. Memories that hung around the less decomposed parts of her brain; of smiles and kindness, caring and compassion.

Coffee.

Although the hooker couldn't remember the *why*, she put on this dress at the same time every fourth Wednesday of the month.

The hooker smoothed the dress over her slim frame and her remaining nipple stiffened at the touch of her wasted hands. She sat down on the edge of her bed with her legs outstretched and stared blankly at the disintegrating toes that peeped out from the ends of her shoes.

And she waited.

FOUR

August's palms were moist and he felt the sweat trickling down his back. He genuinely couldn't think of a time when he'd felt more ill at ease. August gulped down deep breaths and told himself that it had been the walk through the apartment block and up three flights of litter-strewn stairs that had made him overheat, and not that he was as nervous as hell.

He'd parked his car a couple of blocks away – old habits die hard, he supposed. Danielle's neighborhood had never been the most pleasant to walk through in the Before Time, and when zombies had become a *real* problem, slums and drug-infested tenements such as this had been the first to be cleaned out by the Army. They'd systematically swept through and shot indiscriminately at anything that moved, living *or* undead. Then, they had rounded up whoever was left, and shot them as well. The resulting corpses were thrown into the back of garbage trucks and carted away to the incinerators and neighborhoods like this had become some of the safest places to be.

August's footsteps echoed in hollow rhythm on the concrete walkways as he walked. Like most places nowadays, the apartment building had succumbed to the smothering, empty silence.

He fiddled absently with the ring in his pocket and felt like a teenager on a first date. After six months of his whole world – *the* whole world – being turned inside out and upside down, August would have thought that any lingering anxiety he might have had of hearing the word '*no*' from a girl would have been diminished. But sadly no, the fear of rejection was as deeply ingrained in him as with any man and although things were different now, there were some things that *never* changed.

One more deep breath and August knocked on the door.

FIVE

Stirred by the timid knock on her door, the hooker struggled from the edge of her bed. She stood up, wobbled as her ankles threatened to give way in her precipitous shoes and steadied herself against the dresser. A cascade of make-up paraphernalia fell to the floor with a plastic clatter. She shuffled towards the door and grasped the handle on her third attempt.

Opened it.

"Hi," August said, feeling awkward and very much like a rain-soaked Hugh Grant on Andi McDowell's doorstep. "It's wonderful to see you again," as polite as his mother had taught him. "You look beautiful."

The hooker stepped aside to allow August in, holding onto the doorframe as she stumbled slightly. August thought that she looked pleased to see him, fancied he saw a smile on her rotting lips. He looked into her eyes, searching for that remnant of the Danielle she had been before. To his absolute delight, August saw that her eyes were still the same iridescent blue that he had fallen in love with, albeit sunken into her skull some and marred by cloudy cataracts.

The rest of her, however, didn't look so good.

Her skin had the sickly bluish-gray sallowness that was common amongst the dead, it was cracked, split and oozed a foul green/brown slime. In places, eruptions of liquid putrescence pushed to the surface and threatened to burst through like miniature, pustulant volcanoes.

Danielle's body seemed far thinner, more angular than when August had last been this close to her and the soft flesh of her prominent cheeks was now peeling away to reveal the yellowing bone beneath. Clumps of his love's red hair were sloughing from her wasted scalp, and stuck in the viscid ooze of her face like ancient creatures in a tar pit.

A stink of rot and decay wafted from the hooker like some gruesome perfume but like all survivors, August had grown used to the pervading stench of death and it barely bothered him.

August noticed that Danielle had on the dress that he'd bought for her to wear during their liaisons – *their* dress – and it gladdened his aching heart. She had been waiting for him. Did he dare hope that this was a sign that she felt the same way as him?

"How have you been?" August's wilted attempt to make small talk was met with a guttural grunt. "I'm sorry I haven't been around for a while. But, you know how crazy things have been lately." He stopped himself short and felt embarrassed at his *faux-pas;* he was babbling again, always did with Danielle, damned nerves.

August clamped his tongue firmly between his front teeth to force himself to stay silent. The last thing he wanted to do right now was to put the gal off with his incessant jibber-jabber. He followed Danielle towards the bed that had been the scene of many trysts. Unfortunately, it looked a little less inviting than he remembered it, the covers were crumpled in an unruly heap at the foot of the bed to leave the bare mattress exposed and there were ominous-looking stains splashed across the mattress in dried patches that spanned the spectrum between dried blood red and the greenish-black of putrefaction.

Despite the sickening lurch in his gut, August smiled at Danielle and fiddled with the ring in his pocket. The gold felt warm and smooth and the huge diamond dug into his fingertips.

The hooker turned to face her client and something that could easily have been a smile forced itself across her face. She reached both hands behind her neck and plucked at the zipper with uncooperative fingers.

"No." August pulled her arms away. "Leave it on."

SIX

The hooker's lips split open and wept a rust-red fluid

beneath the tawdry lip-gloss as her face contorted into some semblance of a seductive smile. Her eyes burned into August's with animal lust and something else quite intangible that he just couldn't quite put a handle on.

She bent forwards to reach beneath the hem of her dress, hooked her bony thumbs through the waistband of her panties and slid them down. As she did so, viscous globs of snot-green slime snaked downwards along her legs and pooled between her feet. Delicate tendrils of the putrescent gloop made translucent strings between her thighs as they slopped noisily to the floor.

It made August think of melted cheese on fresh-from-the-oven pizza.

August undressed himself, taking great care to slip the ring onto his left pinkie finger, diamond facing inwards. Didn't want to ruin any surprises now, did he?

Danielle climbed onto the bed and reclined with her arms above her head to create an illusion of sexy.

August's eyes wandered up along Danielle's legs and peeked beneath her dress. There he saw her ruined vulva; once deliciously pink and slick and inviting, now it glistened with the silvery green of suppurating flesh. Base instinct overrode disgust and August's penis twitched to life.

August climbed onto the reeking bed and lay beside his love. He stroked her body and reacquainted with every line and curve. His hand rose with the twin mounds of her breasts and dipped with the hollow of her flat belly. And then August ventured down towards that special place where he found a slick, inviting wetness into which his fingers sank. And when he pulled his sticky fingers out of her, Danielle delighted him by licking the discolored rot from them.

Danielle rolled August over on to his back and heaved her decaying body on top of him. She straddled him as one would a steer and her stiletto heels dug into the soft meat of his thighs, just how she remembered he liked it. The hooker positioned her dripping sex just so and lowered herself down on to August's penis.

August gasped as he slipped with ease between Danielle's labia and slid deep into her vagina. She was pleasingly wet for him, so much so that her juices drenched his groin and soaked into the mattress under his plump ass. August groaned at the delightful moisture that made their bodies slick, although he understood that it was more the by-product of her putrefaction than of arousal.

But he was happy to pretend for the sake of love.

The hooker ground herself hard against August, using her hands to support herself against the wall above his head. As she made love to him, a cacophony of grunts escaped from her throat and gave the impression that she was truly enjoying their copulation.

August squirmed and bucked his hips as the pressure in his dick built towards an unbearable, almost painful crescendo. It had been an age since he'd done this, and there had been only so much frustration that onanism could alleviate.

August thrust his fingers into Danielle's hair as he came and accidentally dislodged her left ear. It slid down her neck and hit his chest with a *splat*. The hooker clamped his hips tightly with her thighs and grunted with her own orgasm.

SEVEN

It was done.

The hooker looked down at August, his face and torso flushed red in the afterglow, his eyes half closed.

August looked up at his Danielle and for the first time in six months felt entirely at peace. She had always accepted him for who he was; there had never been the need for pretence. In that respect, she was the one who had found his awkwardness *cute*.

"Thank you," he said, forever the consummate gentleman. "You are quite exquisite."

Taking her hands from the wall, Danielle placed one on either side of his chest and lowered her face towards his. She smiled again and her peeling lips parted to display discolored teeth.

"I love you, Danielle," August blurted out, unable to help himself. He then liberated the diamond ring from his sweating finger. "And I was going to ask you if you would –"

A rasping snarl spewed from the hooker's rotting lips and she lunged at August's exposed throat, her teeth bared in an obscene grin, mouth dripping its fetid juice, August struggled as his lover's teeth sank deep into his neck and he felt some snap off in his flesh. He opened his mouth wide to cry out, but no sound came save a strangled mewling noise as the air whistled through the rip in his windpipe. He tried to push her away but she was too strong and he could feel his life drain away along with the blood that Danielle slurped from his lacerated throat.

August tunnelled his fingers into Danielle's hair and in a macabre emulation of their recent passion, he drew her closer to him.

EIGHT

August S Phillips and Danielle – *his* Danielle – walked along the street hand-in-hand. They had the slow, unsteady gait of the living dead and they looked for all the world like besotted lovers.

He was naked with a scarlet bib of blood covering his chest, she wore spiked heels and the tiny black dress that showed off her shapely legs, clung to her rounded buttocks and exposed the sensuous curve of her spine. The engagement ring hung loosely from the remnants of the fourth finger of her left hand, the diamond glinting in what light remained from the bloated, setting sun.

They shuffled their way towards their favorite coffee shop.

There they would sit amongst the debris and ruins of a world that once was, and wait patiently for someone who would never come to serve them. And neither of them would care all that much, because they were together and in love and because things were very much different now.

OTHER HELLBOUND BOOKS
www.hellboundbooks.com

Anthology of Campfire Stories

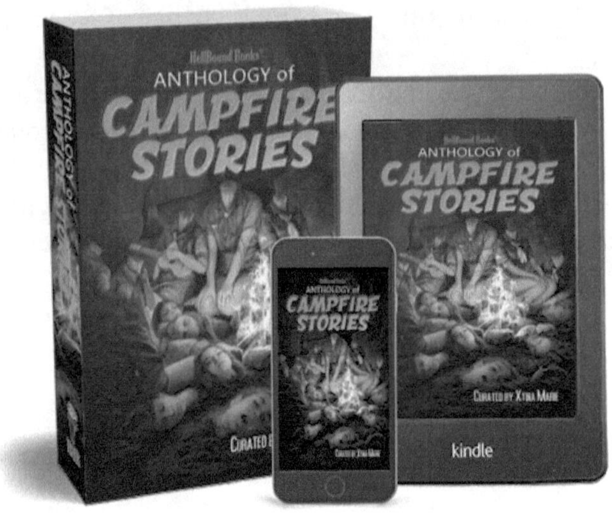

Ever since our ancestors first discovered fire, we have used it to sit around and scare one another silly with creepy tales of ghosts, ghouls, bloodthirsty creatures, maniac killers, and everything in between.

But, what if those stories, related in the dark of night with trembling voices, flashlight held resolutely beneath the chin, are more than just horrifying tales meant to send shivers down the spine and cause a few sleepless nights? What if the snapping of a twig deep in the woods is *actually* a real-life serial killer looking to brutally slaughter his next victim and steal her eyeballs? Or what if the wasp that stung you was no ordinary insect but something far, far more menacing…?

And, how about that very nice stranger you met on earlier on the hiking trail? His odd behavior was merely his fun eccentricities, and definitely nothing nefarious whatsoever.

Right?

Right?

So, why not shuffle your sturdy log an inch or two closer to the warm, flickering comfort of the campfire and chill your blood with 21 strange and dreadful tales that will have you glancing over your shoulder in terror as you make your way to your tent tonight. But never fear, after all… they're just campfire stories.

Anthology of Extreme Horror

If you prefer to take your horror yarns with copious amounts of spilled blood, eviscerated guts, dollops of messy gore, and dark, disturbing themes, then boy howdy, does HellBound Books have a terrifying treat in store for you!

If not, please not this book is definitely *not* for the faint of heart!

With a foreword and brand-spanking-new, never-read-before short story by the grand maestro of extreme horror himself, Matt Shaw, this collection of eighteen stomach-churning tales of terror is guaranteed to have the bile rising and heart thumping with each turn of the page.

So, buckle in, dear reader, and brace yourself for a blood-soaked ride littered with assorted body parts and particularly nasty doers of evil. And, for heaven's sakes, please don't attempt to eat while you're reading this anthology!

You have been warned…

Eighteen exceptional tales from: Matt Shaw, Taylor Z. Adams, Priyanuj Mazumdar, Gabriel Giddings, Dave Davis, Paul Lonardo, Anthony Ferguson, Keith Durocher, Ronan Grey, Galo Romero, Kira Blackwood, James Patrick Riser, Dewey L. Yeatts, Daniel Rust, Brit Jones, HellBound Books' very own James H Longmore, and British national treasure, Joe Pasquale

Anthology of Splatterpunk Volume II

splat·ter·punk
noun
informal
noun: splatterpunk
Definition: "A literary genre characterized by graphically described scenes of an extremely gory nature."

Welcome once again, fellow gore lovers, to HellBound Books' second foray into the deliciously bloody, innards-strewn world of splatterpunk!

Death, dismemberment, and destruction abound within these pages, as we bring to you nineteen perfectly ghoulish tales of terror that are definitely not to be read while eating!

Go on, we dare you!

You have short tales from: Shannon Blake Skelton, Juan Ozuna, Sarah Moon, Seaton Kay-Smith, S.C. Vincent, S. Michael Wilson, Carson Demmans, Diana Parrilla, Michael Errol Swaim, John Schlimm, P.J. Verfall, Karly Foland, W.L. Lewis, Caleb James K., Brian J. Smith, D.J. Tuskmor, Terry Grimwood, Dave Davis, and Paul Allih.

Anthology of Creature Features

Come on, admit it, we all love a gripping tale of our fellow creatures gone bad. Think *Jaws*, *The Rats*, *The Crabs*, *Pede*, *Them!* – the list is practically endless (hell, they even made a movie about killer bunny rabbits! *Night of the Lepus*, 1972, anyone?).

There's just something so inherently terrifying about the animals we see every day and take for granted are going to stay in their dens, burrows, nests, swamps, and crevices going on a murderous rampage of mayhem and outright slaughter against us poor human beings. Knowing what they are truly capable of has us keeping one wary eye on the critters, that's for sure.

And so, gathered within the pages of this skin-crawling, nerve-jangling anthology, you'll discover a collection of the most horrifying examples of Mother Nature gone psycho we could unearth. We have killer goldfish, a murderous mantis, a hellish giant arachnid, giant lizards, turtles, something altogether indescribable with tentacles, and so much more. Heck, there's even a tale of butterflies we guarantee will chill you to your very soul!

Featuring zoological tales of terror from: *Tim Newton Anderson, R. D. Tyler, Chad Barger, Seaton Kay-Smith, Milan Kovačević, Julien Jayus, Robb White, Serena Daniels, Rose Strickman, Janna Layton, J. Neira*, and the amazing *Cliff McNish.*

The Last Customer

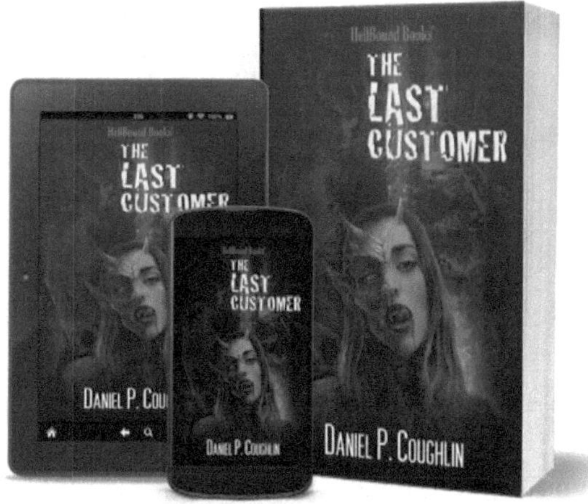

One hot August evening in the small town of Dodge Junction, Wisconsin, Win and Garth Gasper close their family-owned liquor store for the night.

When the demons Sammael and Jezebeth show up in search of Father Leslie Gardner—the priest that many years ago exorcised Sammael—the Gaspers are forced to confront the most terrifying customers they have ever experienced!

Up the hill from the liquor store, Father Gardner senses he is being challenged by the demons. Unable to ignore their foul presence, he makes his way to where the demons have kicked off their destructively sinister plans for the evening.

Now, Garth, Win, Gardner and three unexpected armed robbers must fight their way out of the liquor store where their flesh and souls are being shredded by the denizens of Hell.

Father Gardner must revisit his terrifying past and renew his faith to defeat the nastiest demon he's ever encountered and protect the lives of his neighbors against the last - and by far the worst - customer of the night.

And Then You Die

Following a drunken, hedonistic night out in New Orleans, highly successful businesswoman and sexual deviant, Claire Jepson, accidentally soils herself in her car. The resulting excrement comes to life as a sardonic fecal spirit, and not only dishes out a gruesome death to Claire's unfaithful, gold-digging fiancé, but also thwarts a kidnap/murder plot by her employees. It then introduces Claire to a world of depraved pleasures beyond her imagination.

A year later, the errant spirit has spiraled wildly out of control - its insatiable appetite for perverted sex and human flesh and has destroyed Claire's life. Then, to her horror, Claire discovers the fecal spirit must consume her unborn child to attain immortality; she must return to the seedy underbelly of the Big Easy in a heart-pounding race against time to confront the spirit's creator - a high priest of an ancient, deadly order, who is the only one who can put a stop to the spirit's murderous intentions.

A wicked, fast-paced story laced with tongue-in-cheek, dark humor, which is at the same time incredibly erotic and stomach churning. Most definitely not one to be read whilst eating!

Anthology of Bizarro

Welcome to the wonderfully horrific world of Bizarro - that dark, forbidding corner of the horror genre where absolutely anything goes and one may delve into the farthest recesses of the authors' warped imaginations. Prepare yourself, dear reader, for a journey into the unknown reaches of terror, from which you can only hope you will return with your sanity intact...

Enjoy 16 outstanding stories from:

Scott McGregor, A.L. King, Garvan Giltinan, Keith Kennedy, Robert Prescott, T.M. Morgan, Lee Rozelle, John W. Leonard, A.L. King, Matthew McKiernan, Aron Beauregard, Ken Goldman, Victor Marrow, Ryan Woods, and Stephen Daultrey

A HellBound Books Publishing LLC Publication

www.hellboundbooks.com

Printed in the United States